VOICES IN HER SONG

CLARE C. MARSHALL

BOOK FIVE

THE SPARKSTONE SAGA

Other books by Clare C. Marshall:

The Violet Fox Series:
The Violet Fox
The Silver Spear
The Emerald Cloth
The Midnight Tablet

The Sparkstone Saga:
Stars In Her Eyes
Dreams In Her Head
Hunger In Her Bones
Darkness In Her Reach
Voices In Her Song

Other Titles:
Within
Gear and Sea

PART ONE

What has happened before, will happen again.
More or less.

—J.G.C., *Campbell's Multiple Verses*

CHAPTER 1

After I bury Wil in a secret place that my Future Self will disturb once, I return to the place I hate most to pluck him out of time.

This is how I'll save Wil and Ethan and the rest of the students at Sparkstone University. By using the power in my blood and bones.

I enter this time and the grass rushes up to meet me. So, so cold. I huddle on the ground, staring up at the clouds as the smell of wet earth and the distant sounds of the campus culminate in the fearsome shock that I've really done it. There's no going back now. I've returned to Sparkstone, again.

I don't remember how I chose *this* moment. My time in the between-space slips through my mental sieve like a dream. Those *things* chased me. They nearly touched me...

Someone had been calling my name.

I shake it off and find an uncertain stance on familiar ground. The open field of Sparkstone. Large swatches of bladed too-green grass lined with paths leading to each brick and stone building, projecting prestige and exclusivity, overshadowed by the menacing wall surrounding the entire town.

I clutch my collar, steadying myself as the brisk Alberta air swirls about my bare arms. It's early November again. Right before the Brigade gained true power, before the Collective rounded up all the students who weren't showing signs of superpowers, and before my parents forgot about my existence.

Before Ethan and the others perished in the explosion in the underground library.

There are multiple changes I could make, though right now I'm only interested in one.

My past self is easy to spot in the field. The wind picks up my starkly recognizable, dark red hair and whips it around like a ragged flag in a storm. I don't remember seeing myself, but if I can truly change the past, could I change my own memories? How can I trust my own mind if—?

No. I can't think like that. Not now.

Several feet away, I see Wil. He's on his phone, back to me, and when he looks up, my stomach curls with the unsettling feeling that I get when he reads my mind. He doesn't look my way, not yet. But he already knows I'm here. His powers are extraordinary.

I start towards him, single-minded in my mission. There is he is. Alive. Breathing...

Younger.

His dead face had been burned into my mind that I'd almost forgotten what *my* Wil looked like. The differences are stunning, now that I know to look for them. Dead Wil—*Future Wil*—looked like he rarely slept. Not old, per se, but grizzled. He'd carried himself with the tired confidence of a soldier who had seen the same battle on repeat. If only I had asked him, point-blank, what was in store. He wouldn't have told me anyway.

This Wil has no idea what's coming.

"You're..." He trails off. He can read me plainly as he puts his phone in his pocket, ready to give me his full attention.

I don't know how to hide my thoughts or emotions from him, so I nod. There is no lying to him. He knows who I am, and from where and when I have come.

"I'm here to save your life," I tell him. "I won't let you die again."

"No, no. Hold on." He waves his finger at me. "Appearing and whisk me away? You can't do that. The Collective just made an announcement that changes everything."

"I know. They've formed a student brigade and they're going to start a more aggressive, hostile takeover." I pause, remembering. Wil from the future appeared out of time to us and *helped us survive.* "But if you come with me, we can launch an offensive, away from the school."

"Jadore attacked your family when you tried to escape," Wil replies.

"I'm from the future, where we've already made an escape," I explain to him. "And she eliminated that leverage when she erased our existence from our families' minds."

"Why would she do that?" Wil asks, making a face. "And how?"

I sigh. I thought this would be easier. Wil can see into my mind and know I'm speaking the truth. It's in his best interest to come with me, so he can be saved.

Again, he shifts, taking a quick survey of the surroundings. "Look, I don't think it's a good idea for you to be here. Disrupting the past. Inadvertently changing things. You should go back to your time."

"Don't you want to live?" I ask.

"I'm living now," he says, annoyed. "Go, Ingrid."

"Disrupting the past is what I want to do. It might be our only chance to defeat a power that requires my body to bring fish people through an alternate universe just to replenish their own troops—"

"Alternate universe? So that's where you're from."

"No. I'm from this universe." At least, I think I am. I don't know if I would know if this universe wasn't mine. I go with my gut. "I told you, I'm from the future. *Our* future. Look. See, over there?" I point in the far distance. There they are, the burgeoning beginnings of the Brigade, doing drills in the field, their dark jackets standing out among the fading green grass. "On this day, you come to me here in this field and tell me that you're leaving to protect us."

This makes him pause. He evaluates me with renewed interest. "I was considering that. Just now. My power is too dangerous to remain here. If they ever got a hold of me..."

I nod. He doesn't have to finish that thought. "We can't let that happen. If you help me, I'm going to do my best so that this time, we succeed."

"This time." He throws an uncertain glance at the Brigade. "And where would we be going?"

"Back to my present. In January. Just a few months into this future. You should be safe there, for now."

He glances about the quad. "Wait here. There's something else I have to do before I take you up on this."

"Me too," I reply, relieved.

"The music trailer," he says quietly, like reading an echo in my mind.

I nod. That's where we'll meet. Did he choose it because that's where Future Wil told me to find him? Or is it simply a convenient spot? Or is there another reason he asked me to meet him there? Time travel is confusing.

Wil jogs towards the main campus like a man on a mission. I squint, realizing he's not going towards any of the buildings, but to the marching parade of students in black jackets, and a young woman with flaming red hair, inappropriately dressed for the cold.

Me.

Like a terrible writhing snake in the pit of my stomach, I recall the conversation about to happen, that has already happened on this day. Wil wanted *me* to teleport him off campus. Past Me, that is. He's not going to say goodbye and settle his affairs. He's going to try—and fail—to convince Past Me to help him escape. Did he ask Past Me this, fearing what would happen to him if Future Me plucked him from time?

It's freezing. I also can't stand around out here and risk being spotted by my past self. I take the long way around the campus, behind several buildings as I head towards Raylene House. I don't want to be noticed, so I crouch by a cluster of trees while Wil and I carry out our destiny. Wil orders Shane and the Brigade away with his powers, and they trudge through the plains of the quad like zombies. Wil makes his request of Past Me, and Past Me declines. He storms away, dejected. My past self disappears into Raylene House and I breathe a sigh of relief. She doesn't see me. No weird paradoxes to contend with, at least not today.

My fingers are numb. I wish I could teleport seconds into the future to escape the bitter cold. Next time I come to the past, I'm bringing a hoodie. I'm about to head for the music trailer when in the far distance, I spot Ethan. Dazed, perturbed, and handsome, stumbling out of Rogers Hall.

I press myself against the trees, my knees against my chin. My breath warms my fingers. I could wave and shout, but he's in no condition to notice or know me. He's lost core memories, precious to his identity. Notably, his relationship with me. He's trapped by a cruel experiment wringing a cure from his biology for an alien disease. Agailya's science has robbed him of his mind. For what? What gives the ahmei people the right to come to our planet and conduct unethical experiments on us—on *him?*

My mind reels. I can take him too. Save him from his fate. Even if his memories are already gone, at least he won't be *dead.*

As I consider this bold intrusion upon Ethan's life, another person hurriedly emerges from Rogers Hall. I shrink further back, behind the rough bark. Mira. Or, as I now know them—Gayarnu. An alien of the ahmei species, like Agailya, in human form. Unlike the other aliens who disguise their true natures, Gayarnu actually succeeded at fooling us, with their unique sense of style, warm presence, and knowledge of Ethan's life. Gayarnu pretended to be Ethan's fake girlfriend from London, to better control him. Outside Rogers Hall, Gayarnu-as-Mira fusses over him. I'm too far to hear their conversation. Frustrated, Ethan pushes Gayarnu away and storms off towards his dorm with determination. At least he knows his way.

Gayarnu huffs their frustration into a cloudy fog. Their silver earrings glint in the breeze, but their concern never waivers. They watch Ethan trudge through the cold as they retrieve a cell phone from their pocket. Uttering a report into the phone, Gayarnu steps back into Rogers Hall.

Strange, now that I'm thinking of it. There are others in Agailya's experiment. Did they also suffer the side effect of losing their memories? Tilly Newman was Agailya's subject too. She *died* in a human-sized test tube. A lot of trouble to go through, to have one of your own colleagues disguise themselves as a young university student, pretend to be in love with your subject, just to keep him calm and complacent.

Agailya favoured Ethan, even before his memories disappeared.

She wanted me to keep him safe. She used my feelings for him against me. Perhaps he really is her most promising subject.

"The Collective is strange and inefficient," I mutter to myself.

I return to the path between the campus buildings, following Ethan at a great distance. The quad is quiet. I think everyone's holed up in their dorms, buzzing from the Collective's presentation in the cafeteria.

Taking Wil is one thing. He disappears from campus for the next several weeks, and that tells me that this has already happened, and so it will happen again. I take this version of Wil into the future, unsticking him from time, where he will eventually return to help us fight the Collective and the Brigade, and bring Sunni through the multiverse portal in the underground library.

For me to take Ethan from time, when he's watched by Gayarnu? That will not go unnoticed. Ethan remains on campus, as far as I'm aware, in my past. I interact with him and I try to get him to remember me, and it doesn't work—not until the very end, when we're all about to die. If I take him now, it will create a paradox.

But he will be safe.

I must change the future. No matter the cost. I can't let Wil die and I can't save Ethan from the self-destructing portal if I also don't cure the side effects of his trauma.

I'm humming to keep calm, and then he's there beside me. Campbell. Summoned against his will to my side, out of time just like me.

"There are two versions of you here," he says curiously, with a hint of pride.

To look at him would be to descend into madness. I don't know why, but it's tempting. At least in madness, I would escape the expectations placed upon me, by me. "I'm from January. In six weeks, a portal will explode here in the underground library, preventing an alternate universe Collective invasion. It will also destroy lives. I'm here to save those lives."

"What has happened before will happen again."

"No. Maybe." I turn and nearly glimpse his face. A swirl of dark hair. Endless black-hole eyes. Pride and confusion in squiggled, multi-dimensional lines that hurt my brain to process. I promptly look away, focussing on his leather boots instead. Crunching the light frosted grass next to mine as we march forward. So human-like. In sync. "I have to take Wil out of time because it's clear to me that I've already done that. That's why Wil kept showing up when I was here fighting the Brigade. A future version of him, doing who knows what. But Ethan? I don't know how to save him yet. If I could take him to the future—my present—let him remain there until I can sort out his trauma, and then return him to THIS moment, maybe that will fix him."

Campbell laughs. It's an odd, gargling sound, like identical audio tracks of a growl playing five seconds out of sync. "You are welcome to try, but as I've said, the past is immutable."

"That can't be true. You altered *my* life, didn't you?" A photograph of a family vacation, slightly altered—

—or was it? Memories of that time pass through the sieve of my brain and I can no longer recall if I am a victim of past alteration or if I am simply misremembering.

"That's different, because you're different," Campbell explains. "I must have told you before, haven't I? There's only one of you. You exist singularly—or as near singularly as can be—throughout the multiverse. That is why we are bound. Why you, alone, can carry out the single most important task any sentient creature can perform, and why I alone have managed to cross all known forces to aid you in this task. Didn't I write that in my tome? Didn't you read it?"

"I know you want me to take you somewhere or perform some kind of great task," I say bitterly. "But you and your past and future selves won't tell me anything else about it. And I'm not going to sit around here anymore waiting for you to give me more cryptic information. My friends are in danger. My planet is in danger and I have the power to not only stop, but *prevent* all of it from ever happening."

"Perhaps," he replies coolly. "The invasion of worlds upon worlds isn't necessarily my concern. Although." He considers my position, scuffing his boots on the path. "Perhaps in attempting this foolhardy exercise, our bond will be fulfilled. Do as you will. I've given you all the help I can."

"I don't think you have," I say, stopping. I face him, staring at his boots. They look brand new. "But maybe you'll appear again before I see you at the portal."

His boots pivot toward me like a bloodhound's nose pulled by a magnetic force. The intensity of his presence melts the frost around us in a perfect circle. "What was that you said about a portal?"

My heart pounds. I know something he doesn't. I am ahead of this version of him. "Just something you said to me once. I have to meet you in six months, at a portal. You said that to me about three months ago in my timeline. The only portal I know is..." I trail off. The only portal I know is the one I brought Sunni through. He's enigmatic with me, so I'll reciprocate. "Well, I'm sure you'll figure it out."

"Hmm. I'm sure I will, and once we're both ready, we'll appear there." I hear him smack his lips and he digs a heel into the path. "You'll have to watch out for them."

"Who?" I turn towards Rogers Hall. Three people clamber out of the building on their hands and knees, as if they're learning how to walk. They don't look like students or professors. Visitors to the school? The parents and guardians won't visit until tomorrow in our timeline. I've never seen anyone with transparent skin before. It stretches over their oblong skulls like plastic wrap. A terrible dread fills my stomach. I want to look away from their awkward scramble from the steps, onto the grass. They're not in a hurry. But they seem to know where they're going, and it's towards us.

Campbell scoffs. "*My* people. Call them my far-flung nieces and nephews. They are the keepers of the Untraver. They don't like unauthorized persons ambling around their domain. Especially humans. And well, any sentient life that isn't supposed to be tip-toing from time to time, universe to universe."

"The Untraver." The name sounds familiar in Campbell's voice, and strange in mine.

"Not its true name. A moniker from—well, you'll find out someday. I never told you?"

A tingling sensation crawls down my throat. Now the creatures are running, a dressage on two legs, their tattered robes bouncing with the effort. Now that they're closer, I see it: their forms blink in and out of time. A faint memory tugs at me. In the hallway maze between realities stand ugly, robed guardians, erasing doors from existence, and if they catch wind of my presence, I'll be erased too.

"You've never told me about these...Untrakeepers," I say, backing away from the buildings, brandishing my fists in front of me unsteadily.

"Untrakeepers. I like that. Perhaps now is when I fill you in. Don't let them catch you. You're unauthorized and I'm afraid they're sticklers about that. They're not going to allow you to zip around your own timeline. They're doing a wonderful job, manifesting." He waves at them—I see the motion from the shadow on the grass—and yet the Untrakeepers don't pay him much mind. "Seems like I'm of no use. It's strange that they—" His words crumble into dust in my ears. I glance over, and he's gone.

My ears clog from a steady buzz and a hiss emanating from all around me. I stumble backwards, shaking my head to let the blockage drain, but my ears are dry.

I look up. They're closer. Their out-of-phase, dark mouths expand and contract. They're speaking. Their language clogs my ears. I don't have to understand the details to get the message.

"You won't stop me," I spit at them. "I won't let you."

This only makes the sensation worse. The pressure on my ears is nearly unbearable.

I whip around and run. Another two spring from the grass ten feet away like shadowy, shambling trees. My stomach lurches. Looking or thinking about them makes me retch. I focus on not falling as I head for the music trailer, passing multiple students, bumping into others. Hopefully I don't change their lives too much.

Wil leans against the music trailer, waiting for me. He pushes away from the building as he spots me running. His concern suddenly mirrors mine.

Three Untrakeepers emerge from behind the trailer and shuffle towards him. He turns his head, as if he's heard them, but can't place their position.

Where? he asks, looking around for the monsters.

Words are slow. "C'mon!"

He runs towards me and stretches out a hand. Beyond him, the shufflers advance, blinking in and out of reality like a strobe light.

A flash of green and red beside the music trailer draws creatures' attention. They trip over themselves, confused, looking between me and somewhere between the trailers.

"What's wrong?" Wil asks again, this time out loud.

Whatever that flash of colour is, it's gone now. All of the more reason to get out of the past and back to the present. The Untrakeepers have set their sights on us again.

I take Wil's arm and put Campbell's cousins from my mind. Their ghostly hands reach for us and I phase out of time, out of their reach. For now.

CHAPTER 2

The snowflakes dot our faces as we trudge through the deepening snow. Wil checks his phone and raises his eyebrows in surprise, probably at the date. It's got to be past midnight. Aside from the gleaming stars above, the porch light of Jia's family home, and an extremely faint orangey glow from within the dilapidated barn, it is dark as pitch out here. And freezing. I press my fingers under my armpits for warmth.

"Should have let me take some supplies," Wil says.

I find his arm again and I unceremoniously guide him toward the barn, filling him in on the last several months. He doesn't need for me to speak. He can mine my brain for diamonds with his power. I speak to fill the icy silence in the field and to distract myself from the desire to jump out of this barren place to somewhere warmer.

Every time I pass through the Untraver, my memory adapts. Grows stronger. Still, the vast corridor maze only raises more questions: is the space truly infinite? Why are the Untrakeepers erasing the doors? If the space is infinite, why bother to scorch the doors?

"It's hard for me to remember, so not sure if I can be of much help there," Wil says quietly, in response to my thoughts, not to my spoken words.

"I should be mapping it. Keeping better track," I mutter. I return to the story of the last few months to distract him; a futile attempt to lead him away from my true desires. Mapping the infinite hallways means a swift return to the place my heart aches to go. A final mission I'll undertake, even if it takes me ten months or ten years to complete.

Wil isn't easily fooled. "You're going to go for Ethan after you've settled me here." It's not a question.

I swipe the snot dripping from my nose on the back of my hand and sniff in more of the cold Alberta air. "There is a moment in time when I can grab him. Just as my past self teleports away with everyone else, and just before the explosion obliterates the underground."

"And the others? Agailya and her folk? The other students who escaped?"

My stomach sinks as I recall the chaos in the last two minutes before the explosion. Agailya and the others, minus Gayarnu, had been at the exit, with Jadore's unconscious body. Gayarnu prevented me from taking Ethan with me with their ironclad grasp. "I might be able to grab them too." If I choose to save them.

Wil is quiet. I can infer what he's thinking, even if it's not accurate. I'm cherry-picking who to save with my powers. We all know that that leads to. Tyranny. Twisted, justified morality. Ethan gets saved because I love him, Wil gets saved because we're friends, but Gayarnu has to die, because they deceived me?

He doesn't weigh in on my swirling thoughts as we approach the barn. I let go of Wil. I can't feel my fingers. The snow comes in buckets now. Hopefully it covers our prints. I see no tracks outside the barn as I pull aside the door and gesture for Wil to enter first.

There's no one inside.

At least, that's what my senses believe.

But then, they appear, rippling out of Jia's invisible world all at once like statues come to life. Cautiously, my friends release each other and venture closer to us, their expressions alight with disbelief as Misty's hand flares with orange flame. I expect her to speak first. She's always had trouble containing her temper. But it's Jia who pushes to the fore. The half of her face scarred with Jadore's wrath glares angrily in Misty's firelight as she marches toward me and Wil. Scars she obtained from saving Wil's life, when we'd thought that was when he was fated to die.

"Where have you been?" she demands. "You've been gone for two weeks."

"Two weeks?" Internally, I swear and check my phone. It's the end of January. Dammit. "Sorry," I say to her and Wil. "I thought I'd gotten it right this time."

Jia's confidence falters under my apology, and Wil's presence. She draws back from him, as if he's a hole in the thin ice where we're all skating. Jia and Wil, in particular, are teetering on the edge. She'd admitted her feelings to him, he'd erased her memories of the event, and yet the feelings remained. And round and round things went. Until she found out, and had it out with Future Wil. This Wil still has that to look forward to. It's with that intensity that Jia's gaze narrows at me. I don't have to explain the mechanics of time travel to her. She can work it out. Now, she has to endure *this* Wil, who is still living in denial that what he did to her was wrong.

Campbell's words are on my lips, but I cannot say them. In this instance, he has been proven right. *What has happened, will happen again.*

I have saved Wil. For now. But I have committed a terrible, irreversible act, and cursed my friends to endure it as well.

Not only have I taken my friend out of time, but this is the *beginning* of Wil's end. I have already set in motion a series of events that leads to his death. How am I supposed to know what will change the future, if I keep acting as I have in the past? As Jia turns away from us to process her shock, the others surround Wil with grateful greetings and fill the air with cautious questions about his presence here. To them, this is a miracle.

"She pulled me out of the past. She's filled me in up to this point," Wil assures them. He seems more astonished by Sunni's presence than the others' reactions to his. Even a mind-reader has to see to believe.

Misty and Sunni exchange peculiar glances, though Sunni regards me with a renewed interest. She looks exactly like the young woman I encountered on my first day at Sparkstone University: a spirited, light-haired Texan, who spoke with certainty about the future, because she saw it at night in her dreams. It was she who told me that she herself would die. That my arrival at Sparkstone marked an important shift in their private war against the invading Collective, a group of aliens with mysterious scientific objectives, which involved the hostile, silent takeover of Earth. But the Sunniva Harris before me was not that same Sunniva Harris who died by Jadore's hand on the mother ship. This Sunniva Harris had a more brutal, devastating experience with the Collective in her universe. There, the Collective *won*. She reached out to me across the universes with her power and urged me to open the door between our worlds, to allow her to find refuge her and assist our rebellion. Because hers ended in absolute failure.

Sunni holds onto Kimberly, who has been stunned into speechlessness. Rare, for her. Kimberly has held a candle for Wil, and he for her, for longer than I've known them. She has many false starts at a greeting, tries to go in for a hug, but then recoils when Wil makes no reciprocal move.

"We're all together again." Misty's voice shakes with a rare vulnerability as her gaze rests on me, Sunni, Jia, and Wil.

"And us. We're here too," Greg says in a pretend sulk, smirking and clapping his hands on Elisha and Lynn's shoulders.

Greg, Elisha, and Lynn are all that's left of the group running the *Don't Read Zine* at Sparkstone. They were onto the Collective's unusual agenda. My thoughts dwell on Tilly Newman, their other friend who paid dearly at Agailya's hand for her forthright curiosity. I can't believe now I stayed in that vent like a coward, watching Tilly shape-change in the cell uncontrollably, her limbs contorting and devolving until she was no longer human.

I close my eyes. I can change that now. Can I pop back into that lab for just a moment, pull Tilly out before she expires, and pop out, without her dying? Can I go back further, and take her out of time before that happens, without unsetting the timeline? It is worth trying if it means saving her life.

Every mistake I've made is waiting to be fixed. All in good time.

Jia's gaze fixes hard on me, doing everything it can to not look at Wil. "We were just talking about making a new plan, before you showed up."

Truthfully, I'm exhausted. There's a bed of old hay in the loft calling my name, even if it belongs to someone else. I remain steadfast in my spot. If my friends are ready to enact a plan, then I must be vigilant.

Wil, feeling my impatience, cocks an eyebrow and voices a more polite consideration: "I'd like to know what you've all been up to here, if you're up for that?"

My friends look to Elisha. She's the most organized of us all. "We can add that to the agenda."

I keep my mouth shut. *We don't have time for agendas,* I want to scream. *We have the power to travel to whatever point in time we want—so let's go already!*

Elisha snags a clipboard from a hoard of pens, markers, and other stationary supplies scattered on a splintery table. Judging by the scribbles on the marked-up paper, this isn't their first planning session, and most of their plans have involved stealing supplies. Since my departure, the barn has amassed a hodge-podge of new items, organized discretely so as to avoid notice at a quick glance. They are, after all, in hiding from everyone, including Jia's parents, who own the ground beneath our feet.

Greg and Lynn grab a large whiteboard on steel legs—that must have been difficult to steal—while Misty, Sunni, and Kimberly arrange logs, folding chairs, and heavy cardboard boxes into a semi-circle. Elisha gathers a collection of markers from the table and tests them on the board. Wanting to help, I pick up a black marker, doodle on the whiteboard to ensure it's a juicy one, and then slip it into my pocket. I want to make sure I can write my suggestions on the board. Remnants of past markings on the board are barely visible in the dim light cast by a flame in the fire pit. Jia stands guard over it, her arms crossed grumpily. No doubt they need to keep evidence of their presence to a minimum. We have to be ready to pack up, scatter, or teleport away in a heartbeat.

The one organized pile, enshrined before a pile of hay acting as a makeshift table-and-chairs set, is their food stash. There are two jumbo candy bars and a smattering of wrapped treats, three of cans of beans, and the all-important can opener. A tablet, gone dark without a power supply, serves as a plate for a hard, rectangular brick of cheddar. There's even a bottle of non-alcoholic wine. Judging from the peeled away foil at the top and the dents in the cork, they don't appear to have a corkscrew.

"We'd offer you something, but we're low on supplies. If we can keep this quick, we'll have time for another run into the house," Misty says to me and Wil.

"Doesn't your family notice the missing food?" I ask Jia.

Jia grimaces. I can't imagine living this close to a family who doesn't recognize me. Her invisibility power is a saving grace. "Paige thinks the house is haunted. She ordered a spirit board online the other day."

Throwing up his hands, Greg says in exasperation, "I thought you'd stopped watching her!"

"I was just checking her room again for supplies. The markers are running out of ink." Jia gestures to the whiteboard.

Elisha clears her throat. She stands before the whiteboard like an elected official. "The neighbouring farmsteads have also been... generous, we'll say, with their stuff. We've been careful. But..."

As my friends grab a seat around the whiteboard, I feel an immense pride to be standing here, with them. We escaped Sparkstone and they've managed to survive for two weeks without the university raiding the barn and dragging them back.

They survived *without me,* says my inner voice, heavy with disdain.

With her clipboard as her guide, Elisha continues with her agenda, as if this is a council meeting and we are citizens of a brave new world. "We can't ignore our biggest problem. I'm sorry Jia, but I've got to say it. We can't stay here anymore."

Jia stares at her feet, her face resting in her palms as she stews silently.

Continuing, Elisha delicately addresses the rest of us—namely, Wil and I. "We need to relocate to a better hideout. One with better access to technology and resources. I've been looking into this, and I don't think it would be hard for a couple of us to rent an apartment in somewhere like Olds. Or, a remote Alberta town with access to the basics. With all of our powers, I'm sure we can make it work."

Misty sighs and runs a frustrated hand through her short, black hair. Clearly, this isn't the first time this has been broached. "The Collective will find us if we move any closer to civilization."

"Last week, Elisha suggested we split up, and you pooh-poohed that idea too!" Greg exclaims.

"You're all forgetting," I venture, "that with my power, I can transport us anywhere. Now that I'm back, we may not have to move—or at least, not far." I quickly spit out the last few words as Jia throws me an indignant glance.

"You went outside for one second and disappeared for two weeks. That's not reliable transportation," Lynn chimes in quietly from her place at the end of the semi-circle.

"It's safer than getting a part-time job and saving up money for one-way tickets to anywhere else," Sunni says in my defense, clasping Misty's hand for support.

"Why doesn't she just beam into the nearest bank and steal everything there?" Greg says sarcastically.

Misty, Sunni, and Jia give the idea serious consideration while Elisha admonishes us all. "Just because we're superpowered doesn't mean we're above the law. We can't stoop to the Collective's level. Other ideas?" On the board, she writes, "*Relocation?*"

I absently itch the inside of my ear. "Yeah. We travel back to the beginning of all of this and prevent it from happening."

I really thought they'd be excited by this. But no. Stony silence meets my words, as if I've just admitted to being the mastermind behind the Collective this whole time.

"Your solution to an *alien invasion* is *literal* time travel to erase the past?" Greg says harshly. "Why don't we just travel back to nineteen-forties Germany and *fix* that world problem too? Or prevent the African slave trade? Or uh...c'mon, everyone, what else?"

"Lead and aggressively champion women's suffrage for women of colour hundreds of years earlier?" Elisha suggests.

"Drastically alter or prevent the colonization of North America to protect the Indigenous people?" Lynn offers.

"Inoculate people against the bubonic plague?" Kimberly quips. She glances at Wil with her gleaming, large eyes. The corners of his lips twitch, ever so slightly, and she beams at him.

"We haven't even touched on what's happening to the Burmese people," Jia comments, taking in the exchange between Kimberly and Wil with disdain.

"I mean..." I swallow over the lump in my throat. "Technically... we *could* do all of those things."

Misty weighs in, "Hang on, what about preventing the invention of fossil fuels? Try to get everyone on board with clean energy in the sixties? Or the eighteen-sixties? Saving people and preventing genocides is great, but we have to have an Earth that's healthy enough to sustain us."

"They're not going to go for that then," Wil says dismissively. "We might as well just take what technology we can, and go back to, I don't know, Ancient Mesopotamia, and start again."

"Start again? Wow. Harsh. So glad you're thinking of everyone here," Jia retorts coldly.

"Starting over or altering major historical events won't prevent the Collective arriving *when* it does, as far as we know," I point out, while simultaneously wondering if I could travel back in time to Agailya's planet's past—

—to prevent the phage that devastated her people.

The thought alarms and excites me, and as the rest of my friends offer other historical changes, and Wil starts to defend his and Kimberly's suggestions, I throw up my hands in surrender. "Okay, okay. I get your point. It's an extreme solution. But it's an option we have, with my power. The Collective can't get us if we're dipping in and out of time. They won't see us coming if we attack them from behind." I pause. "Behind in time, I mean. Not like a physical—"

"We can speculate all we want. We don't know what will happen if we start foolin' around in the past," Sunni interrupts me, not unkindly.

"That's easy for you to say. You came here from a different reality. Technically, our past isn't yours. We can't say for certain what the differences are," Elisha reminds her.

"I thought I was living in the best version of reality. Until I was living in the worst. You're right, I don't know all the differences, and maybe the only difference is that Ingrid didn't exist in my world," Sunni concedes with a respectful nod to Elisha and me. "It took a lot for me to get out of there, and bring what I know here. To this reality. Where things are better, because of what you've all done—and because of what others have done—up until this point."

I'm scratching at my ear again. Wil's expression changes in rapid clicks, like a camera shutter. First, confusion as he grasps my hand, wanting me to cut it out. Then, a foredrawn, fearful conclusion clouds his features.

Do you feel that? he asks me telepathically. *Someone is coming.*

My heart pounds. My voice muffled by the unexplained change in pressure. "So, there are these monster things..."

"What THE—?"

Jia's sister, Paige, grips the barn door with white-knuckles as her explication drowns out my explanation of the Untrakeepers. "Get out of our—" she starts to say, but trails off as the flashlight on her phone sweeps the barn. Paige re-evaluates us once more: young people huddled by a fire, hoarding non-perishable food, planning "re-location."

"Do you need...help?" she asks hesitantly. She holds her phone like a talisman between herself and the rest of us, notably Jia, who hurries forward with an outstretched, calming hand.

"We're not going to hurt you," Jia says firmly.

Paige draws back. I don't think the thought of physical harm had occurred to her. "I thought there was a ghost," she says absently. Her shaking hands tap the phone screen. "It's freezing out here. I...I could find some blankets, but you should leave in the morning. My parents want to tear this down." She gestures to the ceiling of the decrepit barn. With no insulation in the structure, the fire is likely the only thing keeping my friends from freezing to death in here.

"They always talked about doing that," Jia says, holding back a sob.

Paige gives her a suspicious look. "How do you know them?"

Jia holds Paige's gaze like a taunt leash, unwilling to let go. She's shaking her head, unable to stop, as she unconsciously puts distance between herself and her sister.

I know this strangeness too. I had to look into my mother's eyes as she claimed to have no daughter. I catch her as she crumbles into a thousand pieces and do my best to keep her skin from touching the splintery floor. This rejection lands different with Jia. Chinese-born, Jia had been adopted as a baby by her white parents, before Paige had been conceived. At least with my parents, they had seen the genetic resemblance and I had hope that they'd find the lost memory within that familiarity. I can see the fading determination in Jia's eyes. Fierce, familial love isn't enough to stir recognition in Paige.

It's just something else I have to undo.

"Those blankets sound great," I tell Paige. "And don't worry, we're leaving. We aren't here to cause trouble. You won't even know we've—"

Ingridwhatisanuntraver—?

Wil's lightspeed string of thought-speech floods my brain as the air shifts. My chest tightens and I pull Jia upright like a human-sized, limp puppet before I can articulate what is wrong. But my body has been through this before, in another place, out of time, even if the mind can't recall the specific nature of the disturbance.

"Stay back!" I yell as three Untrakeepers phase into view in the doorway like glowing grey moths, drawn to the flame. Nightmarish, black-hole mouths expand until their taut skin looks ready to snap. They flutter with stuttering steps into the barn and take in each of us with their beady white pupils trapped in two dark pools of swirling nothing.

I double over, dry-heaving.

Jia bends over me, the tips of her hair brushing against my cheek. Now she's alert. "Ingrid, what—?"

"Is she okay?" Paige asks warily—and then she screams.

One of the creatures slams her into the wall, out of its way as it beelines for me.

I scuttle backward, trying *not* to look at them. To do so induces an overpowering nausea, just like with Campbell.

Their feet. I can look at those, just like with Campbell, and not feel disgusting. Toeless, round, and silver, glowing faintly, phasing in and out of reality with each half step. It seems throwing Paige took considerable effort. It struggles to maintain cohesion and balance as it hobbles for me.

"Any time you want to join the fight, that would be appreciated!" I yell at my friends.

Not a peep from them. Jia helps a bewildered Paige to her feet, though her gaze flits around the deteriorating barn wildly. I recall Wil's difficulty in pinpointing the creatures, back at Sparkstone.

"What's going on? Is someone there?" Jia demands. She releases Paige, disappears from reality, and returns bewildered. Even she, in her watery, invisible world, cannot see them.

The other two Untrakeepers hover by the entrance, struggling to remain in this reality. Their phasing stutters like uneven, raspy breaths. In. Out. In. Out.

"Something pushed me. A ghost?" Paige says, her voice wavering. She doesn't seem to mind Jia holding her tightly, or even notice as Jia flickers in and out of view, trying to search for the out-of-phase, out-of-time aliens.

The Untrakeeper advancing toward me blinks back in, and this time, its claw hands brush dangerously close to my neck. I fidget in distress and crab-walk backward. I have no weapons. No offensive, superhero abilities.

"We should get out of here," I say, swallowing over my gag reflex. "Everyone, c'mon, I can jump us!"

But no one moves, and when they can't aid me, I realize: only I can see this alien threat.

"Someone is there, but I can't pinpoint them," Wil says, flustered, as he studies the air between me and him.

"How many?" Misty asks uncertainly.

This is bad. Very bad. "Three!" I shout, and climb to my feet. I side-step and back into the barn wall. The Untrakeeper phases in. Its grey, long-fingered hand reaches for my tangled hair. I duck out of the Untrakeeper's way as the hand phases through the wall. My ears depressurize with my sudden movement and I swallow against it. The world seems to tilt. The Untrakeeper turns and widens its black maw. The jaw stretches to twice its length and snaps back like a rubber band.

They're furious. And they're here for me.

"Wil?" I manage to say, forcing myself to stare into its black void of a mouth.

"Got it." He begins shouting instructions at Misty and the others. They're fighting blind, but Wil can sense what I see, so I can be their unwilling eyes, and Wil, their commander in battle.

I steady myself as I back away, narrowly missing a cracked wooden support beam. Focussing on the aliens takes incredible concentration. The three of them stride confidently for me now, the two at the door marching in tandem. Their feet discordantly drum against the creaky floor, as loud and disturbing as off-beat snare drums, conjuring disturbing browns and lance-sharp blacks. I taste the colours in my mouth now and it's like I've been forced to eat compost. Looking at them induces the sickly, *you aren't meant to see that* sensation in my body, as if I had touched a finger to an exposed organ. The feeling punches me in the gut and recedes as the creatures phase in and out.

The act of looking at them, even as out of focus as they are, induces vomiting. They are not meant to be here, in our world. Their low, gurgling chatter corrupts and de-pressurizes my ears. I shove my palms against the sides of my head to no avail. I feel like I'm floating or falling. I wait to hit the floor but I fall into bristly hay. I close my eyes, suddenly dizzy, but force them open again: only I can see them. And they know it.

I'm shouting to my friends above it so I don't lose my balance or concentration entirely, "They're from another realm. They're mad about my power."

Sunni says something I don't catch as Misty's fireball lands between me and the Untrakeeper who had attacked Paige. It pauses, nearly losing its balance. That's gotten their attention of all three attackers.

"Uh oh," I say, because that's all I can muster as I find and lean against the wall. At least, I think I'm leaning on a wall. With my ever-degrading sense of balance, it could be a floor. This hard surface is splintery and the pain keeps me present.

Wil calls my name. The sound floats over my plugged ears. Another blind shot, and this one hits. The aliens' screams and hisses clog my ears further. I clutch my ears in pain.

"Did we get 'em?" Misty shouts.

I force myself to look. The three pairs of feet move in different directions. Two for my friends. Another for me.

"Coming for you!" I warn as I scramble out of the alien's reach.

And then pandemonium breaks out.

Misty lobs an ice-ball at the Untrakeeper. It side-steps and swipes at me as it shifts weight from one foot to the other. I duck and the alien strikes the wooden beam instead with considerable strength. It splinters. Cracks. The barn moans.

From somewhere on the other side of the barn, Paige's concern quickly substitutes her confusion. "Everyone OUT!"

A rush of footfalls and panicked screaming erupts from my friends as they stampede the door. I hobble after my friends, using the wall as a guide to help me stay upright. The pursuing alien repeatedly punches through the structure, narrowly missing me each time. Cold air rushes against my back. The barn creaks and I hear a thundering crash.

"Have to get out of here," I mumble. Not just out of this barn, but out of this time. I swing around to find my friends. My hand brushes Elisha and she clasps my forearm as we fall into step.

"Teleport. NOW!" she demands.

I'm not leaving anyone behind. "Where's everyone else?"

Behind me, the Untrakeepers trip over the fallen beams and crushed furniture as they stumble forward, unconcerned by the collapsing barn.

My right arm flails as Elisha yanks me out into the cold, snowy night. A blurry yellow spot in a haze of black and cold and wet: the porch light. That's where Jia's parents are, hopefully tucked away from this horrible mess, blissfully unaware of their daughters' fates. We don't head in that direction. We run straight ahead into the blinding, chunky snowfall, trying to put distance between the Untrakeepers and the falling barn. Wet snow soaks my feet, though the cold air slicing my throat abates the urge to faint.

"Everyone. Over here. Come here!" I yell hoarsely into the night.

Elisha and I press into each other for warmth. She smells like a campfire and that's a comforting thought I can save for later. Finally, my ear pops. The crunch of boots and sneakers on snow grows louder, and I try to find the aliens again, but everyone is a shadowy figure now, scattered on the open, dimly lit farmstead. The nearest street lamp is down the road somewhere. I squint at the partially collapsed barn and see a sleeping, smoldering behemoth in the darkness.

"Did we get them?" Elisha asks.

"I don't think so," I reply. I have no idea if they can be killed with physical means. I don't know anything about their race beyond their difficulty with infiltrating this reality.

Over at the house, Jia shouts at Paige, who has climbed the porch steps, determined to retreat from the supernatural. A bedroom light snaps on upstairs.

"Let's go!" I shout at the entire field, taking a step towards the house. Each step is fresh avenue for the snow to penetrate my non-winter clothes. I'm rubbing my arms with one hand as Elisha clings to the other. "Over here. C'mon! Before they come back!"

"Everyone! To Ingrid!" Wil shouts, and repeats it telepathically, sounding my location like a beacon to everyone.

Twin shapes trudge for us from the direction of the barn. It's not the Untrakeepers. Kimberly's dramatic, fearful breathing can be heard from across the property. She grasps Wil's arm like it's the only thing keeping her upright. She seems physically unharmed and mentally raddled. Wil grabs my free arm, ready for me to whisk them away.

"What the hell are those things? Why can't we see them?" he asks, for the non-mind-readers' benefit.

Steeling myself, I squint against the blustering snow as my tangled hair whips around us. Elisha kindly holds it back as I scan the darkness. Finally, my other ear pops. I can hear normally again. "They're from the between-place. They're upset with me."

Misty's fire blasts the night. She's throwing flames at the snow out of frustration and anger. She pounds on the front door with Sunni, pleading with Jia, who has locked herself inside with Paige. I urge the four of us forward, towards the house. We have to get ourselves away from Jia's family, just in case the Collective descends upon us and decides to murder them in retaliation for our escape.

As a fireball hits the snow a few feet away from the porch, Misty and I make eye contact—and I catch a flickering glimpse of an

Untrakeeper ascending the three steps up to the porch. It reaches for Sunni's frizzy blonde hair.

"Sunni, behind you!"

My warning rings true across the flat property. Misty pivots and throws another fireball over Sunni's head. The flame hisses as it finds its target. The fire eagerly envelops the Untrakeeper, haloing the creature sinisterly. Its mouth twists and emits a screeching howl that forces me to my knees. My ears plug again. Elisha and Wil hook their arms under my armpits and try to haul me up, but I resist their efforts wholeheartedly. Only the cold, thick snow gives relief to the throbbing noise flooding my mind. It reminds me that I'm here in this physical world and that I have a job to do.

"Ingrid! Stop screaming!" Elisha demands, because now I'm the only one making noise. She yanks me up forcefully, holding me by the forearms like a ragdoll. I can barely stand on my own.

The front door to the house creaks open and the interior light floods the porch. Paige peers through the glass storm door, hands splayed on the glass as the alien form burns brightly as a smoking, orange effigy.

I blink, unable to look away. I didn't think we could kill them. I didn't *want* to kill them. But what choice did we have? The Untrakeeper collapses into an ashy heap as the fire hisses and settles. Hopefully that's an example to the others.

"Where are the other two Untrakeepers?" I demand, mostly to myself, snot-nosed and groggy, as I search the farmland in vain. Maybe the collapsed barn really did them in after all.

"Misty. Sunni. C'mon, get Jia out here." Misty shakes her head and waves dismissively at him as she and Sunni try to barter with Paige and Jia through the storm door. "Greg, Lynn? Why are they in the garage?" Wil asks in rushed, hushed tones, as he too scans the perimeter. Kimberly's death grip on him tightens, determined to never let him go. Then, to me: "You have to jump away. With whoever you can. It's the only way to save them."

"Ingrid, we can't leave them here. Misty, Jia, *come on!*" Elisha shouts at the porch. Frustrated, she releases me and runs towards the smoldering alien, beckoning Misty and Sunni to hurry along.

"No one gets left behind. Not this time," I say to Wil. "Let's get Lynn and Greg. Is the garage around—?"

"I'll find them! I'm good at that!" Kimberly volunteers. Shooting Wil a hopeful, longing smile, she dashes around the side of the house.

I'm about to protest against splitting up when an Untrakeeper abruptly blinks into reality beside Elisha. Noticing Elisha isn't the human they want, the alien launches my friend backward into the snow. Snow clings and falls from their robe as their presence blinks intermittently, their footfalls punctuating the ankle-deep snow as they trudge toward me and Wil.

"Misty, here!" I say, throwing snow at the creature and pointing at the visible tracks.

She moves to the railing of the porch and squints into the night, preparing her fire. I draw back to avoid getting hit. Wil releases me as the creature stalks closer and Elisha scrambles to her feet.

The storm door to the Fields' residence flies open, banging against the siding. Sunni is startled backward, caught by Misty as the fire in her hand extinguishes. Even the Untrakeeper is momentarily distracted as Jia's parents emerge, dragging a frightened Paige onto the porch to escape Jia. Flustered, Jia tries to explain for the umpteenth time who she is and why they have to leave *right now.*

Sunni drags Misty down the stairs and she prepares her fire once more.

The Untrakeeper returns their attention to me, gaping in twisted agony. I stare at the alien's feet. It hesitates before me as it flickers, using all of its strength just to remain in this world. I retch, swallow, and cough hoarsely.

"I didn't mean to invade your territory!" I shout, both at the looming alien and Jia's parents, who stare bewildered at the destructive scene that has unfolded on their property. "It's just the nature of my power. I'm still learning to control it."

The alien blinks an inner eyelid—stark white like the untrodden snow blanketing the farmstead—and screeches as it jabs its pointed finger at the center of my forehead.

I inhale as if I'm preparing to go deep underwater. Images swallow my consciousness. My brain will aneurysm if I attempt to parse them.

HE HAS /SHARED/ HIS SOUL, the Untrakeeper drills into my mind, in a simultaneously ethereal and hissing tone. The words reverberate in my skull and splatter in my mind's eye like captions. *WHEN YOU ARE /FINISHED/ HE WILL /REMOVE/ IT.*

Some of their words are lost in the translation, wavering like a garbled portmanteau from their telepathic alien language that disintegrates my senses as I ingest the speech. When I try to reply, my lips feel sluggish, as if in sleep. Is this a dream again?

I manage to utter one word. "Who?"

THE TWENTY-SEVENTH.

I reach deep. Very deep. I recall his many names: Campbell.

Campbell is trying to help me. You are trying to destroy me, I think. My brow furrows against their cold finger on my skull. "Help?" I'm speaking to it and to my friends. I have to know more.

YOU ARE AN /ITCH./

Then: a blast of intense heat against the dotted cold.

Misty's fire momentarily blinds me and Wil yanks me backward into a heap in the snow. I blink violently against the bright halo invading my sight, but the screams of the alien and the smell of his burning flesh are omnipresent. They thrash against the flames, and not only can I hear it, but I feel it in my bones, as if I am tethered to them too.

"No, stop!" I scramble to my feet, desperate for concrete understanding and a foothold in the sticky, mounting snow. Where are they? I rub at my eyes, desperate to see clearly. The Untrakeeper's shape traipses through the snow. Elisha runs from the creature, retracing Kimberly's footfalls to the garage. I create a snowball and throw it at the Untrakeeper, to beat out the fire, and to ensure it doesn't follow Elisha. They don't know how to stop, drop, and roll. It doubles back towards my snowball. This one won't go down without a fight.

I put myself between it and Misty, and hold up my hands in submission. Misty, her hand red-orange with fire, stares at me in shock.

"Don't hurt them. It's me you want." My vision clears. As I stomach a look at the Untrakeeper, I note that the fireball has scorched their left arm and leg. The bright outline surrounding their features has dimmed significantly.

It hesitates and slowly tilts its head. Considering. It raises a finger to my forehead.

Unfortunately, Misty mistakes the well-intentioned gesture as hostile. Another fireball, and the Untrakeeper lights up like a tinderbox. I recoil backward into the snow as their screams pierce my eardrums.

I'm not the only one screaming. Mr. and Mrs. Fields have dragged Paige down the porch steps. They seem to be heading towards the garage, unable to access it from the inside with Misty, Sunni, and Jia blocking the entrance to the house. Now that they can see the alien threat tearing up the night, they hug the side walls, reconsidering our position as the bad guys.

"You all right?" I ask my friends through plugged ears, as Wil helps me up. We watch the Untrakeeper disintegrate into ash. The wind blows snow over them, as if they never existed at all.

"Let's just gather everyone," Wil says curtly.

He won't let go of my arm as we head towards Misty, Sunni, and Jia, who are continuing plead hopelessly with Jia's family. Jia waivers in and out of existence. She's lost all control. "You have to believe me. We're here to help you." She gestures to me as Wil and I approach. "Ingrid will take us away. Where are the others?"

"We're not going anywhere with you," Mrs. Fields says, her patience wearing thin. "The police will be here in five minutes. Maybe less."

If the police hear about this, no doubt Sparkstone University will too.

"No, no police," Wil says. He tries to extend a hand to them, but they recoil, clutching Paige closer. "I can explain."

"Don't you *dare* touch them." Jia stands between them and Wil, challenging Wil with a pointed finger. "You should be *dead*."

Wil hesitates. "I'm not here to hurt anyone. Least of all your family, Jia."

"You keep saying that," Paige says, with uncertainty. Then, to Jia: "You keep phasing in and out. Just like...those things."

Sunni and Misty gently take Jia by the shoulders as she breaks down once more. Sunni glances at me. I can see everything in that look. I nod. I can barely stomach this, and I've lived my own version of it, with my parents, but we have to go, now, before sirens pierce the night.

"Those things"—I gesture to where the two ash piles have been swept away by the snowfall—"were aliens. Aliens are real. I know. It's a lot. So are superpowers. You might have already known this, or suspected it, because of what you've seen here. The Collective has made you forget about Jia. They're aliens too, and bad ones. They're after us because of our powers. I can get us all out of here with my powers."

"No," says Mr. Fields, just as Paige asks, "How?"

But our responses and outcry are overtaken by the sound of a garage door whirring open. The blinding headlights of a four-door sedan roll out from around the corner of the house. The wheels crunch as it conquers the snowy driveway and the vehicle squeals as Greg hits the breaks. The window slides down. Greg leans out. "Let's get out of here!"

"They've got our car!" Mrs. Fields rages as Mr. Fields shouts expletives at Greg.

Greg promptly rolls up the window and hits the gas before they can grasp him or Elisha in the front seat. The car rolls further down the driveway and stops a little further down as the three members of the Fields family run after the car thieves in the deep snow. They tug at the locked doors. In the backseat, Kimberly and Lynn recoil from the windows and try to shout explanations at the Fields' family.

Jia pulls us along after them, our arms tightening like a strained dog leash. "I'm not leaving her!"

The third Untrakeeper steps out of the night, blazing into my vision as it runs for the car and everyone trying to get inside. A rush of nausea overcomes me. I double over, pulled forward by my friends' tug-of-war with Jia.

"There!" I manage, gesturing with my chin to the Untrakeeper's location.

Fire streaks overhead.

The Untrakeeper moves towards Paige.

So do the flames.

Jia's hand, for just a split second, releases mine. "Paige! Look out!"

Paige wrestles out of her parents' grip, stayed by Jia's warning, eyes widening at the approaching hellfire.

"Get in!" Elisha shouts at the Fields family, throwing open the car door.

The fireball sets the Untrakeeper ablaze—just as the alien grabs Paige's hand.

"NO!" Jia launches herself forward.

I catch Jia's flailing arm, hope for the best, and teleport us into darkness.

CHAPTER 3

The smell of the dull tile in the hallway hits me first and alights a cacophony of colours in my synesthetic brain. Thick dust: a warm green. Lemon-scented cleaner: self-explanatory yellow, wrapped in a cocktail of strong chemicals eliciting red and black. A trace of old shoes, possibly leather: a gradient of dotted brown into a thick grey line of despair and obligation.

Are we in a school? An elevator door with an *up* button to our left and the corridor continues at a ninety-degree angle ahead of us. The flickering warm fluorescents creep me out and tug at my memory.

We've all made it—wherever and *whenever* we are.

Jia grabs me with both hands and surprising strength. "Take me back. Now."

"What were those things?" Sunni asks, taking Jia swiftly by the arms and settling her down.

"I had to get us away." My heart pounds and everything sounds like it's underwater. "There are these *things* that came after me before, in the place..." I feel like I'm describing a dream. With every sentence, my sense of my teleportation powers drifts further out of reach. My words can't approach the level of complexity required to convey my dread. "They guard the doors in the place between time. They *change* the doors. I don't know. They don't like it that I go there. It's their domain. They know I can travel. They're after me." Shivers run up and down my front just thinking about them. My entire being rejects the thought of them. "If they catch me…" I shake my head uncontrollably.

Misty grabs my wrists swiftly; the gesture is gentle, like a kindergarten teacher comforting a young student. "They're not here right now, right?"

"I…no. Don't think so." I glance at Wil for confirmation, but even he looks unsure. I don't like when Wil is unsure. I especially hate that I'm the only one who can see the interdimensional demons harassing us. Harassing *me*.

"Kimberly got in the car with Greg and Elisha and Lynn," I say, trying to change the subject. "They probably got away, right?"

"Yeah," Misty says, with equal uncertainty. "You saw that, right?"

Sunni nods obediently. We exchange hopeful glances, willing it to be true.

Except Jia. She's fuming. "You have to go back and *change* it!"

"No one is changing anything," Misty says flatly.

"Right, because it's all about *you!*" Jia retorts.

QUIET. Wil's booming voice echoes in our minds, a telepathic hand-to-the-mouth. I flatten against the wall, and it's then the familiarity of the hallway unravels into recognition. I know exactly where we are.

I storm to the end of the corridor and round it. No guards. Just the double doors leading into the hangar. We're in Conrod building. We infiltrated this place when I first arrived here, and strange tones drove me insane, and we stole a spacecraft to sneak onto the mother ship.

"When are we?" I ask nervously, more to myself than to my friends. A knot twists in my stomach. I've made a terrible mistake in coming here. I've dug us deeper into a time-travelling hole from which we can never hope to escape.

"You don't know?" Sunni asks. The four of them follow me towards the hangar doors.

"Huh. I think I recognize this place..." Misty orients herself, checks her phone, and paces the corridor, ever watchful for enemies. "It's January twentieth. We're nine days in the past."

"Should you be throwing us around like this? Blindly?" Sunni asks diplomatically.

"Better here than back at the barn," I reply quietly. How long will it take for the Untraver aliens to find me? *Can* they find me in the past? To be fair, it's in the past for my friends, excluding Wil. For me, only a day or so has passed since the explosion in the underground library, plus the time spent wandering the Untraver, which I'm having trouble recalling with extreme clarity. It seems one doesn't age or require food while travelling through there, which is convenient, because it's easy to get lost in there.

What if the Untrakeepers are right behind—?

I shake my appendages to physically flick the spiraling thoughts from my brain. I must think of something, anything else.

Ethan. I grasp onto the thought like a drowning woman to buoyant debris. I was aiming to return to Sparkstone at the end of December, to the day of the portal explosion, and I've obviously failed. I want desperately to save Ethan, and the others, from certain death.

Unless...they survived? It seems unlikely, but the thought sparks hope. We're at Sparkstone nearly a month after the explosion. As my friends case the corridors, kill cameras, and bicker about their reactions to the creatures and Jia's family at the farmstead, I spiral once more into fantastical self-indulgence. What has happened here at Sparkstone in our absence? This building appears intact. The lack of guards suggests they've abandoned the place entirely. But why would the lights still be on?

"Any way you could just take us out?" Misty asks me, exhausted from a circular argument with Jia.

My silence is answer enough. I'm too embarrassed to act. For the longest time, I'd thought love triggered my power. My passion for Ethan had fuelled and propelled me through space and time. But it's hope—not love—that gives my body the lightness and untethers me from our linear timelines. I have little hope within me, more of a curiosity, and a despair that I can't navigate to the one place I can prevent my despair.

"I'm sorry," I say quietly. I hate failing. I hate *being* the problem. "Except..."

There is a way to fix this.

Wil tries to stop me as I barrel for the hangar doors. He shouts for Jia to pull me into her invisible world. My desire to know is faster than my good sense. I throw open the double doors like a Nor'easter rampaging through the home of my ancestors.

The last time we tore through here, it had been more of a warehouse than a hangar bay, littered with crates and spooky red lights, and a shuttlecraft that called to Wil and served as our vehicle to the stars. Now, it's a fully operational bay. The red lights are blue-white, reflecting off dozens of shuttlecrafts, fighter ships, small cargo runners, and other ship designs I can't name. Regardless of class, most are flat on top with an underbelly and a long tail, like a stingray. None of them match the grandeur of the mother ship, of course, but the largest of the stingrays rivals a yacht. A trace of new-car smell lingers on each shiny grey-green craft we pass, and I detect ozone too. Some of these have been to space, but if my superpowered nose is to be believed, I don't think these ships have seen the sun—or the stars—in a little while.

The technology dazzles my brain as I nervously navigate the around, under, and between the ships. It's as if we've snuck into a dealership. Money and resources beyond imagination built this place. We saw it before it was fully realized and these ships display a fraction of the Collective's power. No one's here that we can see guarding the fleet. With all of these grounded ships, the Collective must still be ruling over the students...right? They wouldn't leave alien technology unattended.

"Cameras? People?" Misty whispers to Wil as we file into the seemingly deserted shipyard.

A pause. I wait for a team of hafelglob or fishmen to materialize and take us on. Our shoes scrape and click on the pristine floor, threading ribbons of animated colour between my ears. My synesthesia has become more acute as my teleportation power ripened. Not even my senses can be anchored to one lane.

He closes his eyes and presses a finger to his temple. "A few in the floors above us. No one on this floor. I doubt they're concerned about anyone stealing ships. Security footage, I already scrubbed it. Not a problem, for now. I remember there being more cameras last time." He squints and gestures to the double doors. "The ceiling opens, as we all know. The controls can be accessed in the control room up there." He points discreetly to a dark, windowed room above us that I haven't noticed before. The window stretches across the entire width of the hangar. A blue-purple light, potentially from a computer monitor, bathes the dark room above in a spooky glow.

I crane my neck to the ceiling, where the secret, closed hangar door waits to open to the sky. What if Ethan is up there, in the care of alien scientists? Or worse: have they left him in the ruins of the underground library, buried beneath the rubble?

"We should find out if..." I say, realizing only after I've breathed that I've uttered my thoughts out loud.

As if tugged by an invisible string, I angle my body back towards the double doors. I have to get out of this building and find him.

Sunni catches my arm, kindly, as if I am a demented grandmother who has forgotten her family. "We can't go messin' around out there right now."

I know that. She knows I know that, and Wil knows I know that, and it takes every ounce of willpower in me to face them. "We're not going to run into our past selves. Right now, you're back at Jia's barn, and I'm in the Untraver. The in-between place."

I hear the objections to my argument before they're said. I know I'm wrong. Their words wash over me anyway.

"Whatever is going on out there is our past," Wil says with a frown, as if calculating his personal position within our consolidated timeline. It's his future, but he belongs here with us now. I've sealed that for him.

"Yeah, we shouldn't touch anythin'," Misty agrees and scrubs her eyes with her ringed hands. "I hate time travel."

The corners of Sunni's lips twitch into a smile. "We'll figure out something."

Jia takes out her phone and stares at the screen, distracted.

In my shame, I nod. I didn't mean to bring them here to this day. We are at the mercy of my deepest desires.

Thankfully, Wil takes pity on my feelings and changes the subject. "There are so many of them."

"We could take one," I say. I'm joking. Mostly. There's an unusual allure to the idea, akin to entering a fully-stocked store during an apocalypse. No one's around. We can take anything without consequences. Go anywhere in space and time.

Misty looks excited by the prospect. Sunni quells her enthusiasm. "It looks abandoned now, but what if they're rigged with explosives or something? What if our actions here change something important, for everyone? How do we explain that?"

We don't have to explain anything, I want to tell her. We don't belong in this time. Let the Collective create their own explanations. They will never catch us, not while I'm alive.

Wil throws me a concerned glance at these thoughts. "It would be useful to have a travelling base."

"We had a *base* until you came and brought the aliens and destroyed it," Jia scolds him, not looking up from her phone.

"We have to rescue them and having a ship would make that easier. Can't have Ingrid dipping in and out of time while we're trying to fight a battle across every front," Wil replies.

Jia regards him coldly. "Isn't that what we're doing now?"

Sunni's gaze darts about the hangar. She looks pale. "Let's just get on with it before we're spotted. We should disable the ships we don't steal. So they can't follow."

Wil nods. "I'll help you."

"Who will release the hangar controls?" I ask, pointing at the ceiling. Wil is the obvious choice for the job, as he's the one with a special connection to machines, but he's only one man.

"Someone go up there and see what they can do without me." He points to the spooky control room. "Otherwise, I can help after I disable these ships."

Jia sighs. "By someone, you mean me."

Brushing off his pants with his knuckles, he replies nonchalantly without looking at her, "If you wouldn't mind. Some stairs are over—"

"I see them," Jia cuts him off, shoving her phone back into her pocket. She's about to snag Misty for company, but Sunni drags her off to a nearby ship. They're speaking in hushed tones about the Collective occupation in Sunni's universe, as Sunni points out features on the various ships in the hangar. Wil shadows them, listening intently.

Resigned, Jia's gaze falls on me. I have flashbacks to being the last person picked in gym class. She turns and heads for the stairs with determination. I follow her cautiously, aware that a rogue hafelglob, a wayward student, or the Untrakeepers might jump out at any moment.

We pass under an archway. Stairs spin round lazily to our left, haloed beneath blue lighting, and lead directly into the control room. I put a hesitant foot on the first step when Jia doesn't lead the way. It goes without saying between us that entering the control room within Jia's invisible shroud is smarter than strutting into traps that Wil hasn't foreseen.

"I'm angry with you," she says as she grasps my arm, preparing to activate her powers.

I swallow over the lump in my throat. "I know. I'm sorry."

"You're not sorry. Don't pretend to be," she hisses. "And really? Wil? You had to bring him here, after everything?"

"I wasn't going to let him die."

"You're not going to let anyone die," Jia says with a menacing finality. "We're going back there."

"Now?" I ask her.

The idea burns greedily in her gaze. "Can you?"

I've never seen her like this before. It makes me uneasy. "What am I supposed to do when we're there? We don't have any way to heal your sister. Do you really want to take her out of her time, and explain all this to her? To have her chased by interdimensional beings? All that, when she doesn't even *know* you?"

She wants to hit me. I deserve it. I would hit me, if our situations became reversed.

"Look," I say, hands splayed to perform damage control. "She will always be at that moment in time. In pain, yes. But we can go back when we're more prepared to help her. When we know more about"—*don't think about them*—"the attack. Time is on our side."

The realization passes over Jia's face like curtains opening an anticipated Broadway show. "You're going to go back and save Ethan, aren't you."

It's not a question. My face heats. "When I'm ready."

"Add my sister to your list. And all of our families," she says.

"They're on there," I reply.

"I wish you had left him be," Jia says, jutting her head towards the ships. "I won't forgive you for bringing him here. I don't think I can forgive him, for what he did. I thought I did, when he..." She trails off. She doesn't need to rehash Wil's death.

"I know," I reply quietly. "I'm sorry. But it's...already been done."

"And Wil's body?"

The question catches me by surprise. "It's safe."

"Where?"

Seeing that I'm not going to release that information easily, she curls her lip in resignation. We are a team again. Planning and plotting against the Collective. Just as we had done before Wil and Sunni died.

We climb the curved stairway. The blue LED lights create strange shadows on the floor; it's going to be difficult to hide our presence if the Collective shows up. I search for cameras and wonder how much time we have until someone discovers us trespassing and raises the alarm.

The control room has no door, just an archway to match the oblong, giant window overlooking the hangar. The controls are a mix of digital panels on light-up screens and physical buttons, switches, and knobs. It looks like an old recording studio underwent a half-hearted glow-up to join the twenty-ninth century.

"Why doesn't he just open the hangar?" I mutter to Jia, resisting the urge to press the buttons just to see what will happen.

She fails to hide her grimace as she peruses the controls. "Wil does what he wants, and sends others to do his bidding. He's only friends with us so long as he can control us. With words or otherwise."

"You don't really think that, do you?"

"Ingrid. Remember what he did to you."

So much has happened since Wil used his power against me, when he created a secret plan to expose the Collective, breaking our boundaries of our friendship. "But Future Wil was different, remember? Whatever we do now changes him." And if people can change, the events surrounding us can too.

Peering into the hangar, I watch Wil, Sunni, and Misty inspect the ships. Wil, caressing the hulls of each gently, like a craftsperson who had just put the finishing touches on each. Sunni, her hand gripping Misty's as if letting go meant death, inspecting the docking wheels and occasionally noting damage for each vehicle. Misty, along for the ride, living in each moment fully as if she would never see Sunni again.

"All of the controls are in English, at least," Jia says, snapping me out of my thoughts and changing the subject away from Wil.

"Humans must also work here?"

I frown. The Collective has only recently exposed the existence of aliens to Sparkstone University, and they only did so under the guise of being humans themselves. "Sometimes in human form the aliens speak English, so I guess that makes sense. Or maybe they have the Brigade working here." I remember Shane slinking out of the underground library, right before the explosion. Had he lived? I fight the urge to run to the infirmary and find out.

Jia sits at a console connected to the panels, a keyboard, and mouse. While the hardware is modern, the screen awakens to a simple program that looks like it was made in the eighties. A green bulleted list greets us: *Camera 1, Camera 2, Log A, Log B.* The numbers continue up to thirty and the letters through to *X.*

"I guess this isn't the docking controls," I say, but we've both been soured by our conversation about Wil, and neither of us can resist the urge to look through the Collective's files.

First, we check the footage from the camera in the hall outside the hangar. There's a split-second blip where Wil mentally altered the footage to erase our presence. Otherwise, the place is devoid of life.

Clumsily at first, but then more confidently, Jia cycles through every security camera on the list. Unlike the security office we broke into during my first twenty-four hours at Sparkstone, this terminal only has cameras in this building. There's no audio. And as Wil had confirmed, life signs only exist on the upper levels of the building. A few bored-looking Brigade humans scroll mindlessly on their phones as they amble the halls. No hafelglob or aliens-in-disguise.

"They're human. Shouldn't there be more aliens in this building? Given, you know, the ships?" I say, mostly to myself.

"We could go ask them about it," Jia suggests. "That is, if you *really* don't care about disrupting a timeline."

The idea hangs in the air. Access to the security footage is a far too tempting boon and easier than risking a social interaction.

"How far back does the footage go?" I ask, trying to seem casual.

The screen changes as Jia taps the keys and finds the footage archive. Lines of files flicker past as she scrolls madly. "Pretty far. The Collective keeps everything."

I consider the situation carefully. "Go back to the day of the portal explosion."

Jia presses her lip in a fine line and heeds my request.

We flip through the camera logs. Humans in Brigade uniforms patrol the halls and exchange curt words. They're armed with alien weapons. They enter each room in the building in an orderly fashion, and file out again, shaking their heads. They're led by a student I don't recognize. All of the footage on the day the underground library explosion features Brigaders searching the building. Not helpful to my personal crusade.

"Are they looking for us?" I wonder aloud.

Jia flips to the next day, and the next, and silently we examine the following days of the explosion, from the perspective of this building. As the Brigade searches wane, the hafelglob maintenance workers return to their normal duties. They clean the hallways with robotic efficiency. When they're finished, they stare at the walls. For hours. Sometimes, they throw a glance at the camera. As if knowing I'm watching them, in the future.

The other workers in the building—aliens, disguised as humans— ignore the hafelglob's strange behaviour. They've got problems. A security person with large, pus-filled hives strolls through the corridor, absently scratches one of his wounds, freaks out, and faints. An office worker coughs up dark blood, stares at their hand for five minutes, and doesn't resist as two mask-wearing Brigade members escort them out of the room and the building.

Soon, the Brigade members, who have given up wearing masks, are carrying unconscious aliens-as-humans through the hallways. Others are leaving in body-bags, dragged by college-aged kids who probably didn't sign up for this. One alien-in-disguise catches my eye.

"Can we pause?" I ask.

Jia manipulates the keyboard and mouse, figures out the controls, and manages to rewind the footage and zoom in on an unconscious person being carried.

It's not someone we know. The image pixelates as we zoom in. But there's something off about their face. It's human, and yet it's *not*. All of the aliens we've encountered at Sparkstone University—aside from the fishmen guards and Jadore—have gone to great lengths to conceal their true race from the rest of us. They appear to us as humans, even if they're unusual in appearance or behaviour. This person appears to be a fish-human hybrid, complete with gills, scales on their face, and large fish-eyes. This isn't like Tilly Newman, who under torture, lost control of her shapeshifting powers and became a mix of creatures. This unconscious fish-person is a deliberate mix of humanoid and aquatic traits.

"Another experiment?" Jia guesses.

"Or a mutation," I say slowly.

Brigade members escort doubled-over scientists from their offices and posts. Others collapse and have to be carried from the building. Jia stops at one image of a seemingly empty corridor, not unlike the one where we just arrived. A long, scaled hand reaches out delicately from the door and stretches four fingers outward, splayed and begging for help. They tremble. And then fall flat on the tile floor.

As we peruse through the days, the number of workers in Conrod Building dwindles. Even the hafelglob vanish. The diligence of the Brigade collapses. Fewer patrols. Unregulated changes to the black uniform. The older teens perform their daily corridor checks with less precision and in a rush to return to the lobby, open their phones, and scroll mindlessly.

Then, we see a face we do recognize. Emerging from the hangar into the hallway, is Agailya. She's sweating and paler than usual. She's helped through the doors by two humans I don't recognize, though from their graceful movements and lithe bodies, I assume they're ahmei in disguise.

Agailya lived. If Agailya lived...perhaps the rest survived. My heart jumps—

—until she crumples to the ground. Viscous purple liquid drips from her eyes and lips. The hafelglob custodians quickly help her to her feet, and she fails to brush them away. She exchanges a few words with the hafelglob, and although there's no audio, I recognize one word: *Jadore*. The custodians usher her out of view.

Is this a side effect of her survival? What battle is she fighting with Jadore now? As we scroll forward in time, more aliens in human disguise succumb to similar and stranger symptoms: nosebleeds, spontaneous fainting, and vomiting. A once-bustling, professional space for engineering and science becomes the sight of a violent outbreak.

The date on the bottom of the screen is two days ago.

Whatever happened here seems to have only affected the aliens. The humans that remain must still be on a payroll—or receiving some kind of benefit—otherwise, why stay? They don't care about the security of the Collective.

Something terrible happened to the Collective after we left, and my excited heart pounds with excitement as the unbidden thought blooms.

What do *we* do to cause this?

Are you two having any luck up there? Wil asks telepathically.

Startled by his telepathic intrusion, I wince and step to the window, leaning over the consoles lined against it. He stands in front of a sleek ship the size of a car, hands in his pockets, staring up at me expectantly.

I shake my head and shrug at him.

I suppose I can come have a look, he replies.

Jia sighs and pushes the wheely chair backwards. "No, we can find it. We can't..."

A ringing in my ear overtakes Jia's voice. I absently rub at it. It abates, briefly. "Sorry, what did you say?"

She's on the other side of the room now, examining the consoles. "I mean, there's got to be a button or handle that says *open hangar*, right? Foolproof, in case..."

I'm itching my ear again, this time violently. The buzzing noise comes from within my mind and eats all other sounds. This means one thing. The Untrakeepers are nearby.

Not again.

If they disrupt my past, there's no telling what changes they'll bring about.

Changes that will prove to Campbell that the past is mutable.

Movement on the terminal monitor catches me off-guard. We've stopped on a live camera feed from the lobby. The front doors of the building fly open. Of all the people in the universe, Jadore stumbles into the building and nearly trips over her own feet. Maybe it's the low quality of the monitor, or injuries suffered from the portal explosion; she looks terrible. She hesitates, as if trying to remember which way to go, and then heads for the elevator.

The buzzing in my ear intensifies.

"We have to hide," I say, tapping Jia on the shoulder.

She brushes me off as she continues to examine the controls. "I think I can find it! Just give me—"

I hear Jadore, Wil warns us. *And others...*

"Jia!" I shake her.

She sighs in exasperation and gives up. "Fine, fine, let's go."

We run out of the control room and down the curved stairs. Perhaps we can hide in one of the ships? The hatches on each appear closed and some don't have ramps leading up. Sunni, Misty, and Wil gather around and we grasp each other tightly. Jia's power works through touch, and can extend through another person or object as necessary.

Just as she closes her eyes in concentration, Jadore bursts into the room. Like prey, my friends and I freeze, collectively hoping that lack of movement will deter Jadore from acting against us. We could have disappeared from her view in a blink. Yet the five of us remain in shock as we take in our principal nemesis, the person who has tormented us since day one—and the mess she had become. I have seen Jadore as the blind professor, a powerful alien queen of her domain in a throne, and a deranged, driven soul desperate to master the secrets of the universe. This look is new.

The explosion must have burned away much of her reptilian-human hybrid flesh, as her exposed skin—patchy red and white, stitched with green scales—from beneath the hospital gown appears grafted. Her fingernails have receded into pointed, curved claws, which extend towards the parked ships like antennas evaluating signals. Her dark lizard-like eyes dart from one craft to another as she starts towards one in fits, stops, and turns towards another, as if searching for the perfect one. With purple lips, she hisses strange alien words under her breath.

But she seems uninterested in frying us with her stolen power. She marvels at us, as if truly seeing us for the first time. "How did…?" Her sultry croak trails off when she spots Wil. "I see."

Shouting from beyond the door startles us all into action. Including Jadore. Blue-white sparks dance between her fingers; that's all they do as she points them at equally confused guards, who push their way into the room. They are hafelglob in human form, from the look of them. Puzzled, Jadore stares at her hands as if they don't belong to her. She mouths something inaudible.

The hafelglob make up most of the campus maintenance and security at Sparkstone University. While in human form, they speak in a strange accent. Their true form is a grotesque tentacled blob that oozes the stench of garbage. Never-ending teeth spiral down a singular mouth—the only part of its body that isn't a flesh-coloured lump. Despite my distaste for them, the hafelglob seem to have an unearned reverence for me. They identified me as the Crosskey the moment I arrived at Sparkstone, a title they gave me before knowing my true power. I don't understand why they continue to be loyal to Jadore *and* help me. Perhaps I will never know.

"Mistress. You shouldn't be in—" The hafelglob clock me and my friends, which seems to interrupt their justified concern for Jadore. "Crosskey. You survived. The others—"

"Yeah," I say sharply, cutting him off. My face colours. Not knowing what happened to the others means Wil and the others can't accuse me of knowingly changing the past. If Jadore survived— as terrible as she looks—and if Agailya made it, perhaps Ethan *is* all right.

Jadore cocks her head.

"Oh…" A smug smile slides up her face, taunting me. She throws back her head and a cackle escapes her. Tiny sparks flicker between her too-white teeth.

I don't like this. "What's so funny?" I demand.

"Stupid, stupid girl…" Jadore says between her laughing fits.

I advance towards her without a plan, but the hafelglob in disguise shake their heads in unison as they take advantage of her stupor and drag her towards the door.

"Do not trifle," says one, over Jadore's uncontrollable howls.

"Dangerous," says another.

Glued in place, I think about Ohz, the hafelglob trapped in the Untraver. He can't leave without me guiding him to the right door.

And in thinking about the Untraver, the buzzing in my ears reaches a tipping point. It rips through my brain and I double over. Jia grabs my torso to prevent me from crumpling completely. From the corner of my darkening vision, the hafelglob pause, concerned.

"Am fine," I say. Or I think I say this, because I can't hear myself over the cursed noise that has transformed into a cacophony of strained voices. The Untrakeepers, taunting me.

HERE/WHEN YOU ARE, SO ARE WE.

They bleed from the walls and floors in a terrifying, soundless display of grace. Some tumble down the stairs from the control room, others throw open the double doors and strut with frighteningly large legs, and thankfully precious few materialize from the ceiling and crawl down the walls. Two of the Untrakeepers, in unconcerned haste, clamber around one of the parked ships behind us. Their long fingers scrape against the metal and reduce the technology to shards. I register twelve as I shield my friends to protect them, as if it will do any good.

"They're back," I say needlessly.

The dazzling display of their power has left the two hafelglob stunned. Jadore bears her pointed teeth. Impotent electricity sparks and then dies around her fists. They cannot see the Untrakeepers, but the aftermath of their destruction sends a clear message.

"You can't scare me!" Jadore warns, and another laugh escapes her. With a suspicious glance at Wil, she leaves the hafelglob in the dust and heads for a small shuttlecraft a few feet away "I'm going to…"

I don't care to hear the rest. Jadore is the least of our present concerns. The Untrakeepers are closing in. Wil reads the positions of the Untrakeepers from my mind like a beeping radar and tosses them to my friends. As the hafelglob regain their senses and chase after the crazed Jadore, Wil thinks quicker than the rest of us and points at the nearest ship. "In here."

The craft isn't the largest or the most advanced looking of the fleet, though its landing gear rivals my height and props the ship at least a foot above many of the others in the hangar. The weathered, charcoal-colored hull has been recently patched with panels made of a shimmering alloy on its port side, and as the ship hums to life, these panels faintly glow an ethereal blue along the ripple-lines, like highway traffic seen from an airplane window. An outer door opens in welcome to an airlock and a ramp slides out like a tongue, beckoning us to venture into its sleek belly.

An alarm blares in the hangar and the blue light flips to an ominous blood red. Whether the trigger is Wil's illicit mind-hacking of the cameras finally catching up with us, Jadore's bizarre intrusion, or the Untrakeepers shattering a ship, we're cooked if we stay. Misty's hand is in mine, and we're all gripping each other for dear life as we ascend the ramp into this strange Collective ship.

One of the Untrakeepers reaches the bottom of the ramp and puts a tentative foot on the studded metal, as if unsure about the change in elevation. "Behind!" I shout.

Misty releases me, pushes Sunni and Jia ahead, and I feel Wil touch both of our minds as he guides Misty's fireball towards the target. It hits the otherworldly alien square in the chest. It screams as it falls on its back.

An onslaught of images slams me simultaneously. I grit my teeth as my brain struggles to interpret the whisper-sounds interlaced within the visual components of the mind communication: *YOU DO NOT /KNOW/INJEST WHAT YOU DO.*

"Yeah, I know," I mutter.

A couple more steps, and then the airlock, and then another interior door. Someone helps me navigate these hurtles as I shrug off the Untrakeeper's mental attack. My friends and I ensconce ourselves in the cockpit as the airlock doors shut with a hiss behind us. I let out a breath of relief. This buys us a few minutes, at least. Unless they can tear this ship to shreds as well.

At first, I feel like I'm in a museum. The controls are a mix of knobs, sliders, and LED-like screens flashing a logogram language I've seen before on the mother ship. I see a similar recognition on my friends' faces, save Sunni. The cockpit is similar to the ship we hijacked when we rescued our universe's Sunni from Jadore, all those months ago, when we didn't know each other and our time together had just begun. Instead of lockers, two built-in benches line the walls of the cockpit, with accompanying seat-belt-like straps. The domed glass canopy serving as a view screen over the cockpit reminds me of a fishbowl. Except we're the fish.

Misty shouts at Wil to figure out the controls. Jia braces the door with her shoulder, even though the door is airtight. The porthole window shows the empty airlock, though the dull blaring of the alarm reminds us of the danger outside.

Both Wil and Sunni sprawl over the cockpit and slide into the pair of seats beneath the canopy. One of the Untrakeepers crawls down the window and yawns its black mouth at me menacingly.

YOUR BEGINNING IS THIS PLACE, it says to my mind. It lifts a long, spindly finger and curls it into a hook, threatening to break the glass.

"Don't!" I shout, distracting Wil and Sunni.

But the Untrakeeper doesn't claw the ship to pieces. It crawls up the canopy and clambers on top of the ship. My friends hear the sounds and tense up. Wil and Sunni return to the controls.

It could have broken us. Prevented our escape. Why do they hesitate? *My beginning is this place.* But it's not. Unless it's talking about the ship?

What has happened before, will happen again.

Wil raises his eyebrows at me expectantly. We couldn't figure out how to open the bay doors. We're trapped unless we can blast our way through. I return the expectant stare. We blasted our way through before, so—

Our battle of wits is interrupted as the ship rocks violently on its landing gear. We fall like rag dolls. Above us, I hear the multiple, scrambling feet of Untrakeepers. More climb the sides. They're trying to tip us over, to scare us into exiting the ship.

Wil and Sunni trade technical babble, but it quickly dawns on me that there is a way out that doesn't involve destroying property or abandoning ship.

"You want me to...?" I ask, looking to the rest of them as we scramble to hang on. My heart sinks, realizing how stupid I am to bring them to this place. I hadn't thought about the consequences.

Just skipping around my memories to get away from the Untrakeepers.

I'm so done with this. Time travelling all over the place, messing with the past without actually rescuing anyone, trying to outrun strange aliens and demanding answers from another? Campbell chose me because I am destined for greatness. I must live into that. I reach deep down into the feelings I'm not allowed to express. *I just want this to be over. Take us to the end. Let's just go there and do what we need to do and then, maybe—*

When I open my eyes, we're sailing the high seas.

A brisk breeze whips my cheeks and sweat drenches my clothes, as if someone has pointed a pressure-washer at me. A scream gurgles up inside and I try to move. The small raft holds my feet captive. Is this a dream? Sunni is here. It's dark and cold. The air is oddly stale, despite the taste of salt on my tongue and the billowing blue sails above.

Yet as I stretch my arms and splay the fingers on my left hand, the ship lists and veers to port, lightly bumping into the wall of the endless corridors. Black water sloshes onto the wooden raft. Misty and Sunni grab each other for safety. Jia catches her balance readily. Wil stares at me with a mix of awe and concern.

I am the ship. I'm bringing it with us, through the Untraver. I just have to find the right door that will bring us to the end.

The corridor stretches and retracts to accommodate the width of the ship like a dark, artificial bowel. Our ship in this liminal space is a slab of tied-together wooden logs, fixed with a sturdy mast and three healthy sails glowing a strange, brilliant blue. They breathe with me my lungs tingle, as if overtaken with goose flesh. My stomach growls. I wasn't hungry before; now I'm starving. Part of me wonders if the walls are edible.

Stop! That's silly! I have to find the correct door.

My friends marvel at the Untraver, but their voices are distant, as if I am hearing them through a vent. I feel the correct door's presence, somewhere to port, many turns ahead. I direct us ninety degrees, around a sharp corner. I hear shouting. Jia taps me on the shoulder, warning me of the water flooding the stern.

Then, things get hazy. I don't always remember my time in the Untraver. I recall drifting. The sounds of danger. Far off cries of the Untrakeepers—had I brought them back here? They'd been touching the ship when I'd teleported, so maybe. They're long gone now, perhaps lost beneath the waves of time. My boots soak through, but not *really*, because the water isn't real.

We bump against the correct door. I'm jolted back into awareness. Wil turns the knob. It's locked.

My friends look to me.

I stretch—and stretch *further*. Now, my arm is the mast and it bends too, as flexible as a cheese string. As the blue, glowing sails touch the door, there's a *click*. The door swings open with a satisfying *thwamp*, as if recoiling from us.

The threshold widens as we pass through. A white light flashes. I gasp for air and blink, and collapse to the rough metallic floor. I keep moving, sliding down, and then forward, then...up?

The air is still stale. We're still onboard the spaceship. But we're not in the Untraver anymore. The low-level light from the controls is the only thing I can see. Something orange blinks softly. The uncontrollable pang of hunger has evaporated, replaced with faint nausea and disgust. Had I actually thought about eating the walls of the Untraver? I really hope I didn't.

I bump against the wall. Turns out, it's the ceiling.

No gravity. No sound. No power. We're dead in space.

CHAPTER 4

My friends wake from the dream-state around me. The cabin fills with red and yellow light as comet-like streaks of brilliance flash across our hull. A battle rages outside, in space. A distance sound swirls yellow and purple and tastes like stomach acid. The alien alloys of the ship tremble, struggling to protect us from the vacuum and chaos outside. Smaller ships dart in and out of view, firing streaky beams and missiles.

The hair on my arms lifts in trepidation as a massive cruiser looms above us, gliding through the void like a predatory shark stalking its prey. A sleek shadow darts across the cruiser's port bow, and suddenly a short-lived, white-hot flame erupts from the smaller vessel's underbelly, scorching the cruiser's hull. The nimble attacker, like a tiny dragon breathing fire, banks sharply away as the wounded behemoth gives lumbering chase, its engines flaring blue-white in pursuit.

Sunni's eyes grow large. She grabs onto me as we float together in lonely darkness. "Where did you bring us?"

"I wanted to go to the end," I say, my tongue thick with sleep.

An orangey-red light continues to flash silently on the cockpit control panel as the cabin darkens again.

"What happened to the power?" Misty demands as she desperately searches the cockpit from her position below me, as if looking for an instructional manual. We're caught off-guard as another shadow-ship tears by. Our ship tilts forty-five degrees in its wake and we drift port-side. Sunni and Wil grab onto their seats, trying to not to float away.

Panic-stricken, Wil splays a hand across the paneling, closing his eyes, connecting with the machine.

"I just wanted it all to end," I say, though my friends aren't listening. What about this place—this *time*—signals my end? This isn't where Campbell told me to meet.

Why did the Untrakeeper tell me I was at my *beginning?*

"Try to grab something," Wil warns.

Whatever he's doing works and gravity is restored. The five of us are thrown starboard. Jia and Misty's heads smack into the bench. I crash into Misty in a tangled heap. I scramble up and help her to her feet, muttering an apology as we take in the chaos illuminated on the curved view screen.

It's like we're participating in a virtual reality simulation. My brain screams that this can't be real, and yet, here we are. I have a moment outside my body that nearly untethers me to the moment. I shake my head. I can't afford to jump again. Not until I know more.

A sleek ship veers around the large cruiser. Its design appears unlike the others. With multiple weapons across its hull, it looks over-engineered to destroy. As it points its nose our way, a sickening thud in the pit of my stomach signals the danger seconds before it fires bright missiles.

Words are too slow. I point and yell something incomprehensible. Sunni does the same. Wil is already maneuvering.

I blink. Another flash of light, somewhere on our starboard side. The enemy ship shatters into hundreds of shards as several targeted missiles explode upon impact. A second ship, larger and bulkier than the enemy, scatters the debris as it whips past us. Something about the design rings a bell. It might be the same class as this ship.

The orange light flashes more insistently this time.

"What's that flashing?" I yell, as Misty says, "Seems like we have some friends out there."

"Do you know how to fly this thing?" Jia shouts at Wil as we attempt to regain our balance.

"Can you—?" Wil asks Jia and trails off. He doesn't have to finish. She understands intuitively.

"Trying." She crouches and begins an intensive meditation. A ploy to turn the ship invisible, if she has the willpower and stamina. She's done it before. She can do it again.

I hate looking over Wil's shoulder at the controls, ringing my hands like one of my older relatives who doesn't understand technology. We all have our strengths and fighting space battles with alien technology isn't mine. "Do we have weapons?" I ask him.

Sunni's sharp, green gaze scans the controls. She seems at home with them, almost more so than Wil. She brings up a miniature screen covered in coloured dots and triangles. "Another one incoming. We should have some kind of firepower. Just have to find it."

"Should we be firing at ships when we have no idea who is out there?" Jia objects in a calm voice, as she's deep in meditation.

"We have power but no controls," Wil says, and then shoves his fingertips into his temples aggressively. "Ow!"

We're thrown off-kilter as something latches onto us with a terrifying *clunk*. Then, the world swirls around us as we are whipped around and tossed us across the cosmos.

"Something's got us!" Sunni shouts unhelpfully as my stomach does somersaults, along with the ship. I close my eyes and collapse onto the bench, willing whatever is left in my stomach to remain there. The cacophony of our screams shoots through me like rainbows.

We crash into something hard. The ship buckles. Then groans. I groan along with it. The artificial gravity holds. As Sunni assesses the control panels, and Misty inspects Jia's scrapes and bruises, I check on Wil. He's grasping the wall, fingertips to his temples, attempting to mask his pain.

"It doesn't make sense," he whispers. As I kneel before him, he brushes me off. "You're only making it worse."

"Sorry," I say, and a moment later, he mutters an apology too.

"I don't..." Wil trails off and I follow his gaze to the canopy.

Earth is under attack. A blockade made of hundreds of ships surrounds our brilliant blue home like floating, studded armour. Definitely the Collective. The other ships zipping around the inner solar system appear reminiscent of Collective design as well. But they're firing on each other. Dozens of ships dart in and out of the fray and silent explosions obscure our view. When the debris settles, more ships take their place, and the cycle repeats. Jia has a point. It's impossible to tell who is friend or foe. Many of the ships share the design of the one that saved our necks, though they're moving at such speeds that I can't parse individual details. One thing's for sure: they're using the same intense multi-projectile missile on anything that gets in their way.

I attempt to scrub away the eyestrain, quietly thankful that I'm not the pilot right now.

As Wil recovers, Sunni works magic on the controls. We lurch again and the controls light up once more. "Think I got it," she says under her breath.

"I don't see the mother ship," I say.

"She's above us," Sunni says, pointing at the large cruiser wing shadowing the canopy.

"Do they know we're here?" Misty asks.

"I don't know," she says. She looks to Wil as he sits back down in the chair.

As my eyes adjust to the activity outside, I focus again on the Collective ships engaged in battle with each other, and I realize why the designs of some look familiar. Several of them, including the one that rescued us, are doppelgangers of our ship. They appear to be flying in a coordinated dance. They're difficult to count as they dart in and out of view of the canopy. Did I bring us here because I'm in tune with this ship, and this is somehow also its end?

"They look like our ship," I say, pointing to one zipping by.

"Kinda," Misty agrees, squinting.

"One's in trouble," Wil notes, as another fighter launches from the mother ship towards one of our doppelgangers.

"Found gun controls," Sunni intones.

"We shouldn't be shooting—" Jia objects, but Sunni has already activated the weapons. Beneath our feet, there's a *clank* and a *whir*, like machinery waking up from a long nap. A missile flies lazily from our belly towards the enemy ship.

"That's it? These weapons suck," Sunni says.

The enemy ship fires laser-like weapons at our twin and hits them square in the nose, but not before our strike blasts the enemy's port bow. Our doppelganger twists and dives to avoid the enemy ship's momentary loss of control. The orange light flashes again. Wil nearly doubles over.

"So many....voices..."

We may have saved our friend, but now the fighter has decided we're a tastier target.

Jia gives up on meditating and hovers over Wil. He brushes her off too and removes himself from the controls. Misty takes his seat and Sunni quickly tries to teach her the controls with one hand and smashes other buttons with the other. Two more missiles let loose from our belly and fly towards the enemy. It dents their hull, but that's it. It fires red lasers on us again.

The ship shakes. My legs feel like jelly. An alien voice a melodic language intones a warning through hidden speakers.

"I think they've hit our engines. Or, nope, sorry. Fuel? Something is leaking," Sunni says, peering over the controls. "I'll see if I can fix it. C'mon." She motions for Misty to follow her and they disappear out of the cockpit into the unexplored anterior of the ship.

"Uh, hang on—" I try to stop them, but they're both preoccupied. Jia and I share a helpless glance. We definitely don't know anything about ships.

As we shuffle towards the cockpit seats, leaving a toiling Wil to fight his mental demons, a purple beam strikes us head-on. We crash once more into the mother ship to which Sunni had somehow matched orbit and speed. The cabin becomes red once more. The canopy darkens in the top left portion as a virtual screen appears and alien symbols flash menacingly.

"Going to lose gravity soon!" Wil warns with a strained voice.

I don't see our brethren ships anymore. As the mother ship leaves us in its wake, more fighters and a mid-size cruiser bank towards us.

Another warning flashes across the screen, blinking rapidly, in the top right this time.

We're outgunned. Jia isn't the mind-reader, but she nods at me encouragingly. I know what I have to do. I don't know if I have the strength. We have to flee haphazardly or become space debris in an unknown place in Earth's history.

The ships turn their noses towards Earth.

I must lean into my strengths, as the others have done.

From deep within, I conjure happier times. Vacations with my parents. Performing with Ethan in front of the Sparkstone students. Our music captured everyone's attention, even Campbell's. I remember my kiss with Ethan in the music trailer and how safe I felt with him.

My body lightens. I'm ascending—descending?—into the Untraver.

Reality blurs as I open my eyes. Ships fire. Some at us. Some at the blue planet hanging in space. Earth explodes into rock and fire, and the debris floats towards us, until...

We're still in space. The stars outside the canopy twinkle dimly. The battle has disappeared as has the inner solar system, as if I have wiped the scene clean from the alien glass. I remember nothing visual from the Untraver this time; only the impression of being lost, frightened, and desperate. Who knows how much relative body time has passed.

Wil breathes a sigh of relief as he climbs into the empty cockpit seat once more. Whatever was afflicting him seems to have passed. "Thank you."

Jia stares out into space, confused. She rubs at sleep in her eyes. "I think I dreamt the Earth exploded? And now we're here."

I had that dream too. I question my reality as Sunni and Misty reappear in the cockpit.

"We travelled again...right?" Sunni asks.

I nod. "Do we have some kind of star chart or navigation? Or headlights, or something?"

Sunni smirks and nods as she takes the co-pilot seat. She and Wil exchange a few words, and they work together to handle the controls. A couple of screens appear across the canopy, blinking blearily, as if also waking from a wild dream, and then illuminate various viewpoints surrounding our ship. Stars, empty space, and more stars. Then, a brilliant icy blue planet surprises us with its faint rings and silent, orbiting rocky followers.

"Neptune," I say, with stony certainty. My assertion is proved correct with an impressed nod from Sunni.

Jia checks her phone as Sunni and Wil drag us into orbit. "No updates since we were in the hangar."

"Makes sense. No towers in space," Wil says. "But there's probably an internal chronometer...yes, here. Hmm...is that right?" He summons a three-dimensional holographic display above their analog controls that looks like flickering star chart. It blinks to a marginally new display with each ticking second. He glances at Sunni. She shrugs.

"What?" Misty asks. She crosses her arms, mirroring my frustration at being excluded from their expertise.

Wil exhales slowly. "The ship has an internal chronometer so a crew can keep a natural day-night schedule, according to their species' biological needs. It checks and adjusts this chronometer against satellites in orbit and will log any discrepancies, especially if it's been offline for some time. Travelling through space in a spacecraft at near-light speeds means we're dealing with time dilation. Time moves slower for the person in the spacecraft. Usually not by much, but what with the size of the Collective, it's enough that it's worth measuring.

"If it can't find a nearby planet with compatible satellite technology, it will attempt to create a three-dimensional star chart and cross-reference it with its internal database, so it can approximate differences between the time at the original departure location, the passage of time for its crew, and anyone waiting for them at their destination.

"Meaning," he concludes, throwing a glance at me, "When Ingrid jumps the ship in space and time, the ship can approximate the date and time and display that relative to when we left from Earth. We left the Sparkstone hangar on January twentieth. We stopped briefly on April thirteenth, just outside of Earth's orbit. Now, we're in the outer solar system, and it's December twenty-sixth of the previous year."

All eyes turn to me. The portal explosion had been that day. I think. Perhaps it had been Christmas Day. Calendar days are starting to lose their meaning.

"Why are we at *Neptune?*" Misty demands, gesturing to the canopy.

"It's far away from Earth exploding?" I answer with equal sarcasm.

The cockpit descends into thick silence. "I missed that part," Misty says finally in a light tone, but balks as she realizes I'm being serious.

"It…it might have just been a dream. Confusion, from the jump," Jia hedges. "I think everyone could use a minute to just breathe."

No one argues. I cross my arms and make my hands into fists, struggling to hold onto what little body heat I possess. Wil and Sunni fiddle with the consoles, not speaking with each other, but after a few frustrated noises, they manage to find the temperature controls.

"We have a couple of hours of oxygen. Some fuel. Fuel?" Wil ponders this as his fingers dance across the knobs and the digital screens. "Hmm. Nope, that's not right. Looks like there's an oil-based fuel system, but it's not what's powering us right now."

"Oh, we know all about the fuel situation," Misty says, seemingly excited to be the one with the answers. She tilts her head at Sunni. "Can we get this thing on auto-pilot or whatever so we can show them what we found?"

"Yeah. Should be able to."

Wil taps on an LED display beside him, hovering above the canopy glass. Little triangles scurry across the screen. Jia and I peer over his shoulder. "What's that?"

"The battle we just experienced. The ship has external and internal sensors. Some were damaged, but with a bit of help from the internal repair system, we should be able to reconstruct everything it picked up so we can figure out *what* it was. And, uh... well, I already told you the *when*."

He meets my gaze and in is my mirrored fear. April thirteenth. We have a precise date when the mother ship fires upon Earth and shatters it to a million pieces. Assuming we didn't just experience a shared delusion.

Sunni and Misty lead us out of the cockpit, towards the stern of the ship. We pass through an open common area, which I suppose is a *mess* or *mess deck*, as we're aboard a ship. A small booth is tucked in the corner beside a series of counters and alien controls. A galley, perhaps? A tightly spiraling staircase disappears into a hatch, likely a loft. My body screams for sleep, but my brain is wired and my temples feel as if they've been trapped in a vice.

We enter a cramped room at the back of the mess. Three glowing pillars, like life-sized lava lamps, triangulate the space. The colour grips me with familiarity: it's the same glow as the sails of our ship when we were in the Untraver. The wall is framed with a mixture of knobbed panels and LED screens, just like the cockpit and the control room in the hangar at Sparkstone. Unlike the hangar or the cockpit, a particular smell strikes me here, like a new car, or freshly laid laminate floors. The gelatinous substance within the pillar-lamps bubbles intermittently and I squint to get a closer look. My eyes might be playing tricks on me, but I see tiny sparkling dots teaming within the gel.

A memory from the Untraver simmers from beneath the surface. I had felt hungry while piloting the ship through the infinite corridors. That's not normal. I wonder if it has anything to do with the ship itself. I don't sleep or eat in the Untraver; the place freezes bodily functions. I shouldn't have felt anything. But I had felt a sensation not unlike butterflies in my stomach, and it had demanded sustenance.

"Renovation?" I say, feeling the wall and looking to Wil for confirmation.

He mimics my movement and communes with the ship with a thoughtful expression. He nods slowly.

"Welcome to engineering," Sunni says with a strange smile on her face. She excitedly points to a crack running along the bottom of one of the tubes that has been patched by a clear gelatin-like substance. A black stain has coloured the grey metal floor ominously. "The fuel leak was this. Containment failure. Nasty buggers got out all over the floor. Don't touch 'em if it happens. Nearly got us."

"You're talking as if the fuel is alive," I say.

"They *are* alive," Wil confirms. He hovers a finger over the glass. A glob the size of my head bubbles together and presses against its prison. Jia and I recoil instinctively. Even Misty looks concerned.

Sunni is the only one who doesn't look curious about the lifeforms. She crouches like a kid at the zoo before an interesting exhibit.

"Biofuel," Sunni explains. Her eyebrows knit together, as if she's reliving an unpleasant memory. "I love weird bugs and creepy-crawlies. Collected 'em growing up."

Misty's lips press together in a firm line as she worries at her lip ring. Our Sunni's major at Sparkstone had involved entomology. When Sunni glances over her shoulder at Misty, the worrying ceases. Misty puts a comforting hand on Sunni's shoulder and the woman from another universe returns to teasing the tiny creatures.

"But, uh, anyway. That's not how I know 'bout these creatures. We have 'em in our universe too. They're in every ship. We just called them 'little buggers' mostly, but their proper name is *sh-winil.*" She sings the syllables in three distinct notes, beginning with E, flowing into a C-natural, and finishing with a clear A. It sounds like the ahmei language I've heard Agailya and Gayarnu speak.

"This ship isn't from *your* universe though, right?" Jia asks.

"What? No," Sunni replies. "Our ships were more advanced. Had to be, to fight the Collective. Once their true intentions became known to everyone, spaceship tech and other instruments of war became more common."

Explains her quick study of the controls. Strange how our Sunnis are so similar and yet the environment diverged their skillsets. Even the Collectives in our two universes have their differences. A terrible vitaphage devastating the ahmei as a species had severally weakened them and made them reliant on the Collective scientifically and politically. In Sunni's universe, this phage had been cured, and the ahmei play a more militaristic role, as opposed to a purely scientific one. I can't help but wonder how much of the ahmei tongue Sunni has mastered during her time as a rebel.

"The Collective has harnessed these buggers to do their bidding. Not a surprise," Misty mutters.

Right. Because the Collective is gross. Nothing can't not be a gross alien.

"What are they thinking?" Jia asks. The resentment in her tone has quieted. She sounds like she hates her own curiosity.

"They're hungry," Wil replies, and then, "They feel related to the Hunger."

Well. That explains the sensation I felt in the Untraver. I suppose my controlling the ship in there means I have a limited access to the creatures' base instincts. The Hunger had been an experimental creature and energy source that had consumed a lot of people on campus until I teleported it into a supermassive black hole. I'd nearly forgotten about that. The word *sh-winil* and Sunni's pronunciation also rings a bell. Jadore had mentioned using Sh-wnilk'def Stones with the portal technology. I wonder if they're related.

Wil continues, "Like Sunni said, these things are biofuel. Powering everything. They're even functioning as a crude repair system. That was why it was in the hangar. The creatures were learning to repair the ship."

"How? They're trapped in here," Jia says.

"Their powers are like mine, it seems," Wil says affectionately.

I smile a little, until I remember Tilly's screams as Agailya and Gayarnu experimented on her, attempting to bring forward and accentuate her powers. I wonder who or what species died so that these creatures serve the function they do now. They're keeping us all alive. I hate that I'm disgusted and grateful.

"The sh-winil don't like the taste of the ship alloy or the molecules making up the container," Wil continues, as if he's talking to us about the weather. He frowns. "Though they could *learn* to like it, if they're not fed regularly."

"We have to feed our fuel?" I ask.

Misty barely stifles a chortle. "It makes sense. We feed fires, and that's a kind of fuel."

I don't like that these tiny creatures are blackmailing us into keeping them alive. "So, what do they like to eat?"

Wil stands to his full height. "They like the same kinds of food we do. But they also sound picky. I guess they recently had a lot of fishy food and they'd prefer not to have that again for a bit."

"We should do inventory of everything here," Jia says. "There must be rations somewhere. And then we'll have to jump the ship again to somewhere with supplies." I take note of the relief in her voice. She no longer has to steal from her parents.

But my body aches as if I've run a marathon without training. It feels like we've been travelling for days without rest. Probably because we have.

BEEEEEEEEP. The sound cuts through the ship like a hot orange-red knife. I wince.

"What's that?" Jia asks.

"Food's ready," Misty mutters with a smirk and Sunni playfully slaps her arm.

"The analysis is done. Should tell us more about the battle we witnessed," Wil says.

We return to the cockpit. The sight of Neptune fills me with wonder again. Despite the tight quarters, the stuffy, artificial air, and the strange groans of the ship as its little beasts work to repair the behemoth holding them captive, I feel as though a childhood dream has sprung to life around me. I'm travelling in a spaceship with my closest friends.

I glance at each of them in turn: Wil, Sunni, Misty, Jia. They're my *closest friends*. We've been through so much together, I don't know if I've stopped to realize that. There's been no time.

Now, *I* control time.

Sunni leans over the navigation controls and scans a series of screens and buttons on the panelling, then gestures to Wil. "Some of this I get, but can you confirm...?"

"Sure." He brushes past me and sidles up to Sunni. "That's not..." He makes a noise and shakes his head. "I was going to say it's not possible, but I'm here, we're all on a spaceship, and we lived through this, so there's no reasoning out of it. All those other ships firing on the Collective?" He draws a deep breath. "They were us."

"How?" Sunni asks. "How is that possible?"

My ears ring with realization. "Time travel."

"Mmm...yeah...but *how?*" Misty asks, worried, as if I've threatened the love of her life. "Are there more versions of us?"

"Time travel. Not alternate-universe travel," I reply, hoping I don't come off as unhelpful and belligerent. "He's saying that those ships were *us*. The *us* here and now on this ship. We jumped into that fight, but we will continue to jump to it, again and again, in the future. Even if we don't know the reason why right now." At least, I hope there's a reason beyond *we saw our future selves doing it so we figured what the hell let's go back there.*

What has happened before will happen again. Wil and I lock eyes as he continues interpreting the read-out. "I scanned at least fourteen ships with the same serial number and energy signature as this ship. But there weren't the same number of life signs on each one. Sometimes there were five. Sometimes four. Sometimes six." He clears his throat. It seems like he wants to say more on that. He doesn't. "The firepower isn't the same either. A few of the ships are weaker. Others have advanced shields and other modifications.

And if I'm understanding this right, the ships are all different *ages*, despite being the same model."

A heavy silence descends upon us.

"How long are we going to be at this?" I ask.

"A while," Wil replies hesitantly.

"Don't hide it from us," Jia warns him.

As if slapped, Wil turns his cheek and reconsiders the question. "The oldest attacking ship with our energy signature had a chrono-date of several decades from now."

"Okay," Misty says slowly. "But if I'm followin' this, doesn't that mean it comes from the future? Like, Ingrid could jump us to the year 3000, and then back to the battle? Wouldn't that affect the date registering within the ship?"

Wil acknowledges the question with an appreciative nod, taps a few more buttons, and references another readout. "Maybe. If we can trust the operating system, this ship has been in service for about a year. We've already jumped a couple of times and while the chronometer does its best to adjust to the current time, just like our phones do when we change time zones, it looks like it also maintains an up-time log as well. Meaning, it's been counting time since it started its service a year ago, which is important, since that determines its true age, not the part of the chronometer that displays dates and times. Does that make sense?"

I'm wringing my hands absently. "And just because that other ship is ancient, doesn't mean we're zipping around the galaxy as old-timers. Assuming we're going to be doing our fair share of time travelling, there are related time-travel reasons why the ship would age more rapidly than us. You didn't happen to get a read on how old the life signs on each ship are?"

"Nope, no data on that," Wil says firmly. "Just the number of people on board. Mostly five. Sometimes six and sometimes four."

Sometimes six. I cling to that like a lifeline. Ethan could be that sixth person. I will find a way to save him, rules be damned.

The five of us remain quiet for uncountable minutes, mulling over the commitment promised by our future selves to our Herculean—and possibly, Sisyphean—task of taking down the Collective, piece by piece. Time by time.

All I'd wanted was to skip ahead to the part where Campbell validates my efforts, and Ethan is saved. Now, I've tangled our timelines in this mess. "What has happened, has already happened, and will happen again," I mutter.

"How?" Misty asks. "Wouldn't the existence of too many versions of ourselves be, I dunno, against the laws of nature and time?"

I clear my throat. "They are all us, as Wil said. It's not about *versions*, even though that's the best way our language can articulate it. This combat isn't in a parallel universe." At least, I feel it's not. I continue on. "Picture each person here as threaded needles. Each thread is long. We're stitching our fates on a shared, blank canvas of time. But the pattern isn't always a straight line from A to B. Sometimes the pattern calls for us to loop back around"—I draw a petal shape in the air—"to fill in the blank spaces. If you unravel your personal thread, you don't get multiple pieces of thread. It's all one thread, moving in one direction.

"That's what's happening here. While our threads are stitching forward, sometimes we loop back around to one location—one point in time—where we dip down, and out again. Assuming we're not, you know, interacting with each other in any unusual ways, this is how we beat the Collective. Not by gathering an army, or collecting a ton of resources, but by smartly utilizing the most important resource available to us: time."

Misty expresses her discomfort by pacing the small cockpit, resisting Sunni's efforts to make her stop. "So, we know the flight plans of our future selves?"

Wil shrugs. "More or less. Our data from the battle isn't complete. The more we jump to that location, the more data we'll get and the more accurate picture of the event we'll have."

Jia touches her lip, suddenly lost in thought.

"Uh-huh," Misty continues. "But we *do* have some data of what our future selves are going to do."

"Sure," Wil says.

"Okay. So now that we know what we're going to do, what's the point?" Misty asks. "Isn't the future altered by the fact that we know it's going to happen?"

My stomach tightens, yet I keep quiet.

"If you like ice cream and you want it right now, and you decide to go to the freezer and get it, and does knowing what you want alter that future?" Wil replies.

Misty frowns. "I don't think eating ice cream can be compared to changing the course of our lives. And yeah. It can. What if someone else in my house eats that ice cream before I get a chance? Or, I dunno, it turns out it's a gross ice cream that I don't want to eat?"

"None of those things will stop you from going to the fridge, unless you have the foreknowledge," I say. "I think what Wil means is that we make plans for our future all the time, no matter how insignificant. They're driven by desire. Unless that desire changes deeply, our future remains intact. Meaning, we're always going to *want* to destroy the Collective. So now that we know when we have our final stand against them, and a little bit about how we do it, we can fill in the blanks with what we do now.

"We've been reactive. They move. We move. But we've only acted based on what we have seen on Earth, at Sparkstone University. We don't have a sense of the Collective's scale. We really don't know anything about them. But now? Wil's right. We don't have to go to this...uh...Final Battle again, not right away. We can gear up. Gather resources. All this time, they've had the upper hand. Now, we have all of space and time at our disposal." Calling the chaotic space encounter the "Final Battle" seems appropriate, given the stakes.

"You sound like you're about to take over the universe," Misty says dryly. "I don't like it."

I purse my lips. I know how it sounds. And yet, it feels good to say. Finally. I am no longer under the Collective's thumb. They have nothing on me now. I am out of time. They can try to catch me, but I finally have control of the power they desperately covet.

"Tyrants don't use their power to save the universe," I reply. "Here's what we should do. The explosion in the underground library. We go there, we prevent Jadore from—"

"No." Wil's voice cuts the air thickly.

"No?" Jia and I say in tandem. Then, she continues: "You want to die there?"

"No one *wants* to die," he says. "I am still alive for now. Perhaps, I will live a long time and..." He trails off. I wonder if he realizes he's still a young man, not much older than he is now, when Jadore makes the killing blow. He finds his composure. "We can't go mucking around in the past. I've already died there. We start trying to change things? We don't know what that'll lead to. No travelling to the past, relative to the time when we left Jia's farm."

I clench my fists. "Hang on. I took you out of time. I saved you. Now you're telling me you don't want to be saved?"

He sighs. "I thought we were on the same page about this."

"Yeah, so did I!" I exclaim. "Especially considering you can read everything on my page."

"You and I," he says, pointing between the two of us, "we have to keep each other in check now."

"Um, we're also here," Misty says, swirling her finger around the room.

"Sure," Wil says. "But just as I can implant any idea in your mind"—he swallows uncomfortably, avoiding Jia's furious gaze—"she can theoretically go anywhere, at any time, *to* any time. These are god-like powers in comparison to throwing around fire and ice. Or turning invisible. Or, well, appearing in people's dreams and dreaming about death."

"I'll remember that the next time you want me to cloak the ship," Jia says coldly.

It's too late to retract our words, but Wil tries anyway. "That's not what I—"

"Comparing the relevancy or powerfulness of our talents isn't productive," Sunni interrupts. "Wil has a point. Ingrid, we need to establish some rules. Like, for starters. You can't just take off, willy-nilly, without tellin' us. You do that, we're stranded, wherever and whenever we are."

I lean against wall. I hate being wrong and being put in my place. I've just gotten my freedom, and now I have to obey rules?

"You're right," I say, interrupting that nagging voice of power inside me. "What else?"

"No modifying the past. At all," Wil says bitterly. "Even if we must visit a time in our past, it doesn't mean we're there to make changes. Observation and non-contact only."

"And the butterfly effect?" Jia asks. She's staring off into the distance again, as if in the middle of a deep calculation. "Doesn't our being in the past affect the surroundings?"

Wil smiles. He's enjoying this. He could have been a lecturer, a public speaker, or a researcher. Maybe in a different timeline, he is. Instead, he's stuck with us. With *me*. "If Ingrid says our fate is inevitable, then we have already been to the past, then perhaps our existence in that time has already been baked into the formula."

If what has happened will happen again, then perhaps I've already returned to the past and saved Ethan. I hang onto this thin thread of hope and file it away, hoping Wil doesn't see, and change the subject. "Every time I jump, there's a chance the Untrakeepers will find us and attack again." I feel cold even thinking about it.

Wil toys with the buttons on the control panel. "Then we have to make sure they don't catch you. At least we know they probably don't catch you? We're able to dip in and out of this battle at least fourteen times."

"Yeah. I guess," I say distantly. Gooseflesh prickles my arm and I let out a sudden, sharp breath. Even thinking about them causes my body to physically react. "If we jump and stay on the ship, the Untrakeepers don't come for us."

"How do we know the Untrakeepers weren't on the ships in the battle?" Misty points out.

"I've felt them coming each time," I concede. "They could have materialized on this ship already. They haven't. When I collected Wil, I was attacked. When we were in the barn, attacked. The hangar, attacked. I was in each location approximately, what, twenty minutes?"

"Give or take," Wil agrees.

"We've already been here for how long? Thirty minutes?"

Wil presses a few buttons on the control panel and nods. "Longer."

"What is it about the ship that wards them creatures away?" Sunni asks.

"I wish I knew." I don't want to stay on this ship for the rest of my life. I can't rescue Ethan and then confine him here. Assuming he wants to be with me, by the time I'm able to rescue him. I tap my collarbone absently. What if it takes me decades to make it back to that moment in time? Can I afford to betray my friends like that, considering how much they now rely on my power for survival?

Jia settles on the bench, still lost in thought, and I take a seat next to her. Sunni settles in the co-pilot seat next to Wil and Misty hovers, studying the data from the battle intensely. As they sift through the ocean of information, Wil activates a projection light in the ceiling of the cockpit and creates a 3D model of the battle with gridlines and colourful shapes. Every few minutes, the projection blinks as he re-positions an element or re-calculates a flight path.

"Maybe what we saw was a fancy illusion, cast by incomprehensible technology, good enough to fool our eyes and our ship's sensors," Misty posits after a while, watching the projection with interest.

"Why would anyone do that?" Sunni asks with a strange smile.

Misty shrugs. "To make it look like we have a lot of ships attacking when we only have one?"

"It's a good idea, if we could ever create or steal a piece of technology like that," I say. "But the fact is, we won't know or understand what's happening until we go back there. Intentionally or randomly. We can see anything at any given point in time, but we're only seeing it from one perspective: the point in our personal timeline that we occupy."

Wil clasps his hands into a fine point, pressing them against his chin. "You're right."

I'm surprised. I'd expected a clever rebuttal.

He feels my reaction and smiles a little. "You're right about the perspective part. We have only seen the future from one perspective. There are more than a dozen versions of Future Wils and Ingrids and such in that battle, fighting the Collective. Until we are them, with their experience, we won't see the entire picture. The entire battle."

"The blind men and the elephant," Jia says suddenly, awakening from her pensive state.

"Folk tale?" Sunni asks.

Jia sits up straighter. "It's an old parable. A group of blind men come across a strange creature they've never seen before. One man feels the ear, and concludes the creature is like a basket. The other inspects the tusk, and thinks the creature is spear-like. Another, the tail, and thinks it's like a snake." Jia acts each part out deliberately, remaining seated on the bench. "Each man, confident he's right, expresses his observation as fact, as he believes he's experiencing the entirety of the creature. Once they realize their observations differ, they bicker. In some versions of the story, the conflict becomes violent. In other versions, the men listen to each other and realize they are describing parts of a whole." She flits her gaze to me. "Ingrid is right. Even if the Collective does destroy Earth, there's a lot about that battle we don't know. Why do the life signs on our ship change? What provokes the Collective into open warfare, when historically, they've been cold and deceptive?"

My breath hitches. It's the first time we've acknowledged the destruction of Earth as fact. This settles upon us heavily, and each of us look as though we want to say something meaningful but can't find the appropriate words.

Sunni crosses her arms and breaks the silence. "They'll go

from cold to hot when they're ready, trust me. Which is exactly what they'll do. Or have done." She frowns at the complication of using grammar to describe a future event that has happened in our past.

"But we don't know why we're fighting them at that moment, only that we will, in several months' time, be part of a battle for the fate of our planet." Jia stretches out her legs and bends at the waist, still sitting, to touch her toes. "We don't have to be rash. We also can't afford to be. We need more intel." Jia inhales deeply, pressing her palms together. "We truly don't know anything with certainty until we get to the time and space of the battle, record the event with the sensors, and add it to the 3D model here. Unless." Her eyes widen with inspiration. "Did you receive telepathic communication from your future self during the battle?"

I remember how pained Wil had been during our struggle to navigate through the battle. "You got overwhelmed by all of us there, didn't you." It's not a question. I don't want to aggravate the already strained relationship with Jia and Wil.

He seems to debate with himself on what to say. He resorts to telepathy. *It was like walking blindfolded into a crowded room, where everyone wanted my attention. I couldn't make out any one voice. Just all of us, desperate and determined to win and survive.*

"So, you didn't hear anything that would help us now?" Misty questions.

Wil runs a hand across his bald head. "No. And if we communicate back to our past selves during the battle, to the other blind men in our metaphorical group, who knows what we'd be risking."

I frown, but a thought nags for my attention. "Maybe. The orange light on the console...Wil, Sunni, do we know what that's for?"

"It's connected into the communication system," Wil says. His eyes widen near-imperceptively as he sees my train of thought. "We *are* communicating with ourselves."

"Do we have the logs?"

I'm standing now, abuzz with nervous energy. Our future has called, and we now have the keys to receive the hail. We hover over Wil as he peruses through data on the LED screen with one hand and presses his other palm against the console. His power of reading machines works in tandem with his adeptness of navigating the system. Next to him, Sunni starts her own search through the data they've accumulated. Every few seconds, the projection updates with new information. The model becomes more complex with more shapes and expands to fill more than half the room.

"I suppose we are comrades in the heat of battle, so it makes sense that we find a way to relay messages," Sunni says, mostly to Wil, as if to excuse us from potentially tampering with our timeline.

Misty leans over Sunni, studying the controls, while Jia returns to the bench. She appears to be sifting through her thoughts again. I respect her silence and lean against the wall, beside the airlock, staring out at the distant solar system, trying to pick out the blue ball we call home.

Finally, Wil clears his throat. "The ship's main computer is confused, to say the least, about all the log entries from the other ships. We're all the same ship, with the same signature. It picked up transmissions but categorized them as system errors upon receipt, since it perceived the sender and the receiver as the same... oh, wait." He makes a face. "There are a few that weren't logged as errors." He pulls them up as a digital overlay on the canopy, and all of us except Jia press closer to read them.

FROM BLIND ELEPHANT 2 to BLIND ELEPHANT 1

Ingrid is right about the orange light. You'll figure out how it works soon.

-IS

FROM BLIND ELEPHANT 2 to BLIND ELEPHANT 1

Wil – it's Amara you were thinking of this morning.

-Signed, you.

The messages are silent incantations on our lips. "We're *Blind Elephant 1*, I guess," I say after the words have sunk in. "Do we name the ship *Blind Elephant?* It's not the elephant that's blind."

"It's catchy," Sunni says, looking up to Misty for her opinion.

She nods, her dark hair bobbing. "Us naming the ship is kind of a paradox though, right? If we got the name from the future...?"

"Who is Amara?" Sunni asks, nudging Wil playfully.

"My auntie," Wil says, a little stunned. "When we entered the battle, I was thinking about a family barbeque we had a couple years back. One of my aunties asked why I didn't have a girlfriend or boyfriend yet. Was trying to remember which one had asked, because I remembered her worry as one of the most overpowering feelings at the time." Wil leans back in his chair. "It really bothered me that I couldn't remember."

"We didn't tell ourselves how our communication system works, and you didn't tell yourself anything of importance, so we didn't violate any rules," Misty points out. "Unless *Amara* is code for something, Wil?"

"It is not," he replies tersely.

My stomach turns. What if we had looked at these messages before our present conversation? Would that have changed how we arrived at the here and now?

Wil mulls over the holographic projection, cross-referencing it with information on a LED screen on the navigational controls. "There's something else here. Every other version of the ship, except ours right now, has an arsenal of weapons and technology not originally included in the schematic. Like it's been upgraded. Or *will* be upgraded."

"You already mentioned that the ship changes over time," Jia says.

"Sure. But there's a particular weapon signature constant across the board. The *Blind Elephant 2* has it."

Meaning the next time we jump there, we'll have this new technology. Which might be soon. This peaks Sunni's interest. "Can I take I look?" She pores over the data. Wil attempts to explain it, but she waves him away. "I got it, I got it. I've read a computer or two in my day." She smirks and absently bites loose skin off her lip, considering. "I recognize the *de'macah-nu* frequency." Once again, she sings the alien word, starting in C-natural, moving to A, then D, and finishing in C-natural. It's undoubtably ahmei in origin. "But how could that exist here? There's only one ship I've seen that has this tech." Her gaze rests on me sympathetically. "You're not gonna like this."

"Just tell me," I say, just as Misty says, "You have to tell her. It's gone on long enough."

"What?" I say.

"I tried to warn you about your feelings—" Sunni starts to say to me, but Misty, ever impatient, shakes her head. "Skip to the meat."

Blowing out a sigh, Sunni replies, "I don't think that's *my* place—"

"I'll do it, if you want?" Misty offers. "You don't have to tell her about the—"

"Just say it!" I exclaim.

Sunni is faraway for a long time, wrestling with the past. Whatever she's holding on to, it's dear and she doesn't want to part with it. "I told you already that in my universe, Ethan is in league with the Collective. That's not all."

I brace for the worst. In dreams shared with me by this version of Sunni, I have watched an alternate version of Ethan kill her Misty. I don't know how any Ethan would willingly collaborate with alien invaders determined to manipulate our DNA for their personal and scientific gains. His mind is probably being poisoned and controlled by Agailya and the other ahmei conducting experiments to find a cure for the vitaphage that disseminated their people.

"Ethan's their poster boy. The highest-ranking human in the whole Collective. He commands the fishmen like servants. They handpicked him from day one." She taps a screen on the navigation controls. Several triangles on the holographic model glow with a faint orange aura. "The weapon doing damage to the mother ship? It's the same weapon from Ethan's personal ship in my universe. I recognize the signature embedded in the weapon frequency. I don't think it exists here."

"Are you sure?" Wil asks. "We don't know enough about our Collective to be sure of all of their technology."

"I'm sure," Sunni says with strange finality. "Look at the kind of weapons on the other Collective ships, compared to the ones on every *Blind Elephant*." She taps the screen and brings up two wavelength graphs for Wil to examine on the canopy and then overlays them on the holographic projection. The projection map represents a slice of time with heavy crossfire. Each *Blind Elephant*, except *Blind*

Elephant 1, has a red dotted line depicting the fired weapon. *Blind Elephant 1* has a dashed line in orange. All the Collective ships fire weapons in green, long dashes. "The *Blind Elephants* with the oldest service record have integrated, upgraded tech, but it's from this universe. It matches some of the signatures firing here, here, and here." She points at different circles representing Collective ships around the map, which all look the same to me. "Meaning, at some point, we steal and integrate technology from this universe. But the next time we're in this battle, we have weapon technology from my universe."

There's no excitement to Sunni's words. She seems resigned, as if it's an inescapable fact, like the sky being blue and her hair a rich blonde. Misty touches Sunni's arm. A show of consolation.

"All right." Wil leans back against the controls, adjusting his glasses as he thinks. "Since you've said the ship we're on now isn't from your universe, am I right that you're implying that we somehow travel to your universe to take this particular weapon?"

Everyone looks to me. Besides this version of Wil, we were all there in the underground library when I brought Sunni into our universe. The portal the Collective had built to undertake such a task was massive. It required a lot of power, and it required *me* to focus that power and reach out across time and space. Originally, their plan had been to invade other universes. Potentially absorb other versions of the Collective to create a massive superpower of alien knowledge and strength. Or that's what I've assumed, for what would the Collective do with another version of themselves? Valuable knowledge and resources won't go to waste, assuming they have similar goals. With the portal now destroyed, it's unlikely the Collective has the resources to construct and attempt another cross-universe connection, not without me or the Hunger to power it.

"There has to be an equivalent weapon we can steal instead. I don't know if I can transport this entire craft to another universe," I say.

Unless Wil is suggesting that we travel back to before the day the underground library explodes so that we can cross over?

No, I'm not, he replies telepathically.

So much for that idea. "Okay. Sunni, what makes this weapon so special?"

"It fires a ton of missiles, hiding inside one big missile. You saw it during the battle." A sly, but empty smile crosses Sunni's face. "You've had the benefit of a near-bloodless battle with the Collective. They haven't even begun to bring the brunt of their force against you. But they also haven't had to run against an aggressive resistance either. They had more intense subjects to harvest from to create this weapon."

"Who?" I ask, before I can stop myself.

Sunni looks uncomfortable. "I don't know the whole story. It's third-hand anyway. Sometimes the Collective doesn't conquer and harvest interesting superpowers and DNA in a race, you know? And sometimes they don't conduct sketchy experiments either. Sometimes they just see an aggressive, unorganized, war-like race and they scoop 'em up and dissect 'em like frogs. Or they'll see a race like the hafelglob and mold 'em to their liking so they're infinitely more useful. You know their shapeshiftin' powers are not meant to be used for long stretches of time, right? Originally it was part of their species' mating ritual. But nothing can just be what it is. For the Collective, every mutation or special ability or personal *difference* serves a function. You know, I...I just can't think about it. It makes me too darn frustrated." Her Texas twang intensifies the longer she speaks. "My point is, I know a Collective weapon from my universe when I see it, because I've seen it a thousand times. What I'm seein' here is at some point during our cross-stitch journey, we hop on over to another canvas. To my universe. And we steal this weapon technology to enhance this very ship."

A silence falls upon us as Sunni's words become visceral: the unwilling contribution of DNA, and whatever else, comprises the Collective's technology. They're parasites. They're monsters.

"So, we raid this Alt-Ethan's ship in the other universe," Misty says firmly. "We take his firepower. We install it on this ship. Or we *will* raid his ship, take his firepower, and install it on this ship."

"No," say Sunni and Wil simultaneously. Sunni's cheeks flush in frustration as Wil defers to her. "I mean, yes to raiding the ship. But when I was last there, well, his ship and the weapon was always in for repairs in an underwater facility, deep in the Pacific. If his ship is there, so's the weapon."

And he'll be there too, is what she doesn't say. "So, is that where the ship is most vulnerable?" I ask.

"It's where the weapon was made." She seems hesitant to say more. "It's a prototype. It was still being tested when I left."

"That doesn't answer my question. We could jump to a time when the ship is vulnerable in space somewhere, but the weapon works, so we can steal it and return here."

"It's unsafe wherever we jump," she retorts. "And I don't know *when* the weapon is deemed completely operational. All I know is things were—*are*—really bad there." She crosses her arms and leans into Misty. "If our analysis is right, which it has to be, 'cause we saw it with our own eyes and the onboard computer confirms it multiple times over, the weapon is operational. It *will* work."

Jia frowns. "Why would the weapon be made in an underwater

facility? Why not in a space station? Or in a regular building, like at Sparkstone?"

Sunni's smile is one of sadness and experience. "That's how it was, at first. But as the Collective's influence grew, they built more covert bases planet-side. And because a lot of their member species are aquatic, an underwater facility is more comfortable. The ocean depths offer a natural protection against land-faring rebel forces, especially when ships are hard to come by."

"So, what kind of facility is it, where the ship goes for repairs?" Jia asks.

I clock the unsettled expression that momentarily clouds Sunni's face. "Research."

"High security," Wil says, picking up on one of Sunni's stray thoughts.

She brushes a stray frizzy curl from her cheek. "Sort of. Not really."

"What if the weapon isn't on his ship? Or inside this base?" I ask.

"Well, we'll just have to find it," Misty replies. "We obviously *do* find it, if our future selves are using it against the Collective."

An uneasy silence falls upon us. If we've already done it in the future, it seems unfair for us to have to do the hard work now. I wish I could fall asleep, wake up, and have the work completed, so I can do other, less important things. The strange comfort that comes from glimpsing the future is offset by the worry of not knowing how *long* it will take us to achieve our lofty goal of destroying the Collective. What if all of those future versions of us fighting the Collective are fifty-years-old?

I smile a little, imagining us as senior citizens, fighting a secret war against aliens.

And then I think of Ethan, pale, dripping in sweat, desperate for me to save him.

It sounds so easy. Cross over. Raid the ship that belongs to my boyfriend's counterpart. Take his technology for ourselves.

He's *alive* in that universe.

Maybe I don't have to wait until I'm prepared to return to the past and rescue Ethan. The chances of me succeeding in that are slim.

Sunni and Misty exchange affectionate glances as Sunni runs through the technical specs of her universe's missile weaponry. It seems to make sense to Wil, who nods along. Jia alternates between sitting on the bench and pacing the distance between the holographic projection and the mess. She's not listening either. All of it sounds like gibberish.

I don't exist in this Sunni's universe. But if her Ethan saw me, maybe we could start again. I know Ethan through and through. He wouldn't knowingly or willingly be a poster boy for an alien invasion.

Sometimes six, sometimes four.

He needs rescuing. I'm the only one who can save him.

"If you think this is the kind of weapon we need to destroy the Collective once and for all...then let's do it," I say finally, when Sunni and Wil are finished their exchange. I mirror my friends' determination and try to look like someone who knows how to control an unwieldly power. "Let's visit Sunni's universe."

CHAPTER 5

My circadian clock is out of whack, I'm bone tired, but we can't sleep yet. Misty, Jia, Sunni, and I explore the new ship as Wil familiarizes himself with the controls. Misty rummages through the four lockers in the mess and shows us two tinfoil blankets and two unmarked, wrapped bars. She opens one and gives it a sniff. It's reminiscent of a granola bar, with unidentified raisin-like bits smooshed in for good measure. Before Sunni can stop her, she takes a bite.

Misty grimaces. "Tastes like sawdust, but edible?"

"Don't eat alien food without testing it first!" Sunni chides, snatches the bar from her girlfriend, and takes a bite herself.

"There's no need in both of you being the taste testers," I say, unable to hide my amusement.

"We'll know in a couple hours if it agrees with you," Jia comments dryly. "Um, do we have toilets on this ship?"

Our search becomes more harried. We find a couple more sawdust bars and four spacesuits stashed in the lockers. They're large and humanoid-shaped. There's also a bucket with a mop and a floral-scented, egg-shaped stone. When we touch the stone, a clear gel residue bubbles and evaporates promptly, as if it's a cross between soap and hand sanitizer. We unceremoniously agree that a spare bucket will suffice as a toilet until we can figure out how alien plumbing works.

Beside engineering, a cabin with scraped walls and floors sits empty. We speculate this may have served a purpose before the retrofit. A sturdy, sliding door suggests that something valuable may have existed in here. Or perhaps it was a private bedroom.

We find a few maintenance hatches large enough for someone to crawl through and make repairs as necessary, but no other cabins present themselves. As far as we can tell, there are no escape pods, either. The empty cabin becomes the washroom, for now.

The loft beyond the spiraling stairs smells like old plastic, as if there had been blow-up mattresses in here recently. We find no such thing in the lockers. The stuffy air and the fact that I can't even stand up in here means this can't be my sleeping quarters. Sunni promises she'll find a way to improve the air circulation so we can, eventually, set up mattresses.

When we finish exploring the loft, we find Wil fast asleep in the cockpit. Once Sunni assures us that our orbit is steady and an alarm will notify us of any orbital decay, the four of us retire to the mess. Misty and Sunni snuggle under one of the tinfoil blankets in the booth. Jia and I politely offer the remaining blanket to each other, until she insists I take it.

"I slept more recently than you," she says. "We can take turns until we do a real supply run."

She curls up on the other side of the booth while I wander into the cockpit with the crinkling blanket. Wil stirs as I settle in the co-pilot seat and stare out at the watery planet, until I drift into a dreamless sleep.

After a stiff, patchy sleep lasting approximately ten hours, we do our best to refresh ourselves. Limited running water, created from an unknown recycling process, drips from a spout in the galley. The last thing we can risk is sickness onboard what is effectively a submarine in space, so Misty volunteers to be the taste tester for the water. After consuming the sawdust bar, she's especially parched.

"It doesn't taste bad," Misty says, shrugging.

Once we've had a chance to refresh ourselves, we meet at the booth in the mess to strategize. It hits me as I settle in the booth and nibble on one of the sawdust bars we've rationed between the five of us. They are depending on me to bring us to Sunni's home. I have to attempt this multi-universe journey, not only with my friends, but with this ship as well, and arrive in the right place, at the right time.

"We got spacesuits that might be okay for deep underwater exploration. We got *some* food. But we're going to need more supplies for the heist," Misty says.

"Is that what we're calling it now?" Jia asks from her meditative pose on the floor.

"We are stealing something from a top-secret base in another universe." Misty grins at Sunni, but she seems distracted. Sunni flashes me an uneasy smile. I'm glad she can't feel my trepidatious excitement at the possibility of seeing an alternate Ethan.

I'm inclined to agree. "What will we need?"

Sunni grimaces. "Weapons."

The severity of the task slams into us then, as the other four of us try hard not to be the first to object or question this suggestion. We've occasionally taken weapons from the Collective in the heat of the moment, but for the most part, we rely on our individual powers to outwit, outrun, or outmatch our enemies. We'd found no handheld weapons on the ship.

"I guess we could...jump to a store?" Misty suggests. She doesn't look thrilled at the idea.

"How else are we supposed to get into the base, take down the twisted scientists who—" Sunni stops short and composes herself. "You know what? It's fine. There's a cache a couple of clicks from the facility where my resistance cell stashed some supplies. We can go there. Should be enough to get us through."

I'm relieved. I've been preparing for this jump mentally ever since I woke up and I don't want to make any other stops. I just want it to be done. "Tell me about the cache and the facility."

Sunni describes for us in detail the underwater base in the Pacific where the prototype weapon was created. Every sentence is strained, as if she's forcing the information from a deep, repressed place in her brain. "The facility is comprised of mostly scientific staff. There are some guards, fishmen as you call them. Security cameras will be few and far between. This is a classified facility for research. Cameras will be focussed on their, uh, experiments. There's a dock at the rear. That's where ships refuel. Ships are always comin' and goin'. Most of 'em cargo or scientific in nature. Only time there's a military presence is, well, when Alt-Ethan—as you called him—is there, or any of the councillors." An extra layer of disgust coats Ethan's name as she expels it. "His escort shouldn't be a problem, given Jia and Misty's combined powers."

We don't have any paper for Sunni to draw a map, so Misty lends her a phone, where she sketches a rough layout in a drawing program. She passes it around so we can ask questions and memorize the necessary routes.

"The weapon we're after will either be in the main research and development lab, or at the terminal dock, inside Alt-Ethan's ship. Or in transit between the two." Sunni jabs a finger to the respective places on the phone map. The research lab is in the heart of the facility. "Like I said, the weapon needs constant maintenance. But it's pretty powerful. Once we have it, maybe Wil can manage the improvements."

When the phone makes it to me, I burn the makeshift map into my memory and take note of Misty's phone battery. Less than half. Mine is similar. There aren't any compatible outlets on this ship. We're going to have to find a way to charge our phones eventually.

"Other than Alt-Ethan"—it hurts to say his name; all I want is to live in it—"are there any other threats we should be aware of?" I return the phone to Sunni.

The name also triggers a physical reaction in her. She stiffens and crosses her arms across her chest. "There isn't a lot of heavy security patrolling the building. Most of the trouble will be getting inside and getting back out. It's been a target on our list for some time. We'd been planning an attack, but, now I'm here."

I wait for her to volunteer more information, but she doesn't.

"We should be able to dock at the terminal, if you can trick the computers and the staff into thinking we're just there to refuel?" Sunni says, raising an eyebrow at Wil.

He shrugs. "It'll work, for the amount of time we need it to."

It seems so simple. Arrive at the cache. Grab supplies. Dock. Become invisible. Run around an underwater base. Get the weapon. Escape. Teleport back home.

Sunni beelines out of the booth and paces the room with a fierce alertness. "Let's get this over with, okay?"

"We're comin'," Misty says, following her, reaching a supportive hand to her girlfriend. Sunni recoils at first, as if the gesture was unexpected. "Hey, it's okay…"

Sunni sighs, relaxes, and steels her gaze. "Yeah. I know. I just…"

"I know."

I pretend not to hear them. Space is tight on this ship and we no longer have the luxury of privacy. Is Sunni jumpy because she's nervous about returning to her home universe? Sunni had tried to warn me about Alt-Ethan, before. What is her relationship to him, and what happened between them?

If I manage to save my Ethan, will it happen again, here?

Wil has already disappeared into the cockpit. Jia grazes my arm. "Are you ready?"

I nod. "I guess. You?"

She twists her lips in what feels like an affirmative. I have to get us there, but she has to ensure we stay out of view for the entirety of the mission. There's a kinship from the loneliness of our roles. There's a question in her eyes, and I know without being a mind-reader that it's about her family. It's likely the same one that's been on my mind.

"I want to believe we'll make it back to them," I say to her.

She doesn't meet my gaze. We're like two spies in a public space, trying to have a covert conversation. She just nods. "I hope so too."

We join the others in the cockpit. Wil and Sunni are in the two pilot seats. Misty hovers above Sunni.

"Before we do this. Ingrid, where's your phone?" Wil asks.

My stomach curls at his request. "Why?"

"Open the stopwatch app."

I see where he's going with this. I dig it out, open the app, and press start. Our phones may run with their internal clocks as normal, but having a secondary way to track how much time has passed in the Untraver will benefit us. Even a few minutes can be days in the labyrinth. "Ready."

"Okay. Take a look at this signal." He presses a few buttons on the console, they beep, and he waves his hand. A wavelength appears on a hovering digital screen overlaid on the canopy, and then projects as a three-dimensional object from the ceiling, right in front of me. I recoil instinctively. I'm going to have to get used to this alien holographic technology. Wil laces his fingers. "This is what Sunni pulled from the battle log. It's the weapon signature. I converted it to an audio file. Thought maybe if you heard it, you might be able to follow it to its original source. Assuming your power works something like that?"

I nod. Tentatively, I tap the floating wavelength. The corresponding sound wails on invisible speakers above us, scraping against my skull like metal on bone. I wince and crumple to the floor, scratching at my ears, desperately trying to get the proverbial ice pick out of my brain. Everyone else hears the sound and looks uncomfortable, but my reaction is by far the most extreme.

"Agh, sorry, too loud!" Wil shouts. The audio dims. "How about now?"

"Better, but...yuck." I nearly spit on the floor. The sound tastes like overly sweet syrup, and smells like burnt plastic, and overall, it's as if I've been force-fed bad carnival food. Any remaining appetite for real food vanishes. I climb to my feet and tap the hologram again. The speakers fall silent. Like a bloodhound, I have the scent.

"You sure you're up for this?" Sunni asks hesitantly.

"She can do it," Wil says quickly, throwing me a smile.

"Yeah, she's already navigated the ship through time. And the solar system," Misty chimes in.

I stare at my boots, my face flushing. I wonder if Wil told them to encourage me, knowing that my power runs on hope.

"My powers aren't that precise. But I've usually gotten where I needed to go." Except for the time I teleported to the edge of a supermassive black hole.

"That's all we need," Wil replies, nodding. Then, telepathically to me, he says, *We have the time to get it right. Relax.*

I nod. He's on my side. He wants me to succeed. They all do.

"Okay, ship's ready. We ready?" Wil asks, clapping his hands confidently.

Misty and Jia sit across from one another on the facing benches. I stand between them, breathing deeply, taking one last look at Neptune through the canopy. "Okay. Let's go."

Instead of Ethan, I think on my childhood dreams and love of space. Not only am I onboard an alien spacecraft with my superpowered friends, but now I have the opportunity to visit an alternate universe, where everything is different. No one has done this before. The five of us? We're special. We're chosen.

I close my eyes, bring to mind the sound of the weapon, and then...

The environment fades from grey to black, like a theater plunging into darkness moments before spotlights find their mark. I feel it first in my body, like I've been robbed of cozy blankets, rudely awakened in the morning. I grimace as the sharp, boxy corners of the infinite, dark maze comes into focus. As I focus on my memory of the sound, it appears like shimmering thread before me. The blue-red wavelength wafts through the hallways like a magical thread and winds around the corner some distance ahead.

We made it to the Untraver. I grin, until I take a step forward and nearly lose my balance. "Whoa!"

My voice echoes in the vast corridor as I swing my arms to steady myself, stomach lurching. The floor bobs beneath my footing, glimmering in the dim light emitted from behind the countless closed doors and the thread guiding our way.

The floor isn't solid, and I'm not standing on it. The roughly tied logs beneath my feet float atop a black, soupy liquid that *used* to be the floor. The raft, at least five metres long and two metres across, supports the still-unconscious forms of my friends, and a dark, furled sail and mass.

This has to be the largest thing I've transported, and more shocking is this isn't the first time I've been here with the ship. I'm hyperaware of the moment. The more I think about it, the more unsteady I feel. The blue-red thread whispers eerily. That's right, I'm supposed to follow the wavelength to Sunni's universe.

All while steering this craft, without getting caught by the—

Nope. Not going to think about them, not in here. Too dangerous.

"Awake back there?" I ask my friends.

Wil and Sunni begin to stir. Misty and Jia are still out. I kneel before them, keeping an eye out for threats. There are no oars around, either. How are we supposed to move forward in this? I peer into the floor-water. No reflection stares back. I touch a finger to the surface and wince. I can't scramble backwards fast enough. The raft rocks and my friends groan sleepily.

Touching the water felt *wrong*, as if I've touched an exposed intestine. No getting out and pushing this raft forward, and absolutely no swimming.

Our raft bobs along on the soupy black liquid, aimless, as I ground myself. We're not alone in here. Besides those I dare not think of, there's another sentient being in here who knows of my powers. Ever since the beginning, Ohz identified me and my powers, called me Crosskey. He and his brethren have known more than they've let on about me and my powers.

I reach for him across the divide—

—and then I hear *my voice* call his name from different lips.

There. I stare down a hallway to my right and see my spitting image in a parallel hallway. Except, she's not a mirror image or a reflection. A Future Me? Memory in the Untraver is tricky. I haven't been able to recall most of my time in here. This mirror image could be a Past Me travelling the Untraver, but I don't remember owning her outfit. A long, white sweater dress, thickly belted at the waist with a slash of black elegance, hugs my pencil thin body and hangs off my shoulders. Long, dark boots caked with sandy mud disappear beneath the dress. Aside from the tangled mess of hair? Future Me looks amazing.

She smiles at me. I wonder if she can remember what I'm thinking. As if in response, she gives me a little wave, the kind I'd give someone who has a crush on me that I can't reciprocate. I'm embarrassed.

A tentacle reaches out to Future Me, and a terrifying mouth emerges from the darkness. But neither of us are afraid. It's Ohz, the hafelglob I accidentally trapped here. His appendages slap against the walls and doors as he crawls towards Future Me, gurgling. He's all arms and mouth, no eyes, but all the same he swivels his body to face me. He's trying to say something.

"*False,*" he says to me, and then awkwardly turns his mass of tentacles to face the other version of me and adds, "*Choice.*"

I exchange confused glances with the other me, though her look is steelier. Older, perhaps.

"Two of you are here," Misty says softly, now awake, as she stands and eyes me with suspicion. "Are you our Ingrid?"

"Definitely," I reply. The question sends shivers down to my toes. I've never considered the possibility of losing my friends to another Ingrid. I suppose that is what I've done to Wil.

Future Me points at my hip. "Don't forget to map where you're going."

I feel the whiteboard marker in my pocket. Before I can protest that I don't have paper, I notice the black marks on my Future Self's arm, barely hiding beneath the sleeve. I grin. "You're a genius."

Future Me does finger-guns in my direction. "See you soon."

Ohz lets out a gurgling laugh.

"Where?" I ask. I'm tempted to follow. I *am* her. I would tell me everything that's going to happen, if I were her. She turns tail and Ohz slides after her. The raft sways and jostles against the walls as I attempt to steer us down the hallway between us. It won't fit and the walls aren't budging.

An idea tugs at the back of my mind. The walls *should* move for me. They exist *for* me. I have been chosen to walk these hallways and the image of them should bend to my perception.

Misty's hand clamps my shoulder and refocuses my attention on the mission at hand. Right. I'm here to take us to a different universe. Another reality. I must follow the thread. Next time, I can find myself.

I may be a visitor to this domain, but I exert some control over how I move within it.

I line up the tip of my boot with the edge of the craft. The adage, *"Measure twice, cut once,"* skates through my brain as I spread my arms wide and double-check my positioning.

My lungs fill with air. I feel the presence of the tiny creatures powering the craft and their innate hunger. They want to *move.* I pucker my lips and softly blow.

The raft glides forward and I feel like I'm flying. I *am* the ship.

I steer us after the blue-read thread it like an eager treasure hunter. The muffled sound becomes louder the further we travel. I'm reminded of my first day at Sparkstone, and the mysterious tone that nearly drove me insane.

Then, I'm writing. I don't remember taking out the marker. Maybe someone else on the raft creates the marks on my skin. The passage of time becomes hazy as I give myself over to the ship and the thread and the waters below. My navigation of this labyrinth operates on instinct and I feel a quiet content to be on autopilot.

That is, until I sense *them* drawing near. Their robes slosh against the watery floor in the distance and their strange thought-speech threatens to invade my concentration. I fight to maintain my presence of mind and focus on our guiding thread.

The thread has brought us to part of the labyrinth that doesn't feel familiar. The corridors have fewer doors here and the light of the thread intensifies, as if to say, *yes, this is the way.* It dips around a sharp corner and I follow, and at the end of a hallway is a set of stairs going up and down.

Dream logic takes over. Of course! Going to a different universe means ascending the stairs to a different floor. I only wish it had been an elevator instead. I exhale and we accelerate.

But the Untrakeepers don't like that I'm navigating us to a different floor. They're pitter-pattering behind us in the shallow depths. I don't dare look over my shoulder.

"Hang on," I instruct.

I raise my arms and the sails unfurl. I breathe in. The ship lifts from the inky waters and tilts forty-five degrees. My friends grip my torso and dig their nails into the boards. I feel it all intensely. I am the ship. I can't fail us now.

Creeeak. Gurrrlgl.

The ship groans and scrapes against the stairs. Water trickles in thick droplets from some unseen source, creating a scant waterfall to relieve the boards, and the groaning recedes. My muscles ache with the strain, as if I'm lugging a heavy pack up a mountain.

"They're..." Misty trails off. "Not following?"

At the risk of breaking my concentration, I throw a glance over my shoulder. Three of Untrakeepers idle at the foot of the stairs. They stutter, but cannot lift their feet, as if glued to the watery floor.

They can travel in time and space, but they can't travel between universes.

The infinite flights of stairs continue upwards as far as we can see, broken only by landings which lead to other dimly lit floors. We struggle up two flights, rounding the corners awkwardly as the walls shift to accommodate our craft's size. The blue-red thread glows stronger as we level off on the appropriate floor. It disappears down a hallway filled with doors, not dissimilar to our original floor.

I lower my hands. Misty, Wil, and Sunni watch intently for more Untrakeepers as Jia maps our progress on my arm.

A strong wind picks up and nearly blows us off-course, down a dark corridor unlit by the thread.

"Wind?" I say with surprise, my mouth dry. The air smells sweet. The tiny creatures powering the ship are also surprised. I don't think there should be wind in this place.

A comfortable weight settles upon me, and it occurs to me that I might be dreaming all of this. My body might be tucked away back in Calgary, at home, with my parents who *know* me. This adventure with aliens and superpowered students might be an elaborate concoction of the mind. We drift slowly now down the dark hallway. The urge to sleep, perchance to wake up in the real world, intensifies.

"Focus," Wil commands.

His voice slices the sloth-like comfort bogging me down. Our craft lurches forward abruptly, eliciting a shriek from all of us. We're off-course. The thread waits patiently in an adjacent hallway, where I redirect the craft with deft ease.

"I feel it too," he says. The power of his voice is our new fuel. "We're not supposed to be up here. We have to stay awake, or we might not make it."

Jia crouches at my feet. Her warmth is another comfort that anchors me to the present.

"No weird aliens up here," Misty comments, yawning. It's partly a question directed at me.

"I don't think so," I reply. I can't hear or sense them. They don't exist in this universe. Only in ours. Or, at the very least, they haven't figured out how to climb the stairs to this floor. The thread lights up hundreds of doors in this corridor, awash with symbols I've never seen on our floor. The doors are so jammed together that the wall is barely visible.

The thread winds around and down more door-filled hallways and the waves, rhythmic and soothing, want to lure us into an eternal sleep. Wil engages us all to keep us awake, part fitness coach urging us to the finish line, and part confessor, regaling us with stories to prevent sleep from taking hold. I don't register every word, only their underlying intent. We have to stay awake, or we will be trapped here, forever.

One corner, and then another, and finally, the thread amasses at correct door. The *correctness* of the door washes over me, and in equal measure, the wavelength traces the shape of the door, inviting us to enter. I reach for the knob and at my barest touch, it opens. Inside, white light, dark shapes, and incomprehensible sounds await.

Sunni steps toward the door, rocking the craft with her steps, but Wil and Misty hold her back. "Ship has to go in too. Or we'll lose it."

I clutch the side jamb and with my other hand, angle the craft. My friends squish together as the craft condenses. It doesn't slam into the walls or other doors. It bends to my will. Sunni and Misty curl up with each other. A hypnotic voice made of wind intertwines with Wil's, urging me to lay down and forget this whole endeavour. I slide to my knees as the craft lurches forward, half in the door, half out.

Wil's hand grips my shoulder, and then Sunni's, and Misty's, and Jia's. "We can do this," they whisper.

Inch by inch, the raft glides into the light. Just one more inch. Then I can see Ethan again. Then I can save Jia's parents, and my parents, and then I can sleep.

Just one more inch.

One more.

We're so close. My eyes droop as the raft clears the jamb. I push against the heavy door, trying to shut it, to keep any followers out. Have to keep moving forward, though the thick, watery air. We're almost—

With a sickening thud, I return to my real body.

The guiding thread of light? Long gone. We're back in the spaceship and the clear-skied, open ocean expands before us. A white-wave-crested, Earth-looking ocean. And we're hurtling straight towards it.

"Strap in!" Wil shouts, as Misty screams, "Where are the damned seatbelts?"

Sunni and Jia fall into each other and take me down with them. The floor has turned ninety degrees and we slide like ragdolls towards the pilot seats and controls. A sharp breeze whistles above me. I slam into something cold and slick.

"Don't hurl ice in here!" Wil shouts at Misty. Misty and Wil are strapped in on the benches. The safety belts have emerged from the walls. I don't know why he's not in the pilot seat. Maybe our trip from the Untraver unseated us all. Wil's eyes are firmly shut; he must be struggling for control.

But the ice block is exactly the purchase we need, despite the sharp pain that shoots up my back. Jia and I took the brunt of the hint, while Sunni's limbs splay impossibly around us. Awkwardly, Jia and I use the block as a brace to push Sunni up.

"Again!" I call to Misty.

"Don't hit the equipment!" Wil hisses as Misty shots another ice block, smaller this time, by Sunni's hip. The block holding Jia and I up slides backwards and water seeps into my clothing.

Sunni deftly transfers some of her weight from us to the new foot-hold. It cracks beneath her shoe. As ice shards tumble towards us, Misty throws a ragged hand-hold made of ice towards Sunni. It freezes by her right elbow and she grasps it uncomfortably.

As Misty continues to create ice holds for Sunni to climb, Jia and I attempt to maneuver into the pilot chairs. Sparks erupt from the panels, spraying the chairs with tiny pricks of light. No flames. Yeah, I'm not touching any of that. "Wil...?"

"Nothing I can do from there that I can't do strapped in here at this point. We're going to dive. Brace—!"

CHAPTER 6

Jia and I shift as the ice block slides beneath the flashing controls. We catch our feet on the panels and the chairs. The ocean spills over the canopy as we nose-dive into the abyss. My toes already feel numb. A dark comfort overwhelms me, like a wet blanket enclosing my body. I don't know if it's real or all in my head.

Misty creates handholds made of ice, yet they barely stick to the metallic floor as we climb up towards the stern. Sunni goes, then I push Jia up, and then I follow. As the cold ocean embraces the ship and we sink deeper, the ice handholds slip less. Misty's face reddens with effort.

A thick, sweet smell permeates the ship. The scent isn't from me or anyone else. I breathe in with my mouth. It's the air. This universe tastes different than home, as if reality has been infused with notes of vanilla where there should be, well, no scent or taste at all. I'm going to faint.

Misty strains against her security belt to offer a free hand to Sunni and Jia. Sunni entwines herself like an aerialist around Misty's body and extends her arms to me.

I can leave them.

The thought is unbidden—and forbidden. Suddenly, I feel out of time and free of my responsibilities. I can leave them here in this strange ocean and return to the past and Jia's family and Ethan. And then return to this moment with help and supplies.

I stare at my hands. I can brave the Untraver again. I have the power.

"Ingrid! C'mon!"

Sunni's urgent grip rips away my desires as she throws me up towards Jia's waiting arms.

The power flickers. My eyes are crusty from staring at the glass comprising the canopy, willing it not to break under the increasing pressure as we descend into the depths. The suspicious groans elicit soft gasps from me and Jia.

"It's all right," Sunni says reassuringly. "The ship should hold."

Wil clicks his seat buckle and carefully slides down the floor towards the control panels.

"Can you right us?" Sunni asks.

"I don't know if that's—" I begin, as Misty finishes, "How was it the Titanic sank?"

"It flooded and was pulled down, then snapped in two. Aside from the water of your ice sloshing around the floor, we're not flooding," Wil assures us. "At least..." He doesn't finish that sentence.

This sobers us all. The ship lets out a long creak. "We're sure we don't have escape pods?" Jia asks.

I'm transfixed by the darkness of the ocean. I try to reassure myself. It's like space out there, but better. If I'm ejected from the ship, I can swim to the surface. If I'm not crushed to death first. I wonder if I can teleport while swimming underwater. I teleported next to a supermassive black hole...

"I'm picking up some manmade structures," Wil says, breaking my dark thoughts. "And...uh, everyone hang on!"

I see the jagged rock formation before he finishes the warning. The impact jolts through us and sends my stomach into a freefall. We roll and I hold in my vomit as screams pierce the air. And then, we slow to a stop.

"Damage?" Sunni asks. She's the first one up.

My head spins. We're right-side-up again. It's hard to say that with certainty as Jia and I help each other up and struggle to find our footing. The interior lights flicker unhelpfully as we concentrate on the canopy. The dim orange and white lights exterior to the ship expose some of the ocean floor. We've landed on a craggy bed of rocks, surrounded by sand, and beyond that, rich inky darkness. I try to find any trace of sunlight. Nothing can penetrate the ocean depths from above.

"Hmm," Wil muses. It's not a comforting sound.

"Hmm?" Misty echoes. She grips Sunni, her fingers white. The dark hair on her arms stands erect in the cold. Jia and I continue to cling to each other for warmth.

Wil fiddles with the controls and stabilizes the interior lighting. Then, he projects a flickering hologram of the surrounding topographical area above the navigation controls. "We have limited data from our exterior sensors, as most of them are down from the crash. This is us." He points to a green dot in the center of the data. "Our descent was cushioned by these rocks, in the middle of a ravine, here. Seems to span several kilometres and drops off here." He points to parallel lines on either side of the green dot and a thick line at the edge of the projection. "And, this here"—he points to a blue cube, several inches from our green dot—"is the collection of structures I'd spotted."

"It's one structure, they're connected," Sunni corrects him.

"Where's the cache?" Misty asks.

Sunni examines the hologram carefully. "We missed it. We'd need a working craft to get there at this point."

"And those are the bad guys?" I point to the red triangles surrounding the blue cube. They're flickering more than the hologram and change positions every few seconds. Some move away from the cube, others blink on top of the cube, while the rest drift randomly around the vicinity.

"Other vessels. Probably hostile," Wil confirms, nodding.

"Assume everyone is hostile here," Sunni agrees. "Not sure if any of my allies survived after I went through the portal." Frowning suddenly, she taps a few buttons on the navigation controls. "Does this ship know how to connect to this universe's local satellites? So we can get the date?"

"Hang on, let's try to do that without attracting the wrong kind of attention." Wil closes his eyes and glances around, as if searching inside his mind palace for the correct information.

I check the stopwatch on my phone. "I've got two hours, thirty-seven minutes, ten seconds." I press the stop button.

"Ship's got basically the same, though we have to take into account that you started the timer before we started travelling. So, that's good," Sunni says. She leans into Misty. "Let's get the blankets, okay?"

As Wil communes with the machines around us, Sunni and Misty grab the survival gear. The chrome blankets crinkle like tinfoil, but they're soft enough as we huddle together and take turns. When I hand off a blanket to Wil, he blinks, as if waking from a dream, and takes the blanket appreciatively.

"Hmm, thanks. Satellite data says that it's June eighteenth, and confirms we've landed in the Pacific. For the year, it's giving me a Collective standardization. Fourteen-seventeen. Does that make sense to you?"

Sunni uncurls herself from Misty, stiffens, and replies croakily, "Yeah. But that's..." She reconsiders. "Yeah."

"I didn't get you close enough, did I," I say apologetically. I've got to get better at that. The only way is to practice, but the only way to practice is to return to important events.

"No, it's fine." She settles back against Misty, as if told she has to go to school on a stormy day.

Misty squeezes her close. After a weighty silence, she says lightly, "So...how do we know we're in the right universe?"

"The human engineering in orbit has been replaced by Collective technology," Wil replies just as I say, "Because the air is different here."

"Yes," Jia says slowly. "The consistency is thicker. I feel like I'm moving through pudding."

"The air content and consistency hasn't changed inside the cabin," Wil counters.

"That's not what we mean," I reply, as Jia's face flashes with indignation at Wil's comment. "I don't know how to explain or quantify it for you. It tastes different."

"Sometimes I feel like they got the fun superpowers," Misty mutters.

"Trade you," I say. A ping of regret in my stomach. I don't want to trade her. I need my power desperately.

Because I've been so busy running away from the Untrakeepers, and traversing the Untraver has been pure instinct, I've failed to examine if there's a pattern to the seemingly endless corridors within the Untraver itself. Remembering my time there is like trying to remember a dream.

That's when I notice my left arm. Black scribbles, boxes, and waving arrows cover every bare patch of skin from my elbow to my knuckles. I roll up a sleeve. There's more hurried mapping there too. It's a bit smudged from rolling around on ice, but it's readable. Wordlessly, Jia and I document the skin-map with our phones, so we can make sense of it later.

Flashes of memory return. Me, corralling my friends. Jia, with a marker, making notes when I couldn't. Sneaking around hallways to avoid the Untrakeepers. The stars—I press a finger into three different places on my skin—that's where there *were* doors, but no longer.

Sunni remains in a quiet trance, which makes me nervous. I lean against the airlock. It groans and I jump in surprise. The ship rocks; I'm startled again. I fall to the floor like I'm about to stop, drop, and roll, and curl my knees under my chin.

Jia frowns—and then fails to hold in her laughter. She blows a raspberry and laughs heartily in a way I can't ever recall her doing before. I gape at her, and then I'm smiling too, levying apologies at my jumpiness. Misty scoffs, grinning, and shakes Sunni, as if to wake her up to the levity. Even Wil is amused.

"Stop rocking the boat, Ingrid," Misty chides.

"If you want to get out and push, put on a suit first," Wil adds.

"She'd think the suit is her shadow and jump at that too," Sunni joins in quietly, giving Misty a small smile.

My sigh sounds annoyed, but I'm fighting back a laugh. "Oookay. Good ones. I'm ready to get off this boat, for sure. What's the status, captain? Can we make repairs and get on with the mission?"

As Sunni and Misty protest Wil's appointment as *captain,* Wil waves his hand and details what needs fixing with the ship. It's a laundry list of technical jargon that amounts to: lots of stuff broke when we crashed in the ocean.

"Giving you an estimate of repair times is tricky," he concludes. "The sh-winil are efficient but communicating with them is challenging. They're organic, not machines, so..." He shrugs. "Trickier."

Jia's face says, *Yes, you've always had problems communicating with humans.* She's holding back to keep the mood light.

Wil side-eyes her, but chooses not to reply to her obvious distaste. "We can wait until repairs are made, cloak, and approach the dock."

"I can't keep the ship and anyone inside the base sneaking around invisible at the same time," Jia says coolly.

"Cloak while approaching, then Wil does his thing with the base's computers? Maybe tricks some guards into thinking we're on their team, then we take Jia on our team to explore?" Misty suggests.

"How many of us are on Team Explore?" Since I don't have offensive powers and I can't turn anyone invisible, I'm afraid I'm going to be relegated to staying on the ship with Wil. Which I don't want. My heart aches to see the young man my love might have become.

Wil catches my thoughts. Of course he does. "The fewer people who go, the better."

Sunni holds up a hand. "We can't wait here until repairs are made. The longer we wait, the more chance we'll be discovered." She points at the red triangles on the hologram, blipping and patrolling the perimeter of the base. "The spacesuits we found should be able to withstand the pressure outside. Team Explore should venture out and infiltrate the base, while Team Ship hangs back and keeps an eye out for big threats."

"Won't all the big threats be *inside* the base?" I ask.

"The threats are everywhere, Ingrid," Sunni says darkly. "Even unarmored, snivellin' people can do damage by snitchin'. 'Course, all this depends on the weapon being inside the facility. Wil?"

Wil fiddles with the controls. An orange blinking dot appears in the same spot as the blue cube. "Based on the signature I pulled from the battle log, the weapon is definitely in the facility right now."

I cradle the flame of hope in my chest. Ethan. "Then let's go," I say.

"Yeah. Okay. Let's do this. There's a maintenance hatch not far from us. Here." Sunni points to the holographic map with a blunt fingertip. There's nothing there and it's about an inch from the blue cube. She looks at us expectantly. All she gets are blank stares. She flushes in frustration. "Right. Sorry, I know the terrain, you don't. This hatch is our best way in, assuming my codes still work."

"Assuming?" I say. "Wil, can't you—?"

"I can try, if we need it," he replies before I can finish. "If it's not too far."

"So, we're swimming to the hatch?" I ask.

"Can you swim?" Sunni counters.

"I mean...it's just..." I gesture out to the canopy. "Won't the pressure kill us?"

"We have suits, or I can modify the wristbands," Wil says. "Suits might be bulky for maneuvering, though. Afraid you'll have to be in a suit, Sunni."

Sunni nods curtly and continues. "Maintenance hatches aren't usually guarded, 'cause of the constant repairs and upkeep to maintain the base at this depth. Lots of crews comin' and goin' and not a lot of armed folks. Most of the people here are scientists and researchers. If it is guarded, we may be able to fake our way. To an extent. The guards who are here all have the standard underwater modifications equipped. Only ones I'd be worried 'bout are Ethan's personal entourage. He's handpicked some strange ones in the past to accompany him."

I want her to say more on this. She doesn't. Her chapped lips rest in an unflappable line. She's mentioned a planned attack on the facility, but there's more about this facility that she's not saying. She has codes to the place, because of this unfulfilled plan to attack it, or because she's been here before?

"Let's suit up," Misty says, clapping her hands together.

Wil modifies the alien wristbands perpetually stuck to us and Sunni suits up in one of the alien spacesuits. I'm so nervous about potentially running into Ethan, or anyone else I might recognize, that only now does the agoraphobia hit me. We're about to step into the *ocean*. Surrounded by *nothing* but *more ocean*. With nothing but a bit of alien technology between my lungs and salty ocean.

Wil helps us figure out the tech so we can independently monitor our oxygen levels on the band.

"Two hours is plenty," Sunni says nonchalantly.

Misty turns paler than usual but nods stiffly.

As she tightens the straps on her suit, Sunni cuts through our casual chatter with the bark of a battle-hardened veteran, cold and ruthless. "We're not here to save my universe," Sunni says. "It's unsavable. Got it?"

"Right," I say slowly. I'm not used to seeing her like this.

Sunni's brows twitch at my slow reply. "Ingrid. You're on my turf. I've already lived through what's gone on here. *Un-save-able.* Yes?" She presses her thick-gloved fingers together as she annunciates each syllable.

"Yes. Okay." Having a real mind-reader in the room is bad enough. I fall silent. Jia minds her own business and pretends to play with her wristband.

"I just want to get in, get the weapon, and get out as fast as possible," Sunni says, somewhat apologetically. It's not an apology, though. My face heats. I'm not sorry either. I can't help what I want, and she can't assuage her nerves either.

"We should have a code word. Yeah, I know I'm dead in this universe, and Ingrid doesn't exist, but just in case we run into other versions of one of us or people we know," Misty suggests solemnly, as if mediating a silent battle between me and Sunni.

"I suppose beards and sexy outfits won't be enough of a tell," I say under my breath.

Misty smirks. "Has to be innocuous, something we can slip into conversation, even if it seems a little weird or out of place—"

My heart skips a beat. "Banana," I say, side-eying Wil.

His eyes widen ever so imperceptibly as he readjusts his glasses.

"Seems too silly," Jia replies. "Shouldn't it be a phrase? Like, 'I'm feeling under the weather'?"

"We'll use *banana*," Wil says curtly, not taking his gaze from mine.

Sunni touches my arm. Gentle, but firm. "That's what we chose. Before?"

"It's what we choose now. Because I heard it in the past. From Future Wil." I sigh and smile a little. "It's already done, so we should just get out there and find this weapon." I turn to Sunni. "How will we know where to go?"

"I'll lead," Sunni says shortly.

Stepping off the ship is like sinking into a frigid pool wearing weights that threaten to fall off at any second. I'm not a terrible swimmer, but I'm so terrified of the dark, open ocean around us that I forget to breathe. Sunni undulates like a butterfly before us, as gracefully as one can in a spacesuit. The tiny lights on her suit dance in the water. They're the only visible source of light. We'd found a rope in the lockers and she's attached it to her suit and we all grip it tightly. We lose hold of the rope, we get stranded in the depths.

I bring up the rear and try to remember the breast stroke and regulate my breathing. I awkwardly kick and narrowly avoid being kicked by Jia in front of me. The protective suit slimes around my body like jelly. There's not a lot of air in here, despite what Wil programmed, and the suit from the wristband fails to keep out the frigidness of the deep ocean. It's starting to smell like my own mouth, and I can't remember the last time I brushed my teeth. Oral hygiene takes a backseat to saving the world.

Don't think about the vastness of the ocean, I tell myself as we swim deeper. The rope slides in my slippery grip, and I have to keep stopping to make sure I'm still holding it, that it hasn't slipped and my friends haven't unknowingly left me here. I look back. I can't even see the *Blind Elephant* anymore. I'm just a speck in the thick darkness that a leviathan might swallow on a whim. We're four dust motes floating through the world as we awkwardly swim towards the maintenance airlock.

Sunni will put in her codes. If the codes are good, the hatch will open and flood the airlock. Once inside, we have to re-enter the code, and the airlock cabin will drain the water and pressurize. Then, we'll be clear to remove our protective gear.

After what feels like forever, something kicks me in the shoulder. I've gotten too close to Jia. The force propels me backward. Someone grabs me. Sunni's lights ahead have dimmed. A room of cold blue light emerges from the dark, like a rip in space-time. Sunni swims forward, holding Misty, who holds Jia, who in turn pulls me forward into the airlock.

It takes our combined strength to pull the airlock shut. The blue light permeates the water, and as we float together within the enclosed cabin, I'm reminded of all the times my parents brought me to a public pool. Dad would do laps. Mum would relax in the hot tub and float in the shallow end. I'd pretend to be a mermaid with the other kids and attempt to swim to the very bottom. I tell myself now that we are four mermaids, breaking into an evil lair to steal a dangerous tool.

A gloved hand waves in front of my face. Sunni raises her eyebrows in annoyance, points to me, and sweeps her finger to the circular window on the door connecting the airlock to the rest of the facility. The gestures say, *keep watch.*

I maneuver towards the murky glass. The water makes the dimly lit hallway beyond the glass difficult to see. Eventually, the water recedes around me. My feet touch the ground. Cool, recycled air floods the space between us, and the dark corners of my vision disappear. The wristband suit feels heavier now that the pressurization has been completed.

The hallway beyond remains clear. We switch off our suits and Sunni removes her helmet as the puddles at our feet evaporate. Curly, blond hair spills around her face. Green light floods the airlock. Good to go. Sunni punches in another code at the door to the base. *Hissss.* It pops open.

As if awakening from a dream, I search the area for surveillance as we step into the long hallway. It reminds me of a bunker from a post-apocalyptic movie. Jia hovers near me, ready to whisk us into her world.

"They don't have cameras mounted everywhere, like your Collective," Sunni whispers. Her voice reverberates against the grimy stained walls. "There's no need for that yet until we come to the secure areas. We should be fine."

"Still, we shouldn't be seen." Jia holds out a hand to all of us. "Just as we don't want to disrupt our timeline, we shouldn't endanger yours."

It's a good idea, because as we step through the next corridor, two people gripping tablets stride briskly and exchange curt words in a near-English dialect. Comically large sunglasses cover their eyes and their fingers appear webbed. A new species that has similar physical characteristics as humans? Or superpowered human adults with an altered physique?

My instinct is to watch from afar, but Sunni motions for us to follow them. She must think they're headed for the research and development lab. I wait for either stranger to drop a hint about their role here, or what race they might belong to, but beyond a sentence or two, they're not chatty. I raise my eyebrows at Misty. She's frowning. Deciphering. The words we catch are tonal, half-sang by people without a musical ear. Definitely ahmei.

They stop before a door secured with a wheeled hatch. One inputs the key in an electronic lock. We stare at the shaking scientist's fingers, memorizing the code, and we barely manage to slip through after them before they shut and twist the hatch.

Sunni holds out her free arm and makes a fist: *hold.* We stop and wait for the scientists to disappear around a corner. This hallway appears much the same as the one before, except the floors are pristine. I lift my heels instinctively and take careful steps forward to see if I leave a trail.

"Should be mostly okay for the rest of the way," Sunni whispers.

"Were they speaking a mix of ahmei and English?" I ask Misty.

Misty wrinkles her nose. "Yeah." She looks to Sunni for confirmation.

"Ahmei scientists in mostly human form?" I ask.

"No," Sunni says shortly. She gestures for us to keep moving.

"Humans, adapting to the ahmei language?" That would explain the singing quality. All the ahmei in human form I've encountered are exceptional singers. Many scientists in our Collective are ahmei, so it would make sense for human scientists working with the Collective to adapt alien words and terminology.

"Kind of," Sunni says flatly.

"Ingrid," Jia hisses. "Quiet. Some of us need to concentrate."

"Sorry. Just one more. How do you know this is the right way?" I remark, trying to make my inquiry sound casual as my curiosity burns.

Misty shoots me a warning look and shakes her head. This topic is off-limits and I've asked too many questions already. Sure, we all memorized the map Sunni provided, but following a crudely drawn route is different from navigating the real thing.

"I was here for a while," she says distantly.

Given Sunni's rebel history, I conclude she infiltrated the place and went undercover to gather intelligence. I don't remember reading about this in her journal. Misty's glare subsides when she realizes I'm not going to press the matter.

That doesn't mean I'm not going to think ahead, just in case we have to make a quick exit. "I'm guessing we're in the research section of the base?" I venture.

"It's the hardest place to get into, but usually less guarded. The shipyard is always crawling. Once Wil repairs the ship, he'll have the opportunity to scan the dock for us."

"Should we have checked the docking area first before sneaking into R&D, in case they're in the middle of bringing it back to Ethan's ship?" I reply, wondering if Ethan would stay on his ship while it's docked.

"This isn't a democracy, Ingrid. I'm not taking suggestions on how this operation should be run." Her voice threatens to break her carefully controlled whisper.

"Stop arguing," Jia says. "Ingrid, let's trust Sunni's lead so we can get this thing and get out of here. Sunni, let's try and communicate the plan before we enter invisibility and enemy territory. Everyone agree?"

My pride has been grievously stung as sweat forms between my fingers. This condescending, let's-be-friends tone boils my blood. Am I the only one annoyed by this Sunni's militant approach, her inability to share interesting details about how this universe fell to the very enemy we're trying to defeat back home?

Slowly I nod, hating my anger, hating that I can't let it go for my friends' sakes. "Okay," I say to Sunni, not meaning it at all.

"Right," she says stiffly. "Whatever."

Misty throws me a look that says, *Don't start this again,* as Sunni leads us on.

In the next hallway, floor-to-ceiling rustic aquariums line the walls, as if the scientists decided to put all their creative energy into this one section of the base. The aquariums are framed by ornate, swirling metal. As we pass, I notice the aquariums are bubbling yet empty. Seems like a waste of power and water—until I see three that are filled, and not with fish or other aquatic wildlife.

They're filled with *humans.*

Once again, I *think* they're humans, and as I've been chastised for asking questions, I can only speculate. The humans aren't much older than us. They float without breathing apparatuses. Bubbles emerge rhythmically from their noses and mouths, and they look as if they're having the best sleep of their lives. Skin-tight, appropriately skin-coloured aerobic wear covers their bodies. Their nostrils have been artificially reduced and stringy catfish whiskers protrude from their faces. The bubbles from the tank obscure a close inspection, yet their skin texture appears scalier. One person's hair has been completely removed and replaced with a crown of stalky, spindly digits tipped with a bioluminescent light, as if Medusa had had a child with an anglerfish. The stalks twitch and bob in the water, illuminating their tank in an eerie white-blue. The second person's bioluminescent stalks have been attached below their jaw-line, one on each side, above transparent, delicate blue and yellow wing-shaped fins. Faint scars on the neck denote where they've been attached and successfully obscure their gill augmentation surgery.

The third person—a young woman—catches Sunni's attention, and it's why she has halted, instead of aggressively urging us forward.

Like the others, she's been fitted with gills. Bioluminescent freckles dot her cheeks and continue down her neck and arms. Razor-sharp, hair-like fins protrude from the lower half of her arms and legs. Tiny suckers have been attached to her finger pads and her index fingernails and large toenails have been replaced with pointed claws.

Despite the augmentations, something about this girl is familiar.

"This is horrible," Jia says shakily, and looks away.

I feel the same and yet I can't stop staring. There's no evolutionary purpose to these modifications. They feel cohesively cosmetic. "Why did the Collective do this to them?" I whisper to Sunni.

She wrenches from Jia's grip. Before we can protest, she's out of our invisible bubble and in plain view.

"Sunni!" Misty hisses, reaching out to her from our invisible world.

Sunni doesn't pay us any mind. The suspended young woman has transfixed her.

"It's not a punishment," Sunni says. Her splayed hand presses against the tank as her astonished breath fogs the pristine glass. "They're here to show us the reward for compliance."

I remember how Emily Foller's appearance had been modified to complement her demonic powers, once she'd cozied up to Shane Richmond and Jadore. Even Jadore herself is a strange augmentation, a blend of her true alien origins and human form. "But all of them are being modified to be more fish-like."

Sunni doesn't seem to think this is an important observation. "And?"

"Do all of these people have fish superpowers? Why make everyone more amphibian?"

She breaths in sharply, seeing the divergence in our thinking. "Our Collective hasn't cared about individual superpowers for a long time. Now, humans are assigned suitable jobs. Well. Not a job. It's servitude. And then they augment you to be better at that service, if you're cooperative. My guess is this is the underwater maintenance crew, or people who need to go in and out of the facility frequently, who work close to the nearby reef populated with large, dangerous fish. Maybe they're being asked to hunt or fight some underwater threats."

"Why bother with suits when you can just adapt the human body?" Misty remarks. "I guess that's cheaper and more efficient."

"Is it?" I wonder aloud, noting the tubes disappearing into the walls and the subtle hum permeating the thick, recycled air. I recall the two scientists from earlier. Are there fish-like eyes behind their sunglasses? And their hands, modified to accelerate their work? No wonder Sunni had been hesitant to call them human. How many physical or genetic alterations does one have to make before they lose the right to call themselves human?

Jia shakes her head and utters something under her breath. Distress negatively affects her powers. "We should keep going."

Sunni doesn't take her gaze from the person in the tank as she reaches out her hand. I take it and Sunni slips back into our invisible world.

"Is that someone we know?" Misty asks, concerned.

A bittersweet smile touches her lips. "The transformation is pretty far gone, and she doesn't look quite the same as she does in our world, but that's Kimberly Sharma. Was Kimberly." Her surprise and heartache vanish as quickly as they had come, as if she has shoved it out an airlock. Her hand drops back to her side. Time to go. "Not too much further."

Another long stretch of hallway takes us deeper into the beast, and then there's another security door with a wheeled hatch before us and a ninety-degree turn. I expect to pass through the security door but Sunni abruptly drags us around the corner.

Instead of more locked doors or open rooms with silent alien workers, there's a tinted plexiglass wall. The classroom on the other side of the wall, awash with a rich blue light, teams with human children. At least, I'm pretty certain they're human. They're reminiscent of the altered human scientists from earlier and Kimberly in the tank.

It takes a moment for my eyes to adjust to the lighting and I study the children's strange physique. Purple bruises the size of my fists blot their necks. Gills. Some large flaps of skin, prominent and protruding; others, deep cuts like red ravines. Their heads remind me of lumps of wet clay on a pottery wheel, unfinished and untouched. Curly blonde hair grows in patches, while many of the children are bald. The one similarity across all the children are their eyes: large, bioluminescent yellow in the dim blue light of the room. Some of them engage in familiar games, like tag and hopscotch. They dart around the room and crawl beneath the two long tables and rows of chairs. I remember playing similar games during the long lunch hours when we'd been trapped inside because of the weather. A couple of children are playing what looks like an alien word-guessing game on a wall-mounted tablet. They're chattering and laughing; the sound doesn't carry past the wall.

They're happy enough, though I wonder if this room, this facility, is the only place they've ever known. Have they even seen a regular-looking human before? Do they know what they are?

I side-eye Sunni. She's leaning against the opposite wall, holding Misty's hand, purposefully avoiding the scene before us. Tears roll down her face as she clutches her stomach, as if she's going to be sick.

There's a mix of English and alien writing on the walls, and cartoonishly illustrated signs detailing the rules of the room. *Listen to the friendly alien in the white coat. Don't leave the room without holding a fish-person's large hand. An A+ on the tablet means the child gets a large bowl of wriggling sardine soup.*

This is the future of the human race in this universe. Genetically altered to withstand high-pressure ocean environments. An obedient worker class, intelligent enough to problem-solve and complete complex tasks. As long as they obey their aquatic overlords and don't become smart enough to outwit them.

A fishman in a lab coat enters and instinctively, we freeze. Sunni shakes her head and juts her chin to the window. Doesn't matter if we're visible or not. It's a two-way mirror. My breath fogs the glass and I recoil, yet I can't tear my gaze away just yet. The tug on my arm has similarly fallen lax. Misty and Jia are equally transfixed by the children.

The mutant human children form an orderly line, all except two who remain seated at their game in the corner. Not out of willful disobedience. One mechanically moves their mouth like a fish about to eat and stares into the middle distance. The alien scientist removes a digital pad from their coat pocket, makes a note, and waves in front of the distracted child. No change in behaviour.

The scientist's presence has also gone unnoticed by the second genetically altered child, whose engorged forehead looms over the table and obscures their vision. They adjust their head as needed to see the chess pieces before them. At least, I think it's chess, but the pieces are blue and white, and there are five tiers of boards, lined like shelves up the wall.

The scientist stands between us and the chess players, so I don't see how he kills them. When the scientist moves again, body parts vacuum-packed in plastic have replaced the two children in the chairs. Remains of the disobedient.

None of the children in line flinch or seem surprised that their friends are now packaged meat. The fishman's mouth bobbles as he gestures to the door. The children file out like soldiers.

I point at the glass and tug at Misty's hand, but her strength wins over mine. It's time to go. The subtle shake of her head stills my protest. I drink in the scene until we round a corner.

Sunni addresses my objections before I can raise them. "We can't rescue them, Ingrid."

"They're *kids!*"

The whites of her eyes shine with tears and broken blood vessels, but her voice is a stony wall. "You want to take a hoard of genetically altered, lab-grown children unquestioningly loyal to the Collective away from the only home they've ever known?" She sounds like she's had this argument a thousand times. She probably has. Maybe she's even been on our side of it.

"If we see a way to disrupt their operation, we should take the opportunity," Jia whispers.

"That's not the mission. We're *not* here to save my universe. End of discussion." Her voice wavers. Her despair shouts the opposite of her words. She hides her face in her hands and continues on down the hallway.

She wants to save the blonde little children. But she can't. It's too late for them. We have to follow Sunni, lest we break formation and reveal ourselves to the three scientists who've appeared in the hallway.

Sunni presses her lips firmly in a line as we pass more doors, evade a few more scientists, and come to a fork in the hallway. Ahead, the hallway stretches on. That's where Sunni leads us as we follow one of the scientists. To our right, the corridor ends abruptly in a sealed door. A sign in alien symbols worn from moisture captures Misty's attention, pulling us all to a halt.

"That looks..." Misty wrenches herself from Jia's invisibility and she appears in the real world.

"Misty!" Jia hisses.

But she's not listening. She heads down the other corridor and approaches the alien symbols. "I've seen these before. I think. The kanji, for lack of other word, that the Collective uses in your universe is a little different than ours." She takes out a notebook and copies the symbols down. I remember when we had rules about not writing things down. That feels like a lifetime ago. "Go on! I'll catch up!" she whispers.

I don't like that we're separating, even if it's just for a moment. Sunni's lips twitch into a smile. "The woman can't resist crackin' the code on a new language."

The scientist we had been following is out of sight. We continue straight down the hallway, careful not to trip over an open hatch door. We round another corner. "The lab where they keep it is down this—"

Swormp!

They materialize before us in a blazing flash that sears the eyeballs. Three fishmen and one human, whose face I don't see at first, as he isn't facing me. I bump into one of the fishmen and startle him, causing the human to whip around. I jump back and gasp.

The human is *Ethan*.

He cranes his neck and stares past me. He heard the gasp. He heard *me*. The fishman draws a weapon and gurgles something in his native language. We press soundlessly against the wall and don't dare breathe.

Sunni's description of him as the poster boy of the Collective isn't inaccurate. Silk finery drapes over the love of my life, and the flicker of disdain that mares his features carry a distinguished, royal air. His dark hair has been slicked back and lifted, as if to make him appear taller. He already stands a foot above the fishmen. Yet, like the other humans we've seen, he's fallen beneath the knife of cosmetic, genetic surgery. Blue and green scales line his neck and disappear under his collar. Thin gills flare in frustration at his alien entourage. The alterations *suit* him, and I hate how they accentuate his natural attractiveness.

How many people have volunteered to undergo genetic modification because of him?

"Ethan," I say, and before I can stop myself, I pull myself from my friends' grasps.

"No, Ingrid!" But Sunni's protest cannot stop me. I want him to see me. He needs to.

Jia and Sunni appear in the real world beside me.

Ethan's cold gaze scans the three of us. "Rebels."

CHAPTER 7

No. It's me. Ingrid. But his gaze sweeps over me with no recognition.

It's a different Ethan, not *my* Ethan, but maybe our love can transcend the fabric of dimensional space and time.

His attention isn't on me. Like a homing beacon on a missile, he darts for Sunni. She recoils and runs, but her spacesuit is not built for running. Jia and I run after her. This Ethan is faster. Stronger. He pushes Jia forcefully into the wall and hooks Sunni around the neck.

"Welcome back," he says. "Just had to touch Kimberly Sharma's chamber, didn't you."

He doesn't know who I am. He's been brainwashed by the Collective.

He's so enraptured by Sunni that he doesn't notice Misty rounding the corner. "Hey, there's a bunch of—"

A flash of recognition clouds Ethan's face as Misty appears. He squeezes Sunni against him and presses a button on his wristband.

"Don't come after me," Sunni warns her lover. In a blink, she's gone.

"Personal teleporters," I say like it's a curse word.

There's no time to dwell on her capture. The three fishmen from Ethan's abandoned entourage advance towards us, pressing buttons on their own wristbands, ready to snatch us to an ungodly laboratory where they can modify us to be their slaves.

"Move," Misty commands as she charges the three fishmen. Jia and I know not to get in her way. We scramble backward as Misty hurls fireballs.

But these are not the fishmen from our universe. They nimbly dart out of the way of her volleys and laugh at her attempts to harm them. The temperature in the hallway doubles within seconds. A rusted strip of metal that lines the bottom of the corridor blackens. Embedded inside is a pair of thick, coiled tubes. As Misty prepares to strike again, I strain to hear the whispering current running through the metal. Electricity, maybe? I concentrate on the dancing white and blue flashes in my mind, streaked with yellow, urging them to tell me what's inside.

"You really shouldn't underestimate me," Misty says, and throws more fire their way.

This time, the fire hits true. It catches one of the fishmen like a tinderbox and he screeches, running in the opposite direction down the corridor. The other two fishmen recoil, their faces slick with worry.

"Fire probably isn't a good idea," Jia says, reaching for me, readying to turn us invisible.

"Yeah. For them," Misty agrees.

Her fireball hits the second fishman in the leg and scorches his scales. She doesn't let up. Another massive sphere of flame has him blackened and crawling after his friend. He stops moving halfway down the corridor, smoke swirling from his reptilian flesh.

I catch Misty's arm. "You throw more fire and the whole place is going to lock down from a fire alarm! Do you want Sunni to suffocate?"

She wrenches herself from me as the remaining fishman draws a blade from a scabbard at his waist. The three of us jump back to avoid his blade as Misty switches to ice, aiming at the floor. He slips and slices his arm on the blade, exposing sinew. Blood drips from his wound as he advances again, enraged that we dare trick him.

Jia and I hold Misty's torso and we move as one. Misty thrusts another ice spike at the fishman as he lunges. I feel lightheaded as we recoil; the water Misty draws into her palm forms into a long, icy javelin. Jia looks equally drained. She's taking from us to form her weapon.

"Do what you have to," Jia says, speaking my thoughts exactly.

The ice javelin must be the most detailed weapon Misty has created with her powers. It shines in the dreary lighting, as if it's a metallic weapon encased in glass. As it manifests into realness, the fishman halts his attack and swallows nervously, parting its fat lips and sucking in air loudly.

Misty breaks from us and thrusts the javelin at the alien. There is no hesitation. No room for the ethical quandaries of killing a foot soldier. There is only the weapon and her passion to save Sunni, and the determination that no one will stand in her way.

The weapon pierces the fishman through the torso. He falls backward. The javelin, although ice, does not shatter, but implants into the floor. I look away. The sound of him slumping to the ground, groaning, squelching—I can't. The colours evoke too strong an image. When I turn back, his body is still.

"We gotta go after Sunni!" Misty insists. She storms down the hallway, as if she knows her way. "Well?"

My mind whirls from the battle. "Those devices. Just a second."

I check the charred body of the fishman who had attempted to run from Misty's fury. The personal teleportation device is not unlike the alien bands around our wrists. I attempt to slide a fingernail beneath the metal; it's fused to the flesh. *Tap, tap.* I look for signs of life on the device. Nothing. I move to the impaled fishman. Jia is already inspecting him with a detached look on her face. The band is also fused to his wrist.

Jia understands. "No luck?" She braces the wall for support.

I shake my head.

"You done?" Misty pulls at my arm. She's pale and looks like she hasn't slept in weeks. The fight has exhausted her supply.

I nod. We must save Sunni and Ethan, whatever the cost.

"Wait," Jia insists, touching us both gently on the forearms. "Think about this logically. Sunni is distracting the one person who could upset our plans. We need that weapon if we're going to defeat the Collective and return to our universe." And return to her family, is what she doesn't say.

"She said the weapon is either in the hangar or the R&D section," I say. "We're really close to the lab. Should one of us sneak into the dock? See if Wil made it there?"

"We shouldn't split up," Jia says.

"But we might not have time to search both places *and* rescue Sunni!" Misty retorts.

My gaze flits to the tubes running the length of the ceiling and along the base of the wall. The facility groans and the lights flicker.

"Maybe we do," I say.

Misty's dark blue eyes flash with pride. "Time travel."

"Oh. Well, maybe," I say, not wanting to dismiss the option outright. I point at the tubes. "If we can find a way to shut off the power, we don't have to worry about any alarms or electronic security this universe will throw at us. They get busy fixing that while their oxygen runs out? We buy ourselves time to search and rescue Sunni. We have some oxygen in our wristband suits if we need it."

Nodding slowly, Misty paces, finger tapping her chin. "Okay, okay. Doable. I don't remember what Sunni said about where the electricity comes from in this place. A generator, outside?"

"Wil would know," Jia says softly.

"We may not need him. Misty, can you target your fire on this?" I point to where she'd already blackened the covered wires. "If we can cut power to key areas—"

"We'd be telling the Collective exactly where we are," Misty interrupts.

"We can be quick," Jia says. She looks as exhausted as Misty. We're running on pure adrenaline now.

"Wil can be able to tell us where Sunni is," Misty says, and kneels before the power conduit. "Wil, if you can hear me, tell us where she is."

There's no response. We must be out of his range.

We shield our eyes as the coils spark and emit a hissing sound, first from the base of the wall and then on the ceiling. A blaring alarm screeches and then cuts out. It sounds like it's still sounding at a different part of the facility. The lighting returns, now an ominous red, emanating from tiny beams embedded in the wall. Must be powered by a different source, in case of emergency. A high-pitched tonal message rings over the distant alarm. Jia pulls us close as Misty listens intently.

"It's saying for everyone to prepare to evacuate and repair crews to head to our section," Misty says. "Let's hurry."

From what I can recall from the map, and what Sunni had said before Ethan appeared, the lab is nearby. We hurry down the hallway under cover of Jia's invisibility. People with varying aquatic genetic modifications rush by us with hard drives and tablets under their arms, presumably towards the main hangar. When the coast is clear, Misty continues to disrupt the power conduits in nearby hallways to throw the Collective off our trail.

"That sicko better not be making off with her," Misty mutters under her breath as we approach the entrance to the lab. She's had the same thought as me. That Ethan might escape the facility in his ship with Sunni and the weapon.

"No way," I say to her, to convince all of us. "Her returning from another universe with us makes us valuable. He won't leave until he has us and answers." I'm making a big assumption about his character, based on my own desires. And, if the weapon leaves the area, Wil might be able to pick up the signature in the *Blind Elephant.* "Let's try and get this open."

The main lab has an electronic lock on the twin sliding doors and looks sleeker and cleaner in contrast to the rusted submarine aesthetic of the facility. With the power blown, the doors require only brute strength to force them open. The three of us jam our fingertips between the doors to gain purchase and heave. When we're through, the doors remain open, as if too tired to close.

A frightened person, more fish than human in a white lab coat, peers out from behind a counter and throws up their hands, spitting out a hurried falsetto that feels like an apology and a plea for life. Before Jia and I can stop her, Misty strikes the scientist with an ice shard between the eyes. They fall back, hit their head against the counter, and slump unconscious to the floor.

Jia and I exchange looks of terror, which Misty catches with disdain. "As if I haven't done worse already today. C'mon, do you want them to run off and tell people where we are?" Our stunned silence answers for us. "Great. Let's find this weapon and get out of here."

"How will we know what it looks like without Sunni?" I ask.

"I mean, it's a weapon. So, look for weapon-like..."

Misty trails off as we fan out amongst the rows of counters holding arrays disassembled computers, dissected mechanical parts, bioluminescent flesh lumps infested with cyborg parts, and dozens of enclosed tubes streaked with red-lettered alien warnings. Although power has been cut to the area exterior to the lab, the cool-toned lights and electronically powered machinery hums and churns. I guess this room is important enough to warrant its own power source. Even with the partially open entrance, the distant emergency evacuation alarm and worried chatter from the facility doesn't carry into the lab. Anyone working in here would have no idea of the chaos happening outside and be doomed to work until it's too late to escape.

Along the far side of the room is a row of computer stations and terminals. Only one monitor shines brightly, displaying an intranet document program. The operating system looks similar to the one Jia and I had played with in the hangar at Sparkstone, but retrofitted, as if the older nineteen-eighties aesthetic had been an intentional design choice. The language of the document is mostly alien to me, save a few English words jammed here and there, including JADORE and SUNNIVA HARRIS.

My gaze slides over to the unconscious scientist. I wonder if someone has been reading up on Sunni's activities now that she's been captured. This isn't good.

I call Misty over. "Can you read this?"

"Hmm." Misty grabs a black chair on wheels from a nearby

workstation and slides it over to the terminal. Her eyes flash at Sunni's name. "Give me a minute."

Jia and I search the rest of the lab. I'm panicking because I don't see anything that looks missile-shaped. Jia starts at the opposite side from me and studies each new item with care and consideration, as if there's going to be a pop quiz later. I run my hand absently along the counters near Misty, passing my gaze over the mechanical and biological experiments in circular dishes. Admittedly, I'm distracted by thoughts of Ethan and his genetic modifications in this universe. I have to think of how I'm going to get through to him.

I don't notice it at first because its appearance alludes my understanding of a projectile missile fit for an elite ship. A silver rod half my height rests horizontally in an open glass case gilded with brass. I've passed this three times already, but it's the smell that brings me back. I stick my nose in the case as close to the metal as I dare, and then test other areas of the lab, so I can be sure. It's hard to explain, but this rod smells like blue and red intertwining, but never meeting. I sense cayenne pepper and late nights, and lack of sleep. The scent awakens a deep sorrow and longing, accompanied by a strong moral centre rooted in salt and sand. I feel as if I'm experiencing a movie through my nostrils instead of my eyes and ears.

At least two sentient people have been murdered, dissected, and inserted into this rod. Tablets open to blueprints surround the case with digitally handwritten notes in the margin in a tight English script, detailing formulas about power fluctuations while travelling half the speed of light. Several drawings depict the rod duplicating at least three times and shooting out of a cannon-like structure.

"Wil, can you hear me?" I whisper. "Is this it?" The metal is surprisingly warm to the touch. I put an ear up to it, as if expecting to hear the ocean within a conch. The whine of the frequency that led me to this universe sings within the metal, barely audible, but present.

Looks like it might be it, Wil replies. His voice is barely louder than the hum of the room.

I secure the rod and close the case. "Found it, I think." Cautiously, I pull the case towards me. It moves an inch and my arms strain with effort. "Uh, definitely can't carry it alone. Heavier than it looks."

"Huh?" Misty jumps at my voice and swivels in the chair, turning her bleary eyes to me. "Yeah. Right. Ingrid, there's a ton of stuff on here, all in an ahmei dialect. Even the system documents are in ahmei. Stuff about the portal that sent Sunni to our universe, which Jadore in this universe also worked on. Apparently, this Jadore's dying. Maybe already dead. There are notes here I don't get about some drug the ahmei have administered to her. I don't..." She trails off, overwhelmed.

I see Jia's patience tested as she approaches me and judges the weight of the weapon case. "Does it say anything that will help us right now?"

"I mean, this *does* help us," Misty says, scrubbing her eyes. "The ahmei are in complete control here. Not Jadore, or a council of races, like in our universe."

I remember Sunni mentioning that the vitaphage had been cured here and that the ahmei have a more active military presence. I try to imagine Agailya or Gayarnu as cruel masters, leading the Collective in a scientific mission to enslave and force their idea of genetic perfection on everyone. Everything I know about them has been influenced by the vitaphage that disseminated their population and ensured their cooperation with the Collective. It's difficult for me to picture Ethan, who has suffered in their quest, willingly obeying their commands.

"Wil," Misty says quietly. "If you can hear my thoughts right now, we should download everything we can access from this database into the ship's computer so we can look at it later."

If we can find the cure in a database somewhere in this universe, we can deliver it to Agailya and barter for my Ethan's freedom, before the explosion. I can change history. Or, at the very least, seek the ahmei as an ally against the Collective, if they'll have us.

I wonder if a cured vitaphage means this universe's Ethan was never part of Agailya's experiment. Which means he likely never experienced those horrible side effects, like losing his memories. What leads him to be their poster boy?

"Let's hard copies if we can," I suggest, recalling the evacuating scientists carrying digital copies of their work. "There are enough similarities between our two Collectives that something in there might be of use."

"Yeah, I'll just yoink this out," Misty says. She reaches beneath the counter and pulls out all the plugs. The monitor goes dark and a black box the size of Misty's hand comes free. She coils the chord around the hard drive, tucks it under her arm, and then considers the weapon case on the counter. "Looks awkward?"

"The two of us can try to carry it," I say to Misty.

"That would make it easier for me to keep my focus," Jia says.

Misty and I carefully pull the case into our arms and maneuver it around the counter. It's just like lugging a harp around, I tell myself, trying to think of better days. Jia hovers, watching us both with hands outstretched, preparing her invisibility.

Misty hesitates as we put down the case, so we can catch our breath. "We're going to have to carry this all the way to Sunni. Wherever she is. Wil...?"

"We need to get this back to the ship before more of Alt-Ethan's guard find us," Jia says, regret ringing through her words.

Misty knows she's right. "Wil? You hear me? How far are you? Because I don't want to carry this—"

I'm coming, he replies. His voice, normally booming, is like a static radio turned down too low. *Vessels are evacuating due to whatever stunt you pulled. I think I can dock long enough to get you onboard.*

"We'll do our best, but it might take longer than we think," I tell him.

He doesn't reply right away. When he does, his voice sounds fainter. Like he's just run a marathon, untrained. *Blocked the weapon's signature for now from them. Lots to track now. Can't hold for long. Follow my directions.*

The memory of Sunni's digital map flashes before my eyes, and while I had a rough idea of the route between here and the main hangar, Wil has cemented it in our minds. I feel as if I can make it there on autopilot, as if this facility is my childhood home.

We're just about to figure out the best way to pry open the doors to the lab when they're thrust apart by three fishmen. Jia pulls us into her invisible world and we huddle together around the heavy weapon. The guards are heavily armored and carry what look to be miniature harpoon weapons. Perhaps this is the personal entourage Sunni warned us about. They hiss and sing as they point to the unconscious scientist and promptly fan out to search the lab for intruders.

It's going to be hard to carry this glass case out of the lab without attracting attention, even while invisible. Misty could take them on, but she's done a lot already. Jia could out-maneuver them and run if she didn't have to carry a weapon or worry about hiding anyone else. And then there's me. I could blink us out of existence, but who knows where or when we might end up.

What I feel as I watch the fishmen isn't a sinking feeling, because the result I want isn't born of self-sacrifice. "Both of you, go."

"No, we can all get out!" Jia hisses.

I keep my voice barely above a whisper. "I'll distract Ethan—I mean, Alt-Ethan—and the guards and find Sunni. It will buy you the time you need to get to the ship and install the weapon. I won't come back without her."

Or him, I promise myself.

Misty's terrified face emulates my fears of returning to them years or decades later because of my inability to precisely gauge time as I free myself from Jia's iron grip.

I'm a surprise to the guards as I materialize from nothing. The three of them point their harpoons at me and gurgle. I hold up my hands.

"I surrender," I say steadily. "I have information about the other universe. Take me to Ethan."

The fishmen lead me away from the lab and towards the living quarters. The regular lighting has returned, but the power flickers precariously and I hear the distant chatter of repair crews.

Before us is a handleless sliding door with a damaged keypad. Professionally engraved symbols denoting ownership of the room have been hastily scratched away, and replaced with different symbols in a rough-hewn script. Ethan's name, perhaps, represented in the ahmei language.

The fishmen gurgle an off-key tune and the door slides open to reveal a drab, but surprisingly large suite. The quarters have been draped in blues of all shades. Lipstick on a pig, for all the good it does to disguise the facility's bunker aesthetic. A silver tub half full of water sits in the middle of the main cabin, like a coffee table, as it is surrounded by two mouldy-smelling couches. I spy another silver tub next to the bed in the adjoining room, and a smaller one in what looks to be the washroom.

Sunni sits on one of the couches, next to Alt-Ethan. Someone has removed her suit and dressed her in blue leggings and a thick sweater dress. Our entrance interrupts a heated, but quiet argument, as Ethan stands awkwardly, red-faced. His complexion contrasts his enhanced aquatic colouring. My mind struggles with how I should address him. He's Ethan, and yet, he isn't. This Alt-Ethan struggles to hide his cough as the fishmen guards enter with me in tow. They gurgle something to him. He examines me clinically, and once again I seek recognition in eyes that don't know me.

"I see," he says with a hint of curiosity, and gestures over his shoulder to the person standing behind a shockingly pristine data console.

If Alt-Ethan hadn't pointed out this person, I wouldn't have noticed them, which might be due to their natural powers. It takes me forever to recognize them: a genetically modified human with dark hair spiked to the heavens, protruding gills from their neck, and bulbus fish eyes, sea-green and sparkling. Their skin glows with an otherworldly pearlescence. They only have to part their lips for an entire verse of a song to tumble out, as if they're a master ventriloquist. As they speak in their native tongue, their voice strikes a chord in my memory.

Alt-Gayarnu sings two notes in glorious G and one of the fishmen holding me falls away. He leaves immediately, shutting the door behind him. Alt-Gayarnu sweeps their fishy gaze over me and returns their focus to Ethan. They pretended to be Ethan's girlfriend in our universe. What is their relationship to him here?

Sunni's hands are bound in front of her. Similar metal cuffs secure her ankles. Yet it is not the metal that keeps her from escaping. She stares into the middle distance, trapped within her own dark thoughts.

"Sunni," I whisper to her, eager to free us both.

She lifts her gaze, and like the aliens in the room, she pays me little mind.

Alt-Ethan switches from ahmei to English, and throws a smug look to Sunni. "I don't need all of them around. We can handle these rebels personally." He wants us to hear this. He motions to the fishmen. "Process her."

My heart sinks into my chest as I'm dragged to the console. The last time I saw someone processed, they died in a person-sized test-tube. I refuse to die today, in this terrible place far from home, at the hands of a man who is supposed to love me.

Alt-Gayarnu holds a tablet and speaks calmly to Alt-Ethan in the ahmei tongue. I jerk my arms forward and knock the tablet from their hands, wrench myself from the remaining fishmen's grip, and lunge for Sunni. We can get out of here.

"Stop," says Alt-Gayarnu. Their grasp of our language is crude, compared to the Gayarnu I know. "Hurt less."

Her tone blankets me like a warm towel after an ice bath. My body halts stiffly. I detect a faint comforting scent and my muscles relax. Now is my chance to move. Except I don't. I'm not in control anymore. I don't resist as I'm guided back to the console. Alt-Gayarnu records my fingerprints and swabs my cheek, as if I'm a child again. The induced dream-like calm dissipates as they complete their admin work and I stare at them in horror.

"Pheromones," Sunni confirms.

"Useful," Alt-Ethan says approvingly, nodding at Alt-Gayarnu.

The fishmen who had restrained me have disappeared. Nothing keeps me here. I can grab Sunni and this Alt-Ethan, and jump us out.

"Ingrid," Alt-Ethan says. I feel light, and it's not pheromones. It's my name on his lips. Had I told him my name, or has he intuited the information from our connection across space and time?

"Yes?" I say, my mouth dry.

But he's looking to Sunni now, more interested in her reaction. "You see? I told you we'd get your allies to cooperate. Everything is so much smoother when we don't have to resort to violence."

"You're a filthy collaborator," Sunni says coldly, without looking at him.

He smiles a little and gestures to Alt-Gayarnu. "Everyone collaborates to survive. Suffering makes the enduring meaningful, etcetera, etcetera, as the ahmei say. All of this race-traitor nonsense is beneath you, Sunni. Everyone you know has come 'round."

Sunni sets her lips firmly. "Everyone I know is dead. Or so unrecognizable they might as well be dead."

"So, my eyes were mistaken? That wasn't Mary-Ellen I saw, valiantly defending you? Or what name was she going by?" He seems legitimately interested and a brief tonal answer from Alt-Gayarnu confirms his suspicions. "Yes, you're right, Misty is what we have on file. But I personally oversaw her harvest. So. Either Misty Carter has a twin sister who also shares her affections for you...*or*..." His smile grows wider. "You brought someone back from the Other Side. Multiple someones. Which makes our mission here a success. All that's left is for you to tell us *why* you've returned *now* with these specimens. I suspect they're not a present from an alternative Collective."

My veins feel cold, as if Alt-Gayarnu has injected me with ice. *Our mission.* Alt-Ethan controls the mantle of this ambitious project?

Sunni says nothing.

Alt-Ethan furrows his brows. "Gayarnu, show them what happened to our versions of her companions and their families in this reality. What will happen if they don't cooperate."

For their benefit, Alt-Ethan repeats his request in the ahmei language. Nodding, Alt-Gayarnu taps their tablet and then a button on the console. The tablet projects a series of images and text onto the nearest wall. The text is alien; the images speak for themselves. Blueprints of human beings, detailing the numerous mutations and proposed alterations to our bodies to best serve the Collective. Gills on our necks. Gruesome surgery by alien doctors on screaming, tied-down humans. Modifications to the areas of the brain involved in obedience and decision making. Controlled breeding for optimal physical traits desired in primarily underwater worlds.

Names—in English, and other human languages—flicker across the screen as Gayarnu and the computer processes Alt-Ethan's request. He reads each entry aloud as they're projected.

"Jia Fields. Escaped processing after nearly killing Mistress Jadore. Biological mother, harvested. Adopted family—reassigned. Adopted sister, hmm, in processing." He wheezes and continues as more images cross the screen, too horrible for me to linger on. "Wil McBride. Harvested during Phase Two and integrated into... oh, that's rich. Your friend Wil powers the headquarters, hiding in the nebula. Did you know that, Sunni? I imagine you did. You were here when Mistress Jadore cut him down. And then there's Misty. Well. We won't re-hash her death." His smile is tender, as if he feels affection for her. Sunni's face glows hot, as does mine. "And then we have this one." He scrutinizes my face. "You're not Jia, you're not Wil, you're not Misty or any of the other students from Sparkstone. So. What makes you so special, for our instruments to not recognize you?"

I raise my eyebrows. "You have my name. Why don't you search it in the database?"

"We are searching with more than just that," he replies coolly. He tilts his head, angling his perfect cheek to Alt-Gayarnu. "What are the results of the bio-scan?"

Alt-Gayarnu's long fingers grace the white buttons and lights as they emit a variety of musical tones. The wall projection changes to a yellow error message and the other images disappear.

Whatever Alt-Gayarnu says enrages Alt-Ethan beyond measure. "How? We have everyone. Run the DNA again. She's not a counterpart from the Phase Four batch?"

More melodies from Alt-Gayarnu, this time, frantic and sympathetic.

"I guess that's possible," he says slowly. "But Mistress Jadore never made those kinds of mistakes. So. That means you exist to vex me. Or..." He glances at Sunni suddenly, and hums something to her in the ahmei language.

Sunni shakes her head frantically, and then hums a shaky, threatening melody. Jealousy rushes through me like an electric shock, which only shames me more. She can communicate with him in a way I cannot.

Alt-Ethan laughs. It hurts because I've heard this sound before. His accusing, pointing finger is like a dagger aimed at my heart. "She's a beanpole. What's she going to do? So far, she's demonstrated nothing useful."

Alt-Gayarnu mulls over their controls and does what I interpret to be a shrug. Then: the panel beneath their hands glows red. They try to fix the lockout and sing a frightened, monotone note.

"Classified? By whom?" Ethan fumes.

Now I smile and cross my arms.

"You know what she'll do, you say," Ethan says dangerously as he circles Sunni. "You're rarely wrong…"

Alt-Gayarnu sings an answer to Ethan.

"That's impossible. I received access to all of Mistress Jadore's files after her death."

I raise my eyebrows. Misty had mentioned this Jadore was dying.

Alt-Ethan interrupts Alt-Gayarnu as they attempt to read what they can access. "I'm not interested in the mystic nonsense research she thought would save her life. Talk to me only about the research and the science that would explain Sunni's fear of…this." He gestures at me, as if I'm a piece of furniture.

"You should be afraid," I say, using every ounce of willpower I have to keep my voice steady. "You are not the scariest person I've dealt with today."

"Once our team has decrypted your DNA sample, your potential will become clear, if there is *any* potential," Alt-Ethan replies evenly. "Either we'll reduce you to your most essential parts and employ you as a scraper, or we'll extract your brain and reproductive organs and attempt to duplicate the useful bits."

My throat tightens to hear him speak this way. "You can't."

"I can." He shrugs.

I take a small step forward. I must keep him talking so that Misty and Jia can get the weapon back to the ship. Then, if I can get close to Sunni, and this strange Ethan…

I have to be bold. "You and I are friends in my universe."

This admission surprises the three of them. Sunni shakes her head. But I have to catch him off guard. Alt-Gayarnu pulls their tablet closer and takes notes with a digital stylus.

Perplexed, Alt-Ethan wheezes again. "Is that so?"

"Yes." I choose my words carefully.

He adjusts the lapel on his silk garment, showing off more of his enhanced neck scales and gills. "We can start there, if you insist. Tell me what I'm like in this other reality."

"Weak," Sunni replies coldly.

I inhale sharply, which this Ethan mistakes for surprise at her insolence, instead of the fear of losing his attention. He smirks. "You mean, unmodified?"

Sunni holds my gaze, and keeps quiet.

Alt-Ethan becomes impatient and kneels before Sunni, pressing his face close to her ear. "Tell me what you saw on the other side, or I will dismember your friend."

Sunni huffs indignantly. "She'd be gone before you had the chance."

He slides his gaze to me. "A hint about her potential, Sunni? Now who is the collaborator?"

"Sunni's no collaborator," I say.

"No? Do you really think her participation in our scientific advancement was unwilling? We *all* collaborate to survive."

Sunni bends at the waist and sinks her face into her cuffed arms, shaking her head, as if that will rid her of the trauma she experienced here.

Alt-Ethan stands again, pressing a hand to his upper chest. He pauses, suppresses a cough, and reconsiders me anew. "She's fairly talkative, this one. Maybe she'll tell me. Answer my questions, or I'll dismember Sunni."

I hate that he talks about me as if I'm not here. Now Sunni looks uncertain. Alt-Ethan grins at the discovery that I am the weak link. My stomach sinks. I don't know how to form an intelligent answer. He's here in the flesh, not dying or dead. He's evil and I can't breathe.

Everything in me screams to say nothing. But it's *Ethan.* Cosmetic alterations aside, it's still him in there. Those shoulders I have cried on. Those lips I have kissed.

"All right," he says softly. "As neither of you are cooperating, it seems as though Sunni needs another session in the lab." He nods at Alt-Gayarnu.

Sunni attempts to run, forgets that her ankles have been bound, and falls off the couch. "No. No, no, no!"

"Yes, yes, yes!" Alt-Ethan retorts.

Alt-Gayarnu approaches her and Sunni scrambles against the tub. Water sloshes over the side and coats her front. The ahmei says something in her mother tongue that makes Sunni stop struggling. Limply, my friend stands, glossy-eyed. Her terror shines through every pore. Alt-Ethan waves Alt-Gayarnu and Sunni away as if he is a snooty customer at an expensive restaurant.

I reach after Sunni as they drag her out. Alt-Ethan's words stop me cold. "Do you want to watch the procedure?"

I do and I don't. The doors shut on Sunni's horrified face. "You'll give her gills and fish fins?" I ask.

"She's not being rewarded." His voice is raspy, like he has something caught in his throat. "They'll finish removing what's useful and discard the rest. Just like we do with everyone."

I can't believe his callousness. This isn't real. I'm struggling to fly away from this wretched place yet my feet are planted firmly in the room. We're alone now. I'm disgusted at my delight. Maybe he can change. Maybe *I* can change him.

He's amused by my horrification and starts to unbutton his silks, but he's seized by another round of wheezing. I recoil, feeling as if my spirit is puppeteering my body from somewhere distant and safe while my physical self must endure this moment.

I have to know. "Why did you agree to this?" I point his modifications.

He shrugs. "The ahmei say that suffering is beauty."

"You're not vain."

"Isn't everyone a tad vain?"

"No. You're sick. Just like—"

Alt-Ethan sees where I'm going. "In the other universe, the Other Me is sick."

I nod.

"And you want to help me."

I nod again. I'm getting through to him.

He closes the gap between us, smiling. He's no longer impatient or cruel as he cups my face with a hand. He smells vaguely like sesame oil and vinegar. I allow his touch.

"Bless you," he says softly. "Maybe I won't dismember you after all."

My stomach flips. I fight the instinct to recoil. I'm too terrified to activate my powers. "Ethan. I know something terrible happened to you in the past. Your mind is blocking it, but the ahmei are killing you with their experiments. The unprocessed trauma only makes this worse. Please. Tell me what it is, if you can, so I can help save you."

He tenses. The coldness in his perfect face stabs my heart and he drops the hand from my cheek. "My Other Self told you this?"

I incline my head. I've lost him again. I fear he's going to order me out of the room as he did Sunni.

Instead, he says, "Suffering is beauty. Which means, you are my punishment. My penance. My..." He falls into another coughing fit and I instinctively tense, ready to come to his aid. When he recovers, a blackish tar substance stains his inner elbow.

The ahmei have polluted his mind and body with their experiments. They're the ones who have made him cruel. The sooner he's out of this place, the better. "Tell me what happened to you."

He dips a hand into the tub and rubs off the tar. It dissolves easily. "There are a number of *traumas* you may be referring to, but there is only one I have ever had trouble integrating. They use it to torture me, but I endure it, because that what they wish of me, and it is my honour to do so, because it affords me this life. And because you have travelled far to speak with me, and because it will also cause you suffering to know the truth of it, I'll tell you." He fixes me with his eyes, streaked red with strain. "I murdered my brother."

CHAPTER 8

"We grew up next to each other. Same building. Different units. Our mothers being sisters, we were always at each other's homes. Practically brothers. Forgive my exaggeration. But to me, he was a brother, and I'm sure our mothers would feel the description accurate."

I'm numb. I feel for the couch and have a seat. "I understand." My voice is flat and calm. It doesn't sound like me. It's as if I'm in a soundproof room. My ears ring with warning. Maybe he has implanted pheromones in my mind that have hypnotized me. But I can't leave now. Not when I'm so close to prying the truth from this Ethan's mind.

"He was sickly, even as a baby. We had to be careful in our play. Lots of rules from his mother. *Don't go here or there, don't eat this, don't play with that child as they have that virus.* Didn't matter whether we followed her commands or how many inoculations he had. He always ended up sick. And his final sickness...was quite deadly, I'm afraid. It nestled within him, and none of his mother's tinctures or cures seemed to work.

"For days he languished. Only his mother dared to enter his room and fulfill his basic care needs. But she was not up to the task. She had other obligations. She was tired, yet she wouldn't allow us to help. My mother and I could tell she was resenting her child's sickly nature. Her visits grew less frequent. His health deteriorated."

I'm mortified. "Why didn't a doctor—?"

"There *were* no doctors. None competent enough, not for her standards or *beliefs*." He splashes the water in frustration, grips the edge of the tub, and continues washing his arms. They shimmer with a green pearlescence. More modifications. "We couldn't move him. Our mothers were scared we'd catch his illness too. They forbade anyone from seeing him."

"That sounds awful," I say.

"It was," he replies. "Thank you." He rolls up his sleeve further, and drips water on his forearm. I catch glimpses of purple bruises and red scars amidst the pearlescence. "Eventually, there came a point where he needed urgent care, beyond the remedies offered by family and untrained *healers*." He spits the word. "His mother disagreed. He would pull through with her care alone, she said. As he became worse and worse, I realized there was something I could do to help."

I clear my throat. "So you snuck into his room and put him out of his misery?"

Alt Ethan grows still. "That is exactly what I did."

Instead of putting him in a car and taking him to a hospital, or sneaking him antibiotics, this Ethan thinks that mercy-killing his sick cousin is the best medicine.

The story sounds like a lie, designed to elicit my sympathy. Even my mother's family in rural Cape Breton, with limited access to healthcare, would have found a way to care for a sick child. They would have driven to Sydney or Halifax, if that's what it took. It's news when the healthcare system fails children. But I don't know enough about the British system to comment, and I can't afford to lose Alt-Ethan's trust. Perhaps a nugget of truth shines in his evil river of words. My Ethan is not a murderer.

Unless, when my Ethan had been grasping for me in the underground library, he had been trying to say, *"But I'm not innocent."*

"I do wonder," he says slowly, as I marinate in the silence, "why my Other Self didn't bother to tell you the specifics. Assuming you and he are...*friends.*"

I consider my words carefully. "There's something wrong with his memory. I think it's something to do with the ahmei's experiment on him, in their attempt to cure the vitaphage."

This gives him pause. He stands and flicks droplets towards the tub, and considers me again. "His memory is faulty?"

"He forgets important things. Do you also have that problem?" I search his face, hoping that this is all a test and that of course, he's killed no one.

He circles around the tub and ignores my question. "The vitaphage isn't cured where you're from? I'm involved in an experiment?"

"That's right," I say slowly. I've given him too much information; I don't want to lose the upper hand. I have to get him back. "And another key difference that Sunni has pointed out to me is, I don't exist in this universe. I'm unique."

This intrigues him. "Is that so?"

A thump in the hallway diverts my attention. I struggle to keep my gaze on Alt-Ethan. I can always take him away with me, and then come back to this universe for Sunni. And then deliver us all to the ship. It's a few extra steps, but if this is what I have to do, then so be it.

"Yes," I say, gathering my confidence and my hope. I stand and approach him. "I can show you my power."

He is unafraid as I touch his forearm and lean closer. Our noses touch, and neither of us flinch, as if daring the other to make the next move. That's when I notice his eyes. Not entirely green, or green-blue, like they were when I last saw my poor, tortured Ethan. Since we've started talking, they've enlarged, and streaks of red permeate the irises.

I love you. But I'm...

"Not my Ethan," I finish my thoughts out loud.

His confusion is cut by the flash of black running into the room. He breaks from me, stunned, as he turns to face a force of nature.

"Misty," Ethan says. "I thought I...?"

"Yeah, wrong Misty," she says, and uppercuts him with a flaming fist.

A steady stream of fire catches his finery in an explosive conflagration. He yells obscenities and tries to suppress the flame with his arms, and then screams as his pearlescent scales curl and flake like paper kindling.

He jumps into the tub and submerges all but his head. Steam surrounds him as the fire fades and his face floods with relief.

But Misty's rage is absolute. She switches to ice and in an instant, the tub has frozen over, entombing him. He screams, mouth agape, until he's seized by a coughing fit. Unable to move, he tries to clear his throat and rasps. The ice creeps up towards his twitching gills, freezing them in place.

"Please, Ingrid..." He flits his desperate, enlarged eyes to me.

Misty prepares another blow.

Before she can inflict more harm, I push Misty. She stumbles and loses concentration. The icicles rising from her palm melt instantly into puddles. She flicks her wrists, readying more ice in her hand, and snarls at me. "What the eff are you doin'?"

"What am I doing? What are *you* doing?"

"That's not your Ethan," she hisses.

"And Sunni?" I say, determined to say the unspoken.

"That's different," Misty says with finality. "You don't exist here. Your relationship never existed. He will *never* be your Ethan."

"He could be," I whisper. "With time."

"No. End of sentence." Misty purses her lips. "I'm not going to tell you what he did to Sunni and everyone else here. I don't think you're ready to hear that right now. Maybe your big brain can put together the pieces. But I swear on her journal that *this* Ethan"—she points to the frozen, cowering young man—"isn't worth the atoms he's made of. Understand?"

My vision blurs with tears as I stare at Alt-Ethan, gasping for air like a fish out of water. His eyes roll into the back of his head and the gurgling in his throat calms as he eventually stills.

How could two people from similar realities be so different? What made this Ethan murder his own kin, when my Ethan is so kind? What if *my* Ethan is a secret murderer?

"This isn't why we're here, anyway," I say distantly, attempting to quell the swimming questions within.

"That's right," Misty says with relief. "C'mon. Wil managed to dock. Sunni and Jia are on board. Let's blow this rotten canister."

Misty leads the way to the docking port in a flurry of fire, ice, squeals, and close calls. I cower and hide my head every time Misty engages an alien scientist or an armed fishman. The enemies that don't fall to Misty's might have already been evacuated. Pipes hidden in walls gurgle, and the entire structure moans from the pressure of the sea.

The docking bay doors invite us in as we approach. A countdown and sharp warning in an alien language blares in invisible speakers. Misty grabs my arm because I hesitate at the entrance, unwilling to throw myself into the fray. She pulls me inside and to my surprise, a fight has already occurred here. Unconscious or dead aliens curl around the entrance and a couple have collapsed around a row of adjacent airlocks. No ships remain in the bay, and as we hurry by the windowed airlocks, no other ships remain docked.

All except one. Ours.

One airlock blinks blue and I detect the faint odor of fuel and seaweed. Four unconscious aliens and strange modified humans lay bathing in the eerie light. Not in a heap, but in perfect straight lines, as if they'd all simultaneously decided to have a nap while reaching for the ship. Wil's work. Weapons have been nicked from their holsters.

As we hurry up towards the airlock, the entrance hisses open. Anxiously we dart inside, wait as the system detoxifies us, and then breathe out clouds of chemicals as we exit the facility and board our ship once more.

Our ship. Strange how relieved I am to board this alien technology, this *Blind Elephant* of ours.

"Welcome back," Wil says curtly, and swiftly detaches from the base. The ship groans and we shift as Wil maneuvers us away.

Sunni and Misty embrace tightly, and then Sunni pulls me into a firm hug too. I squeeze her tightly, remembering the awful things Alt-Ethan said in her presence.

"Are you okay?" she whispers.

I draw back. "Are you?"

She nods. A lie. Without letting go of Misty's hand, she hovers over Wil's pilot chair. "Any followers?"

"Not yet." He angles his head, hearing my question before I ask it. "Jia's in the back. She's got nothing left in her for today. How long until we can jump, you think?"

"I don't think I can jump again right now," I say quietly, thinking of my haggard mirror self as the memory slips further from my grasp.

Wil rubs his smooth head and examines the radar. "We're all right for now, as they re-organize and try and save their facility. I'll try to get us to the surface, into orbit, and hide us somewhere. Should be able to..." He closes his eyes and touches the side of the ship and a serene look passes over his face. "Yeah. Should be fine."

I navigate to the back of the ship, giving Sunni and Misty a wide berth. Jia huddles in the booth. She opens her eyes, acknowledges my presence with an exhausted grunt, and then curls up into the fetal position. Wil's sweater has been draped over her like a blanket; she clutches the sleeve like a lifeline.

In engineering, Sunni and Misty are fussing over the fuel. I slide down the wall and stare at our hungry, bioluminescent fuel pillars. Sunni and Misty share affectionate whispers and I pretend not to exist. Eventually, Misty leaves, and it's just me and Sunni.

She sidles up beside me, sitting so close that our knees touch, and plays with her split ends. "Installed the weapon, with Wil's help. It'll give us a leg-up on your Collective, for sure."

"Good," I say, because that's the only thing I can think of to say to that, after everything it cost to get it.

"So..." Sunni says, raising her eyebrows at the floor.

"So," I say, with finality. I'm not sure how to broach the topic of anything that just happened. I hear Misty muttering to herself in the mess. She must be looking through the database. The buzz of the sh-winil grows loud between us. My thoughts are a jumble, but my biggest curiosity hangs heavy like a tempting fruit I long to relieve from its tree.

"How did you know she'd be the same as your Misty?"

She nods, as if expecting the question. "Misty will always be Misty. And I just knew. Like I knew eventually you would save me. I saw her in my dreams, like lookin' through a window. She needed me and I needed her, and that's not gonna change from universe to universe.

"And yeah. We combed our histories. Everythin' that happened to us in childhood, high school, it was all the same. Couple minor differences. I guess the Sunni here was more in the closet. More 'fraid of her powers. Afraid of hurtin' this Misty, we think."

"I'm happy for you," I say. I am happy for both of them, but I can't muster the feeling right now. All I can see is my Ethan, dying in the underground library, and Alt-Ethan, choking on his own bile in a frozen tub. "If you're more or less the same as this universe's Sunni, and Misty will always be Misty, then why are the Ethans so different?"

She stiffens at his name and brings her knees up to her chin. "I..." Sunni stops and starts three times before settling on, "How well did you know him?"

"I love him," I say hoarsely. The words are meaty enough for the sh-winil to eat.

"Ingrid," Sunni admonishes me softly. "That don't mean you know him."

"I know your Ethan—"

"He's not *my* Ethan," she interrupts darkly.

I rephrase. "Alt-Ethan did bad things. My Ethan would never. Has never."

As far as I know, hangs in the air.

She sighs into her knees. "Don't get mad, but I saw your mind, in your dreams. That's the only way I know your Ethan. Pictures of moments of strangeness of him. He's got somethin' funny wrong in his head. You said he did somethin' terrible and his mind won't let him know what it is. What if this block inside him is the very thing keepin' him an inch away from becomin' Alt-Ethan?"

If the Collective can invent and implant memories of a false girlfriend—Gayarnu as Mira—then they can invent a sick relative for him to murder, to create trauma in his mind. "Agailya's experiments have made it hard to tell what's real with him and what's not."

"I only knew Ethan as a corrupt man with too much power. I don't know how he was raised. So maybe the difference is the position the Collective in my universe gave him. Your Ethan is a lab rat. Imagine if the lab rat were put in a white coat and told that his only way out of the maze was to participate as the scientist."

My heart pounds, resonating and fearing this to be true. "My Ethan wouldn't hurt anyone."

She grimaces. "Given time, for the right reasons, any of us would do anything to save the people we love."

The ship rumbles and groans. We're ascending from the depths. I'm willing to leave my friends to save Ethan. It's disgustingly true. But there are limits. I'm not going to leave them until I know they can survive without me. I want to believe my Ethan would make a similar choice, if our roles reverse. I don't think I would've fallen in love with him otherwise.

"Is that what happened to Alt-Ethan?"

She considers this. "I don't know what the ahmei promised him in return for his collaboration. He spent a lot of time with them, when everything ramped up. Whatever his power was, assumin' he has one, they were incredibly interested in it."

So even Sunni doesn't know Ethan's history.

Suddenly, the ship rolls three-hundred-sixty degrees, throwing Sunni and I into each other and the bulkhead. *CLOMP!* From the other room, Jia groans, and a crash and a flurry of swears spews from Misty.

"They found us!" Wil shouts. "Sunni?"

Sunni disentangles herself from me and races to the cockpit. I follow, rubbing my bruised arms. Jia stands behind me, fuelled by obligation. As Sunni slides into the co-pilot seat next to Wil, a faint glow washes the dark water, colouring it a light blue-green. We're almost to the surface.

"Where are they?" I ask.

Wil summons a rectangular window that hovers in the corner of the canopy. Multiple red triangles blip towards a blue dot. The red triangles peel off and begin to surround the blue dot as they increase speed. Their ships are likely designed for underwater flight, whereas ours isn't. Perhaps if we can make it to the surface, we can outrun them.

Something whizzes by our port side. The ship sways to avoid the missile, represented by a yellow dotted line on the radar view.

"Can we speed up?" Misty asks. She runs into the cockpit, the database tucked carefully beneath her armpit.

"Don't think so. The little guys are already giving us all they got," Wil replies.

We break through the surface. Large water droplets slide from the canopy as red and green lasers shoot across the cloudy sky. Collective ships, waiting for us to emerge, advance on our position.

"Oh…" Sunni says, and the radar view populates with several additional red triangles. "Weapon's hooked up, right? Let's test our new baby out." A strange smile passes her face. Guerrilla Warfare Sunni has returned. "Wil, ready?"

Wil doesn't sound confident. "Uh, yeah. One sec…"

The ship convulses. I lose my balance and tumble to the floor. Misty and Jia lean on each other for support. The lights flicker and settle on red. A computerized voice in an alien language calmly spouts off what can only be a warning.

"It says our tortoise covering has been half revealed," Misty yells over the voice, and then does a quick re-translation. "Plating down to half."

"Yikes. I feel that. Jia?" Wil shouts.

"Wil! Where's our weapon?" Sunni says. She's tapping frantically on the navigational controls. "You said—"

"It's connected. It's just taking it a while to—"

As Sunni and Wil exchange techno-babble, the ship jolts and tosses us around. We're narrowly dodging their attacks. Now that we're in the sky our speed has increased, but navigating between the fighters and larger ships as they close in isn't a sustainable strategy. More red triangles flood the holographic radar flashing on Wil's right.

"Jia!" Wil shouts again.

Sweating, Jia kneels gracefully, concentrates, and takes us into her invisible world. But she's physically exhausted. Not only did she run around with us for hours, but she had to hold her concentration too. She's not going to last long.

"Two more coming up on our six," Sunni intones. "You have it for me or not?"

"Ingrid?" comes Wil's voice. "You said you couldn't, but…"

"Yeah, I know." We need to get out of here with our stolen goods, to a place where they can't follow.

The ship convulses. We haven't been hit. It's the weapon, powering up. Jia's sweating buckets and tears run down her face with effort. As the experimental weapon warms up, our speed decreases. Firing and flying at the same time might be an issue.

"They're prepping weapons," Wil says. "Sunni, you—?"

She doesn't wait for Wil's mark. A digital joystick blinks into existence. She punches it forward and slams her palm on the analog controls.

PHOO.

The projectile launches from our belly towards the nearest ship. Just as it hits the target, it fans into five mini-projectiles, which seek and explode the hulls of the adjacent ships. Four triangles on the digital radar blink for the final time as, on the canopy, they erupt into fire and metal. The debris flies towards us and the other Collective ships. Everyone hurries to maneuver around the destruction.

But as the weapon's blast leaves our area of invisibility generated by Jia, it immediately reveals our position. A target has been placed on our backs, and because of our reduced speed, we're not going to easily avoid these strikes.

Wil and Sunni mash the navigational controls like angry gamers. We drift lazily and I close my eyes. This isn't how I want to die either. It's time to get out of here. Once I rescue my Ethan from the underground library, I will uncover the mysteries in his past, and prove to my friends that he will never be like Alt-Ethan.

But first, I have to conserve my strength, and practice my jumps, so that one day I will end up back in the green glow of the underground library. I will save them all, even if they can't see it yet. I will hold the vision in my mind like a painter seeing the final masterpiece before she's lifted her brush. Even if it takes me the rest of my life, I will alter the fates of every person on my list. Ethan. Wil. Jia's family. Our Sparkstone friends. My family.

The entire human race.

Pressing my arms against my chest and thrusting my chin upwards, I use this dash of hope to send us into the place between realities.

I descend the stairs without fear. The inky Untrakeepers have gathered on our floor. That's how I know it's the right place. But they cannot touch this ship. I protect it with my body and soul. They bang on it like mimes hitting an invisible wall with their blotted, dirty fingers. Their movement in the watery floor rocks the raft perilously. My frightened, sleepy friends tremble behind me.

The Untrakeepers block all corridors in this labyrinth, except one. The raft picks up speed as we dash for the calmer waters. They don't follow me down this hallway. It's as if they *want* me to go here. A door glows in the darkness, amidst burnt walls.

I know what's behind this door. I don't want to return here. I glance back, and hundreds of sets of ghoulish eyes peer at me, daring me to turn the ship around and pilot it into their waiting, monstrous claws.

"The Final Battle," I say hoarsely, and I open the door.

I fall into a chaotic reality. Wil and Sunni are still asleep at the controls. Jia sprawls on the floor. Misty slumps in one of the benches. The ship lists to port as our future selves—and one past self—dives around us.

"Hey. Hey!" I cry, shaking them both. The navigation controls are numerous and confusing. A few buttons flash blue and one digital screen spouts a warning. The orange light catches my eye. Our ship-to-ship communications.

My finger is a centimetre from allowing the messages into the cabin when Wil catches my hand. He leaps out of the co-pilot seat, swings us around, and points at a bewildered Jia, now awake. "Do it."

She needs no other instructions. Moments ago, in another universe, she'd been sweating with effort. But now, some of the colour has returned to her cheeks, as if her time in the Untraver has restored her. Jia kneels and begins muttering under her breath, and suddenly, the whole ship is in her watery world.

"Ingrid, get ready to leave once Jia can't hold us anymore," Wil instructs. He releases me and his hands work quickly over the controls.

"This again," Sunni mutters, working in concert with Wil.

I press my lips firmly together. I don't like being told what to do, but I nod. We don't have long. I've brought us to yet another dangerous place so I don't have a foot to stand on in this argument.

Misty appears at my side, and we brace each other as Wil and Sunni execute some tight evasions.

"That's too close," Sunni says suddenly, glaring at Wil as we tailgate a sleek fighter heading right for one of our doppelgangers.

I'm about to suggest that Misty and I strap into the bench when I recognize the overpowered fighter from our previous run. It's going to fire on the past version of the *Blind Elephant*.

Wil's reaction is faster than my words. He and Sunni ready the missile weapon. Our speed drops.

"Can we control how many—?" But the missile has launched before I can finish my question.

PHOO!

A flurry of blows lands on the fighter, blasting it to hundreds of shards. Just like we saw in the previous run.

"Uh, hold on!" Sunni shouts.

Jia groans. We're visible again. Misty and I grip each other and we're screaming as we fly through the remains of the Collective ship. The debris glances harmlessly off the canopy, but the sound of it hitting the hull is like violent hale.

"All right. That's enough," Wil says, to us and to the battle.

The ship deftly navigates between weapon fire, fighters, and other, future selves and takes us to the far side of the moon, which is out of the way of the action. The ships are like flies on the canopy, buzzing around a brilliant Earth.

"Sorry," I say. "We were going to come here sooner or later. We're recording everything with the sensors?"

"Yep," Wil confirms. "We'll just sit tight here and get what we can. And..." He taps the orange communication light. It blinks out. He winces, brings up a digital screen that looks like a chat window, and starts tapping on a digital keyboard hovering over the controls.

"What are you doing?" I ask.

"Sending myself that message," Wil says shortly. "What was it? Oh right."

I purse my lips. "Have you thought about not sending it?"

He pauses for a heartbeat, and side-eyes me. *Have you had a day where you don't think about travelling back in time to save Ethan?*

I glance at the others. They're not paying attention or they're pretending they can't hear us. Jia curls up on one of the benches with a tinfoil blanket and an alien ration bar. Misty and Sunni are speaking in low whispers on the opposing bench. "That's different."

He raises a brow. *Different because I'm sending this message to ensure our timeline doesn't diverge, or whatever? Or different because you're planning to destroy our timeline for your own selfish whims?*

"I'm not going to do it right away, because..." He can see my perspective. He understands my feelings, even if he doesn't agree with them. I don't have to explain myself.

Slowly, he nods. "I'm sorry," Wil whispers. He taps a few more times on the digital keyboard and it beeps contentedly. "You want to send yours now?"

I'd nearly forgotten. I frown, trying to remember the wording. Something about the orange light, and I sign with my initials. Wil shows me how to use the keyboard, and I awkwardly type out the message. Just before I hit send, Wil brings up the message log on a different screen and compares what I'm about to send to what we received after the first run. It's exactly the same.

Sighing, I hit the enter key. The chat window disappears, and history is created.

We spend the next ten or so minutes rationing our food, taking down notes from what we can remember in the Untraver to update the map, and processing everything that's happened in the last, well, *day*. Once again, I've watched Ethan perish, and I couldn't stop it. Once again, I'm going to have to jump us somewhere, just so we can survive. If every day is as action-filled as this day has been, I can't imagine what *decades* of this will be like. I wonder if this is what it's like to be immortal.

"Coming up on time," Wil says softly.

We gather around the canopy in quiet vigil for the death of our planet. Earth explodes into rock and fire. It hurts just as much the second time. More even, as we know it's coming. It just doesn't seem real. Wil winces, rubbing his temples.

But this time, we see something new.

As the rest of the *Blind Elephant* ships vanish, the mother ship and the entire Collective fleet turns their noses to a remaining, single ship—a beaten-up, dust-bucket version of our new home—and fire their weapons.

The explosion is silent. Just as Earth's demise had been. Yet it is no less impactful. Debris from the *Blind Elephant* drifts through the short cloud of flame as the oxygen is sucked into the vacuum. Without ceremony, the Collective ships turn tail and head away from the newly created graveyard.

It's a full thirty seconds before any of us speak. Our gaze is transfixed on the canopy.

"Which *Blind Elephant* was that?" I ask, desperate for anything but destructive silence.

Wil checks the logs and updates the hologram. "*Blind Elephant 13*. The oldest by chronological age."

The colour drains from Jia's face. "We're going to *die* in this fight?"

"That can't be right," Sunni says, and takes a seat in the co-pilot chair once more. She rewinds the three-dimensional, digital simulation. We experience the battle once more in holographic format and as we approach the eldest *Blind Elephant*'s explosion, Sunni slows down the playback. She taps a few times on the controls, and double checks her work, her freckles stark against her pale face.

"Let's not do this now," Wil suggests, looking to me. "We'll have time to analyze it later. We have all the time. We should get out of here before the Collective spots us."

He's right. I don't think I can take any more bad news. He's trying to lift my spirits, so I can make the jump. I turn this over, hanging on to the hope that Future Me will solve the puzzle, and take us back into the Untraver.

Someone is calling my name. I turn, and see only myself. But I'm shockingly old.

"A dream?" I ask, knowing it's not.

As I stare at my older self, her waxy face melts and I can't look away in time.

It's *him*. And I'm staring into his face, but I *shouldn't*, because it's pure madness.

I close my eyes, but it's too late. I can still see the image in my eyelids.

"You left me to *die* in here," he croaks as he sinks desperate fingers into my shoulder.

"No...!"

I take a deep breath—and remember nothing more of the Untraver. I'm back in my body, lying on the floor of the cockpit in the *Blind Elephant*. I rise to my feet, not remembering how I've fallen. I attempt to grasp at what I saw and how I navigated to this point in time, wherever and whenever it is. I can't recall.

I feel as if I've forgotten something important.

Scrawled on my left arm in desperate, capital letters: "LET ME OUT."

I'm holding the uncapped marker in my trembling right hand.

The only person trapped in the Untraver is Ohz. But that creature—that *madness* I'd stared into—there's only one sentient being capable of that. And he's not in the Untraver, I'm sure of it. I would remember seeing him there.

"Everyone all right?" I ask. Maybe the sound of our voices will jog the memory loose.

"Present," Jia mumbles from the bench.

"I think I woke up first this time," Sunni says, stretching her arms up. Misty stands over her supportively. "Kinda weird to fall asleep and not dream."

"My legs hurt. Were we running again?" Misty asks me.

"Maybe," Wil and I reply at the same time. I furrow my brow at him. Does he remember what I saw in there?

My memories of that place aren't as vivid as yours, he replies telepathically, so as not to disturb the other young women. *Whatever you saw this time that scared you has been ripped from your hippocampus.*

It's only because he names the emotion that I realize my heart is racing. I am afraid, and not because I've forgotten, but because we were running from something even scarier than the Untrakeepers or Ohz.

As we rub the exhaustion from our faces, the *Blind Elephant* peers out from behind the moon. The battle has dissipated. To stare at the Earth, the floating asteroids, the blazing sun, and the surrounding tiny dots of light in the depths of space, it's hard to know whether we've travelled backward five minutes, five months, or five years.

The swell of the precious globe we call home burns into my eyes. Everything I love somehow exists down there. And every second I float up here, unpinned from time, is another moment closer to the instant that the Collective destroys our home.

"It's our Earth, right?" Jia asks hesitantly.

I breathe deeply. The air smells normal again. "Yeah."

Wil curses under his breath. "Unless there's another universe where the Collective mother ship is also in orbit?"

I squint against the intense darkness of space, the hovering, ominous moon below us, and the solar activity, and indeed the

Collective mother ship lies in wait like a thick, sated snake above our planet. Its high orbit on the other side of Earth likely means we haven't been spotted, but we have learned not to make assumptions of the Collective.

Wil and Sunni maneuver us into the dark side of the moon as they calculate the best way to approach Earth without being detected by the mother ship, Earth's satellites, or any amateur human who may be watching. I check my phone. It hasn't updated since we left this universe. It still shows the date as January twentieth.

"We need supplies," Misty says. "Let's stock up at some out-of-the-way mega-mall and get this database decrypted."

"An out-of-the-way mega-mall?" Sunni says teasingly. Wil mutters something technical to her and she nods. We move out of the shadow of the moon, towards the northern pole of the Earth.

Misty smiles a little and shrugs. "Yeah, America's full of 'em."

"Buckle up," Wil says sternly. "Jia, assist?"

Earth fills our eyes as we rapidly descend. Jia closes her eyes and leans against the cold walls, and I feel us enter her watery, invisible world as Earth's clouds rush to meet us. I watch, transfixed, holding on to the bench seat, as the North American continent grows in size.

We can use the new weapon on the mother ship right now. We can blow them up and they wouldn't even know what hit them. Will that change our fate?

My stomach flip-flops thinking about it.

Our phones buzz. I check the time as our service returns. January twenty-seventh.

My friends discuss the merits of remaining in orbit versus returning to the outer limits of the solar system, the range and limits of Wil's power to hide us from Earth's astronomers and scientists, and the garbage encircling our home, when a string of held texts are suddenly delivered to my number.

January 21: MIRA ETHAN GIRLFRIEND??

I hope this is still your number. Call when you get this.

January 21: MIRA ETHAN GIRLFRIEND??

*Ingrid—wouldn't be reaching out if it
wasn't an emergency. Call us.*

January 21: MIRA ETHAN GIRLFRIEND??

*Come at once, to Sparkstone. Alone. The ahmei are dying.
Humanity is dying.*

The scenes on the camera in the hangar. The thinning numbers of the Brigade. It suddenly makes so much sense.

My voice cuts through the chatter. "We have to return to Sparkstone."

PART TWO

The soul will guide the girl to her destiny.

—J.G.C., *Campbell's Multiple Verses*

CHAPTER 9

"It's probably a trick," Misty says.

"Definitely *is* a trick," Sunni corrects her. "How can they be alive?"

The question excites me. If they're alive, perhaps they found a way to escape the portal explosion with Ethan. For that reason alone, I must go.

"I don't know. Gayarnu helped us before," I point out. "The ahmei in our universe don't trust the Collective."

"They still are loyal to it out of necessity," Sunni argues.

Jia palms the bulkhead contemplatively, no longer holding us in her invisible realm. We're in a low orbit over the North pole, in a region Wil has assured us is not as monitored. "The security footage we found proves something terrible happened while we were gone. The ahmei are desperate for our help. Which we can use to our advantage. We can't defeat the Collective alone."

We fall silent. Jia is right; none of us want to admit that we need the ahmei's support.

"They want something. It's an opportunity to figure out how we can form an alliance," I say.

Wil considers this. "Jia, how long do you think you can keep the ship invisible?"

"A few minutes?" she guesses. "With more practice, longer."

He nods. "Jia needs rest to keep her powers strong. Misty needs to work on translating and integrating the data we stole, and Sunni has to help me with the weapon maintenance. We'll drop you down, get supplies, and then come get you at your signal. Cool?"

Jia shoots him a silent look, as if to say, *Don't tell me what I need,* but doesn't outwardly object. "At least bring Misty with you," she suggests.

My breath catches. Returning to Sparkstone to see our Gayarnu, after seeing the alternate Gayarnu so fiercely loyal to the ahmei-led Collective, does make me pause. Having someone there watching me means I won't be able to find out what happened to Ethan without fielding some awkward questions.

"Not a bad idea," Misty says. There's hesitation in her voice. She glances at the data drive longingly and puts a hand on Sunni's shoulder. She doesn't want to go.

"If the situation gets hairy, I'll just jump out. We need you up here, working." I gesture to the drive.

Wil holds my gaze. He knows my thoughts. My desires. He turns back to the controls. "Taking us in. Jia, you ready?"

"Yeah." She sinks to the floor and adopts a meditative pose.

Within moments, we're in Jia's invisible world again and we're rolling along the curvature of the Earth. The ice and water of the north blossoms into green-brown land and morphs into distinctive mountains, farmland, and roads. I see the town of Sparkstone, isolated in Northern Alberta. So small. So fragile from above.

"Most of the activity I'm sensing is concentrated in the basement of Rogers Hall. The infirmary," Wil says, pointing. "A lot of power consumption is in that building as well."

The corner of Jia's lip twitches. Her concentration doesn't break. That's where the Collective reconstructed her face, leaving her with Jadore's scars.

"Checkin' for life." Sunni taps some controls and squints at the readout. "Yeah. Confirmin' what Wil said."

"Could still be a trap," Misty says slowly.

I steel my nerve. "If they wanted, they could have destroyed us in orbit. I won't be long."

"I don't think they saw us," Wil says, with a hint of defensiveness in his tone.

"If you're not back in ten minutes, we'll come and get you," Misty says firmly.

I nod, hoping that it won't take that long to figure out what happened to everyone at Sparkstone.

Wil pilots the ship to the open field, away from most of the buildings. Whatever shielding Sparkstone had in place to prevent enemies from spying or entering the campus are long gone. He and Sunni exchange some procedural words around landing and then they shut down the ship. I hover in front of the airlock, anxious to disembark.

"Good luck," Misty says, hugging the data drive to her chest.

"Be safe," Jia intones dully, as she maintains her focus.

Sunni sighs from the co-pilot's chair. "I don't like this. But you better teleport your butt out of there if there's trouble. No hangin' around."

I nod. Wil lifts himself to his full height, taps a few buttons, and releases the airlock controls. The doors slide open with a hiss. I can already smell the fresh air outside. It beckons. I'm so close. Finally, I can find out what happened to Ethan.

I'm trusting you, Wil says to me telepathically. *Don't do what I know you're thinking about.*

My hand stays the airlock door. The thought of Alt-Ethan in the alternate universe, writhing in the tub, unable to breathe—

Was Wil putting that thought in my mind? I search his gaze.

He shakes his head. "That's all you."

I disembark via the studded plank and touch down on the strangely untended grassy fields contained within the grounds of Sparkstone University.

I whip around and catch a glimpse of the vessel as it materializes before me, a twenty-something-metre-long enigma of steel-like metal and light. This is the first time I've seen it clearly since we embarked. Its sleek fins at the stern extend, vibrating as the pointed bow seems to bend light around it. As the ship lifts off, a wave of cool, ozone-scented air washes over me, ruffling my hair. The grass flutters its farewell.

In flight, the vessel becomes a blur of motion. I struggle to keep my eyes on it as it banks sharply, revealing the missile weapon we risked much to obtain. In seconds, it's nothing more than a glinting speck against the sky, and then nothing as Jia takes it back into her watery world, leaving behind a faint trail of shimmering blue particles that quickly dissipate.

And once again I'm back at Sparkstone. Alone.

As I find my bearings and approach Rogers Hall, I search for evidence of the underground library destruction. My gaze returns to Conrod Building in the distance and I cross-reference the time on my phone. It's January twenty-seventh. I've arrived here a week after stealing the *Blind Elephant* from Sparkstone.

The unbidden urge rises within me: if I could find a moment in time where I'm alone, I could meet myself and warn my Past Self about the heartache I will feel about Alt-Ethan, so I can steel myself against him and the confusing time-travel space battle. It makes sense to prepare me and my friends.

Wait. I'm alone right now. Right?

I pivot on my heels in the grass, greedily seeking some Future Self to give me guidance. Have I not been seeing flashes of red here and there in the timeline? That *is* me, isn't it? Why wouldn't I want to help myself?

"Ingrid."

I whirl in surprise in the direction of the voice. It takes me a moment to re-orient myself. All that spinning has made me dizzy. I didn't hear Gayarnu approach. The ahmei has a way of moving silently. I wonder if in yet another alternate universe, they are an assassin.

As a human, Gayarnu has a trustworthy face, dangling hoop earrings, and a flowing bohemian skirt beneath the austere garb of a scientist, which is their primary profession in this universe. Their long, white lab coat shows old stains in blue and red. A disposable mask hangs around their neck. They put it up as they close the distance between us.

"You got my message," they say evenly. "I wasn't sure if you would come. Perhaps you shouldn't have."

"Are you about to lead me into a trap?" I ask, half-joking.

"If I were, wouldn't you escape from here immediately?"

"I would."

"Good. The only trap here is the one we laid for ourselves, years ago."

I eye their mask suspiciously, wondering in equal parts if I should have brought one, or if it means I'm about to become an unwilling participant in an experiment.

Gayarnu reaches into their lab coat pocket and draws out a cylindrical, silver tube that fits easily in their palm. "Can you put out your finger?"

I make my hands into fists.

"It's a blood test," they explain calmly, holding out the tube for inspection. "If you test positive, we have to speak outside. And, well, that will be a whole other conversation. I'm not sure what to say to make you believe me." They pause as their eyebrows knit together, considering. "Only that I am working on saving us both."

Humanity is dying. This is a bad idea. My being here is a bad idea. I have no idea how long we have until the Untrakeepers show themselves. Better to go along rather than waste more time. Begrudgingly, I stick out an index finger.

They nod appreciatively as they position the tube above my finger pad and press down. A pinprick jabs me, not unlike the doors used to here at Sparkstone. I grimace, and just like that, it's over. They mutter something I don't catch and take a step back as they inspect the tube, waiting for results.

A tiny red dot beads on my index finger. I'm about to tell them that I don't have time to wait fifteen to twenty minutes for results when they replace the device in their pocket and pull down their mask. Their smile is grim. "Good. Negative. This way."

I follow them inside the basement of Rogers Hall. I clock the smell, double over, and retch. Alcoholic cleaner barely covers the overpowering scent of rancid fish and stale sweat.

Gayarnu waits for me to compose myself. "I should have warned you. But in a way, I suppose I did."

"You asked me here to help you, but I'm not a doctor. I'm just a girl who can teleport," I mutter, clutching my stomach, begging it to be calm. We pass several private rooms, all suspiciously closed off. Terrible smells emit from within. "Your doctors must be better than anything I can bring you to. Is that what you want, to escape from here, to bring you to better doctors?"

They frown. I'm trying their patience. They turn and continue down the hallway, gesturing for me to follow.

I huff indignantly. My boots clomp on the tile and echo through the long corridor, painted a strange green. "Gayarnu."

"Yes?" They don't stop walking.

"Is Agailya all right? Is Ethan?"

Their gaze is fleeting. Worried. Then, resigned, as if they've been assigned to give me a tour on my first day when they've got an exam tomorrow.

But I'm getting impatient. They're the one who called me here. I deserve answers. "Is she going to be all right?"

"Well, she's..." Gayarnu looks puzzled.

"She's what? Up on the mother ship?" I prompt her.

"No. She's dying." Now they seem indignant. "She's in here. With the rest."

In *here* turns out to be a large emergency room, set up like a combat medic tent. The *rest* is thirty people in various states of transition between alien-fish and human, moaning and resting on lines of cots clearly not meant to be in this room. I'm reminded of the footage of the hybrid from the security camera in Conrod Building, as well as the engineered hybrids we witnessed in the alternate universe. Unlike those hybrids, the transition state of their bodies seems in permanent, fixed flux, like a horror movie paused on the gross monster. The modifications that make their form human—ears, noses, skin—drip like gooey prosthetics onto the floor. As I pass, a few gaze up at me with glossy, protruding eyes, and reach for me. I don't mean to recoil and I know it's rude. I just don't know how I can comfort them, and I've had too many recent run-ins to trust that they aren't preparing to harm me.

Three Brigade members, their jackets stained with blood and bile, note my presence with disdain, and continue their nursing duties. I wonder if the rest of them have abandoned Sparkstone altogether. There's something off about these humans too: two of them have fading rashes on their necks, and another coughs aggressively into their elbow. Besides myself, and Gayarnu's human form, these three are the only humans in sight.

Agailya lays comfortably on a cot at the back of the room like a beached mermaid, her white hair strewn about the short pillow. Her once-glowing skin is sallow with sickness, and a stained blanket covers the bottom half of her body. An IV connects to a vein in her hand, but as we approach, an ahmei in human form looking equally sick strides up to Agailya's sleeping form, disconnects the line, and then wheels the IV stand with the bag of fluid towards another, nearby patient.

I point this out to Gayarnu. They aren't concerned at this apparent medical theft. "Resources are thin, and the Collective isn't sending more. They'll need it too, after all." Then, as if remembering why we're here, they turn their attention to Agailya. "I'll rouse her. She wanted to know when you'd return."

When you'd return. They didn't just expect me—they *knew* I'd come. Keeping a sharp ear out for Untrakeepers, I follow Gayarnu to Agailya's bedside.

Gayarnu hums in hushed tones to Agailya. Agailya responds with halted, weak notes. Somewhat surprised, Gayarnu shifts their weight and clears their throat, hums some more, and then turns to me. "She's awake."

I have so many questions. It's hard to know where to start. *How did you escape the portal explosion?* is the first. Gayarnu should absolutely be dead—they had been next to Ethan, preventing me from whisking him away. Agailya had been by the exit, carrying the unconscious Jadore, blocked by fishmen. Had she made it up to the main floor, she could've had a chance, but no matter how often I turn this over in my mind, it seems impossible. The question of their escape does seem insensitive, given Agailya's state. Perhaps this is further proof that I will return to the moment of the explosion in time to save them. Or maybe there's something else that produced a miracle that allowed their escape. I'll have to work up to that conversation. "Tell me what happened here."

"The phage was altered," Agailya says croakily. "It struck more than half of the Sparkstone staff."

"I'm sorry." It's true. I am a little sorry. The security camera footage Jia and I had found in the hangar suddenly makes a lot more sense. The aliens falling ill and unconscious. The humans, seemingly fine, left to become caretakers. The footage had been terrifying. And yet, my thoughts dwell on everyone her cruel experiments have killed in the name of curing this vile phage, and I can offer her little comfort.

She doesn't seem to mind my cool tone. In fact, she smiles. "I can no longer return to my true form. I must die like this."

"Is that so terrible?" I ask.

"I will endure in my most beautiful of hours," she says, with strange pride.

Suffering is not beautiful, but as this is part of the ahmei's beliefs, I keep quiet on that. "And Ethan? He's safe?"

Her harsh gaze darts to mine, then softens. "We haven't...he's still..." She gestures to the door.

My heart leaps. "Where?"

"I accept that you have asked about him with me in this state to taunt me," she says. "I will endure. This is the way of the ahmei. We hang on and we welcome the strength of suffering. Your mention of him only brings me strength in my most beautiful of hours." Agailya repeats this as if it is gospel. Her breathing becomes laboured. Gayarnu hovers behind me in reverence of their superior. They don't ask me to leave. I want to run and find Ethan, if he's here at all. But I also owe it to my friends to get answers about the altered vitaphage before the Untrakeepers show up and destroy everyone here. Including Ethan.

"When you say the phage was altered, do you mean that it's attacking ahmei who were previously immune? And...maybe humans?" I ask, eying the coughing Brigade nurse.

Gayarnu's jaw clenches. "Yes."

"How did this happen?"

Gayarnu balks at my question, disturbed.

Agailya smiles a little, which lifts her bloodshot, watery eyes. "The project is no longer in my control. The phage should never have...been released to the other places. I never authorized it."

"Other places?" My throat tightens. *Humanity is dying.* She didn't just mean *humanity at Sparkstone.*

"Show her," Agailya instructs Gayarnu croakily. They start to protest; Agailya will hear none of it. "It's all right. This is why she returned. Show her."

"But we promised, and I don't think this is part of the plan, and we don't know if this will—"

"*We* didn't promise her, Gayarnu, and I wouldn't take it as truth."

Agailya takes a deep, wheezing breath. The outburst has tired her. "It won't matter soon anyway. Show her the data."

Promise whom *what?* What *plan?* My heart pounds in my ears as Gayarnu reaches into their lab coat and reveals a tablet. They tap their delicate fingers on the black screen, and a holographic, spinning globe twice the size of my head emerges in the space between us. The blue light glitches as yellow polka dots appear on the continents, pulsing rhythmically as the globe turns on its axis.

"This is a map of the confirmed case sites of the altered vitaphage among humanity, including Sparkstone. Here is the rate of spread." The yellow dots disappear and the globe halts its spin with North America facing me. *Beep.* A single yellow dot flashes into existence in Western Canada. *Beep. Beep.* Another two appear in Southern Ontario and the Eastern seaboard. The beeping sounds overlap and trill aggressively as the dots spread down the coast, into South America, and then Spain and mainland Europe. The globe spins again and every now and then, a stray beep punctuates our conversation.

"Each dot is at least a hundred people. Not every human donates biomatter or visits a doctor to receive a diagnosis, but if the spread becomes—"

"Gayarnu is not leaning into our ways. Ask her," Agailya says shortly.

Flustered like a rebellious teen, Gayarnu hums a low melody in Agailya's direction. The dying alien woman huffs, as if she knows the tune all too well. Seemingly reconsidering any further argument or snide retort, Gayarnu asks me dryly, "Are you responsible for this?"

That's not the question I expect. "Me?"

"You. Your friends. Did you modify or release this altered vitaphage upon our people stationed here on Earth, and humanity?"

"No. Of course not." I spit the words, angry at the accusation.

The room has quieted. The patients and the Brigade humans have a vested interest in this conversation. Gayarnu layers their singing language, directed at Agailya, atop the trilling of the monitors and the rustling and muffled groans of the suffering. Agailya responds with a few notes of her own, joining Gayarnu in perfect harmony. They're in agreement.

Nodding, as if satisfied with the musical exchange, Gayarnu attempts to regain their composure. "We believe you and your friends don't have the means or knowledge to modify the phage and release it as it has been. Your goal has always been to escape our influence, or stop the Collective from furthering its goals. Your tactics have never been this grand in the past. We had to ask you personally, to be sure, before we continue. Although..." They pause and glance at the Brigade members, who hover suspiciously close to the conversation. Gayarnu's gaze acts like bug spray; the dark-jacketed humans scatter to the other side of the room. "Most of the humans we've managed to track had head colds. In the data we've been able to procure, about forty percent of cases have evolved into fatal conditions, or left subjects—I mean, patients—with severe, lasting side effects, including blindness, irreversible gut-biome damage, and extreme brain fog. Releasing a bioweapon that incapacitates your own people to ensure enemy destruction would be in line with your history, no?"

I'm insulted and relieved. Although Gayarnu and the other ahmei have been part of the Collective's agenda on Earth, they have operated as a separate unit, with their own goals. Still, the Collective's hubris shines through Gayarnu's words. *Subjects, I mean, patients.*

"We didn't do this," I tell her emphatically. "But...everyone *thinks* we altered and released this vitaphage?"

"Whispers from the mother ship," Agailya replies hoarsely. She nods to Gayarnu to continue as Agailya coughs up some strange liquid that's too blue to be blood.

"Yes, the Collective believes it is you and your cohort. The Sparkstone division and several other sister schools are split. Many believe it comes from within the Collective, at the highest levels, to remove descenders, nay-sayers, and human sympathizers. However, we don't believe the Collective would be so cruel."

"You don't? Really. Says the person who tortured my classmate in the name of science."

They ignore my jab. "The Collective doesn't bombard populations with dangerous, gene-altering viruses without a multi-step plan that serves their ultimate goal: pursuit of a body of knowledge that benefits the core members of the Collective. The vitaphage brought the ahmei under dominion of the Collective and forced us to serve or die. Here? There is no rhyme or reason for the Collective to target humanity as a whole *and* the sister schools with a dangerous virus. Those sites exist to conduct experiments and gather information. If the altered vitaphage had been genetically productive, perhaps the hypothesis that the Collective released it would hold water."

"Genetically productive," I say spitefully, thinking of Kimberly and the others in the hallway aquariums in the other universe, their changes on display for the scientists to pat themselves on the back while they stroll to work. "You're saying that because it doesn't alter humanity for the *better*, it can't possibly be the Collective's handiwork. Well, what if the Collective ordered it for some grander experiment?"

Gayarnu shakes their head. "The hypothesis doesn't make sense.

Conspiratorial thinking does not serve us here. These strikes—we should call them what they are—are targeted and irrational. They are the work of someone who is trying to undermine the Collective's work and carried out by someone who has intimate knowledge of our operations. Someone who wants to throw us all into disarray."

"Jadore," I say softly, gritting my teeth.

"Correct," Agailya croaks, nodding. "She creates division."

"Between the Collective and her own interests," Gayarnu explains softly.

"So we've discovered. You mentioned something like that before," I say.

They nod. "Jadore has been backed into a dangerous corner. We believe she's planning a coup and she's used our life's work as a smokescreen to throw the Collective into disarray as she plots to take control."

"Where is Jadore now?" I ask.

"She's in and out of custody. We don't have resources or time to keep tabs, what with..." Gayarnu replies, gesturing to the patients. "Jadore has allies and supporters in the Collective. She's never in trouble for long. One division arrests her, and another works to set her free. If the Collective is convinced that humans are to blame for this virus, your race is in danger. By extension, because of our position here at Sparkstone, we share that danger. We have asked you to come so we can share this gift of information and to warn you so you may prepare your race for what is to come. That is all." They incline their head and a flicker of conspiracy passes across their eyes, as if to imply there's more.

"That's all?" A low hum slides into my ear. The Untrakeepers. I don't have much time left here. "Do you have any other allies that could help us get the message out? Any technology or"—I point to

Gayarnu's tablet, still alight with the globe—"any data that we could take about the virus in its current state?"

"Gayarnu will give you what you need." Agailya sounds tired now, though she doesn't tell us we need to leave. That's probably part of the suffering too. Having me here, incessantly asking questions.

The ship battle. It's only January twenty-seventh. The battle is in April. I can warn them. "Look, we know you've got ships in the hangar out there. Take them and leave Earth as soon as you can, okay? Go back to your home planet and get the care you need there. It's only going to get more dangerous here."

"The quarantine blockade will destroy any ships that leave. We are trapped here, and we will die here," Gayarnu says.

"We snuck by the mother ship. I think if you load a ship with your people, and as many humans as you can carry, and then adjust your heading as you climb into orbit..."

Agailya sighs. "No, Ingrid."

"But you have the means to *save people!*" She's giving up. It makes me sick that Agailya would rather stew in her suffering and die than do something about her life's work, no matter how gruesome or disturbing it is. I shouldn't judge the beliefs and practices of her people, but it just feels needlessly helpless.

"This is part of my suffering," Agailya says. "You and Gayarnu may discuss the finer points, if they wish to give you further aid. But here I will remain, unknowing, until my last breath, until I am sung out of this world."

Out in the hallway, a commotion demands our attention. The three Brigade nurses shout an alarm from another room. "She's got a bunch of stuff, Mira! Professor, what do we—"

A crackle of electricity. *Thud.* Another surprised yelp.

"Oh..." Gayarnu checks their tablet, as if they're suddenly late for an important exam. "Oh no, no, no..." They race for the door and I'm on their heels.

In the pit of my stomach, I know who I'll see before she appears in the doorway. Jadore skids to a stop, gripping the door jamb like a lifeline, and fixates on me. Instead of laughing, her jaw slacks into worry. Gone is the smug expression from the hangar, as well as the dirtied johnny. Black, sleek, form-fitting material covers her body. She looks like a caricature of a hypersexualized spy from the sixties. The material of the outfit looks too high quality to be a costume, though everything else about it screams Halloween. She hugs a black box to her chest protectively and cords dangle down her front. A couple of flash drives have been stuffed into her bosom; her outfit can't hide anything. Her grip on the jamb loosens and she stumbles backward.

"Jadore, stop!"

Jadore doesn't listen. She yelps and scurries down the hallway, struggling to run in her chunky boots. One of the Brigade nurses stops to check if her fallen comrade, whom Jadore had fried, is still breathing. The other runs after Jadore, yelling in a broken alien language for her to stop. I try to join them, but Gayarnu grabs my arm. Their grip clamps around me like cold steel.

Jadore makes it to the nearby back exit and throws her shoulder against it. It flies open and Jadore disappears into the quad.

Gayarnu stops the Brigade human with a sharp sing-song yell. "Don't bother. Help them." They point to the human who face-planted on the floor. The nurses obey warily as the door to the building clicks shut.

"She's getting away!" I try to wrest myself from their strong grip. They don't relent. "Don't you want to stop her? We can help."

The ringing in my ears protests against that offer. It won't be long before the Untrakeepers spill into Sparkstone.

"There's no point," Gayarnu mutters. "It's fine."

"It's clearly not."

Releasing me, they move further into the hallway as the two Brigade nurses carry their downed friend into the main recovery room. Gayarnu gives the nurses the barest of concerned glances as they consult their tablet once more.

"Is this part of *your* suffering? To allow the enemy to make off with valuable tech? You just said you're low on resources." I point to the nurse. "What did she take?"

Bewildered, the young woman looks to Gayarnu for permission to speak, but seeing the alien in disguise has no interest, heaves the unconscious Brigade member up and continues walking backwards into the emergency room. "I saw her in the server room, the one that controls all the tanks. I think she made off with the hard drive containing the medical research. We can do inventory later?" She lets it hang as a question as she struggles to keep her Brigade friend aloft.

"Stick to your duties. I'll handle it," Gayarnu says.

The young woman can't hide her relief and returns to helping the other nurse lug the unconscious Brigade member into the emergency room.

"What kind of medical research would she have taken?" I ask Gayarnu.

They don't look up from their tablet and their response contains a measured tone. "The hard drive she took contained information on the Hunger."

My anger pushes down the warning sound of the approaching Untrakeepers. "That's *not good*! What if she tries to rebuild that? What if she's building another portal?"

Gayarnu's blank expression breaks. A red blush forms

around their cheekbones. "We have backups. Jadore would need tremendous resources to rebuild the Hunger, or a portal."

"What if she gets those resources? Who is going to stop her? Do you even *care?*"

A shrug from Gayarnu. That's answer enough. I remember the coldness of Alt-Gayarnu. How easily they gave and followed orders from Alt-Ethan. This coldness manifests in the Gayarnu in front of me, and I shudder to think of where the line is drawn. It's easy to care about the immediate problem when it has the stench of death. Jadore, apparently, isn't their concern.

I'm tired of holding back. "What about Ethan?"

They direct a sharp glare in my direction and put the tablet away with a renewed sense of purpose. To my surprise, their coldness melts. Their hair flops forward as they bow their head respectfully. When they look up, their eyes shine with sorrow and regret, and I feel a strange kinship with them. For a brief moment, Gayarnu is human to me. But with their words, the feeling evaporates. "You already know what happened to him."

"Except that I *don't*," I say emphatically. "You're alive, so he must be too."

The logic is infallible, to me at least. But Gayarnu takes this fact in stride, as if I've just told them that the sun is yellow. They part their lips to reply and hesitate, and there's that look again. Conspiracy. Uncertainty. Perhaps I've already been here after all. I've already saved Gayarnu and Ethan and maybe some others. Is that the hesitation I see in their eyes? The struggle to tell me about the future, and the fear that if it's uttered aloud, everything will change for the worse?

They shake their head. "I don't...I can't. Unless this is...?" They consider me anew. As if they want to tell me a secret, but—

—but have made a *promise* not to tell?

A wash of nerves runs through me. I think I've been here before. I purse my lips and Gayarnu stands awkwardly. Waiting.

But if I've been here before, and I spoke with Gayarnu and Agailya, why didn't I save Ethan? I need to consider my questions carefully. Maybe I haven't gone back far enough. It's been nearly a month since the explosion. My Future Self could have been here dozens of times since. That explains their surprise that I don't know about Ethan's fate.

My phone buzzes. It's Wil. I'm furious at the interruption, but I answer.

"We're coming down. Be ready. We just spotted Jadore in a shuttle," he says.

"Yeah, she was here. She stole a bunch of stuff. Do you think we'll be able to catch her?"

"Not sure." He sounds doubtful. "Just be ready." He hangs up.

I ground myself in the moment. I can always return without my friends if I manage to find my way back to this moment, but just in case I can't, I have only a few minutes to take advantage of the present. "Please, just tell me. Pretend I don't know."

"There is nothing left of him. I'm sorry, Ingrid," Gayarnu says slowly. They clench their long, delicate fingers into fists. Their tone becomes reverent and measured, as if they are reciting a prayer. "We have all been gifted with this suffering. You must bear it now, proudly, as a gift from our people to yours. And then, one day, if you—"

"Nothing left? He's..." I don't want to say *dead*. It's too final. Nothing is final now, not with my power.

They reach out a comforting hand. It hovers above my forearm and then retreats. They look like they don't know what to say. "For some, the altered vitaphage is deadly."

The ringing in my ears intensifies. It's not just the aliens from another dimension. So the portal explosion is only one hurtle. The *altered vitaphage* kills him. A cold sweat breaks out all over my body. I'm afraid Gayarnu will test me again and find me positive for the disease.

It can't be. Ethan *can't* die. I can't think about it without breaking down, and there's no time for that. There's plenty of time, however, to change the past. He and Gayarnu and the other aliens apparently survive the blast, only to become pawns in Jadore's terrible plot to become queen of the Collective or whatever? It sounds like I'll have to navigate back in time to the explosion, snatch Ethan and everyone else, and then deal with the altered vitaphage.

I peer in the emergency room one last time to check on Agailya. She appears as if she's fallen asleep. This won't be the last time I see her. But maybe this is the last time she'll see me.

"This modified phage," I say slowly, lowering my voice so the aliens and nurses can't eavesdrop, "What if we helped you cure it?"

Gayarnu blinks. Their expression remains a practiced calm. "How?"

"You said you think we don't have the technology to infect everyone, and that's true. But we may have uncovered some research that could help your team. Maybe." I want to broach this as a possibility, not a sure thing. I have no idea how much Misty and Wil have decrypted from the alternate universe database. "If we gave that to you, could you help...?" I trail off. Ethan is dead. For now. I try again. "If we gave this research to you, what could—?"

"There are too few of us left here. We have become a medical camp. Not a research lab," they interrupt. Their eyes dart to the ceiling, then back to the open door behind them, leading back to Agailya and the rest of the alien patients. I sense they're not telling me the whole truth. "How do we know your research is sound? What is the source?"

"A place and time where the ahmei cured the vitaphage and control the Collective," I reply.

Gayarnu flushes. Now they are unsettled. "I can't accept anything that disrupts the noble suffering of our people."

"Then tell me who can."

"I'm...not sure..." They clutch their lab coat tightly and anchor themselves in a steely gaze. "You...time travelled, to receive this information?"

The corners of my lips twitch. "Sort of. Whatever you're hiding, please just tell me. You helped me once, and I know that you care...cared...for Ethan, in your own way. Let me help you. For his sake."

Gayarnu takes a deep, calming breath as they reach into their lab coat. Something clinks in their hand as they pull out a rectangular glass tube. Within the tube is a smaller, suspended vial of blue-green, viscous liquid. "I don't know if I should be doing this...but all right. This is a sample of an infected ahmei. I've been working on research of my own, but time is short. Use this vial to test your current research. Take it to the Collective directly. Prove that you have a cure, and you secure the Collective, and us, as allies. Then we can deal with Jadore together."

I accept the sample gingerly. *Secure the Collective as allies.* I thought I'd never hear the words. Not after everything we've seen. "Okay. Easy. The mother ship—"

"No. Their headquarters," they interrupt, as if I should know where that is.

"Where is that?"

"Your power can take you anywhere, can it not?" They gesture to the vial. "There is more of that if you need it. But not that much more."

"Oh." I hold it up to the light, examining it, as I have seen scientists in films do.

They nod, as if we've come to an unspoken understanding, and breezily stride away from me, past the set-up in the emergency room, deeper into the basement.

"Wait!" I reach with splayed fingers. I have more questions. What about the data from their tablet? Where's Ethan's remains? "If the vitaphage also affects humans, won't we need two different cures, one for our species and one for yours?"

Gayarnu frowns and continues down the hall. "You have everything you need, Ingrid."

"But don't you...?" I trail off. They disappear from view. I consider this unusual gift carefully, and start down the corridor towards the entrance when my phone buzzes abruptly. I swear, startled, and drop the vial. It tumbles to the floor, rolls down the hallway, unphased by my poor handling.

"Where are you?" Wil asks through the phone impatiently.

"Coming," I reply, stooping to pick up the tube. The line beeps and I shove the phone back in my pocket. I freeze, listening for the Untrakeepers. I feel the urge to vomit. They are close. I break from the sterile, putrid-smelling environment into the brisk air outside and run towards the open field.

If my Future Self returns to Sparkstone in Gayarnu's past— possibly to rescue them—why hadn't Gayarnu given the sample to my Future Self? Is it too late then? No, because it would be their past, before the outbreak. My head hurts as I attempt to do the mental gymnastics. Whatever. We have the vial now. Together, my friends and I can attempt to develop a cure, for us and for them. And for

Ethan. I clutch the sample close. I'm not sure how we can succeed where the ahmei have failed for generations. But if I can change the ahmei's fate, maybe Agailya will—in the past, when she's not on her deathbed—tell me why she chose Ethan for her cruel experiments.

I meet the ship at the prescribed spot, checking over my shoulder every few seconds. The Untrakeepers can't sneak up on me as I stand on the frigid grass of the plains. The descent of the ship tussles my hair as it lands invisibly, and blinks into existence long enough for me to board. One look from Wil at the cockpit and he knows we only have moments before we're overwhelmed with extradimensional company. I avert my gaze from the canopy as we climb, and Sparkstone University diminishes, and with it, the buzzing and anxiety of the approaching monsters.

My friends have not been idle during my time at Sparkstone. I intended to tell them everything immediately once through the airlock, but Misty and Sunni ambush me with smiles and trip over their own stories. They can't wait to fill me in on their adventure somewhere in the Midwest as Wil pilots us back into orbit with a smug smile. The heavy burden of alien plagues and alternate-universe cures evaporates as my friends regale me with their shopping spree.

"Stole some supplies." Misty points with one hand to six bags of groceries, piled by an exhausted Jia. She's curled up on the bench, barely holding her eyes open, after her deft assistance in keeping the ship cloaked. She acknowledges me with a satisfied smile.

"We paid for some of it," Sunni adds, pointing to the bag filled with canned goods. "Although I suppose Wil manipulating someone into using their card to pay for our groceries *is* stealing."

"I just wanted it known that I snuck these things out of the store, without triggering the guard or an alarm." Misty reveals another bag from behind her back, containing a long fresh baguette, three flattened loaves of bread, and a plastic container of chocolate chip cookies with a discount sticker plastered across the top. "The greeter at the door was *not* paying attention."

"Better to attack on all fronts than just one," Jia says sleepily, nestling further into the bulkhead.

"We have to keep our little friends happy. Wil said they weren't too pleased with the kelp he fed them in my universe," Sunni adds as she takes Misty's bread and one of the bags from the floor, throws it over her shoulder, and heads towards the mess.

I follow her, because the groceries aren't the only items they've procured. I watch my step; there's not an inch that isn't covered in plastic wrap, reusable bags, stuffed grocery bags, boxes of homeware, and other items. Two funky lamps rest on a stout coffee table. A rolled-up rug leans precariously on the crown jewels of this hoard: two unwrapped pallets of food, stacked to the ceiling of the craft next to the staircase. They're encircled by six sleeping bags, a folded tower of blankets, pillows, and an assortment of bedding. Yoga mats laid out before the bean bag chairs appear to be our mattresses, yet on closer inspection, I spot a couple of inflatable camping mattresses. Large garbage bags of clothing, as large as the bean bag chairs, also dot the room, tags and hangers spilling out of the untied openings.

"Had to guess at your size," Sunni says. "You like long-sleeved shirts and long skirts, right? Well, there's a ton of that. And boots and running shoes. And yoga pants. Jia mentioned running a yoga session with us each morning to increase mindfulness?"

It's as if they've teleported an entire supermarket and department store into the belly of our new abode. A mountain of treasure, just for us.

"Bean bag chairs are perfect for zero-G," says Misty. "Unless they get punctured. Then...it's going to be the worst." She collapses onto one and covers her legs with a comfy black sleeping bag, two pillows, a giant energy drink, and a random assortment of candy bars.

My stomach growls. I've been running on adrenaline, so focussed on our mission, that all my basic needs have been neglected. Can't exactly teleport a meal into my stomach. I inspect the crates of food. Three tiers of canned goods, everything from sardines to beans, topped with another three rows of crackers, and then another three rows of non-perishables, and another three rows of ramen noodles. If we ration this carefully, we might be good for a few weeks. Possibly more.

A mini fridge, wrapped hastily in cardboard, sits next to an open wall panel, waiting to be wired. Next to it, a camping stove with several bottles of propane. I dare not to ask if the propane stove is a good idea in our closed, recycled-air environment. One battle at a time. I frown at the bags of milk, cheese, green peppers, and meat. Maintaining perishables seems ambitious, somehow more ambitious than travelling through time to prevent the destruction of our home. *I* certainly don't feel like cooking right now.

Paper towels and toilet paper are piled, to my relief, next to what my friends have newly determined to be the bathroom: a closet-sized room behind a hidden panel door next to the empty cabin with a waste-disposal tube so transparent that left little to the imagination. It empties automatically and stores contents in a larger container in the belly of the ship, below the floor, which would have to be emptied periodically, hopefully into some distant star. Sunni explains that Wil has tried to see if any of it could be hooked up to the sh-winil tanks, in the interest of efficiency and recycling.

According to him, they'd been horrified by the idea of consuming what we considered waste. Beggars can't be choosers, but these little guys *are* powering our ship, so they have the upper hand.

Sunni busies herself with the organization of silver cutlery, including forks, knives, spoons, chopsticks, and sharper knives, into plastic organizers, which fits inside a larger plastic drawer system, which is still wrapped in plastic and has a price tag. "Don't worry," she drawls. "I make a mean shepherd's pie. Among other dishes. Have to maintain some sense of humanity up here while we work."

"Is there anything you didn't get from the store?" I ask, smirking.

"Probably," Sunni replies, with more seriousness than I'm expecting. "You were right, before. We shoulda did this before we got the weapon. I just...I was scared."

"It's okay. We all were," I say, touching her arm.

Misty bounces up from her bean bag throne and wraps her arms around the two of us, hooting like a kid at Christmas. "Honestly, we should Robin Hood our way around the world. Take a bit here, take a bit there. Eliminate poverty and corporate greed. We can make that our side gig while we take down the Collective. Right?"

If the Earth is going to explode, perhaps some light robbery won't matter in the long run. But *no*. I have to *stop* Earth from exploding, save Ethan, save Jia's parents, save our other friends, save our parents and *everyone*. The knot in my stomach twists. Stealing with abandon and Robin-Hooding our way around the timeline *would* be easier.

"How did you get all this stuff up here?" I ask.

"Wil tricked everyone into thinking the ship was a movie set or a children's charity or somethin'," Sunni says dismissively. "A bunch of guys came and loaded them in..." Her face droops coldly and she spins to look at the cockpit. "Why wouldn't I tell her?"

"You let strangers board the ship?" I say, marching back into the cockpit. Jia stirs from her light snooze uncomfortably.

"They will never remember it," Wil says in a low voice. He taps some controls. The Earth is a shining sphere in the distance. He secures our orbit around the dark side of the moon, and then gets up from his seat without meeting my gaze. I'm on his heels as we return to the mess. "And no, no one else that witnessed the ship will remember our presence either. And no, I don't feel bad that I told them it was for charity. We're performing a service for the human race that isn't being compensated. We're outside of our dystopic, capitalist society, and we can't live by their rules. Especially if we're operating outside of time."

I want to feel bad for all of this stolen merchandise. But I don't. Misty tears into the chocolate and exchanges stories with Sunni, who does inventory. Even Jia, exhausted, joins us and takes the energy drink from Misty gratefully, and settles on one of the yoga mats. I plug my phone into one of the stolen portable chargers and set it on the floor with the rest of my friends' devices.

This is what university might have been for us. Hanging out on the floor of a dorm or apartment, eating and talking trash, hoping and wondering about the future. That future is just another thing the Collective stole from us. We have to fight to get it back.

Once our idle chatter draws to a natural close and Jia perks up, Wil gets down to business. "Tell us what the ahmei said."

I rummage through the clothing and find some new boots in my size and slump into one of the beanbag chairs. "They're dying of a modified version of the vitaphage. So is humanity. Other Collective aliens too." I give them a rundown of the data from Gayarnu. "The Collective thinks we did this. But Agailya says the ahmei suspect it was released by Jadore, not long after the explosion in the library."

"The ahmei cured the vitaphage in my universe," Sunni says distantly, picking at her nails.

"Would that cure be in the database we stole?" Jia asks.

Wil and Sunni exchange glances. "Could be," Sunni answers cautiously. She looks to Misty.

Misty shrugs. "There's a lot on there. I was hopin' to continue decryptin' after we get some sleep."

Sunni looks concerned. "You're not considerin'...?"

"It's a bargaining chip," Jia says solemnly.

"They got nothin' we want," Misty scoffs.

They're having the same thoughts I was having hours ago. "They're going to blow up the Earth." I slip my boots back on in one fluid movement. "We have to do something to stop them. Anything."

"Ingrid," Wil says. "They've already destroyed it, in the future. We saw it happen. It *will* happen."

"There's still a lot about that battle we don't know," I reply. "What if we spend the next, I don't know, let's say five years, evacuating people from our planet and taking them to an alternate universe? Besides. Jadore also showed up, and from the stuff she stole, it looks like she's running wild, maybe building another portal. Gayarnu didn't care. They're just trying to heal the sick."

"Jadore stole research *from* Sparkstone?" Misty asks.

"It sounds like there's a widening divide, politically," Wil says gravely.

Sunni regards me coolly. "You didn't promise you'd help the ahmei, did you?"

"If we don't, humanity will also suffer," I reply, matching her tone. I show them Gayarnu's sample and my friends examine it thoughtfully. "They said if we take this to the Collective's headquarters and prove to the Council we have a cure, we can ally with the Collective and stop—"

"No. That's a trap," Sunni interrupts. "This whole visit was designed to elicit your sympathy and trick us into flying into their waiting hands."

"Could be. But the mother ship is *right there*. They could find and come after us now if they want. If Gayarnu is right, the Collective has been weakened by the altered vitaphage. I think we have more of an upper hand than we think." I look up at Wil, who has been pacing the mess thoughtfully. "What do we know about the Council?"

Wil communes with the ship. "Nothing useful. That's a higher paygrade than what the *Blind Elephant* was designed for."

All we have are scraps of information, pulled from hundreds of throwaway conversations. "Do we know if the Council are at the Final Battle? I mean, do we have records of species on board the mother ship that we don't recognize?"

Wil brings up our in-progress Final Battle schematic and zooms in on the mother ship. "Data's sparse. Hard to say. Did Gayarnu tell you where the Collective's headquarters is?"

I shake my head. "The Ethan in the other universe said something about the headquarters being in a nebula? I know it's not the same universe, but we could check?"

"Could check the ship's database," Wil says nonchalantly. "Let's see..."

Wil goes to a panel on the wall. It lights under his touch. Instead of pressing a combination of the three buttons beneath the panel, he closes his eyes and communes with the machine. Sunni stares into the middle distance, as if she can't believe what's happening. Misty tries to comfort her with soft whispers.

From a nodule in the ceiling, a three-dimensional projection rains upon us. The Milky Way zooms in and becomes a cluster of solar systems. They sprinkle our faces with beautiful lights, and although it disrupts the projection, I don't tell my friends to move. Seeing our neighbours in miniature reminds me that I *can* get to where I need to go. If I have to. I spot our solar system easily.

"This is a rendered map of nearby systems. The Collective's headquarters is here." He gently taps the screen. The projection responds. A green dot blinks in the top-right portion of the projection.

"Hmm," I say, my stomach falling. That green dot is in a solar system the furthest distance from our position. I'm hoping he'll tell me it's actually not that far, somehow, though the magic of science. "That seems really far?"

"It would take probably very little time to get there, if you teleported us," Misty points out, gesturing to me.

"Sure," I say dryly. "But what are we talking here? A couple of days in a spaceship, at maximum speed?"

It's depressing and I don't want to know the answer, even though I can guess.

"Approximately four years."

"Four!" We all exclaim some variation of our surprise.

"I don't want to be cooped up here for months or years when Ingrid could get us there in, I dunno, one second? Plus, isn't the Final Battle in April? By the time we get there *and* back, Earth will be dust."

She's right. "It's only one second to you because you aren't practiced at remembering your time in the Untraver," I mutter.

"It's the most efficient way to get there," Jia says. "Uses less supplies, less time..."

I wave my hand. "I know, I know. I'm not...I'm not against it. I just hate that if we do this, we could arrive and crash into the heart of the enemy."

"A very good reason to not go," Sunni says. "It's not like the Collective knows there's going to be a battle in April."

I sigh. "Okay. If we can prove that we have a cure to the altered vitaphage, we can exchange it for Earth's protection. Look at these Collective ships surrounding the planet." I point out the blockade of Earth on the hologram. "Maybe that's why they're there. For all we know, it's not the Collective that blows up Earth, but some third party that has taken control of the mother ship and presses the trigger. If we want to, we can destroy them later." Then, another thought, as quick as a blink. "And, what if by *not* going to the Collective headquarters, we're triggering the destruction of Earth?"

"What if by going, we're triggering the destruction of Earth?" Jia counters.

"Let's not have that argument. It's impossible to win, and we'll just go in circles," Wil says.

"Maybe I'm thinking about this wrong, but what's stopping us from taking this research, developing the cure, and disseminating it to the human population—and the ahmei, if we must?" Jia asks.

I press my back further into the bean bag chair. I've been so caught up in trying to help save everyone that I forgot that everyone can, potentially, save themselves. "I didn't think about that."

Wil shrugs. "We theoretically could do that *and* go to the Collective. The thing stopping us from disseminating a vaccine to an entire race across one planet is that we lack efficient infrastructure. And with a plague coursing across the planet, maybe the best minds are already working on the cure. By the time we enter at the correct moment with a vaccine, maybe humanity will have already developed their own solution. I don't know about you, but I don't want to spend countless *years* organizing and cajoling five billion people into taking a vaccine. Well-intentioned, but logistically, not an ideal use of our strategic position."

"I guess that makes sense," Jia concedes.

"Humanity can maybe develop a vaccine for the altered vitaphage, but they probably can't make a planet-wide shield that blocks the mother ship's blast," I say quietly. "At least, not with our current level of technology."

"I don't even know if humans in my universe have that kind of technology. We'd have to steal it from either Collective," Sunni says.

"Again, I'll state the obvious. We already saw the Earth blow up. I don't think we can prevent that." Wil sighs and then continues, arms behind his back, pacing like a politician refining a speech. "We have a choice. Give the Collective the research we took from the other universe in exchange for Earth's security. Or, we don't. We wait and choose some other cause to champion. Or, ideally, prepare for the Final Battle."

Ohz's words from the Untraver echo in my ears. *"False. Choice."* Was he talking about *this* choice?

What if the Collective destroys the Earth to prevent the further spread of the vitaphage?

"Let's vote," Wil says, his voice slicing through my dark thoughts like a sharp katana.

"You already know what we're all voting for," Misty remarks under her breath, but waves off further instigations with resignation. "Fine, fine. Do we have paper, or we're just saying our—"

"We'll say it. Wil's right. 'Nough talkin'. I'll start." Sunni stands and waves her hands emphatically. "We shouldn't be negotiating with aliens who don't acknowledge our sentience and basic right to live. Vote no for bargainin' with the Collective. Misty?"

Misty plays with her lip ring and stares at her shoes. "I think we should go to them."

"Misty!" Sunni exclaims.

"What?" She climbs to her feet. "The enemy of my enemy, and all that! Yeah, Collective is bad. But Jadore has been our enemy from day one and we need to stop her from building another portal or whatever she's up to! She..." Misty leaves the unsaid reason hanging in the recycled air. Jadore had murdered our universe's Sunni right in front of us. "You got to throw a few punches at yours. I want that chance with mine."

The conflict resonates on Sunni's face like a murky pool. Misty wants justice for the person she loves, the alternate version of Sunni. But that justice has been fed by an angry love.

While Sunni and Misty simmer, Jia casts her vote by touching her scarred face. We all have our reasons for hating Jadore and wanting her gone. "Diplomacy is worth trying. I vote yes for meeting with the Collective."

Wil fails to hide his discomfort. He has already died, in the past, at Jadore's hand. If possible, and I have the chance, I can change that. If Wil cooperates. Which he likely won't.

"I want the chance to read the Council, if I can. I vote yes to visiting the Collective," Wil says finally.

I don't even have to vote. Sunni is the only one firmly against. But I state my position anyway. "We should visit the Collective, if not to get intel on the enemy."

Sunni shakes her head. She doesn't look mad. She's disappointed and disgusted. "All right. I guess if that's what y'all want. But don't be surprised if they turn y'all into canned tuna and feed you to their strongest warriors. Because that tends to happen to people who walk into their den with a sign sayin' 'I'm dinner.'"

"Sunni..."

"No, just...I need to be alone." She throws off Misty's placation attempt and climbs the spiraling staircase, opens the hatch, and crawls into the loft.

I avert my gaze from their lover's quarrel and curl up in the booth. My chin finds the coziest place on my knee as I squeeze every drop of warmth from my bony body. It's not the same as a hug from Ethan, or my parents, or anyone else in my life. We're going to make a deal with the devil, even though it might be frivolous.

And if we discern the cure for the vitaphage within the database, maybe I can administer it somehow to Ethan. Perhaps that will set his addled soul to right.

After everything we've been through, I can't afford to not sleep with boots or shoes on. We may have to jump at a moment's notice.

I'm afraid I'm not going to sleep, but the events of the day—has it only been one day?—sink me into a rich dream. I've travelled to the alternate universe and my Ethan is there—he's followed me, because he has powers just like mine now. I take him in my arms and together we teleport across the stars, away from the aliens who want to take everything from us...

I wake with a start. Sunni and Jia are up, whispering as they complete a morning yoga routine. I hear Misty and Wil in the cockpit. The smell of coffee and tea and oatmeal permeates the mess, and I'm overwhelmed with hunger.

"You were talking in your sleep," Sunni says, with a side-long glance.

"Sorry." *She knows my secret wish*, I think with a sudden spike of anxiety.

I get up, stretch, and debate joining them in their yoga routine. But not showering has caught up with me. I rummage in our supplies and find hand sanitizer, a wash cloth, soap, and a jug of water.

As I wash in the scant privacy of the water closet, I can't shake the guilt. My friends have procured everything we need to survive while I tried to selfishly glean more information about a dead boyfriend.

Well. The whole endeavour wasn't entirely selfish. I learned more about Jadore's plan and how the intwined fate of the ahmei and the human race.

"Are you there?" I whisper as I gather my things, and change into fresh clothing.

Nothing but the sound of my friends outside the closet. Campbell isn't coming to my aid this time. As far as I know, it's all on me.

CHAPTER 10

When we arrive at the Collective's headquarters, we spend countless minutes gazing out the canopy at the beautiful nebula, within which lies the heart of the beast.

The nebula stretches across the void like an open wound. Luminous gas swirls and pulses in shades of violet and electric blue, the remnants of a long-dead star that once shredded an entire solar system, caught now in perpetual aftershock. Jagged asteroids drift in slow, stately orbits, their surfaces glittering with frozen methane and ammonia. The ice catches the light of the nebula and refracts it into spectral ribbons that coil and dance through the vacuum like ghostly currents in a cosmic ocean.

Nestled atop the largest of the asteroids, sits a vast metallic dome. It clings to the rock like a parasite. It's hard to believe everything that we've experienced has originated from this very spot. The urge to destroy it all rises within me, if not to protect the surrounding beauty.

It's been a few days since our adventure in the other universe. We did some recon on the mother ship, organized our stash, and settled as best we could into the *Blind Elephant*. It takes that long for the tension between Misty and Sunni to subside. Sunni channels her discontentment into teaching me how to use the hand weapons Misty and Jia stole from the alternate universe.

Now, my arm reveals the journey we took while in the Untraver. The lines are decisively drawn. Up, up, right, right, up, right, down, down. A star, marking the door we stepped through. A black dot, marking an Untrakeeper. I try to recall the journey. It's not fuzzy because of the dream-like quality of our time there; I feel flashes of hurried running and I remember the confidence in my stride. I don't remember it because my brain categorizes it as unimportant. Instinct. I've done a route like this many times before, and I have felt confident before, therefore it is not distinct enough to be memorable. Why I chose this door, and this moment, I'm unsure. That aspect of my power remains a mystery. Jia has been helping me organize the markings we've collected so far so Sunni and Wil can add it to the three-dimensional rendering later.

Wil analyzes the spectacular sight with the help of the ship's sensors. "If I'm reading this right, I'm picking up old Collective technology, dating back thousands of years. When they say this is their headquarters, this really might be the birthplace of the Collective."

"And then their star went supernova?" I ask.

"Yes," Wil says slowly. "Though...if I'm right...they may have had a hand in that."

"They took and they took and they took." Sunni's drawl is soft over the hum of the equipment. "Until their home had nothing left to give."

Bleep-bleep! An approaching craft sets off an automated alarm and cuts our admiration of the nebula short. We spent a day creating contingency plans and doing drills in the event of a surprise Collective attack. Feeling overwhelmed, we spring into action. Sunni activates our new weapon controls. Jia buckles herself into the bench and closes her eyes. Misty and I rush to the newly organized lockers in the mess and grab weapons to distribute to everyone. I also take a hair elastic, because there's no way I'm letting my freshly washed hair get ruined in a gun fight. Especially when the laser in this gun could slice my hair off.

When I return to the cockpit, I meet our visiting ship. It looks exactly like the overpowered, sleek fighter we destroy in the Final Battle. An uneasy feeling settles in my stomach. The laser weapon feels heavy in its holster around my waist.

The orange light flashes on the navigation console. Wil taps a few buttons. An AI voice reads the message as captions appear on a digital overlay over the canopy.

"Thank you for arriving at the appointed hour and coordinates," says the friendly voice, as if we've called an automated customer help line. "After disinfection procedures, your envoy will be accompanied with hospitality to the assigned point. Please follow the leader."

"How did it know we were coming?" Jia asks under her breath.

Sunni appears ill. "Please don't tell me one of you sold us out."

"C'mon Sunni," Misty says.

I exchange a curious glance with Wil. Do we arrange this appointment at some future date? Perhaps this means we *are* supposed to be here, and that our bargaining works. It's hopeful thinking. Twice we've been to the Final Battle, and twice the Earth exploded at the Collective's hand. Trusting in my future self to make the right moves that will lead us on the right path frightens me, as it requires my present self to make the most of the opportunities presented.

Wil stands casually and leans over the controls, as if considering the next move on a late-game chess board. "If anyone on this ship betrayed us, I'd know. Unless it was me. Then no one would know."

There's one other explanation that presently makes sense. "Time travel. Someone, at some point in the future, travels to the past and uses their knowledge to inform the—"

Another message interrupts me through the speakers in the same customer service voice. "We repeat. Stolen Sparkstone University ship. Welcome to your appointed coordinates. After disinfection procedures—"

Wil cuts the audio and jams a finger into one of the control buttons. "Roger that. We will follow the lead ship to the appropriate docking bay. Send disinfection procedures so we can prepare. Over."

Misty crosses her arms. "The altered vitaphage is out here too?"

I haven't thought much about the spread of the altered vitaphage beyond humanity and the alien staff at Sparkstone, but Gayarnu and Agailya had speculated that Jadore had released the phage to the Collective. I took that to mean the Collective presence within our solar system. For it to travel out here to the headquarters is troubling.

My head spins, worrying how long we've been travelling through the Untraver and trying to calculate the potential incubation period for the vitaphage. "What's the date?"

"According to the timestamps from the Collective's messages, and cross-referencing the calendars, we're at March thirteenth," Wil says. "A month before the Final Battle."

"How long were we travelling?" Jia asks, alarmed.

I check the timer on my phone and the number makes me feel nauseous. "Just ten minutes."

"Ten minutes, and two and a half months have passed?" Misty says. "Are you sure?"

"Body time is different than in-universe time. The ship's internal chronometer confirms that only ten minutes have passed since we jumped," Wil confirms. "This is a good opportunity to take the temperature of the Collective's current influence. The vitaphage's spread might be an important factor in their decision to destroy Earth."

I imagine a spectral hand pressing a giant red button stamped 'decontaminate' in yellow letters.

Our two pilots guide us into an open hangar bay at the base of the anchored dome-city. Just like the Conrod Building at Sparkstone, this hangar houses dozens of ships. They're similar to the *Blind Elephant* in size and shape. No war ships in sight. Our military escort exits the hangar as soon as we set down. Perhaps they're headed toward Earth right now, preparing for the battle to come.

"Is there air out there?" Misty asks.

"Looks safe for us," Wil says, looking at a flurry of data appearing on digital overlays.

The ship jostles suddenly. Outside in the shipyard, I see humanoid forms in full-body suits. I try to catch a better glimpse but they hurry out of sight, down a set of bay doors connecting to the rest of the city. It looks like they've attached something to the ship.

"I'll stay," Sunni says, stretching her arms and settling deeper into the co-pilot chair. "No use of them seein' me."

Misty starts to protest and the rest of us quickly convince her it's in our interest to hide Sunni. "Regardless of their relationship to Jadore, we can assume she's reported the results of her portal experiment. And I'd feel better knowing someone is with the ship," Wil notes.

Sunni readily agrees. "Don't worry. I can handle myself. And the ship. And our little friends." She glances over her shoulder towards the blue glow emanating from engineering. "If any trouble sprouts, well, you'll know about it."

After a curt goodbye, we step into the *Blind Elephant*'s airlock. We're about to venture into the belly of the enemy.

We disembark into another airlock, sickeningly white and medical. It smells like a plastic hospital. I gag. There's a windowless door in front of us with a red light shining like a beacon above. As Sunni closes up the ship, the airlock behind us locks, and the room fills with thick, blue smoke. Misty spreads her arms against us, ready to fire at the shower-head nozzles in the ceiling.

"Let it," Wil says.

We breathe in the disinfection gas. It smells and tastes like hand sanitizer, sending a flurry of colours through my mind. We cough and sputter together, but we don't fall unconscious. After a few moments, a light above the exit door shines green. A computerized voice says something as the door swings open.

We scurry into the massive ship hangar, sucking in more recycled air. At least it tastes normal. I'm expecting a battalion of fishmen armed with futuristic weapons and aquatic armour. Behind us, the boxy, portable decontamination unit rests, attached to the *Blind Elephant*.

"I can't believe we subjected ourselves to that," Misty mutters, spitting on the gritty concrete. Her saliva glistens with a blue tint.

"They could have vaporized our ship when we materialized. They don't mean to kill us, at least, not right now," Wil says nonchalantly.

I listen for Untrakeepers. Nothing. I wonder how long it will take for them to find me, all the way out here, in some distant solar system. If they can find me at all. My shoulders lower as some of the tension dissipates and we stop coughing. "Maybe we arrived before our escort?" I say, glancing around for signs of life.

"I'm sensing thousands of lifeforms," Wil says. "This dome-city houses hundreds of thousands."

A chill settles over us. We're used to the Collective playing mind games. Asserting their military strength when convenient. Quietly killing their enemy. We fan out, remaining within arm-reach, in case we need to disappear into Jia's watery world.

The hangar bay doors whisper open, and the four of us turn towards them, hands on our weapons. Misty has already conjured a flame in her hand. But instead of guards, or nasty-looking aliens, a single, silver construct rolls towards us on four small wheels, like a narrow, portable kitchen island. A round digital eye—definitely a camera—whirs as it scans the four of us. Then, it runs through a blazing-fast list of sound and glyphs, which project in a holographic format above its head. I shield my eyes, overwhelmed.

"It's identifying our species," Misty explains.

It settles on an item from the list, blinks twice, and then another list comes up—this time, in a language I somewhat recognize. A primitive robotic voice says something in Mandarin.

"Uh..." Misty and Jia exchange glances as they work out the translation. Misty arrives at the solution first. "It's asking us to wait."

The holographic characters flicker again. The Chinese characters morph into roman letters.

"New language detected in cabin," the robotic voice says, with a Texan accent. "Wait, to be pleased." It repeats the translation in Mandarin.

"That thing must have shown us hundreds of thousands of languages," Misty says with awe. "So, I know that we're on a ticking clock or whatever, but it would be great if we could stay here for like…a day? To see if we can download any of their databases? Know your enemy, all that jazz?"

The construct's accent flattens, making me jump out of my skin. "Error number six-five-oh-seven. Unable to parse phrase, *"ticking clock or whatever"* and *"all that jazz."* Please restate conversation so all records remain unbroken."

"Creepy," Misty says, examining the rolling machine for hidden microphones.

They must record every conversation everywhere, Wil says telepathically. *Let's not give them any unnecessary information about humanity, our lives, or our mission.*

The three of us nod imperceptively at Wil.

"Follow this way," it says, and leads us towards the bay doors and a long bridge, crossing like a plus-fifteen over a buzzing metropolis. The four of us slow to take in the sight below. It reminds me of the industrial areas of Calgary. Swaths of flat space with rectangular buildings. Few people, but lots of machines, and rivers of dark water instead of roads. Drones zip by in organized lanes above the water, going about their likely nefarious business. A bustling empire inside a metropolis capable of conquering entire civilizations, and it's all at our feet.

"Following, please," the construct says again in the Texan drawl.

Misty smirks. As Sunni had remarked earlier, the woman can't help herself. She addresses the computer once more. "So, how and when did you acquire human languages?"

Wil frowns disapprovingly at Misty and I expect the computer to throw an error or an access restricted message. Instead, it answers the question. "First human contact registered eighty years prior to present date. Language brains assessed and acquired utilizing standard operating procedures in local research facilities ten years prior to present date."

Big gap. Misty slicks back her hair and steps back from the camera. *Language brains* and *standard operating procedures* hit hard.

"Why'd it take seventy years from first contact to learn our languages?" I ask.

What I really want to ask is: who did they abduct first? I hadn't thought about first contact with the Collective being a mutual or friendly event. It seems like one day they'd settled and created a ton of schools to reap our superpowers. At the same time, I don't want to know what poor soul likely died at the Collective's hands during that fateful encounter.

"Portal construction to human origin planet delayed due to ERROR. INFORMATION NOT FOUND. PLEASE RESTATE QUESTION." The jovial, feminine Texan drawl becomes a booming, growling automaton without skipping beat.

"Whoa, whoa," Misty says, and I similarly recoil, expecting the construct to explode or turn on us violently.

It doesn't stop moving. It's as if nothing sinister has happened. The Texan, feminine voice returns. "Please restate question."

As portals seem central to the Collective travelling vast distances, and given Jadore's interests, I wonder if Jadore had a hand in erasing or modifying any Collective knowledge about them. If I were building a portal, I wouldn't want my enemy working on one too.

We descend into silence as the bot leads us into a nearby elevator. An assault of foreign scents smacks my brain as colour, meaning, and history converges. Wil slides an arm through mine to help stabilize me. He too looks uncomfortable.

The construct hits what the button for what appears to be the top-most floor of the structure and the doors close. We barely feel movement. A few moments later, the elevator opens to a small foyer with an immersive, panoramic view of the nebula. It flares around us, dangerously beautiful. It's striking from the ship, but here, it's breathtaking. The four of us pause here and take in the view, speechless. When I first saw Earth from space, I could scarcely believe my good fortune, despite the tragedy and trials. This vision strikes a similar chord, yet it feels more unreal.

I squint. Occasional flashes of light, like a welding torch, blink on the icy asteroids. "The Collective is mining the asteroids?" I guess.

"Minerals continue to be harvested from the remnants of— CLASSIFIED. DISENGAGE FROM CONVERSATIONAL THREAD."

The AI has improved its English grammar within minutes of discussion. Convenient, but irksome. I don't want to give the Collective any more information about us.

"This way, please," the construct says, returning to its conversational tone.

The floor transitions from carpet to shimmering tile just beyond the elevator foyer as we head down a long hallway. The floor-to-ceiling view continues. I can see why the Council would want to have their meetings here.

As we round the corner, the wheel on the construct rolls aggressively over the transition strip. *Klur-UMPH. Clang.* The jolt upsets the top panel and it flies open for a second. Inside, I see a flash of grey and a smattering of lights. The panel snaps shut again and rattles quietly as it rolls along. The construct makes no mention of an error. It's probably too busy listening to Misty and Jia commenting on the spectacular view.

I frown and catch up with the girls, trying to act natural as one can when surrounded by alien opulence and cruelty.

Every piece of technology we've encountered so far has had a biological component, Wil remarks telepathically, because he also saw what I saw.

The deep-seeded fear returns like a blooming flower within my guts. I clear my throat. "You mentioned before about standard operating procedures and acquiring language brains? Tell me what that means."

It doesn't answer right away. "Biomatter containing desired information is harvested, processed, and assessed for usefulness within the network. Once assessed, biomatter is assigned, grafted, and integrated into the appropriate management team."

I knew there was something off about this thing. It's not an AI in the way we're thinking, Wil clarifies for us.

I'm more shocked that it doesn't consider this classified information. Unable to hold back my curiosity—and emboldened by the fact that I can leave this place behind if I choose—I throw open the top panel.

Snaking wires and flashing computer chips have been inserted into a perfectly sectioned neocortex. It's undoubtably human. The brain fragment sits in a glass dish of viscous blue liquid, atop a hard drive and other computer parts.

The construct halts. I recoil, expecting retaliation, or an alarm.

"Temperature disruption detected in cabin. Compensating." I detect the faint hum of a fan within the construct. Its wheels restart and it continues towards the doors at the end of the hallway.

I glance at my friends. They're stunned into silence as we share identical thoughts, daring not to voice them aloud.

"Coming?" the construct asks.

The word sparks us into action. We meet the construct before the doors and it's raddling of instructions.

"The Council has granted you fifteen minutes. At any time,

standard operating procedures may apply. When they have concluded the meeting, you will be escorted back to your vessel. Please stick to the prescribed agenda."

"You're...alive?" Jia says numbly.

"We are alive," the construct confirms.

Jia kneels to the camera's eye level. "I'm so sorry they did this to you."

Steely silence. Then, "Why?"

I touch Jia's shoulder, urging her to get up. "We should go in."

She wants to protest. The four of us hold our breath and dare not say another word.

Inside the expansive room, our shoes *click* and *clomp* against the large, silver tiles. Swirling coloured light emanates between the grouting, as if we're walking across a high-tech dance floor. Our footsteps leave impressions on the tile and glow in ever-changing rainbows before evaporating.

I sense mechanisms beneath the floor, Wil tells us. *Storage. Electrical power. This is a conference room.*

This is a room built to show off the magnificence of the Collective. Its grandness makes its emptiness seem more opulent.

I turn to say goodbye to the construct, but it has already disappeared.

Towards the back of the room, there are thirteen plump chairs in various colours and sizes, built to the specifications of each alien councillor, but only four lifeforms enter the room through thick curtains sectioning the hall. I instinctively recoil.

We haven't encountered these species before. The first councillor is a hunched, fungal-smelling creature with multiple black-and-white spotted caps. I detect faint whirring from the spots, as if they're embedded cameras. A singular mouth at the connecting stalk oozes red, which is promptly wiped away by one of the spotted caps as it elongates into an appendage suitable for the task. It chooses a seat near the middle and emits a cloudy huff, as if this is the tenth meeting of the day and it can't wait for five-o'clock.

A dashing, yellow-bellied avian sways its long neck as it crosses the room to a chair in four long strides. Its three-toed bird claws click on the tile like a scampering cat. Rapid, bulging eyes flit to each of us. Every wet blink is an incremental head movement. Blink. Head-tilt. Its beak pecks at the table.

The third councillor looks like a raccoon, down to the black mask across its eyes. While the avian alien has the most impressive natural presence, this raccoon alien has adorned itself with layers of colourful fabrics and golden, shimmering chains, as if it glanced at the pop culture from the eighties and nineties and decided that was the epidemy of style. An air of arrogance accompanies the creature as it settles near the bird and they exchange squawks and clicking sounds.

The fourth alien shows off the Collective's efforts to integrate technology and biology. I count eight tentacles; six of them have been outfitted with metal surgical tools. It is a permanent Swiss Army knife. Unlike the hafelglob, which are also tentacled, this alien has stalk eyes and several other face-holes that could be nostrils or mouths, or both. It slides up onto its flat chair, gurgling something to the others. They cluck in response.

Just when we think the meeting is about to commence, a fifth alien skitters from behind the curtain. It has the long mandibles of an ant, five dark eyes across the upper half of its face, and a human-like appearance and colouring. Its mandibles move, and the creature emits a near-imperceptible chittering sound. I sense that if I had not been endowed with my power, I wouldn't have heard it, nor detected its distinctive smell: fresh grass and something medicinal. The other councillors acknowledge it with an air of annoyance. At least, that's what I think is happening. I'm not an expert in alien body language.

The four of us form a defensive line. We're ready to launch an assault, if necessary.

"Hello," Wil says.

The unique languages of the Council die beneath Wil's voice, which echoes in the grand emptiness.

The tentacle alien waves. Not a friendly gesture. It's signing.

"Wow," Misty says.

Directly in front of us, as if in response to the alien's sign-language, vine-like wires erupt from the floor with a disturbing crack to support an emerging, stalky brown trunk. We're watching a timelapse of a growing tree. When it's as tall as me, the growth halts, and four oblong leaf-shapes emerge from the top. They fall open enticingly to reveal a flatscreen panel. The material comprising the panel appears to be chitin, and as the screen comes to life, the vines glow with a faint bioluminescence. It even smells alive, vaguely fungal and wet.

"Interpreter ready. Waiting for Council confirmation of meeting start!" says a chipper voice from the panel. A green wavelength appears on the panel matching the speech pattern. This voice isn't the same as the Texas drawl from the construct. It has received pronunciation and a peppy manner, as if it can't wait to serve us.

The pit in my stomach deepens as I wonder *who* this voice used to belong to, and if they know where they are, and what function they currently serve. From its sentence structure, I surmise that the individual cyber-fitted intelligences don't share their language models, or, if they do, it's on a delay.

The five aliens before us seem unconcerned with this artificial emergence. In front of each alien sits a half-moon-shaped speaker. They glow blue.

"Council language database loaded. Council is waiting excitedly for your speaking words," the interpreter says.

"They are not excited to see us," Wil clarifies.

The interpreter clicks and squeaks. The raccoon alien clicks in reply and gestures with tiny fingers to Wil. A deep-registered human voice with a heavy Texan accent emanates from the alien's speaker. "You are the one Ja'Dor'Esss had trouble gardening."

"The language model is still learning our idioms, I see," Misty explains. "They mean, *harvesting.*"

Again, the strange voice interprets Misty's words, assigning it an individual voice for easy aural recognition. The bird alien speaks up. The chosen voice is close to the interpreter's voice, with quick, strangely clipped delivery. "We do our best with lesser race languages! It will be fast to fix, only a second-hand's tick until it is complete!"

The four of us share a moment of awkward silence. None of us want to be the next person to speak and have our words jumbled, translated, and replied to by these beings who came to our planet to secretly dominate, assimilate, and torture our people. They're not interested in introducing themselves or wasting time with diplomatic niceties. We shouldn't concern ourselves with that either.

I don't want to be afraid of them; I don't want them to know I came all this way and then became too cowardly to speak. I remember my power; I remember my purpose.

"My name is Ingrid Stanley," I tell them. The translator clicks my words to the Council. "My friends and I are from the planet Earth.

You're right that Jadore, as we call her, has been after us and our abilities for months now. Even though we're strongly opposed to everything you're doing to our people, we've come to you to strike a bargain.

"We have the cure to the altered vitaphage originally created for the ahmei people, then modified and released by Jadore. We're willing to trade this cure for the immediate departure and cessation of all Collective activities on Earth." Not a complete truth. We don't know everything that's on the alternate universe database. But Misty's reasonably certain that it's in there somewhere.

I expect silence and contemplation as they process my words, but as the translator finishes, their chatter is shamelessly translated back to us as they cluck like hens.

"The vitaphage? Which one is that?" asks the fungal alien, whose translated voice sounds as airy and tired as it looks.

"Didn't you listen? It mentioned the ahmei, so it is the one we crafted for the ahmei," the raccoon alien says.

"The tall one speaks like a person! The *three* vitaphage strains are not comprehensible to human scientists!" says the bird alien, exasperated.

"A barter. These lesser-beings have nothing we want. Tell them we will suck the cure from their marrow," says the tentacled alien, whose exaggerated deep voice sounds ready to perform on Broadway.

"The vitaphage has been modified so it now infects non-ahmei races. As you may have noticed," Wil adds pointedly. "The research we've collected is in your interest if you want to resume normalcy. We know the altered vitaphage has disrupted your operations significantly."

"Ah. *That* vitaphage! These humans! They are the ones who

released the bioweapon as a terrorist plot!" screams the bird alien.

"It wasn't us. It was Jadore!" Misty retorts.

Both outbursts send them into an explosion of clicks, squawks, and the translator feeds it all back to us in a cloud of confusing accusations, exclamations, and misused idioms.

"Ja'Dor'Esss put these humans up to it! The two-eyed primitive leads the blind primitives!"

"Let's tell them we'll consider their bargain, and then put their bodies in the hafelglob pens."

"At least let me have the mind-reader, for study. And the one with invisible-touch."

"Files say the one with metal bits in her face can generate fire and ice, but only from her limbs. Perhaps we could enhance that within the cells, extract, and then..."

They must have no clue we can understand them, for them to expose their chatter like this.

Oh, they understand perfectly. They just don't care, Wil says telepathically.

"Where is the evidence of this cure?" asks the raccoon alien finally.

Wil produces a flash drive from his pocket and places it on the desk. "This contains a quarter of the data required to create a cure. We will transmit you the rest once your fleet is clear of our solar system."

The raccoon examines the drive between two fingers. "Clever, very clever."

"Ja'Dor'Esss has been promising cures to her followers," says the fungal alien. "It is how she has been able to amass more influence in this eleven-o'clock hour. We have only to obtain it, and we will have no need of these humans!"

"Reptile cure," says the tentacle alien, swirling one of its modified appendages.

"Snake oil," Misty says.

Two caps from the fungal alien stretch into snake-like appendages and snatch the flash drive from the raccoon alien. They connect with the flash drive and hum in a low G-minor chord. Then, it discards the drive in the direction of the tentacle alien, as if tossing an empty juice box. "The investment in Earth is significant. This so-called cure research is not sufficient value to discontinue operations on Earth," the fungal alien says. "We require additional currency."

Misty and Jia look concerned. I also can't hide my worry. Wil remains stony-faced. "What did you have in mind?"

"Your brain. And..." The raccoon protrudes a bejewelled finger and swirls it menacingly at me. "The body of the teleporter."

"No deal," Wil says firmly.

"What makes your mind believe we don't already have a cure? The human race must offer value equal to our lost investment in Earth," says the raccoon alien.

I shiver. Wil wasn't wrong about his assessment of our combined powers. The two of us, in exchange for the safety of our race?

Not a chance, Wil says telepathically to me. *Our powers are too dangerous to hand over to the biggest threat in the galaxy.*

"You don't have a cure," Jia says, speaking up finally. "If you did, your facilities here and on Earth wouldn't be abandoned. You would have caught Jadore by now. You could have taken over the entire planet by now. Before now, we struggled for every victory. Now, you let us walk through your halls with no resistance. It doesn't matter if you believe us. We have a cure that will restore you, and your arrogance blinds you to the possibility of rising to meet your former glory."

As the translator trips over Jia's speech with its clicks, I regard the only alien who hasn't addressed us or added to the mindless chatter. The humanoid ant doesn't seem to be paying attention to anyone in the room—except me. When it finally speaks, cutting off the inane replies from the others, its chosen voice sounds like an entitled young man in his twenties. "Dispose of their mouth-flesh and feed the rest to the feral hafelglob in the northwest camps. It will be their final feed before the faur devour the remains."

"Feral hafelglob," I say under my breath, before I can stop myself.

"You and your people will eat what they are given," mutters the tentacle alien.

The humanoid ant fixes all of its eyes on me as my muttering is translated. It chitters softly, almost like a laugh. "Why do you care about those animals?"

My face heats. "Who says I do?"

"I have seen it," it says simply.

"You haven't been in the field for years!" chides the bird alien. "You see nothing! Your ships have been squelched by rebels in the—" The human voice halts and switches to a clicking, squawky language as it encounters foreign concepts and words. This sparks another argument amongst the Council.

Wil takes this opportunity to cautiously break our formation. He's studying the quietest alien. No one protests as he approaches the council table with interest. The aliens' squawking subsides momentarily as they regard Wil like a ladybug who has dared to join their picnic lunch.

"Such curiosity!" says the bird alien.

The humanoid ant twitches nervously as Wil circles it. My friend is careful to give the Council a wide berth. Misty is about to chide

Wil, but Jia and I touch her hands. She frowns at us as we shake our heads. Best to let Wil do what Wil does best.

"You're ill with the modified vitaphage," Wil says simply.

The humanoid ant stands with outrage. "Lies! Kill the mind-creep now!"

"Councillor Ari-Faur!" exclaims the raccoon alien. "I knew your scent was off today!"

"You have broken protocol for the final time," says the fungal alien.

"Do you want us ALL to perish?" the tentacle alien gestures to the curtains. "Escort Councillor Ari-Faur to quarantine immediately."

"You should have kept your mouth-flesh quiet, mind-creeper," says the humanoid ant, as a single armed fishman appears from beyond the curtain and points a spear at the councillor. It once again and regards me with pure malice. "We've all suffered from the consequences of *your* actions."

It hisses at everyone as it heads towards the curtain at the behest of the fishman. The final look I see from the alien is one of pure fear. It knows something about me.

What did I do in his past that could have him so riled?

"New bargain. Bring Ja'Dor'Esss to us, and we will consider your request," the fungal alien says.

Misty, Jia, and I are about to protest, but Wil holds out a hand. Telepathically to us, he says, *Let's hear them out on this.* To the council, he asks, "Why should Jadore be our problem?"

The question surprises me. Jadore kills Wil. Wrecked Jia's face. Killed Sunni. Threatened the people we love. She's our problem because she is everything we hate about the Collective, personified.

The bird councillor huffs and wrestles his feathers. "The implications of a headstrong, uplifted lifeform sprinkling technology on primitive pond scum concern us to the extreme. All of the ideas we've heard from her flock violate our standards and ethics."

Ethics. Uh-huh. And yet...

We don't know all the secrets and technology Jadore has stolen from the Collective. What if she uplifts a fast-breeding, invasive species? One of the Collective's weaknesses is that it is a bureaucracy of alien scientists, with factions seemingly vying for control of its combined power. If one person took all of the research and effort and used it to their own ends, unchecked, that could have devastating consequences.

Wil puts a hand to his chin and exaggerates a thoughtful expression. "Jadore has always coveted my power. All of our abilities, really. And, she's already modified one of your biological weapons. It's in our interest to bring her to you."

"Yes! The mind-reader understands. As an uplifted primitive, her mental capacity has always impressed," says the tentacle alien.

"Her unhealthy obsession with body modification is trouble," concedes the raccoon alien. "She already violated laws about uplifted primitives exceeding two modifications. And she had those two pilakee wrapped around her digits." It gestures to two empty seats.

"What if she plans to uplift other reptiles on her home planet?" asks the raccoon alien.

"She cannot!" shrieks the bird alien.

"We can take care of Ja'Dor'Esss," says the tentacle alien. "We don't need these primitives to chase another primitive. That would be the opposite of sanity."

The raccoon alien shakes its little head. "All of our hunters are ill or containing other crises. Let the lesser-beings hunt the lesser being."

"Yes, I think we can do this," Wil says, looking to us with an exaggerated nod. I nod slowly, because it seems like that's what he wants. Misty sighs and shrugs. Jia looks concerned and crosses her arms. Wil turns back to the Council. "Would you like her dead or alive?"

"Her body intact. Either," the fungal alien replies.

"Alive!" the bird alien squawks.

"If you don't have her on board the mother ship in"—the fungal alien's human voice drops and is replaced with clicking for a solid thirty seconds, until the human voice returns—"one Earth standard month from this moment's date, we will consider any bargain struck in this meeting void, and standard harvesting procedures will be implemented."

My stomach drops. If we don't present Jadore to the Council during the Final Battle, we're toast.

"All right," Wil says.

"Wait," I say.

A speech roils within me: I could travel back to the beginning of your sentience and crush you all.

If you say that, it can't be unsaid, Wil warns me telepathically. *We should take this deal and get out of here.*

I shoot him a look. He's right. I shouldn't give our enemy any more information about my time-travel powers, any more than they might already have. But they're sitting here, thinking us the bugs, when they have no idea how much I could squish them, if I wanted. My cheeks burn because I don't want to be this person. They've made me become what I hate.

I hate being underestimated. I hate not being *seen*.

"There is more to say?" the raccoon alien asks.

"No. We accept your terms," Wil replies, nodding.

For the first time, the Council regards us silently.

The tentacle alien twists an appendage and a black rectangle replaces the wavelength on the flatscreen panel. He taps his right temple three times. The others do the same and stare ahead, as if watching something invisible.

Wil frowns; he fixes me with a curious stare. *They're watching a recording of you. But I can't get a fix on it.*

It's as if they've finally figured out how to mute themselves and convene silently. I wonder if they're watching the video feed of when Jadore had locked me in a room and created an experiment with me and Ohz. Because of this, I accidentally left him in the Untraver, where he roams still. If they're watching that feed, they may have just recognized my time travel abilities.

The black box disappears from the flatscreen and the Council's chatter returns.

"A trick of technology?" asks the fungal alien.

"And yet, she exists here," the tentacle alien says, gesturing. "Was there, and then..."

"A strong ability. But strong enough?" the raccoon questions.

"This benefits us!" screeches the bird alien.

I step forward and once again, they fall into unusual silence.

Don't say anything, Wil warns me.

As usual, I don't listen to Wil.

"If we're entering into a pact with you, to deliver you Jadore and our full research," I say slowly, "you cannot touch Earth. Ever, or ever again. Or any member of the human race, anywhere. They're protected now."

"Ohhhh!" the bird alien says excitedly. "What stops you from laying waste to us once we agree to your terms?"

I shrug. "What stops you from destroying our civilization once we give you Jadore or the cure? It's mutually assured destruction." And for us, the destruction truly is assured.

Unless I can stop it during the battle.

The four remaining aliens at the table consider our words more carefully. Clicks, gurgles, and the tentacle alien intones music to my ears: "Prepare the pact."

CHAPTER 11

"Bring them not only the cure, but *Jadore*, and they'll leave humanity alone?"

Back on the ship, piloting away from the gorgeous nebula, Sunni doesn't believe us when we tell her about our deal with the Collective. She *really* doesn't believe the Collective will hold up their end of the bargain.

"We all want to catch Jadore, and if we can get a few punches in before the Collective gets to her, that's good," Misty says steadily.

"You're doing their dirty work," Sunni argues. "You bring them Jadore, and they'll blow up Earth anyway."

"Maybe Jadore is the one holding the trigger," Jia replies.

We're escorted to the edge of the system by two sleek fighters. They remain at a distance as we set a course for the nearest system and accelerate. None of us want to hover in the belly of Collective space as we contemplate our next jump.

"Jia's right," Misty says, settling in on the bench. "Why would the Collective blow up Earth when it's their prized investment? Like, they'd have to be pretty desperate to incinerate literal money to them. It would have to be so valuable that they determine *no one* should have it. Maybe Jadore is the one behind the destruction of Earth.”

Or the Collective is blowing it up to spite me and my powers. I shake my head. That’s incredibly self-centered. “I don’t know if pure destruction is Jadore’s thing. Whoever controls the Collective fleet at the Final Battle decides that for some reason, Earth needs destroying, out of malice or fear of vitaphage spread. Who do we know with those interests?”

“Vitaphage spread is a good one,” Jia concedes. “At some point, we have to deliberately visit the battle so we can get another look at the elephant.”

“Agree. Let’s go,” Wil says, slapping his hands on the controls.

“Now?” I say incredulously.

He raises an eyebrow. “Are you busy with something else?”

Even though it’s our third rodeo, and we’ve tied the flight paths of every moving object into main navigation to help us avoid any collisions, we’re off to a bumpy start. We arrive beneath the mother ship and Jia, strapped into the bench, brings us into her watery world. Fighters emerge from a hangar bay in the mother ship and spill onto the battle like a handful of shiny dice scattering across a cosmic table.

Spinning in the co-pilot chair, Wil brings up the in-progress hologram of the Final Battle. It bathes the room and our bodies in a red-blue glow, and once again I’m filled with awe and terror that this event may be unpreventable. Unchangeable.

“She’s here,” Wil says, waving his hand in the vicinity of the blip representing the mother ship. “At least, I’m pretty sure. Compared to the thousands upon thousands of people on the mother ship, she's got a unique bio-sign. And...hmm. I'm picking up what I think is a councillor's sign. That one with mandibles for a mouth. Councillor Ari-Faur."

The one who had given me the stink eye. Well, five stink eyes. He survives the vitaphage. I wonder if he's the only one on the Council to do so, or if he has been sent as a representative to collect Jadore.

"If she's on the mother ship, aren't we just stealing Jadore from Collective custody?" Misty says.

Wil sighs. "Perhaps Jadore or another faction has commandeered the ship. With the state of the Collective being what it is, maybe they're already in pieces by now, and we are truly only fighting Jadore on that day. The only way to know is to be on the ship while it's happening." He frowns. "I'm not getting her bio-sign anymore. It doesn't seem to leave the mother ship. But I'm picking up a ship that's registered to her specifically, leaving the mother ship, and heading away from the battle."

We stealthily follow, and we're not the only ones. A convoy of small Collective ships fall into formation. Seems like the Council had been correct. Jadore has a following.

"Our computer's saying there are thousands of life signs on these ships. But I..." He looks pensive and touches his temple. "I don't feel there's that many."

"A trick?" I ask.

"Maybe." Wil sounds unsure. With his power, he's not used to people deceiving him. "There are people on board. Frightened. But then there are those that feel nothing at all."

"Could there be more of those brains wired up to machines," Misty points out.

"I don't think it's..." Wil trails off. "We'll cross-reference it against the sensors later."

The hodge-podge fleet, made of at least twenty ships, head towards a bright star in the distance. It gleams an unnatural blue-green.

"I see it. Sunni?" Wil says.

"Yeah. Got it. The sensors are saying it's a celestial body, but...?" She sounds unsure.

A flash of circular, ringed light emanates from the strange star. The ships scurry towards it, attracted to its greatness.

Circular ringed light.

The stolen research.

"It's not a star. It's a portal," I say shakily. "How long has it been there?"

Wil closes his eyes and focusses his power. "A couple months. I could get more if we get closer."

We accelerate closer to the convoy. Wil and Sunni perform an analysis on the portal and study the ships zooming towards it. Wil summons a digital overlay on the canopy of a small vessel nestled in the middle of the convoy. The larger ships have overtaken the vessel in speed, and to me, there's nothing except its size that makes it distinct within the twenty-odd crafts beelining for the portal.

"Now I'm reading a thousand life-signs on this one. That has to be a malfunction." Wil shakes his head in frustration. "Sunni, can you...?"

Sunni double-checks his work. "I thought I read that, but now it's just showing two humans. Um...one human? One alien." She brings up a separate digital overlay with sensor data on the other ships in the convoy. "Some humans. Some aliens with human DNA, so, aliens with modifications..."

Jia grunts something behind us.

"Hmm?" I ask her.

She shakes her head and then returns to a deep meditative state, just as the proximity alarm starts beeping.

"Fighters!" Sunni says.

Wil and Sunni maneuver the invisible *Blind Elephant* out of the way as the fighters exchange volleys with the convoy. The small vessel suffers a direct hit from the fighters and veers off course. Two minutes later, it explodes.

"Hey, I think there were—" She frowns. "Never mind. Thought there were survivors that jettisoned, but I'm not getting anything now."

"Can the *Blind Elephant* identify the humans on the convoy?" Misty asks.

"We need better tech for that," Sunni replies. "Or Wil's brain."

"Wil's brain is busy keeping out the chaos of this place," he mutters.

The battle culminates once more with the destruction of Earth, which we watch from a distance this time. My third time watching it explode, I think about my parents. They don't know who I am and they're going about their normal life when suddenly, BAM! Their life is over. If I can't figure out how to stop the destruction, I'll figure out a way to get them off-planet.

"Still doing okay?" I ask Jia.

Sweat has soaked her clothes and she's deep in a trance.

We stay a little longer. The mother ship drifts away from the remnants of Earth, in the direction of the portal. The portal flashes. Something has activated the device, but the convoy hasn't reached it yet.

"Can we get a little closer?" Sunni asks.

Jia moans and scrunches up her face. She's reached her limit.

"All right, we don't want to risk being seen," Wil concedes. "Ingrid, take us out?"

Jia spends time washing up in the water closet once we're clear of the battle as Wil and Sunni update the Final Battle hologram. I also record my markings from the Untraver and punch them into a tablet program Wil has designed. The two-dimensional map isn't as elaborate as the hologram of the Final Battle, but it's better than nothing.

"Progress?" Wil asks, when he's finished.

"Some. I think we can safely say I don't enter at the same point each time," I reply, feeling shame and disappointment at not being a computer with automatic sensors, taking in and categorizing every piece of encountered data. With every jump, I discover new scribbles on my left arm, leg, and sometimes my stomach. My skin has been rubbed raw with the effort to wash it off—once I've documented every line on paper and within the ship's computer. Wil and Sunni have been helping to create a model. It's slow work.

"We'll get there," he says. "We should also make sure there's no other markings on anyone or anywhere else. In case you run out of space and decide to use another surface."

The five of us meet in the mess to strategize once we're refreshed. Wil pulls up the updated hologram of the final battle. "Here's what we got. The battle is approximately twenty minutes long, if we count the first instance of the *Blind Elephant* appearing as the beginning, and the explosion of Earth as the end." He waves a hand at the hologram as it fast-forwards. Timestamps appear at the top. He zooms in to the symbol representing the mother ship and it's replaced by blueprints. "Sorry, we don't have quite enough for specifics, but Councillor Ari-Faur remains on the mother ship for most of the battle, around here." He points to an aft part of the ship. "Jadore starts here, then goes here, and disappears around here." He gestures to various points of the ship, nowhere near Councillor Ari-Faur. "Does she die, or does she have some kind of biological masking ability? I think it's the latter, personally. But she's on the mother ship, clearly up to *something*. And hey, if you don't care what it is, that's fine for our purposes. But I was thinking, maybe if we understood her motivations, maybe we'd have better insight into how to approach her when we encounter her on the ship."

"We catch her, then?" Jia asks, studying the blueprints with interest.

Wil looks uncomfortable. He rubs his head. "I believe so. It's tough to parse when there's so much chaos, but the data we got suggests she's surrounded by humans at various times while on the ship, before she disappears." Wil straightens his glasses. "Clearly from the time the underground library explodes to the Final Battle, she's been busy. Releasing a bioweapon. Allegedly gathering influence. But why now? She's had her own agenda this whole time, but she's probably had access to that vitaphage data for years now. She could've done this years ago. We find out why she ramped up in January? We find out what she's doing and how we can pick her up."

Sunni and Misty sit together at the booth, holding hands and sharing some leftover shepherd's pie. I'm across from them, picking at the leftovers. I set down my fork and clear my throat. I've been thinking about this too.

"Let's run through where and what we've seen of her,

chronologically," I suggest. It's hard to think straight when we've been all over our own timeline. "On the day of the explosion, she's got me connected up to a giant portal, ready to invade an alternate universe, perhaps join forces with another Collective. Who knows. That fails. Portal explodes. A near-death experience. She barely makes it out alive with the ahmei, somehow." I don't mention that I believe I make it back there at some point. "Some point between the explosion at the end of December and when we acquire the *Blind Elephant* on January twentieth, Jadore releases the modified vitaphage. Jia and I saw security footage at Sparkstone of sick aliens."

"Jadore wasn't looking so hot herself," Misty says, gesturing to her front to remind us of the johnny Jadore had been sporting. "And hafelglob had been chasing her. Maybe she'd been prisoner that whole time, but she manages to tweak the vitaphage, because she'd have access to everything at Sparkstone. Then when everyone had been weakened enough, she tries to steal a ship and runs into us."

"Do we think Jadore had the vitaphage and survived?" Sunni asks.

"It seems pretty fatal, especially to aliens." But something nags me. "In Sunni's universe, Alt-Ethan said that Jadore had been doing 'mystic nonsense research' before she died." I point at Sunni. "You said there aren't many divergences between our two realities. Have we searched the stolen database for anything about Jadore's fate?"

I'm also curious about the classified file that Alt-Ethan couldn't access that may have something to do with my power.

Wil and Sunni have stuck the drive onto the wall next to the booth and connected it with our systems. Misty taps her wristband and the drive turns on. Holographic documents in the ahmei language sprout up from the middle of the table.

"I did manage to translate some of it, but there's lots of technical jargon," Misty says, flicking through them. A crease appears between her perfect eyebrows. "This make sense to you? Something about her DNA eating itself?"

Steeling herself, Sunni scans the data. "Yeah, here it says that because of her modifications, many ill-advised and self-inflicted without a medical professional, her DNA started to, umm, disintegrate?" She also frowns. "Her symptoms included extreme pain, paranoia, an increased nesting instinct, hallucinations, and delusions surrounding her position within the Collective. She was forced to take medical leave. Then she was restrained and..." She trails off. "Tortured, essentially."

"Increased nesting instinct? Gross," Misty says.

"She was uplifted," I say offhandedly.

Wil and I exchange glances. He sees my train of thought, and as if plucking it from my brain, says, "Of course...she wants to perfect herself. And if she believes herself to be dying, what would be her number one priority?"

"Survival," Sunni says.

"Survive long enough to pass her genes on to the next generation," Jia says quietly. "Did she manage that, in your universe?"

Sunni removes herself from the booth and refuses to read more. Misty takes over. "Uhh, yeah. She was injected with some kind of compound that accelerated her decline, which ultimately killed her. There's lots of notes about her genetic material, but not seeing anything about—oh. Hang on." Misty looks uncomfortable. "Post-mortem extraction of ova material, success. Fertilization attempts in a lab setting proved unsuccessful with unmodified genetic material from native male species. Autopsy findings from mid-section reveal unknown, uncategorized fluid sacs, containing broken uh, egg shells? Whatever the word is. Which might be the specimen's potential attempt at autogamy."

The five of us say nothing for a long while. A dusty memory springs to mind of my family going fishing in a stream somewhere in Cape Breton. I remember my father explaining how salmon returned to the same place to spawn, each year. Their instinct is so powerful, he'd said, that they could jump upstream.

I don't know the ins and outs of Jadore's biology. But I think now on the salmon, swimming against the current, and Jadore, smashing the Collective in the face with an altered vitaphage, gathering followers around a giant portal.

I look to Wil for confirmation. He nods slowly. "Could be."

"What?" Misty asks.

"Well, if we continue the timeline," I say, "When I was down at Sparkstone on January twenty-seventh with Gayarnu and Agailya, Jadore appeared and stole a ton of technology. Then disappeared before anyone could grab her. At the Final Battle, we see a portal. I don't think the portal is to another universe. It's to her home world. Maybe, Jadore's following her natural nesting instinct, and is just trying to get home."

"Why now? She's chock-full of mods," Misty exclaims. "She could have returned to her home world when she first made the portal."

"There was something off about her when we were in the hangar," Wil muses. "The Jadore we know doesn't run from hafelglob guards. And it was only a week from that time that Ingrid returned to Sparkstone at Gayarnu's request. I think she either caught the vitaphage or..." He pauses, shifting uncomfortably. "Or, maybe the ahmei, in retaliation, dose her with something to accelerate her cell decline, which would trigger this nesting instinct."

Jia rolls out a yoga mat and begins stretching. "Is there anything wrong with that? I don't understand how that has anything to do with her destroying Earth."

"A genetically modified species, with the ability to self-replicate, power-hungry, with no natural enemies arrives on a world. Minus the superintelligence, if this was just on Earth, we'd be treating this as an invasive species issue. But in space? A race of Jadores left unchecked, with portal technology, could easily invade and populate—" Wil's words from our examination of the Final Battle slam into me and I leap to my feet. "What do our sensors say now about the number of life-signs on the convoy? Because if it's *thousands...*"

Tiny symbols appear above the blips representing the convoy on the holographic projection. "Thousands, for sure," he confirms, keeping his gaze steadily on me.

Jia rises to her feet, flushed. "How can she carry thousands of fertilized eggs?"

"Extraction," Misty and I say together, with equal parts fascination and disgust. "Hidden in that convoy."

Sunni twists her lips. "The ship that gets destroyed...that's where the thousands of life-signs were. That's what I read, but it was confusing."

Wil re-checks the data in the holographic projection. He frowns. "I see confusing data here. Like someone has tried to mess with the sensors. Or maybe it's something to do with how Jadore can mask or change her bio-reading sometimes, and that's a trait manifesting in her eggs. They're on one ship, and then they're on another." He points to various ships in the convoy.

"So, we're going to separate Jadore from her *children* and give her over to the Collective? And maybe let those children die?" Jia asks disapprovingly.

We're getting into some sticky ethical territory. "You want Jadore to raise them to be like her, power-hungry, so they can create another Collective?"

Jia sets her jaw squarely. "We can't play gods and pass judgements on how her children will turn out. Though I suppose if you want, we can travel to the future and settle this quickly."

Wil looks thoughtful as he carefully comes between the two of us. "As long as we get Jadore and give her over to Councillor Ari-Faur so we can gauge the reaction, we can worry about the eggs and the portal on our next run. I'm inclined to agree that the Collective shouldn't have Jadore's eggs. Maybe the convoy disbands when they hear Jadore is gone, and the eggs are lost. Maybe Ari-Faur is the last surviving member of the Council and he's behind the explosion of Earth and we deal with him while we're on the ship. Maybe once Jadore and Ari-Faur are in this same place, they'll cancel each other out, and that will be that.

"We can speculate about the details, but we won't know more until we get onto the mother ship and see with our own senses what's going on and who is moving all the pieces. We have to set priorities for each run."

Jia sighs slowly and returns to her stretching. "Fine. I just don't want murdered unborn babies on my conscience."

They're fertilized embryos, I want to say, but Wil shakes his head at me. He's right. Now's not the time for that argument.

Misty breaks the tension. "So, priority for this run is, we grab Jadore when she's on the mother ship. We deal with the ant councillor, whether or not he's legit. And we try to see what happens to the eggs on the convoy. Uh, wait…" Misty trails off as she calls after Sunni as she ascends the staircase.

"Do whatever," Sunni says shortly, waving her hand over the

hologram. She stuffs earbuds into her ears. "I'm at my limit with this conversation." She disappears into the loft.

I think we all are. We spend the next few minutes making a list of items we need, and where I should jump to retrieve them: we decide to pick up handcuffs and heavy-duty gloves to protect against Jadore's electric powers. We also rummage through our supplies to ensure we have sacks and clothing suitable for sneaking around the mother ship.

Later, I join Sunni in the loft. It's still stuffy up here, but Misty and Sunni have moved their sleeping gear and decorated the room with stringed Christmas lights, posters of their favourite bands and movies, and small end tables that house tablets and even a few coffee table books.

Sunni sprawls across the large mattress, reading something on a tablet. When I poke my head through, she raises her eyebrows in question.

"Can I come up?" I ask.

"Sure," she says slowly. "You okay?"

I sit near the loft door and leave it open to let air circulate. Wil still needs to fix that.

Sunni shrugs. "For a fortune-teller, I'm not that good at knowin' if I'll ever be okay."

I smirk. "Has anything you've dreamt ever not come true?"

She doesn't answer immediately. "I think everything has come true, one way or another."

"One way or another?"

"Dreams aren't precise. Mine can be literal but sometimes they're layered. Complex. Just like any language. 'Sides. It's not like I get a dream each night about somethin' I wanna know. I spent a lot of time in someone else's head, tryin' send her messages. That's what I've gotten real good at."

Without those dreams, I wouldn't have known how to retrieve Sunni. "Have you had any more, since coming here?"

She fiddles with her tablet. "Ingrid..."

"If you've dreamt about..." I can't say his name to her. It's too cruel. I sigh. "If there's something you think I should know...I want to know it."

Again, she's quiet for a long while. "Whatever experiments your Agailya and Gayarnu are doin'...it's not enough. I don't know if the research we have is enough to help 'em, either. We can grab people outta time, but we can't bring 'em back from the dead."

It's not what I want to hear. Lips trembling, I nod, and I descend through the hatch, onto the staircase. It's all right. Once I travel back in time to rescue Ethan and the rest of them, I'll jump Ethan to our present time. He can't catch the altered vitaphage if he's not exposed to it. Dreams or no dreams, I won't let the future win.

CHAPTER 12

"Approaching mother ship. Ready?"

We've arrived at our fourth run through the Final Battle. In less than fifteen minutes, Jadore will be in our custody. We'll be one step closer to figuring out how to save all of humanity when Earth explodes.

And maybe, just maybe, we'll be one step closer to figuring out how to prevent all of this destruction in the first place.

Jia has cloaked us, and with Wil's talents, we've snuck through the forcefield protecting the hangar bay on the Collective mother ship. From the moment we arrive, the place buzzes with the remaining pilots, which include a mix of fishmen and a squat bug-like race, who man the last of the sleek fighters. They zip into the fray. As far as we know, our entrance into the mouth of the mother ship has gone unnoticed.

That's about to change as Jia prepares to disembark with Misty, Wil, and myself. We're wearing flat backpacks stuffed with prepared goodies, holsters with alt-universe tech on belts, and outfits fit for sneaking around in enemy territory. I chose dark leggings, layered with a stretchy dark skirt with pockets, a long-sleeved green shirt, and of course, heelless, tall boots with soft soles. Jia sports dark yoga pants and a loose-fitting tank; Misty comes armed with a green army jacket and track pants; Wil wears comfortable denim and a dark t-shirt.

As soon as the four of us touch down on the mother ship, the *Blind Elephant* becomes visible in the bay. The remaining aliens in the bay shout in confusion and raise an alarm. A squad of well-armoured—and well-armed—fishmen run into the bay from a double-sliding door. The four of us run for the door as the aliens fire their laser weapons indiscriminately around the room. They know our tricks. Wil catches his arm in the door as the last of the squad makes it in the room and holds it open for us as we slip into the passageway.

The passageway lighting blinks yellow with alarm. A low thrum ripples through our feet in time with a wail, to accommodate and remind every potential alien physiology that the ship is under attack. It's not even safe to talk next steps. Weapons fire narrowly grazes my shoulder and I yelp as we duck.

My sound is barely audible above the squabbling of the two factions on either side of the passageway. Fishmen exchange volleys with humans that I immediately clock as ahmei in disguise: tall, lithe, washed-out hair, and sharp pale eyes. One even has green scaly webbing between their fingers. They struggle to pull a trigger on their weapon as three fishmen blast laser-fire in their direction. The heat of the missiles singes my hair, darkens Misty's shirt, and one bolt catches Wil in the boot. He shakes it, grimacing. Superficial wound.

The ahmei fighting the fishmen? Is this happening because we deliver Jadore to the Collective – or because we *don't?*

"Says something about a mutiny in progress!" Misty shouts over the alien intercom warnings.

We scurry towards the ahmei, squeeze behind them, and find the adjoining passageway empty, for now. But with all the screaming and blasting going on, that will change in a moment. I rub my shoulder gingerly. We can't continue like this. Someone is going to run into us or worse, we'll be incinerated. Jia's cloak doesn't shield us from firepower.

"I sense Jadore better now. She's up a couple of floors. Get in there." Wil feels around a bulkhead and it unlatches. The hatch opens to a narrow vertical shaft, lined with a ladder that runs seamlessly between the decks. Metal rungs disappear into the darkness above and below. It's going to be a snug fit, but at least it's difficult to fire weapons in there.

We squeeze inside and secure the bulkhead behind us, becoming momentarily visible so we can climb with ease.

"Did Gayarnu or any of the ahmei at Sparkstone talk about mutinies?" Jia asks.

"No, they sounded like they didn't want to get involved in Collective politics, what with everyone dying and all." I already feel a cramp coming on. I need to take Jia up on that daily exercise routine she's been pushing.

"Maybe Agailya's death changes things," Wil says. "Let's get off here."

We emerge into a near-identical passageway, minus the fighting. The alarms continue to blare. Just as Wil picks a direction, a fishmen guard steps out of the nearest doorway, weapon at the ready, and speeds towards us. We dart out of his way and enter from where he came, and come face-to-face with a holding cell filled with dozens of humans.

The cramped space, no larger than my bedroom back home,

contains one data console, set before a blue forcefield sectioning a third of the room. The humans behind the forcefield are young; they can't be more than twenty-five. Their dirtied clothes and roughed-up faces tell the story of a group of refugees who have attempted to fight for their freedom, but have been caught by the enemy. Some of the faces I recognize from around Sparkstone. Others aren't familiar. From the multitude of ethnicities present, and the sprinkling of Spanish and an Eastern European language I don't recognize, I conclude they're from the sister schools across the world. The thought of them lined up in aquatic transformation pods, altered against their will to serve the Collective, makes my stomach turn. Judging by the fact that they're stuck behind a forcefield and not using any talents to escape, I assume they don't have any useful manifested superpowers. Regardless, the Collective will find a way to make use of them.

We don't dare speak. I implore my friends silently to help me rescue them.

Wil shakes his head. I can imagine what he's thinking: we don't have time for this. They're safer behind that forcefield than in the line of fire outside.

But if Earth is truly doomed, then these students are among the remaining members of our species. We can't leave them here among the sparring factions of the Collective.

Misty presses her lips together and shakes her head at me. The distrust in her gaze is palpable. We have to be *so* quiet. Who knows what kind of power these folks have and what their allegiances are? Jia quickly examines the fifty-odd students and regards me sceptically. She can't possibly hide that many people while we traverse the ship for Jadore.

They're right. We can't take them with us. Even packing them onto the *Blind Elephant* would be a tight squeeze. Unless we reveal ourselves, hijack another ship, and shepherd them to safety, these confused students are staying put.

The first time we embarked on this ship, Jadore had captured us and murdered Sunni.

The last time I was here, I'd witnessed Tilly's murder in the name of science.

The murdering stops today, even if we have to repeat this day thousands of times to get it right.

The door we came through automatically closes. It's the only way in and out. Wil pulls us towards it: there's a momentary lull in the hallway. We should take our chance and move. As the four of us reposition within the room, I accidently bump my hip into the console. Unfortunately, it hasn't been secured to the floor. This room isn't normally a holding cell. The console wobbles.

The humans can't see us, as we're invisible. But some of them look up, their interests piqued.

"That thing moved!" yells one of the students, pointing at the console workstation.

Another student sighs. "Stop, no it didn't. For the last time, you're not telekinetic, okay?"

A third student mocks the previous in a condescending tone, which sparks an argument within the group.

The doors spring open. Wil recoils. He didn't trigger the mechanism. The four of us quietly scramble backwards as two people we recognize march into the room.

Shane Richmond has manifested no powers, and he likely never will. He relies on bullying and his large, imposing frame to intimidate folks into submission. His collaboration with the Collective began when he believed they were a secret agency fighting aliens. I wonder what he believes now, and how he has twisted his personal beliefs to remain in his position of power.

Emily Foller strides in after him. Her demonic bodily modifications have intensified. I only recognize her by her psychopathic, fanged smile. Striking orange-red eyes appraise the trapped humans, as if they're prime cuts of meat. Her horns curl behind her head, and she's bedazzled them with cheap, gold gems. I hold my breath, wondering if she can sense body heat.

Laura, the third in their trio, appears strangely absent. She's the real problem. Her super-enhanced hearing will expose us in seconds.

My friends and I exchange worried glances. Shane and Emily unknowingly guard the only way in and out of the room.

"Time's up, freaks. Gotta choose," Shane says. "Mistress-Commander Jadore has a generous offer on the table. Join us, we get to go to the promised land and build a better human race with technology beyond our wildest dreams. Or, well, you can be processed into food for said journey. Pretty easy choice, right? Let's get going."

The students exchange glances. Someone steps forward.

"We'll go," she says nervously.

"Yeah. Figures. Remember, if you try anything..." He pats a holstered weapon at his belt and gestures to Emily. She strikes a pose, as if she's about to perform an elaborate tap number. To her, this is a game.

Misty pulls me closer to her as Shane rounds the console and operates the controls. It wobbles like an unsteady table beneath his touch. He scowls. "Didn't those fish-brains bolt this down?"

"No time," Emily replies. She licks a finger and presses it against the forcefield. It steams and sparks at her touch, which elicits a delighted yelp from her throat. The people within the forcefield recoil, uninterested in turning into bacon.

An opening large enough for one person to pass through appears in the field. The closest person steps out as Emily opens the door. Out in the hallway, four fishmen stand on high alert with massive weapons.

"Bay Two," Shane says to them.

Emily repeats Shane's words in a hiss language. They hiss an affirmative.

"And hey, good behaviour gets rewarded," Shane says to everyone as they obediently wait to exit the forcefield. "You want to breathe underwater? Well, now you can. You want different coloured eyes, or get rid of that ugly mole? We can do that for you."

Emily's toothy grin reveals her sharpened fangs. "You're all getting gills, is what I've been told. You're all little fishies, isn't that right?"

One by one, the students file out from behind the forcefield and into the hallway with the guards. The students could overpower the guards, knock out Shane, and take on Emily. But none of them do. The despair and hopelessness of the situation shackles them to this ship. I can only imagine what has gone down on Earth during the past few months: disease, upheaval, overt alien invasion.

Once again, I implore my friends with my unspoken concern. We have to rescue these people.

We don't have time for this, Wil says telepathically.

A couple students shift their gazes and linger on our position. Perhaps some of them can hear us or maybe even see us. We aren't so far gone in our humanity that we can't help them.

Not on this run, Wil replies, to my thoughts and theirs. *But now that we know they are here, we can plan a rescue.*

In the hallway, the captured humans march with the fishmen guards towards Bay Two, wherever that might be. Wil has started to become antsy, and Misty, holding onto him, shoots him an annoyed look. Once the last of the humans have left the room, more fishmen guards bring up the rear and Emily hovers in the doorway. "You heard from Mistress-Commander Jadore yet?"

"Yeah, she's taking care of something in the big lab. If you see any more rebel aliens, just throw them out an airlock." He deactivates the forcefield and joins her at the door. "Did I overhear you talking to those fish people about a lock on the systems? 'Cause I couldn't access much from there. Is that because of my status, or...?"

"Yeah, no, that's all part of Mistress Jadore's plan to make sure we're not followed. C'mon, I made sure you got one of the good seats in the shuttle."

Emily pulls him out of the room by the cuff of his shirt. Just as the doors are about to close, Wil jams his hand between them and using his talents, implores it to remain half-open for the four of us to squeeze through.

Shane recoils from Emily and spins, staring directly through us.

"What?" Emily demands, impatient. She follows his gaze. "Mutineers?"

Furrowing his brow, he searches the area and reaches for his weapon. They continue down the hallway on high alert. "What's the intelligence on Jia Fields, Ingrid Stanley, and that bunch?"

We follow behind them, each step a deliberate art. Emily's laugh echoes above the alien alarm. "Oh, they supposedly died in that giant portal explosion at Sparkstone, but the Mistress has been telling everyone they're alive. She saw them. She has this whole plan to get back at them. Very hush-hush."

I tense up. Emily and Shane get further ahead due to our slow-but-steady pace.

"Hush-hush? Like, if you have status, you can know about it?"

"I mean, I know a *little*, but you know how Jadore is." She smacks him suddenly upside the head. "You don't think they're here, do you? Did you see them?"

"No, I..." He looks concerned as he trails off. "Can you sense them?"

Emily stops. We halt. It's a long thirty seconds.

She touches something behind her ear. "Laura? You free? How are internal sensors at my location?" A pause. Emily scoffs. "Well, what are they called? I don't know how an alien *ship* works! Just tell me if we're the only two humans on this floor." More silence. Shane begins to pace. "What do you mean my life-sign isn't registering? Didn't maintenance fix that yesterday? Yes of *course* I know there's a battle going on, why do you think I'm trying to get the subhumans to a shuttle?"

Wil gestures for us to turn around. We pick up the pace and run as quietly as we can away from Shane and Emily's position, round a corner, and come to an elevator shaft with an accompanying ladder. The passageway appears to bend and double back the way we came, running parallel to Shane and Emily's position and out of their sight.

"Did you hear that...?" Shane's voice is faint.

We can bypass them, Wil says. *It will take an extra minute or so. Let's run for it.*

Misty hits a button by the elevator to cause a distraction, and then we make a run for it.

As quickly and as quietly as we can, we scoot down the parallel passageway. Misty readies an icy shuriken as we pass Emily. Her orange stare flits to our position as we rush by.

"Do the alien rebels have body cloaks?" Emily shouts. Then: "Laura, you *told* me this floor was *secure!*" And: "I don't care what an ant-person told you, we're *not* taking orders from *ants!* Or weird fish-humans!" Her voice fades. "I don't know, they're *all* aliens, just fight them if they're not with us!"

The ahmei, Jadore's splinter group, and Councillor Ari-Faur are battling for control of the mother ship, while every part of our thread winds through the tapestry, willing the art we create to live for twenty more minutes.

We reach another fork in the passageway, a set of elevators, and a security door. Wil sets to work on the security door while Misty breaks formation, opens the elevator, and presses every button. She rejoins us triumphantly.

"So, on the next run we take care of Jadore's eggs, and then we deal with the humans trapped on the mother ship?" I whisper.

"We should do it now, instead of getting Jadore. We can get her next time," Jia hisses.

"We're prepared for Jadore now," Wil replies steadily, placing another hand on the massive security door.

Jia regards him sarcastically. "Are you prepared for what's behind this door?"

"Are you?" he retorts. "I'm following Jadore's mental and physiological signals."

"Emily's still here, shh," I say.

"Once Jadore is taken care of, we can do whatever we want," Misty says impatiently, as if I haven't spoken. "But if Jadore's in charge on the mother ship, who—?"

Her words sputter into unintelligible syllables as Wil hacks the security door and it slides open, revealing the scientific heart of the Collective mother ship.

The testing chamber where I watched Tilly die had been just a fraction of the Collective's devotion to science on this ship. This lab sprawls across multiple transparent platforms suspended in a vast cylindrical chamber, each level connected by shimmering ladders and slopes that pulse with prismatic light. Holographic displays hover at workstations on each level, their alien symbols cycling through countless permutations in a hypnotic dance. The air hums with static-like energy, punctuated by the vibration of the alarm outside, and the whirring of bio-mechanical arms grasping and depositing bottled specimens into various machines and stations infused with similar bio-tech as the Collective's headquarters. The science never stops, despite the turmoil.

Curved walls of a silver, pearlescent material rise from floor to ceiling. Emergency lighting bathes everything in an intense blue glow, reflecting off the polished surfaces. My eyes become strained as I drink in the multitude of technology, but soon I focus on the prize.

Through the floor I see Jadore, standing at a station directly above us. She's not alone. Seems like we're not the only ones after her today.

"—and according to the treaties signed by our people—" Gayarnu intones above us as they point a firearm at Jadore's forehead.

A tremor runs through the lab, caused by the conflicts outside, as we scramble up the nearest suspended slope to the platform where Gayarnu and a group of heavily armed ahmei-human hybrids hold Jadore hostage.

Gayarnu's physicality has changed dramatically since I last saw them at Sparkstone. They look frighteningly close to the alternate universe version of themselves, but instead of controlling the Earth, they're leading a band of fish-human rebels in a revolution.

The six ahmei would be easy to mistake as humans with aquatic modifications, were it not for their ethereal movements, beautiful voices, and the vocal range required for the ahmei language. Only two of the group have opted for human-like eyes, and both are an unnaturally bright shade of turquoise and blue.

Although there's a weapon pointed at her, Jadore seems unperturbed. Just like the last time I saw her, she's dressed in a tight black body suit, but she's wearing a lab coat over it. Her long black hair, once luscious, has lost some of its shine. It's curled in a messy updo. "I don't recognize your treaties with the Collective. Most of the councillors have been dead for days. Or haven't you noticed, with your own little insurrection?"

"What are the codes?" Gayarnu demands, jerking their weapon impatiently.

"Not telling," Jadore replies. Her tone mocks the ahmei modular way of speaking, which irritates several of the modified ahmei.

If the Collective has been defeated—or is being defeated, in this battle—then they don't need Jadore, and maybe we never deliver her to Councillor Ari-Faur.

We should still make the attempt, if only to gather the data. If they don't leave within thirty seconds, we'll have to expose ourselves, Wil says. *We're fast approaching the point where I lose track of Jadore.*

"We don't have to be enemies," Gayarnu says, attempting to introduce calm into their tone. "We can create a new council, or any kind of rulership we want."

"I already have my own Collective, thank you, and my future doesn't include you. You can drop that weapon. Today is not my death day. But you already know that." She glares at Gayarnu.

Something passes over Gayarnu's face at that, the same expression I saw in them when I visited them at Sparkstone. A secret knowing of the future, that comes from time travel.

I can't wait any longer. I draw my firearm from its holster, point it at Jadore, and break from the grip of invisibility.

Oh, fine, Wil concedes, and Jia releases my friends from her world as well.

Jadore is the only alien who isn't surprised by our appearance. "You're here. Finally."

Gayarnu and the ahmei turn their weapons towards us in shock. One of the ahmei with human eyes attempts to move against us, but Gayarnu stays them with an outstretched hand. "Not now." Then, they add, "You're here."

"You see, they're desperate to attack anyone and everyone who boards the mother ship," Jadore says dryly.

"We're here to defend our research against you and the puritan humans who have somehow fallen into your pond," Gayarnu retorts. Although they have the best grasp of human idioms, their anger has affected their delivery. The surprise at their appearance must be plain on our faces, because Gayarnu adds, "We have married our ahmei bodies with our human forms. Some research suggests this will keep us resilient against the altered vitaphage. And it allows us to breathe the air here."

Of course, the ahmei are primarily aquatic. Jadore sneers. "Ugly." She removes a data chip resembling a USB and hides it in a fist and shakes it at me. "You really think you could capture and deliver me to the Collective?"

How could she know of our plan? I hold her self-satisfied stare, knowing that I cannot hide my surprise. She flicks her fingers at me and I recoil. Lightning isn't forthcoming. A single spark emits from her thumb and falls limply to the tile. A guffaw escapes her, covering the flash of annoyance that rocks her unlined, smooth face.

"What's happened to the Collective?" Jia asks.

"The councillors I control have joined me on my quest for the promised land. The rest? Dead by now. I'm surprised you five haven't gotten sick yet. Maybe you'll get a tickle in your throats after you're done on this ship, if you're not caught in the crossfire."

"The member species with sway who haven't been bullied to her side stand with the ahmei and the dozens of other cultures who have been conquered and unfairly treated as second-class citizens within the Collective. We are striking back against tyranny, and those on this ship still loyal to a dead organization that doesn't care about them, and never has." Rage burns in Gayarnu's eyes, matched in intensity by her fellows.

"What are the codes for?" I ask.

"Jadore has compromised key systems on the mother ship to prevent anyone from chasing her people to this promised land," Gayarnu replies.

"Give them the codes," I say.

Once again, a strange look passes Jadore's face, not unlike the one she had when we stole the *Blind Elephant*. A kind of smug amusement. As if she's immune to hardship and believes herself the protagonist of this epic.

"What?" I step forward and press the weapon to her forehead.

"Don't kill her," Gayarnu says in warning. "She needs to suffer for her crimes."

"Yes, don't kill me, Ingrid," Jadore says. "You and I have work to do."

"We do?" I match her sick sweetness with contempt. "If that's the case, give them the codes so we can talk."

Misty's hands swirl with ice and fire. Wil and Jia raise their weapons. But Jadore seems oddly unconcerned. She considers me carefully, and as she holds my gaze, she flicks her hand at the altered ahmei. They duck instinctively. Misty creates a ball of flame that hovers above her palm, ready to be thrown. But no lightning emerges from Jadore's fingertips. She waves the ahmei away as she begins a recitation as intense as casting a spell. It's a string of English numbers, long clear notes in the ahmei tongue, and a three-syllable word in a language I don't recognize, but it's hiss-heavy. The d'ntak native tongue.

It's possible these aren't the real codes. Maybe at this point, it doesn't matter. We just need to get Jadore alone so we can remove her from this battle.

Gayarnu nods briskly at Jadore's admission, sings something to her team, and then says in English, "We'll see if she's telling the truth. If she's not, we'll return and force it out in a different manner."

I doubt they'll return in time to see her before she disappears, Wil says.

As Gayarnu leads her reticent team across the transparent platform towards the nearest exit, I call after them. Giving Jadore as wide a berth as I can without losing my balance on the platform, I circumnavigate the console workstation and close the distance between myself and Gayarnu. "I know this is a big ask, but if you have the manpower, please find a way to rescue the humans on their way to Bay Two."

"Say no more," Gayarnu says, and sings brightly to her comrades. They reply in harmony, each with a different, rich voice that creates a tapestry in my mind: several fighters intercepting the convoy, surrounding the ships in a web-like beam, and pulling them away from the portal. I have a long way to go in learning their language, but the synesthesia bridges a gap. I wonder if we can last long enough in a future run to see them carry out this plan.

"Thank you," I say, bowing my head.

A few of the ahmei peer at me with their curious fish eyes, and I wonder if they are the same ones from the underground library, who came to sing during Wil's death and the destruction of the portal. The one with the human eyes, who had attempted to move against us, stands unnaturally close and doesn't take their gaze from me. There is something familiar about this one. Had they been part of Agailya's group, who had come to sing at the portal? If so, perhaps this is evidence that I have already gone back to save them—and Ethan.

"Thank *you*," Gayarnu says, mimicking my bow. They whistle and intone a series of notes—a war call. The ahmei return the call, and follow their new leader out the exit, back into the fray.

Wil looks disapprovingly at me. I don't care. He takes a bold step towards Jadore. "Let's move."

"Don't insult me with that weapon," Jadore says smoothly. She places a hand on a strange, heavy-looking canister. "There's nothing you can do to stop me, dead man."

"The certainty of knowing my death means I can take this risk," he replies.

"Hmm. Wise words. All the more reason to ensure your legacy."

Misty approaches Wil with a fireball at the ready. "Yeah. Okay. 'Nough talking. Come with us, or we'll fry your eggs!"

She reduces her fireball and throws it at Jadore's shoulder, deliberately missing. While Jadore is distracted, Misty snatches the canister with one hand. Despite the liquid within, she palms it easily. Her hand glows orange and the smell of plastic fills the air.

"No!" Jadore attempts to retaliate with desperate lightning, but Misty holds out an icy hand and holds the canister even tighter with her heated grip. Jadore stops short. She spits curses in her native tongue.

"Misty," Jia says disapprovingly under her breath.

"Don't—don't," Jadore sputters. She holds out her hands, not to attack, but to plead. "Put down the container. Don't hurt them."

"I won't put down the container," Misty replies, just as sweetly. "Surrender to us. Do what we say. And we'll leave these things alone."

Jadore searches each of us for pity and finds none. I feel torn, but after all the suffering she has put us through? We've finally found something she cares more about than herself.

"My loyal followers will come and turn you all into paste," she says. Her voice wavers.

No one is coming, Wil confirms.

Jadore swivels her body to me. An icicle shoots from Misty's hand and sails across Jadore's front, missing her by a centimetre. It falls to a lower platform and shatters on the transparent floor. A warning shot. Jadore closes her dark eyes and presses her palms together. "You must leave my eggs be. Tell Misty to put them down...and I'll go with you."

We make no guarantees, Wil says telepathically. I'm unsure if he says it to everyone or only to me.

I stare at the canister. Wil's comment about life with no *feeling* springs to mind. My stomach drops.

"I take it by your behaviour that this is the only container," I say evenly.

"It is," she replies.

If that's true, it's possible it still ends up on the convoy and potentially destroyed, if our data from the Final Battle is correct. I look to Wil for confirmation.

I believe she's being sincere, but she's not the easiest one to read, he replies. *We need to get to Councillor Ari-Faur. I'll tell Sunni to come 'round.*

I remove the heavy-duty gloves and handcuffs from my pack, slip the gloves on, and secure Jadore's wrists. Just in case her powers decide to work.

"I'm keeping this, for now," Misty says. "If you try to escape, it burns. If someone comes for us with weapons, it burns."

"You've been clear," Jadore intones.

"Follow us," Wil says.

When we step into the passageway, the fighting has died down considerably. The alarm continues to warn us through sound, sensation, and sight to watch for intruders. We're no longer invisible. If we take the elevator down a couple of decks, we'll reach Councillor Ari-Faur in a couple of minutes.

Jadore side-eyes me. "I gave him his book back." Her voice is a whisper.

I frown. She's talking about Campbell and his treatise, I think. "Why?"

"It's part of the plan," she says simply, as if this answers the question. "I ensured my legacy. If you were smart, you'd do the same."

I don't like this line of conversation one bit. "We're fine, thanks."

"No, you're not."

I'm taken aback by the seriousness in her tone, and maybe that's why she manages to catch me off guard. The cuffs clatter to the floor with a hair pin and the cold barrel of a weapon presses against my temple.

My friends spin around defensively, weapons trained on Jadore. "Give her up, or we destroy this," Misty shouts, shaking the container.

Go, Ingrid. You have her, Wil says.

It's true. With Jadore this close, I can teleport us both out. Which will strand my friends here.

Jadore's hand trembles. For the briefest moment, uncertainty passes over her green face. Then, she slams her body against the bulkhead and something unlatches. A hidden door slides open. She yanks me inside and the door hisses shut.

Jadore throws me to the floor and hits a button. *HISS. PHOO!*

My stomach drops into my intestines violently, like an elevator plummeting twenty storeys. I'm screaming. Jadore's laughing. I'm upside down until gravity rights me, and as I stare out a giant port, I realize this isn't part of the mother ship.

We're in an escape pod, tumbling into the battle.

The craft is about the size of the *Blind Elephant* cockpit and has a similar layout. As Jadore climbs to her feet, sputtering and poorly attempting to hide the pain in her stomach, I notice the ship is flying on autopilot towards the budding convoy.

It starts with a few ships, but others quickly join the group. She hails the other ships and speaks in the d'ntak hiss language, and then in English, she says, "Power source secure. Hurry for the portal. Home and a new start await us!"

"You gave up your legacy for me?" I say spitefully.

Jadore sneers as she holsters her weapon, pulls the controls towards her, removes the autopilot settings, and taps a heel against a cylinder resting at her feet. "Don't flatter yourself."

A near-identical canister. This one doesn't tremble with the ship's turbulence, lacks sheen in its material, and is completely solid. Perhaps she has several canisters, or the one in Misty's hands is fake. My heart sinks into my stomach as I remember the sensor malfunction Wil and Sunni experienced. Thousands of life-signs on a tiny vessel—

—that's going to get destroyed *real* soon.

My heart pounds in my ears. I can get myself out of here, and Jadore if I choose, but there's so much I need to know first. "How did you know we were coming to capture you on the Council's behalf?"

"Campbell filled in the gaps for me. Don't try any tricks." She catches my surprise and makes a face. "Why are you surprised? You knew this would happen. All of it."

He's working with her. No wonder she was able to amass this much power, this fast. "He's been feeding you information?"

She looks smug. "If I say yes, would you be jealous?"

"No," I lie. He refuses to tell me anything. Which has made life harder than it should be. Jadore hasn't been chosen for a special mission. She's a pox on the entire galaxy. The only reason he'd deal with her is to get something he wants.

Jadore continues to prattle on as we pick up speed. The portal, a bright artificial fish-eye resting on top of an asteroid, blinks as if waking up from a long nap. The interior of the portal shimmers in a green, swirling light, like a whirlpool. I feel ill.

"This promised land everyone's talking about. It's your home world, isn't it."

"For now," she replies. "My children will burrow into the mud and grow strong there. Campbell has foreseen it."

"And what about you?"

"Of course, I'll be there to guide them." She says nothing more on that.

I wonder what's happening within her now—how much she's aware that she's likely going to die. I feel a pang of guilt for even broaching the subject. I try to shake that feeling. If Campbell told her we'd attempt to capture her and trade her to the Collective, she must have released the vitaphage upon the Collective first, killing them and endangering humanity. We thought we'd be sparing lives by turning in Jadore. In reality, our timing was all wrong.

I stare at the canister. Campbell couldn't have told her everything. This vessel is going to explode soon. Those eggs are toast.

Unless I teleport them out with me.

"So, you rebuilt the portal with stolen technology. How's it different than before?" If I can keep her talking, she won't notice if I creep closer to the canister.

"This version is far more sophisticated. With a few hints from Campbell, I found the right materials. And so much faster when I don't have to go through the official channels. I won't have to strap you in this time, will I? We have to time this right." She summons a digital window over the canopy. "We have three minutes left."

My stomach tightens. No, we probably have less than a minute until the fighters swoop in. "Until what, Jadore?"

"Don't be obtuse, Ingrid."

I'm so done with this. I grab the thick hairs growing out of her scaly arms and yank them. Surprised, she yelps. Sparks dance from her fingers and land on the equipment. Alarms blare. I ignore them and press her chest with my boot, slamming her into the console.

"The mother ship engine isn't the only thing you rigged to explode, is it."

Jadore doesn't fight me. She just shrugs. The ship continues on autopilot towards its destination. "You want me to spell it out for you or have you figured it out yet?"

I don't want her to say it. She's the one who rigged the mother ship to fire on Earth. I shake my head at her, disgusted. "You didn't have to rig any explosions. You didn't have to do *any* of this."

"Didn't I?" Her voice is suddenly cold. Hollow.

"So why do it?" I demand.

"Because," she replies stonily, "it's inevitable, given your power, that humanity will attempt to eliminate me and my kind. I'm ensuring my legacy."

The way she says it, I believe it. I'm not going to travel to her home planet and destroy it. That's not the kind of person I am. Not yet. But it could be, if I continuously watch my home shatter from a new perspective every time I return here. By destroying Earth, she has instigated the very action she has sought to prevent. Filled with rage and remorse, staring at the person who destroys my home, I want nothing more to hurt her the way she has hurt me.

She's planned it all. Blow up a planet, disrupt the battle, give people something to focus on as the convoy rushes for the portal. My friends had been right. The Collective wouldn't destroy their prized investment.

"Campbell doesn't know everything," I say darkly. "And you shouldn't trust everything he says, either."

"And you do?"

The shuttle jostles us before I can answer. I attempt to understand what's happening from the myriads of digital screens populating the canopy. The convoy ships cradle us as we accelerate towards the portal and appear to be hailing us with concern. Jadore swings in the pilot seat as more warnings pop up in intrusive windows. She waves them away.

"Nothing will hurt us. He promised," Jadore mutters.

Ingrid, are you on the craft I think you're on? Wil asks telepathically. *We're coming for you and we're cloaked. Hang on.*

And that's when I see the radar view, in the top right corner of the canopy. The digital window border flashes yellow in warning, and though I can't read any of the Collective languages, I step closer to the canister and prepare to jump.

A dotted line slides out from the largest red triangle on the radar view and beelines for us. Even though I know I'm on the vessel that is destroyed by fighters, and that I can teleport away from danger at any time, I have a sudden, strong urge to change the future.

"Evade!" I scream at Jadore. I shove her shoulder to get her to move, even though I know nothing about the controls. "Incoming—"

The enemy missile hits us square in the stern. Jadore and I slam into the canopy, which is just a digital screen, not a real window. I slide down the bulkhead and onto the floor, bruised and dizzy. I don't have time to be hurt. We're about to be space dust.

It's hot in here. Fires engulf every surface. It feels like we're spinning out of control, but gravity's still intact. Jadore's on the floor. Groaning. Sparks fly from the controls. Panels, hanging. Wires, exposed. An astronaut in a spacesuit, standing before me, untouched by the disaster. She's offering me a pile of laundry and a space helmet. The visor slides open. It's me. Her eyes crinkle with knowing.

"Go," she says.

"Can we save Earth?" I ask her, accepting the pile, wondering for a moment if I'm dreaming. Some of the folded pile drops to the floor. It's a spacesuit. Just one.

"You know you can," she replies.

I blink and she's gone.

Swearing, I throw the suit and its accompanying gloves and helmet at Jadore. She groans. Blood pours from a wound on her head.

"This ship is going to explode. Put that on and get into the airlock."

Panicking, she looks to the broken digital screen and climbs to her feet. "But—"

"Fine, your eggs are going to die with the ship. Good luck surviving in space without my help." I activate my wristband and a cool, slimy substance covers my body. I breathe in. It smells like rubber and my own breath. I fiddle with the airlock. Sparks singe my hands. If nothing had been protecting me, I would have gotten a burn. "Open this!"

Jadore struggles to put on the suit. "I'm trying to get dressed!"

Wil's voice invades our heads. *Ingrid, incoming!*

Under one arm, Jadore holds her helmet, and scoops down to pick up her canister. "He said you'd help me in my time of duress. And I knew—"

It's as if Jadore's body has been attached to a long fishing rod, and the person reeling her in has yanked her across a fiery, starry night. The shuttle? One moment, it's all metal and fire. The next, the dead vacuum swallows it whole and everything around me spins. I can't swim in this strange ocean but I'm not drowning. I can't find right side up. Colours blur around me, and my flesh crawls.

Ingrid. Grab—now!

Wil's voice is the only thing I can trust. I hug something soft and wriggling. It's Jadore. Her face is exposed to the vacuum. Her helmet is nowhere in sight. But she's gripping her canister like it's a life raft.

We're still cartwheeling in zero-gravity. Jadore has seconds. I'm not going to let her die. Not today. Because today, I'm not a monster.

I press my wristband against her head and brush some of the slimy substance across her frosty skin. It starts to spread towards her left eye. It's not extending fast enough. I'm going to have to teleport us out.

Something grabs me hard. I scream, but the slime muffles the sound.

SWOOSH. HISS.

A familiar airlock encloses us. My body remembers which way is down as Jadore and I hit the floor. Hot air and the smell of hand sanitizer wash over my senses. As the clouds dissipate with another hiss from behind us, I hear Jadore cough and sputter.

"They're okay!" Misty shouts.

Someone helps me to my feet and taps my wrist. Jia. I tap my wristband obligingly and the body-forming slime reverse-oozes back into the band. I never thought the recycled air of the *Blind Elephant* would smell so sweet.

We set Jadore on the bench in the cockpit. The blood from her head wound seeps everywhere. Misty keeps on iron grip on the alien's shoulder. Jia straps back in to the opposite bench and resumes concentrating on her invisibility.

"What will you do with me now?" Jadore demands.

"You'll answer for your crimes," Jia replies.

Jadore sputters a laugh. "And you are to be my jury and executioner?"

Don't say anything else to provoke her, Wil warns. *I might be able to reach Councillor Ari-Faur telepathically to let him know we have her.*

She cranes her neck to see the controls. "Where are you taking me?"

Misty clamps down on her. "Stop."

"No," Jadore says. "You won't succeed."

When she'd attempted to use her powers in the hangar, she'd failed. I'd believed the gloves would have prevented some of the damage to come. Turns out, she's been holding back, waiting for the perfect moment to let loose.

A hot, white sensation rips through the floor, travels up my body and the bodies of my friends, and passes throughout the cabin.

We're suddenly hurdling through space. The navigation controls sizzle. The ship has been engulfed with white lightning. I search for the convoy from the canopy, but the ship is doing cartwheels. Everything's a blur.

My friends cry my name and urge me to jump anywhere else but here. At this rate, we might be hurtling into the sun. Low level shocks rattle my teeth as I grasp a happy thought. Jadore's container remains with us and is not on that convoy. They were not destroyed, as we had thought. I feel as if I have changed the future in a small way, and I can't wait to tell Campbell the next time I see him.

Perhaps then, he'll trust me enough to let me in on his grand plans. Like he did with Jadore.

As I come to, I'm pushing against metal. My body screams for safety. Around me, voices and clambering. We all want the same thing: escape this metal prison.

What remains of the airlock hisses open, releasing a plume of acrid smoke into the humid air. I stumble out, my friends close behind, coughing and squinting against the harsh sunlight. My boots sink into hot sand, the grains finding their way through the seams and shifting beneath my soles.

An island unfolds before us, a mere speck in the vast ocean, barely five hundred meters across at its widest point. Thick, clustered palm trees crowd us, their fronds whispering above the relentless rhythm of waves. A ragged gash of blackened earth and debris—our ship's violent path of descent—bisects this tiny refuge.

I take a few unsteady steps, my legs wobbly from the crash. Twisted metal and shattered hull fragments litter the ground, some still hot to the touch. Our ship, once sleek and powerful, now lies crumpled and half-buried at the island's center, its form grotesquely folded in on itself. Sparks dance across exposed circuitry, and the faint pulse of the sh-winil trapped in their tubes cast an eerie blue glow over the wreckage. The air hangs heavy with the mingled scents of ozone, salt spray, and something metallic—blood? I can't tell.

Jadore is the last one to crawl from the wreckage, carrying a canister under one arm, and deftly scurries across the sand towards the lapping waves of the shore.

Heat—close and more searing than the sun above—whizzes past my shoulder. Misty. The fireball cuts off Jadore's path and paints the sand black. Jadore recoils and falls backwards onto the sand, hugging the canister to her chest as she collapses.

"Don't even think about it," Misty says.

Jadore opens her mouth and hisses. She lifts a hand and sparks fly between her fingers.

Sunni raises her gun and points it at the canister, advancing slowly towards our enemy. "Who's the faster shot?"

"You wouldn't." Jadore moves her lightning hand and points it at Sunni.

Misty prepares another fireball and tears towards Jadore. "Not again."

"Stop!" I yell. "No one wants to do anything they'd regret later, right?"

"I will not regret killing her," Misty says sinisterly.

The wind picks up, blowing the smoke of the wreckage towards us. We share a sputtered cough. Above, there are no signs of battle. We must have arrived sometime before the battle. And before the destruction of our planet.

"Everyone check your phones." Wil's command carries over the wind, filled with urgency.

Sunni, Misty, and I share a glance. None of us want to take our attention from Jadore, lest she dive into the ocean and escape our reach. Misty raises her prepared fireball slowly and nods to me.

I slowly reach into my pocket. My phone is hotter than the air around us and takes a minute to respond to my touch. Jadore's frantic gaze flits from me to Misty's fireball.

"No cell service," I say.

"We're in the middle of the freakin' ocean," Sunni spits. But she too checks her newly acquired device and frowns.

"Exactly," Wil says as he approaches us, carrying a small piece of the shattered hull. He bends it playfully in his grip, shaping it like clay.

Now Sunni looks worried. "Does your phone say April thirteenth?"

"What are you chattering about?" Jadore moves her leg and Misty shifts her blazing fireball towards her. The alien lets out a terrified gasp, clutches her canister, and moves her hand to Misty. The sparks fade.

"Yeah." My stomach drops. "But...the Earth should be...?" I don't want to say it, because my words might make it real. No signs of battle. We're all in one piece. Our cell phones might not have updated to reflect the current time, depending on the trajectory of our crash and where exactly we are on Earth. But momentary hope lightens me. Did we *change* the future?

"The *Blind Elephant* gave me her chrono readings, before she couldn't anymore." He shoots a glance at me apologetically. "Barring a rogue Spanish, Portuguese, English, or some other colonist vessel, I doubt we'll see anyone. We're about three hundred years in our past."

PART THREE

Even if there is only one door, it will open in every direction
conceivable to the one who enters.

—J.G.C., *Campbell's Multiple Verses*

CHAPTER 13

"The past? Earth history? In our universe?" Jia wipes sweat from her forehead and flicks it into the sand.

I sink to the ground. The pebbles dig into my leggings and serve as tiny anchors tethering me to this spot in time. Without a ship, I am solely responsible for our transportation and survival. And I have crashed us here, away from the Final Battle, into our past. I have flung us here randomly and trapped us on a tropical island.

What if I can't return to Jia's house, or the portal explosion, or anywhere? What if we're stuck here forever?

Jadore climbs to her feet, mindful of Misty and Sunni's weapons. "Lies. Preposterous *lies*."

Wil shrugs, strangely unbothered. "It doesn't matter if you believe us. We're equally trapped."

Misty's fireball fizzles and shrinks. Her veins shimmer and shift, as if she has taken the fire back into her soul. She keeps one hand fixed on Jadore. Just in case. "But the ship can be fixed, right?"

Wil bends and inspects the alien metal between his fingers. "Eventually."

"Ingrid can take us to where we need to go!" Jia insists, pointing at me.

As my friends consider this, a presence sits at the edge of my mind. I spin, feeling eyes upon me, but no one is there.

Jadore raises a singed eyebrow. "The only place I need to go is my homeland. If you touch me, I will kill you." But there's very little bite to her words. She's desperate. She turns on her heels and hurries toward the water with her canister.

"Where are you going?" Misty sneers. Fire returns to one palm and ice to another, ready to freeze Jadore to the ocean if needs be. "Good luck swimming in the middle of the ocean with your modded bod. Not really fit for the swamps anymore, is it."

"I have tuned my body for—"

"Yeah. To some perverted human standard. Because that's all they taught you. You're an experiment too."

"That is why I maimed their organization from within, stole their technology, and built a new way forward, before you imbeciles stranded me here! Someone on this planet will aid me. None of you, with all of your powers, will dare to—"

She pivots as she reaches the shore. A crack of lightning splits Misty's icy lance in half in mid-air. Misty lops a fireball. Jadore ducks and the fire lands in the water, creating a cloud of steam. Sunni's firearm erupts and catches Jadore in the leg. Jadore crumples, yelps, and then leaps back up angrily and prepares another lightning bolt. The canister rolls listlessly on the sand.

"Enough." With a flick of his hand, Jadore's canister flies towards Wil. He catches and tucks it beneath his armpit. Jadore stops in her tracks. "There's nowhere to go, Jadore. The simple mechanical lock can be easily overridden on this canister. Unlike the other canister, made of plastic, which has already melted in the crash. Besides, if

I'm right, what you're thinking won't work."

"You don't know me," she says pointedly. Her hands light up again.

"You don't know our history," Misty says, equally prepared to fire. "Even if you managed to swim far enough to reach civilization, we're in the past. Pre-Collective, pre- a LOT of technologies, and also, we're in pre-modern feminism. No one will listen to you. You'll be institutionalized and dissected. Brutally. And then you'll be back where you started."

"I can make them listen to me," she says icily. Sparks cackle between her fingers as she digs her toes into the sand. "I will cow them into silence with my gifts. Now give me *back* my eggs!"

I promised Gayarnu I wouldn't trust the Collective. Look where that landed us. Literally in the past, with no food or supplies. And no way off this island. Except teleportation.

"It doesn't matter if we're here or up there, or in the future or the past," I interrupt them, digging the toe of my boot into the sand. "The Untrakeepers are still chasing us. Me. So, I'll go. Keep them away from the rest of you, while you fix the ship."

I feel them at the edge of my consciousness, as if I'm pressing a fingertip into the point of a blade. The more I focus, the harder I push, and it's only a matter of minutes before the blood pours.

My friends share a stony silence. Jia inhales sharply, as if to object, but then asks, "Where will you go?"

I shrug and bombard my mind with random eras of time, a kind of mental smokescreen. Pompeii. An isolated forest. A crowded market in an idealistic vision of the Middle Ages. I avoid Wil's gaze.

"You can't go on your own," Sunni chides. "What if you can't make it back?"

A chance I'll have to take. "How long will it take to repair the ship?"

Wil considers the folded wreck, unperturbed, as if our situation is less dire. "A few weeks for sure. Maybe a few months?"

"A few months?" Sunni exclaims. "We're supposed to survive that long?" In turn, she looks to each of us. "Do any of you know anything about tropical plants? Crafting crude weapons?"

As Jia pales and rattles off her limited knowledge of the subject, and Misty keeps watch on an antsy Jadore, and Wil twists the piece of hull with his mind, my role crystalizes. "I will bring you supplies."

"I'll come with you, and we'll take Jadore," Misty suggests. "Ingrid can take us back to the councillor. We'll deliver her and return here with a bigger and better ship."

Sunni brightens. "Then I'll go too, to fly the ship."

"I don't want to endanger you more than I already have," I say. The familiar ringing fills my ears. The Untrakeepers know I'm back on Earth. I back away from my friends. "Those *things* will keep coming and we will never get the ship fixed if I'm around. Wil will need all of you helping him."

"What if...what if you can't make it back?" Sunni asks.

"She has to," Jia says. "She promised."

I nod. I have promised to return to so many times and spaces. This is just another door I will have to find, again and again, for my friends' sakes. I can't leave anyone else behind. Not anymore.

"And how will you contribute?" Sunni asks Jadore, jutting her weapon in her direction.

Jadore has fallen silent amidst our back and forth. I imagine the thought of being stranded here with the people she's tortured and hunted sickens her, just as it sickens us. "If I had my eggs—"

"If you contribute, we can talk about you getting the canister back," Wil interrupts, patting the metal firmly. "Answer Sunni's question."

She snarls and drops her gaze to the lapping waves against her green legs peeking through her ripped bodysuit. "I will catch fish."

"And if you try to swim away, we'll destroy—" Misty starts to say, but Wil finishes with, "That'll be fine, Jadore. Thank you."

Misty and Sunni exchange annoyed glances. I press a palm against my temple. I want to stay with my friends. I want to see how many times Jadore will attempt escape; if Jia and Wil can make peace with each other; how Misty and Sunni continue to reconcile their pasts as we create our futures.

Wil tosses the hull fragment onto the sand and grabs a cast-off branch. He draws a large circle in the sand, about a twenty-foot radius from the shoreline and the trees. "That's your spot, Ingrid. Always try to return here. We'll set up regular watches to check for you."

I nod and gravitate towards it. The ringing is growing louder. My window in this moment draws to a close.

They all hug me. I can't remember when we've last done this. If ever. We're often so at odds that we forget to show each other human decency.

Jadore watches from a distance, eyes narrowed with distaste and, perhaps, jealousy. I wonder if she remembers the song I sang at her, so long ago now. She casts her gaze to the setting sun in the horizon.

My friends step away from me. I take in their gleaming faces. And then, I am gone.

Freedom feels as vast as a desert and equally as dangerous. With my friends safely deposited in the past with Jadore, I can finally pursue my ultimate goal: save Ethan. Save *everyone* I've left behind.

Prevent the Earth's destruction. Bring down the Collective.

Once my skills are honed, I can bring Ethan, Elisha, Greg, Lynn, Kimberly, our parents, and any other important person back to the island. I will continue to bring supplies until we are ready. Then, as one, we can escape on the repaired ship and attack the Collective. Maybe by then, Jadore will come to her senses. If not, we can attempt to bargain with the Councillor Ari-Faur or whatever remains of the Collective. Maybe Gayarnu and her ahmei followers will have successfully taken over by then. Either way. Time is on our side. *My* side.

I step lightly on the reflective floor of the Untraver. I just have to find the right door to get back to Sparkstone on the day of the library explosion, before the Untrakeepers realize I'm here. I conjure Ethan to my mind. My memory twists. What was he wearing, again? I remember his bloodshot eyes. The desperation and waiver in his voice. Gayarnu, in the infirmary, when they told me he had perished from the vitaphage.

No. I'm here to *change* that future. *I* am the one who can travel through time and space. Once I've cleared this up, they won't remember any of that.

I no longer have the computer model map of the Untraver, and it may be lost to us now, but that's all right. I take a fresh marker from my pocket and mark on the walls, and create a matching mark on my skin. I will create my own path.

A guttural shriek echoes through the endless structure. The Untrakeepers know I'm in their domain. The presence of one close by feels like a migraine manifesting as a skittering shadow. I have to hurry.

My feet pound against the metallic floor as I sprint through the maze-like corridors, each thunderous footfall of the creature behind me sending tremors up through my legs and into my ribcage. My lungs burn as I take sharp turns past an endless parade of identical doors. The air grows thick and oppressive, as if reality is warping around the pursuing horror. I fight the overwhelming urge to glance back, knowing that even a fleeting glimpse could shatter my sanity and break my focus on finding the right exit.

TRESPASSER/TRAVELLER OF WORLDS. YOU WILL /END/ BEGIN.

I pass an intersection of corridors. Straight ahead or right. I continue straight; there's another fork to the left ahead.

Movement beyond me, from the right fork. Another one. But this monster doesn't reach for me. In my peripheral vision, I catch a flash of writhing tentacles.

I skid to a stop and spin to peek. The creature crawls for the Untrakeeper behind me, roaring with intelligent frustration and hunger. The monster wraps his large, decaying tentacles around the Untrakeeper, and in one swift motion devours my pursuer down its infinite hatch-mouth. He smacks his gob shut. There's a shattering crunch. A scream cut short.

"Ohz," I say, fascinated and disgusted.

The hafelglob turns to me. No eyes, only mouth and tentacles. The lizard part of my brain screams for me to run. Saliva mixed with dark ooze drips out of his mouth and stains his tentacles as he advances and feels his way through the corridor towards me. His tentacles touch each door with lingering curiosity; every time he touches a handle, he yelps in pain.

"What...?" He struggles to form words. His mouth snaps hungrily.

"I'm Ingrid. The Crosskey. Remember?" I say hesitantly, avoiding a massive tentacle as it flops up and down like a drowning fish beside me.

He hesitates. His flesh has greyed and his stench is unbearable. Time might not exist in the same way in the Untraver but it has had an undeniable effect on the hafelglob.

"Door," he says finally, stretching a tentacle towards a burnt section of the wall between two nearby doors.

"There's a lot of them," I concede unhelpfully.

"No," he says, urgently now, as if trying to grasp his train of thought. When he can't, he lets out a massive roar and his teeth snap at me.

I turn and run, and I hear him tumbling after me. I can't save him, not in this state. He'll tear my arms off. I've waited too long to save him and now he's deteriorated to this.

"No choice," he gurgles after me. "One door!"

I want to understand. I have near-infinite time in this place between places. But I'm not invincible or ageless.

"I'll try to help you!" I promise. Because I'm really good at throwing promises around.

I see a glowing door ahead on the left and the familiar pull to investigate. My exit, where I belong. Right beside it: another burn mark. Where another door used to be.

A memory: I recall the Untrakeepers convening to burn a door.

What if the Untrakeepers have already burned the way back to Ethan? I tug on the glowing doorknob. The door opens easily, loosing a searing blade of light on my face.

No, this is the door I need right now. This is where I'm supposed to be.

"Supposed to be?" I murmur to myself, squinting against the light. "How can I go where I'm supposed to be if I need to change the future?"

Can I trust myself anymore to know what is best?

Ohz has caught up to me. He lays a tentacle over the door as if to hold it shut, but I manage to pry it open and squeeze through into the heat. The tip of a tentacle catches in the door as it closes and his outraged scream and my apology fade as I gasp for clean, fresh air.

I stumble forward. But this is *not* where I belong. Not even close.

Flat, dead behemoths litter the cracked, dry plains like shadows. No matter how much the wind whips the grains, the large shadow-shapes remain, as if tattooed on rippling skin. There are hundreds of them scattered across the beige landscape. Beside them, spiked trunks. Husks of a former forest. The big violet sky hangs above and stretches on forever, reminding me of home.

"Earth, after the battle?" I ask aloud. Anything to hear the voice of someone familiar.

But Earth will become bits after the Collective blasts it with their technology. It wouldn't be able to support me here, now.

I venture to touch a shadowy shape with sweaty hands. It's cold, hard, and smears like mascara. I wipe it on my calves, stand up, and continue. Some distance through the collection of shadows, I find piles of spike-like teeth and metallic trinkets.

I'm walking through an alien graveyard.

I squint against the hot sun—no, *suns*, I think blearily, barely distinguishing between the blots in the sky—wishing I had a hat or other adequate protection. Squat structures, bulbus and oblong, offer shade in the relative distance. The village is surrounded by dark craters dotted with greenery. Farms, perhaps. Where there is green, there is life. Maybe something edible. My body moves before I can think it through. I will make it there before I die of thirst or heatstroke.

Food first, then back to the Untraver, and away from this dead place.

At my three o'clock, a much taller structure looms across the pitted plains and casts eerie, long shadows. The closer I walk towards the village and this structure, the stronger the smell. Garbage. Vomit. Rotten food. The stench I associate with Ohz. Although the shadows from the imposing tower offer respite to my heated skin, the repeated, bird-like screeches from within and the sound of scurrying on stone gives me pause. A warm breeze picks up my hair and as I struggle to bring it under control, I note the dark cloud circling the building, like a flock of swallows. Dread settles in my stomach. I know to listen. I hold my nose until I adjust to the smell and continue towards the village, hoping whatever creatures within the tower decide I'm not worth the trouble.

The craters multiply the closer I venture towards the village, and I notice now there are not just one-storey buildings, but rolling hills, the same height as the structures. The smell is stronger here. I pass on trying the venomous-looking green flora growing in spurts around the craters. Above, clouds form. They're as dark and as menacing as the tower. Just because I'm on a different planet doesn't mean the precipitation is going to be friendly. I recall lessons from my childhood on acid rain.

Then: squelching. Not the same as the sounds from the tower. This sound is familiar, but it's cacophonous. I spin on my heels.

Hafelglob slither up from the deep pit. Hundreds of them. I step back, but the only escape is through time and I'm anchored by the fear of the writhing forms emerging before me, flexing and widening their mouths, the sand and rocks wet with their saliva.

"Wait!" I call. My shrill voice echoes across the expanse, above their gurgling language. They surround me without pause in a perfect circle and hold position, as if waiting for the pop of a starting pistol.

They're going to eat me.

Four figures emerge from the impatient crowd: three large and one small hafelglob. Three adult hafelglob coo and gurgle encouragingly to the child. Metal chunks have been seared to their flesh. The freshly cauterized wounds bubble around the improvised armour. The little one is adorned with similar metal trinkets I found arranged across the plains.

Very few other hafelglob have this treatment. Most others have rotten, sopping bandages covering recent wounds. These three and the little one must be leaders.

The little creature gestures one of eight nubby tentacles at me and opens its mouth lazily. Two short gurgles and something that sounds like a hiccup emerges from it.

"Uh, hi," I say cautiously. I point to my chest. "I'm not here to hurt you. I just got lost." As I wipe my brow, sweat drips to the cracked ground. The hafelglob around me gurgle a little louder.

One of the adults protecting the child jabs its tentacle at me and belches more aggressively this time. Behind me, a few hafelglob with spears and other weapons advance.

I throw my hands up defensively. "Yeah, you're right, I shouldn't have come. I guess I was just thinking about one of you I know, Ohz, who was chasing me, and then that broke my concentration, because I'm trying to find my—"

"Ohzzzzzz?" says the little hafelglob, with curiosity.

"Yeah, that's his name, Ohz. He calls me Crosskey," I say, relief washing over me. I just have to communicate to them that Ohz and his buddies are on *my* side. "Does that mean anything to—?"

I trail off as a mechanical hum rises above the din of the hafelglob. The sky above darkens, but not from clouds. Some of the creatures crawl with terrifying speed towards the craters. The three adult leaders raise their tentacles and screech, howl, and emit a disgusting garbage stench from their pores. I recoil as some of the retreating hafelglob reconsider their choices.

"Hey, what's happening?" I ask, though my question is drowned out by the emergence of a colossal ship from the swirling alien clouds. Its metallic hull gleams in the eerie violet light of this world's twin suns. A deafening hum fills the air as the vessel descends, dwarfing everything around it, like a giant boot threatening to squish us from the heavens.

I recognize the ship immediately. The mother ship. Though it looks far more patched up since the Final Battle. Why would it leave its post around Earth to come to the hafelglob's planet? I don't know how far I am from my solar system, yet even at top speed, it would take a ship of its size a long time to reach here without additional acceleration technology. How far in the future—or the past—am I?

And if I am in the future, am I still bound by the deal we negotiated with the Collective, if Councillor Ari-Faur is on board?

"Hey, these guys are bad news," I shout at the hafelglob, pointing up at the ship. "If this thing came to get you to fight against my people, don't listen to them."

This time, they hear me. One spins and advances on me, growling and pointing a sharp spear at my chest.

I raise my arms to protect my face. "Whoa, whoa, I'm just—"

Blinding beams of energy erupt from the underside of the mother ship and slice through the air towards my position. I dive to the ground as the lasers singe my hair and blast the place I stood moments ago. The tentacled creatures screech and writhe, and their gelatinous bodies pulse with an otherworldly glow. As dust and debris rain down, I frantically search for an escape, my mind racing to make sense of this chaos.

The healing wounds. The seared armour. They're fighting a war. *Against* the Collective.

The circle around me has broken. Half of the hafelglob have retreated. Others lay in a sizzling heap. The ship above hums again, preparing another strike.

"Hey! No!" I shout at the ship, waving my arms. "Get away from them! We are protecting this planet now!" If the remnants of the Collective are against the hafelglob now, perhaps we *are* in the future, and our fight continues as the Collective falls from galactic power.

Which means, I'm certainly not bound by *any* agreement I made with them.

I yank a tall spear from the sand left by a deserter—one of the hafelglob snarls at my aggressive act—but I chuck it like a javelin at the spaceship. It sails through the air and glances off the hull like a toothpick against a wall. There's a noticeable dent on the otherwise shiny exterior.

"Get away!" I shout again at the roaring ship.

My screaming startles the hafelglob, but all it takes is one follower—a leader—to legitimize my attack. One of the leaders that had been protecting the little one takes their spear and hurls it at the mother ship deftly. Others catapult their weapons at the ship, two and three at a time with their multiple appendages.

The mother ship hums louder in retaliation. Another beam bursts from its underbelly, right for the three leaders and their child.

I act as though I'm puppeteering myself from the sky. I'm moving toward the dangerous beam, not away. The familiarity of the hafelglob odour hits me again. Yes, the garbage stinks, but it's a specific kind of abhorrent stench that tugs at my memories and urges me to act, not recoil, from the small alien.

I grab the creature, and immediately, I regret it. Needle-like spines pierce my palms from beneath its slimy skin. I jump in surprise and try to shake the alien, but it's attached to me now. Hot liquid gushes into my bloodstream and I feel it coursing up my arms, towards my heart.

"Ohz!" it says to me defiantly.

"Ohz," I say dizzily. "Little Ohz."

Where Little Ohz had been, scorched sand sizzled.

"Ohz," I say again, the only word I know in his language. I'm so heavy. So tired. The sand and tiny rocks that had irritated the soles of my boots now beckoned. I sink to the ground, eager to rest. Just for a moment. Just until after this battle, and all of the other battles, until I can reach the end I've been promised.

The ship has quieted its laser. Suddenly there are two ships, three. No—it's just a mirage within my shrinking vision.

The hafelglob shriek a war cry and advance towards the ship. They're woefully outmatched. Space lasers versus gooey tentacle blobs with spears. The lasers are, unsurprisingly, winning.

A group of hafelglob fill my vision, and something slimy touches my neck, and my injured hand. I try to bat it away but I'm too woozy to move. My vision shrinks to a point and the sound of battle dims. Even the scent doesn't bother me anymore, nor is it layered with extrasensory information.

It would be easy to die.

Except, now my vision is blurring white.

A slobbering chant bubbles up from the aliens like a drunken song. "*Kala-sha-keen!*" Some are pointing above my body, to some place beyond.

Another voice joins in. "*Kahn-sha-kee!*"

"*Kars-keen-sha-kee!*" says a third, pointing in the opposite direction of the first.

"Kahn-sha-kee! Kala-sha-keen! Kars-keen-sha-kee!"

In my dizzied state, I hear, "Crosskey. Crosskey. Crosskey."

I don't understand. That's what they call me on Earth. "Crosskey," I say, affirmatively.

The cracked sand and the surrounding craters twist and blur in my deceived vision, but through the putrid stench of their bodies, another layer beckons. The wet smell of compost. I isolate the colour-smell and ask it to tell me more. The land hasn't always been this way. The craters are just a pox of war. The cracks are a sign of dry skin. The water that once flowed through this place has been sucked away. Two dead rivers, criss-crossing, remain. Is that what they're saying?

I collapse again, exhausted. I lift my hand. The pinpricks are shrinking red dots in my palm. The tentacles attached to my neck recede and wave in front of my face. My gaze follows them attentively. Satisfied that I'm conscious, they retract and give me space.

No wonder the Collective want them. Their bodies work magic.

Ohz has known me, this whole time. They all have. They have been subjugated, their natural inclinations controlled and manipulated by the colonizers, and yet, they have vowed to help me.

A renewed strength fills me as the hafelglob's natural talent works its way through my body. There are too many of them to take with me through the Untraver. I could make multiple trips, though there's no guarantee I'll arrive back at the same moment each time.

More ships whir across the darkening sky. They won't stop coming until they've captured and enslaved them all.

What has happened before will happen again.

But...

I can give them a fighting chance. They have helped me. Now I will help them, so they can help me again, until the end of time.

"I'll be right back," I say to the hafelglob keeping vigil, hoping I can keep this promise. The hope unmoors me from this planet and their startled gurgles fade as I find myself once again in the Untraver.

"Ohz!" I cry, knowing it will attract unwanted attention as well as the hafelglob.

I pass through several hallways, many with burnt doors. Eventually, I find him, listlessly feeling the walls, as if he too is searching for the correct door. It's time to take him home.

"I get it now!" I tell him excitedly. I feel like I'm speaking to him from underwater, the way one feels when talking in their sleep and being aware of it in the dream.

Reluctantly, I reach to touch him. One of his tentacles whips me in the torso and I stumble backwards. But I try again. I'm not going to leave him this time.

"I'm taking you home!" I scream at him.

Ohz's mouth widens, showing off the spiraling teeth. I shift my weight backwards, preparing to run.

"Home...?" he asks.

"I saved you," I tell him, smiling.

"Agh," he says. "Agh...!"

A full-bodied laughter erupts from his terrifying mouth, and despite myself, I fall to the floor and join him. This disturbing creature has been nothing but strange towards me since the moment I arrived at Sparkstone, I've trapped him in a nightmare, and now we're forever linked—all because of my power.

Our amusement fades with the distant shriek of an Untrakeeper. An ominous feeling settles on top of my glee, as if I've forgotten something important I was supposed to do.

"Okay. Enough. Let's get on with this." I stand and suddenly experience a flooding, full-body experience that someone is watching me. Even before I gaze into the alley, I know who it is, and the sickening sense of déjà vu submerges me into a thick uncertainty.

She wants me to tell her what's going on.

I could tell her, says something inside. *I don't have to do what was done to me.*

I smile knowingly at this. And what, risk not being the person I am now? I wave to her. She looks so desperately hopeful.

It happens as it did before. "*False,*" says Ohz to Past Me, and then to me, "*Choice.*"

Past Me looks horribly confused. Misty climbs to her feet on the raft and stares at me, sharing Past Me's concern. I'm also unclear on what Ohz means.

I realize I'm a distraction to them. They've got important work to do, as do I. I remind Past Me to map the Untraver, and in my glee, I do finger guns at her. I never do that, and I remember thinking it silly when I was on the receiving end, but I literally almost died—I can do anything.

Ohz and I take off together down the hallway, and then I remember something else.

My memory of myself in this moment was of a beautiful woman wearing a white dress. Not this dark skirt and leggings number.

Does this mean the future *can* be changed? Or did I witness a different universe-version of me, travelling the Untraver with my friends?

Campbell had said there's only one of me—right?

"No choice," Ohz says, as if in reply. "Only one direction."

"I'm not sure that's true," I say, wiping off my shirt.

I concentrate on finding the right door, but I can't shake the feeling that I'm accomplishing the impossible. Yes, wearing a different outfit might be the most mundane change one can make, but if *that* can change...

Once we step through the correct door and return to the arid landscape of the hafelglob planet, the scene has changed for the worse. Two cruisers, mere school buses compared to the mother ship, have joined the fray. The scent of garbage invades my nostrils and I double over, gagging into a squishy, mutilated hafelglob corpse.

Before I can come to my senses and prepare Ohz, he has already taken off towards the ships, which fire indiscriminately at the scattering hafelglob army. Ohz's diet of Untrakeepers has given him strength beyond that of his ancestors. As soon as his tentacles sense the enemy hovering above us, he leaps into the air. The mother ship lists to port and prepares to fire, but the gigantic ship is too slow for the kraken-like entity.

To say he lands on the cruiser would be inaccurate. Ohz's tentacles latch onto the bow as he approaches the craft, and he extends his mouth over the ship, pushing it fully into the deep spiral of teeth. The Collective ship crumples and twists unnaturally like a tin can as Ohz ingests it fully. Having nothing to hold onto, Ohz falls ninety feet to the ground, leaving a crater of his own on impact.

The regular hafelglob, inspired by this daring trick, make several failed jump attempts upon the mother ship. A few try a smarter approach, and pile on top of each other and stretch out their tentacles towards the imperial craft. They just don't have Ohz's speed or size. The mother ship fires on Ohz's location, but when the dust clears, he's already in the sky, devouring the second ship.

Soon, only the mother ship remains. As it fires on a pile of regular hafelglob, splattering ooze across the craters, Ohz attempts another jump. But he's taken on a lot of mass, and instead, flubs the maneuver and flops onto the ground.

As the mother ship prepares another blast, I run again into the fray, waving my arms as a distraction. "Hey! I'm a more interesting target! Look at me!"

To my surprise, lasers burning in the underbelly like dragon fire dim somewhat, as the nose of the ship lists lazily in my direction.

Uh oh. I haven't thought this far.

But it has given the hafelglob enough time to rethink their strategy. Their pile has become a flesh wall, a sloping cone with a curved tip, like soft-serve ice cream. One hafelglob leaps off the top and pancakes on the port side. It sinks its teeth into the hull. Another follows, and lands just behind the first. Their confidence grows as the deserter hafelglob emerge from their craters, see what's on the menu, and join the unique assault.

I run again as the mother ship decides to fire. The heat burns my arms, but I dodge the worst of it, or perhaps their aim has been skewed by the dozens of hafelglob now tearing into the ship with their hungry maws.

Ohz lumbers upright and crawls towards his brethren, dripping with more unnaturally blue-coloured ooze. His tentacles assess the mother ship above him and he gurgles.

"You made a bad choice coming here!" I shout at the ship, because I'm definitely not launching myself up there. "I, Ingrid Stanley of the human race, planet Earth, am one of the protectors of this planet, and all planets, in time!"

I feel silly as the words leave my lips. I am an ant to this giant. I haven't done much of anything in this fight. I just brought the champion and threw him into the ring. But I'm the only one with this power, and if I can't express myself, then what's the point?

As if I have cast a spell, the mother ship's engines roar. The colossal ship spins and moves, whale-like, across the sky. Tiny pinpricks of light flash across its starboard side as the hum intensifies. The hafelglob snacking on the hull begin jumping like water-striders onto their flesh wall. The mother ship shutters as it shrinks into the atmosphere and a deadening *CRACK* splits the air, billowing the dry sand into clouds around us.

Once the dust settles, the hafelglob disassemble their wall and gather not just around me, but Ohz as well. Seeing side-by-side the hafelglob who survived the Untraver and the natives is like comparing a wild wolf and a domesticated dog. Ohz towers over his ancestors, and they marvel over him, as if he is a god.

Perhaps, he is.

I clear my throat. "I'm sorry I locked you in there. I didn't mean it."

Ohz transforms back into his human self, much to the surprise of the surrounding hafelglob. He quiets them with reassuring throaty sounds and then nods in my direction. "Was to be, Crosskey."

I look to Little Ohz, who nestles against two of his parents. "What now?"

"I am to stay, if to be pleased. Hafelglob need help against Collective. Can return through the door, when it is her time."

"But...didn't we change the future? Won't this deter them from enslaving you?"

Ohz chuckles. "Am not oracle, is this the word, thank you very much? Go through unburnt doors and return to say if is different. What matters is protecting hafelglob at this now." He sweeps his human hand over gathering hafelglob, who peer with open mouths at us.

I smile and nod, though I have one more question before I can leave him. "You said there's a false choice. What does that mean?"

He struggles to answer, opening and shutting his mouth like a cow chewing cud. The surrounding hafelglob mimic him and gurgle in delight. Finally, he spits out the words. "Ohz has seen through the cracks of the door. Pieces. The memories..." He flicks his wrist by his ear. "Tricky. Saw the Crosskey wind the hall many times, and the monsters too, round and round. Monsters, burning doors. Terrible cries." He looks genuinely sad. "When Crosskey only runs, no choice—*is* choice. But is to be also, false choice. In the end, when monsters finish, Ohz thinks there is be only one door."

I think it's a lot of nonsense, but I nod as if I understand. Maybe my Future Self can parse it. If the Untrakeepers continue to burn doors, this limits my options considerably. Not just for my own ends, but for me to keep my promise to Hojshz and the hafelglob: find a Collective-free world for the hafelglob to settle. Challenging, but if there are universes where the Collective has won against the rebels of Earth, then there must be versions of Earth where we've defeated them.

My boots scrape the cracked sandy ground and I turn towards the twin suns, basking in our victory. Today, I helped save the hafelglob race.

I may have *changed* their fate.

If I can do this, I can save Ethan.

I return to my prescribed circle on the island, and at first, I'm unsure if I'm in the right place. Or in the correct universe.

A small village has grown up around my circle in the sand.

Four handsome huts with frond roofs, constructed from palm-tree wood and plastic tarps, surround a communal fire pit at a safe distance. The smell of smoked fish fills my nostrils and my mouth salivates. On a grouping of logs around the simmering fire, there's a smattering of camping supplies, including a propane stove, pots and pans, plastic dishes, and giant water jugs. The modern cooking supplies look well used and different than the ones my friends had acquired previously.

Encircling the site are various water collecting devices, mostly tarps connected to bottles and small tanks. I see Jia in the distance, checking on them. She wears a ball cap, a long cardigan I haven't seen before, and rolled-up cargo pants.

Behind the huts, the *Blind Elephant* has never looked better, or grander. The ship towers like a silent sentry god protecting my friends.

Sunni ducks out of the nearest hut, spots me, and throws her arms wide. She wraps me in a giant hug. She smells like the campfire and incense. Sunni's body has been tanned and her frizzy blonde hair, which she wears tied back with twine, has been sun-bleached. She grins at me expectantly. "Hey. Welcome!"

"Thanks. Things have...really progressed," I say, gesturing to the entire set-up and feeling a little sick to my stomach.

"Yep," Sunni says nonchalantly. "You bring me that soda?"

"No?" I frown. "What soda?"

Sunni lets out a frustrated groan, spins, and heads in the opposite direction towards the huts. "She forgot *again*, Misty!"

"No! Ingrid!" comes Misty's complaint from afar. "C'mere, so I can write it on your arm so you don't forget!"

Wil emerges from a different hut. He has a tool belt around his waist and wears a frond hat. He's looking trimmer; gaunter. His confident stride slows as he approaches and takes me in. Hesitates. "Banana?" he asks.

"Yeah, I'm banana," I reply slowly, walking out of my circle. "Why are you saying it like that?"

A small pause accompanies his reply. He shakes his head. "The ship's ready."

"Oh." Even though the evidence is before me, my reply is filled with surprise. There are things here they couldn't have acquired themselves. Which means I've brought supplies for them in my future—their past.

It's all right, Wil says telepathically, with a small smile. *I won't tell them. We just have to remember to send you back here, with all the right supplies, in the future.*

"Sorry," I mutter beneath my breath. "How long?"

He looks as if he doesn't want to say. "A year."

I've been gone barely a day, and my friends have endured a year on this island with Jadore?

Jia disembarks the ship, wipes her hands on her yoga pants, and grins when she sees me. She gives Wil a curious look I can't decipher. "Now?"

"Yeah. I think it's time, but we'll have to be quick," Wil agrees. "We can come back and clean up later. Ingrid, you up for a jump in the ship?"

"Oh. You're ready?" My gaze darts around to the elaborate camp site.

"We'll return to dismantle these, so we can leave no trace. I know you don't have a ton of time."

He's right. A low hum buzzes just below the lapping waves.

As Jia and Wil start loading supplies onto the ship, I walk towards a makeshift gurney beneath an open-air tent constructed from palm fronds and a blue tarp. Jadore rests there in the shade and looks terrible. Her thick, long hair has faded to wispy strands. One of the alien tinfoil blankets covers most of her body. I notice her skintight outfit has been replaced with a loose-fitting, drab dress.

Sunni and Misty trudge through the sand to Jadore's side. Jadore looks me over with the barest interest and recognition.

"Soda?" Jadore rasps, with a voice like sandpaper.

"No soda," Sunni replies, just as disappointed.

"Can we get some, when we go back?" Jadore implores.

I raise my eyebrows and try to contain my surprise. Where does she think we're going? Even if we brought her to Councillor Ari-Faur and the remnants of the Collective now, what can they do that's worse than what she's already suffered?

"Yeah, we'll make it our first stop when we're back in the future. Right?" Misty throws a glance at me.

"Yep," I reply, nodding emphatically. The less I say, the better.

"All right," Misty says begrudgingly. Her and Sunni position themselves at the head and toe of the makeshift gurney and lift with their knees. I shift out of the way and watch them maneuver her out of the tent and into the *Blind Elephant*.

Ever watchful for Untrakeepers, I help carry supplies into the refurbished ship. The interior looks better than it did before the crash. "The technology and its attached metal tell me the memories of its shape," Wil tells me cryptically, "but I made some suggestions, and here we are."

The bulkheads and the floor panelling gleam with a blue tint. The sh-winil's work, I imagine, as they would have been a great help to my friends in the reconstruction. Everything looks as it did before in the cockpit, though the seatbelts are more intuitively placed, and someone has created signs for the bulkheads by the benches that say, *"Don't forget to buckle up before a jump!"*

And to think that I'll have to gather all of these supplies from the future, in the future.

Don't worry, I give you a list, Wil assures me telepathically.

To my surprise, Misty and Sunni have strapped Jadore into the gurney with a plastic buckle and have left her on the floor of the cockpit. I poke my head into the mess. The layout remains, but there's more seating, a better kitchen, and the staircase has been reconstructed with reclaimed wood. Surely Jadore would be more comfortable in there.

As Sunni joins Wil at the controls and Misty sits on the bench across from Jia, Wil continues in his regular voice, "I was able to restore most of our data from the battle, and your Untraver project as well."

"That's good news," I reply, stepping over Jadore to sit next to Jia.

Once everyone is secure, the ship begins to climb into Earth's atmosphere. My friends cheer and clap; I imagine outside of test flights, this is the first time they've flown in a year. I notice Misty has a foot on the gurney to secure it and smirks down at Jadore, who hoots along with the rest of them.

"Future, and then home," Jadore mutters. Her head whips suddenly to the side and she begins hissing uncontrollably.

"She's seein' things again," Sunni says over her shoulder to me. "Gettin' more frequent."

"Shh!" Jia hushes us. "She can still understand us."

"We're taking Jadore to her home? That's what we've landed on?" I ask carefully.

"Yeah," Misty says without meeting my eye.

That seems ill-advised, but I'll take it up with Wil, who can speak without Jadore hearing. I glance at the canister, which sits next to the gurney. "But without that?"

"No, of course that's coming too," Jadore snaps, scooping it up and cradling it like a newborn. Realizing she's strapped into the gurney, she begins tugging at it with one hand, determined to unbuckle it, but unsure of the mechanism. "I had another one around, have you seen it?"

"That one is gone," Jia says, as if she's said it a thousand times. "Remember?"

"Yes," Jadore says slowly. "But it's not really gone, right?"

I don't want to deal with Jadore right now and I'm too ecstatic about my achievements with the hafelglob to care about whatever deal she's negotiated with my friends. I'm too busy imagining Ethan on board the ship with us. We'll have to pick up a few more supplies. Maybe Wil and Sunni could learn how to add pieces onto the ship. We'll have to figure out how to house Jia's family, our other Sparkstone friends, and the rest of our families, once I rescue them as well.

It's all worked out.

"I just want to return to my home," she says again, this time more pained. She looks up at me and gestures to the straps. "Will you help?"

"I think that has to stay on," I say, leaning over to pat her hand. "It might be a bumpy ride."

"Oh. Right. Because I'm going home."

Once we're out of Earth's gravity well, our pilots slow their acceleration and head leisurely towards Mercury. I stand and head towards Wil. "So, we're ready to jump?"

Sunni unbuckles from her seat and joins Misty. Jadore has become unsettled again.

We might need you to stay a little longer, Wil says telepathically. *Could you sit at the controls for a minute?*

"Longer? Because we need to go back to the island?" I do as he asks. As long as I'm on the ship, I'm safe. But I don't want to risk sticking around too long. I'm pretty sure if I'm on the ship while it's on Earth, the Untrakeepers will still come and cause a terrible scene.

Wil passes Mercury and the two of us admire the celestial body. *Eventually we'll need to return there. But—*

"No. You can't have it!" Jadore shouts.

Jadore has been unsecured from the gurney and has become upset with Jia, who tries to remove the canister from the alien's protective grip. I notice the three of them are wearing the heavy-duty gloves as they maneuver around her, speaking in calm tones.

Ingrid, Wil says, and I turn my gaze back to him. *What's this I'm seeing in your mind about the hafelglob?*

I'm a little taken aback by the intrusion. "I saved them. I think I changed the future?"

Why do you think that? He returns his attention to the controls. He's since removed his hat. A bead of sweat appears at the top of his forehead.

My brain fills with the reasons why, and as I'm sifting through the events of the past day, hoping that Wil can parse them without me having to explain, the airlock hisses open and then slams shut.

I leap from the chair. Sunni and Misty press against the door. Jia hugs the canister tightly. Jadore pounds on the structure, confused and deranged, crying for her eggs and for her home.

"Now," Sunni says, pointing at Wil.

"No," I whisper. "No, you can't be..."

HISS. WHRRRRR.

The outer airlock door flies open. Misty and Sunni hold me back as I foolishly try to open the inner door. Through the port, I see Jadore's eyes bulge from her skull as the silent vacuum freezes her beauty eternally in one final, horror-filled expression.

CHAPTER 14

I'm at a loss. They've *killed* Jadore. Not only that, the murder had been premeditated. "Why did you do that?"

"There was *no way* we were going to let her live, Ingrid," Sunni says, her voice steely and calm.

"But..." I gesture out the airlock. Through the canopy, I see Jadore's body, floating in darkness. "She helped you survive on the island. You bonded with her. She was dying, and you just murdered her."

Misty points a sharp finger in my face. "If we let her go to the Collective or back to her home world, she would have created another Collective. This is justice. She killed Sunni and so many others. We're doing the entire universe a favour."

I look to each of my friends in turn. I can't believe what I'm hearing.

"People change," I say, more determined than ever.

"Only if they want to," Jia says. "A woman who spent all of her sentient life stepping on others for her own vanity? Nothing in the few months she would have had left would have made a difference."

"A lot can be done in a few months. We are proof," I reply.

"Yes, including becoming a martyr for her new, planned Collective and spawning others like her," Misty says.

"Did you know she was going to do this?" I ask Wil.

"Whose idea do you think it was?" Jia says quietly.

The four of them exchange quiet glances. They *planned* this, right under my nose. "All of you knew except me?"

They waited until I was gone, busy providing for them so they could all survive, *including* Jadore, and they plotted against me. Meanwhile, I've been making my own plans, ever so conscious that I can't act until the right moment. I've gone along with their requests. I've stayed with them, when I could have taken off on my own.

My thoughts have never been private. Wil reads them all, and he probably shares them too. They probably entertained themselves on their cold island nights by gossiping about me.

Then, a quiet realization: "You're scared that if I know the future, I'll try to change it without you."

"None of us wants to alter time. Only you want that," Wil says.

"I don't think any of us want to watch you die!"

"We all have to die sometime, Ingrid," he says. "At least I know when and how I go. There's power in that."

"And that?" I point at the canister.

"It stays as it is," Jia says, with finality. "We are its guardians now. We aren't murderers, but if Wil and the others are right, we can't let these creatures free. At least, not all at once." She looks conflicted. She doesn't know if she believes what she's saying.

"You are literally murderers."

"She figured out the Final Battle," Misty says. "I guess we were talking about it and her hearing is pretty good, although...no, it doesn't matter how she found out. We can't have her trying to escape this solar system and repopulate her home world and the Collective in her image."

"I'm pretty sure Campbell told her everything," I retort. "And why does it matter. Her home is what, super far from Earth? Let the sick and dying Collective deal with it."

"Ingrid. You yourself said it. Letting her loose on her home world with her modified eggs is the equivalent of releasing a non-native species into an environment," Misty says. "If all of the Collective, and humanity, has the altered vitaphage, but Jadore's descendants are immune to the vitaphage and can quickly populate an area, it's not going to be long before they take control of the remnants of the Collective and use its technology to take over, well, everything. Including potentially other universes."

"She already had ships going. What happens to those ships now during the battle? What if they're not there? What if by killing her here, you've altered our fates at the final hour?"

"There's only one way to find out," Sunni says, gesturing to me. "Take us there."

I balk at her presumption that I'd take *orders* from her. "No. I'm done. You want to go back to the island? That's fine. But if we're no longer making decisions as a group about who gets saved and who dies, then I guess I'm on my own."

Before they can stop me, I teleport away.

They don't care about saving anyone, even themselves. It's only me who cares. Yes, Jadore is a problem. I can stop her before she even *begins* to spread herself across the galaxy.

Then, my friends will not act behind my back, because there will be nothing to act against. Perhaps Alt-Sunni will never cross over, and our Sunni will still be alive.

They would thank me. But they probably won't, because after I make a change, they won't remember.

I don't need the four of them anyway, or a ship. Let them drift through space for a while and when they're ready to apologize to me, and when I'm ready to hear it, I'll return.

Before that, it's time for me to do what I should have done a long time ago.

I'm ready to finally save Ethan.

I step through the correct door like a quiet mouse, arriving behind the console. I've gone over this scene hundreds of thousands of times in my head. I'd seen a flash of colour there, before I teleported out. It had been me. Elisha is just a few inches away, but she's so engrossed in the controls that she doesn't notice my appearance.

Wil calls for Past Me. He knows I'm there, of course. That's why he pulled me to his side, to prevent me from seeing myself. He tells me to meet him in the music trailer, which I realize I haven't done yet. I file that away for later.

Goodbye, Wil. I love you, and where I'm from, you are still alive and well, as are the rest of us. I'm sorry that I haven't figured out a way to save you, yet. But maybe, I will yet.

He doesn't speak to me. I listen as the scene unfolds as before, because I don't wish to meddle with this part. I need to hear the rest of Ethan's words.

I peer from behind the console. This is it.

"I love you," I hear him say once more, to Past Me. "But I'm—"

I watch myself disappear with our friends. And I wait for Ethan to finish his sentence. But his words stall. Whatever he is, I will not know, not right now.

No matter. I've practiced for this moment, like a general plotting a critical battle maneuver, and now it's finally happening. I dive out from behind the console and reach for him.

Ethan fixes his confused gaze on me. He looks different from what I remember. Young. So scared and fragile. So much has happened since I've seen this version of him. Alt-Ethan has completely overtaken my memory of him. I falter. What if this Ethan isn't mine? What if I've come to the wrong place?

No time for hesitation. Everything I've worked towards is in the palm of my hands. I snatch Gayarnu too, and they're confused, but I'm grinning. We're going to be okay.

"Ingrid, I'm not..." He falters again, and slumps against me.

The room roars with heat and the portal starts to erupt. But it can't get me. I'm the master of this moment in time. Agailya sees me running with Gayarnu and Ethan in tow. She doesn't hesitate. She hoists Jadore's unconscious form with imperious strength and a couple other ahmei as humans appear at her side, hustling past bewildered fishmen, and we run towards each other, arms outstretched. She emits a song that I know means, "GO!"

Green flames lick our skin and engulf the library. The ahmei, with Jadore and Ethan, wrap their arms around me, humming a hopeful song that deadens the heat. The outline of an Untrakeeper emerges from the portal. Not today.

"I win," I scream at it, and because it's the best feeling, I soar out of there.

My time in the Untraver is a fever dream. Leading all of them through dim hallways with burnt, darkened doors. Their songs light my heart, and the correct door blazes before me. I step through, and—

I don't awake immediately. I'm floating in an ocean. I reach for

Ethan, knowing he's nearby, but I can't feel him. A heavy sense of calm has been forced upon my chest, removing all fear. My limbs wave awkwardly in the water.

I have to find Ethan. I have to *wake up.*

When I finally come back to consciousness and reality, I sit up in bed, gulping air with desperation. The smell informs me I'm in the infirmary in the basement of Rogers Hall, at Sparkstone University. I'm in a private room, similar to what Jia had been given when she'd recovered from Jadore's lightning.

I throw off the white sheets. Death has not visited this place yet. We must be pre-vitaphage. An IV has been inserted in my forearm. I attempt to read the packet hanging on the stand; the clear liquid seems innocuous, though I will take no chances. Awkwardly, I search for gauze with the stand in tow.

My clothes have been washed and folded neatly on the chair; my boots, cleaned, and placed beside them. My phone rests on top of the pile, plugged into a nearby outlet. I check it apprehensively. December twenty-seventh.

How long have I been here—the entire day? My heart races as I listen for Untrakeepers. Maybe they can't get me while I'm asleep. Does this mean my soul isn't in my body while I sleep? Nope, can't have an existential crisis now.

I search for cameras out of habit. The loneliness of my situation strikes me like a sharp explosion in the chest. Even if they're watching, it doesn't matter. I rip off the gown and the IV and dress. Shoving into my leggings, I realize somberly this is the first time I've been alone in a room in ages.

When I'm decent, I try the door. The handle stalls in my grip. I try it again. Locked. I'm a prisoner. Great.

Futilely, I jiggle the handle and then launch backwards, emitting a groan. Door is a no-go. Vents? I cross the room. A small one above the bed. We've been surviving on a lean diet, and I've always been a beanpole, but that vent could fit a determined kitten. Not me.

The door clicks thickly behind me and I whirl around. Agailya emerges through the threshold. Colour fills her pale cheeks; she looks as she did the first day I met her. Calm. Poised. Jadore has not yet released the modified vitaphage that will wreak havoc on the Sparkstone alien community.

"You're awake," Agailya says softly.

"Where's everyone else?" I ask. The hallway beckons. I dodge Agailya's lithe form, slip away, and follow my instincts until I find the man I love.

"They're in the recovery room or in tanks. Resting." She closes the door and clasps her hands diplomatically. "You have done my people an undeserving service. Even Ja'Dor'Esss. You have prolonged her suffering. We will care for her wounds and keep her under our protection. For which we are grateful."

"We all have more suffering to go," I tell her hurriedly. I take a step towards the door, testing the waters. "You can't keep me here."

"We would never dream of doing so. You are free to come and go as you wish. We have no technology to stop your power."

That's true. Still, she blocks my way. My throat tightens. I have to know. "And Ethan?"

Her gaze hardens. "He's in critical condition. You cannot see him."

"You have no idea what I went through to get back here. I will find him, even if it takes me years to pinpoint the time and the space."

She wets her lips and considers me. "Ingrid Stanley grows angrier and more resolved in our future, does she?"

"I just want to see him, Agailya. One last time. Even if...even if it's too late for me to do anything...medically speaking." My eyes sting and I wipe the tears away. I don't have patience for sadness right now. "The next time I come here, it's all bad and too late. The ahmei value suffering, I get that. I have suffered, I guarantee you. I left everyone and everything to be here, in this moment in time—to risk seeing him, even if it's just for a few minutes."

"I recognize your service," she says devotedly, and opens the door. "But I ask you again. Another suffering lies before you. One I am unsure you are prepared for. Once you lay eyes on him, you cannot un-see what has become of him. Are you prepared to endure?"

"I'm prepared."

She nods respectfully. "Then I will show you."

I follow Agailya into the corridor. She glides past numerous rooms, and never once does she check to see if I'm following; she acts as if I'm not there. I hear faint whispers and far-off conversations behind closed doors. Each sound makes me jump, because any of them could be made by Ethan.

A few minutes later, we're no longer in the infirmary. A faint chemical layers on top of the scent of the sea, as if we've entered an oceanside motel that also houses a pool. The fluorescent lighting dims to a cool blue. Agailya's pace slows.

"What part of Rogers Hall is this?" I ask hesitantly.

She doesn't reply. We pass a room with floor-to-ceiling windows, revealing rows of person-sized tanks filled with bubbling turquoise liquid. I'm struck by their similarity to the transformation tanks in the alternate universe. Within one is Gayarnu, in human form, unconscious, attached to a breathing apparatus and a variety of other tubes lodged beneath the skin in her forearms.

I stop short. "Oh! Are they okay?"

Agailya doesn't stop. "They will be."

I'm unsure and struck by Agailya's lack of care; I scamper after her.

We pass other tank rooms; some are filled with humans, others with humanoid aliens I've never seen before. All of them, unconscious, floating in the healing liquid, and affixed with tubes or wires. I drink them in. More intel for my friends, when I return to them in triumph with my love.

"Through here," Agailya says, gesturing to a secure entrance. No glass walls; just a slit of a window at eye-level on the door. She taps deftly at a keypad beside the door jamb and there's a soft *click* from the lock. She looks at me expectantly and steps aside.

"Why have you locked him in?" I ask, apprehensive as I stand before the door. I look through the window. A similar green glow emanates from within, though it's too dark to see anything. My hand hovers over the handle.

Like Schrödinger's cat, in this moment, Ethan is both alive and dead. I sink into the second, relishing and treasuring it, because in a moment, the uncertainty will be gone, and I will only have him one way or the other, forever.

Agailya senses my fear. "You are free to leave," she reminds me.

I shake my head. "I've come too far."

"I will check on the others," she says, and returns the way we came. I watch her go, realizing this may be the final time I see her alive.

It's happening now, it's happening now and it hasn't happened before and it won't happen again, I remind myself, and I push into the room.

The light from the hallway fills the rectangular space. I feel the wall for a light and my finger flicks a switch. In the corner, a large tank abruptly bubbles to life and fills the room with a brilliant emerald green light.

The figure within the tank lifts his chin, as if waking from a nap. And the mystery of Ethan's final words to me crashes into my prefrontal cortex.

He'd tried to tell me.

But I'm—

His bulbus blue-green eyes meet mine and blink horizontally.

—not human.

CHAPTER 15

My knowing Ethan is the being within the tank goes beyond physical recognition. He doesn't look like my Ethan. He has no dark hair. Fins for ears, green-blue scales that ripple gently as he swims for the glass to examine me. Humanoid, yes. He wears a loose-fitting dark shift, akin to a hospital gown. An IV has been attached to his left webbed hand. He breathes through gills in his neck.

The door swings and slows, not quite closing, as I approach the tank.

The way Alt-Ethan had regarded me, so curious about my relationship with his counterpart. His position as poster boy, one so unrealistic in retrospect for a mere human to hold. His gills had likely not been modifications at all, but an accentuation to represent his role as ambassador between two races.

I feel incredibly stupid. How could I have not seen the signs?

"You're ahmei," I say, breathless.

He opens his mouth and a faint note emanates through the water. I note a speaker-like device within the tank, and another on the ceiling above me. His webbed fingers point to a panel embedded into the tank. There's one green button and an 8-bit screen displaying

"READY" in English, French, and words in the ahmei script. I'm hesitant to touch anything, but he insists with silent, swirling hands. At least we can communicate.

I fiddle with it, sticking a tentative finger in. It pings and vibrates the water. He presses a suctioned finger against the glass and holds it there. I try again.

"Can you hear me?" I ask.

A curt nod. The water ripples and I hear a soft, gurgled song. The panel beeps and I recoil. Words appear on the primitive screen.

I thought I'd never see you again, they read.

I press my cheek against the tank. I'd just wanted to save him. Now, I've reduced him to this. I don't know what to say. I hold down the button for a while and then release. There's so much to tell him. All this time has passed for me, and he's always been here, in this tank. An alien.

Gayarnu and Agailya had told me he'd died. Perhaps to cause me suffering. Or he has died by the time my past self arrives to learn about the vitaphage.

He presses a hand where my cheeks and breath have fogged the glass, and sings some more. *I tried to tell you, but it's hard to remember in human form.*

"Maybe I can..." I study the tank and follow the multiple tubes. They disappear into the wall. "Can you get out?"

He hums more notes. *I cannot breathe your air in my true skin.*

My heart sinks. No wonder the Agailya and Gayarnu have adopted and remained in human form. Even if I separate Ethan's tank from its power source, he'll be stuck in there. And if he transforms into a human, he may not remember me, or anything else that makes him truly *him.*

There are so many things I want to say. But one question

tumbles from my lips. "Did you really kill your cousin?" I ask.

His large eyes blink vertically in surprise. The notes in the water are frantic. *She told you?*

I don't know who *she* is, though I can assume it refers to Agailya. "An alternate universe version of yourself told me."

The water stills with this news. The whole story threatens to spill from me like a pent-up waterfall, and as he sings his response, I try to think of the best way to condense everything I want to say and ask of him before the Untrakeepers show themselves.

What appears on the terminal, however, is not what I'm expecting.

The vitaphage is uncurable. My brother-cousin was close to the end, and in terrible pain. They refused to heed his cries to alleviate his pain, to end it all. So I ended his suffering. I couldn't bear to watch him toil. It was cruel. Our people are...cruel. That's why I'm alone here, he says. *And why my aunt doomed me to be an experiment. To punish me for what I did to her son. To forget and re-remember with each transformation back to my true form.*

"Your aunt is Agailya?" Blood rushes to my face. She experimented on her own nephew, in the name of saving her race. To punish him for what he did to *her son*. Agailya's favouritism of Ethan makes so much more sense in retrospect. Of course she'd want Gayarnu, her trusted servant, to spy on Ethan. His suffering had to be ultimate. He had to endure sleepless nights, painting his pain, trying to remember the trauma that alien science buried deep in his altered brain.

Please don't hurt her, comes the soothing song and accompanying message on the screen. *We are all in pain. Pain only begets more pain. I only want happiness with you but I have only sadness to share.*

"I want happiness with you too," I reply, shaking with sobs.

My heartache resonates with the faint ring in my ears. Go away, I whisper to the universe. Let me live with this heartache longer, because I'd rather feel this than nothing at all.

Then I am sorry to share this with you, but I must be truthful, he says. *I have the vitaphage.*

My tears slide on the glass. He touches one with his webbed fingers. What had Agailya told me once? That the survival rate was fifty percent? "We'll get the cure," I say, but I forget to press the button when I'm speaking. I shove my finger hard, creating a hangnail. I ignore the pain. "I'll find a way to cure you. We have some of the research, we just have to put it together. Then we can save you."

Except...

I can never truly save him. His choice to help someone he loved in the only way he knew how, on a different world, altered his life forever. Nothing I can do or have done will free him from the Collective or Agailya's experiment. *But I'm not human.* A feeble, last-ditch attempt to tell me the truth, just when he thought we were going to die.

A new message: *My aunt and Gayarnu have been experimenting for months with little to show. According to them, I have weeks.*

Weeks, if that. Perhaps Gayarnu had been telling me the truth. Perhaps by the time I return to Sparkstone University and witness Jadore stealing technology, he is already dead.

This may be the final time I speak with him.

"I risked everything to come here. I don't want this to be the last time," I say softly, more to myself than him.

Do you regret it? he asks.

I shake my head. It's still him in there. I asked for my moment in time to see him again, and that time is now. I accept this gift. I have to make the most of it.

I ignore the growing warning sound and reposition myself on my knees. "So much has happened. You've missed so much."

Tell me, he says.

My ear itches. Soon, they'll come. I talk quickly. "There's going to be an epic battle. Between us and the Collective, orchestrated by my time-travelling power. They will be weakened by an altered version of the vitaphage. We think because of Jadore. We will try to capture her and her eggs and deliver her to the council to stop the fighting, but—"

The ring in my ear modulates. They're going to find me soon. It's the end of December. At this moment, Past Me is hurtling through the Untraver with my friends. Perhaps I am fighting them in there, unknowingly buying me time here.

"We have a new base," I tell him, knowing he wouldn't understand the context. "It's on an island. You could go in the ocean and..."

More music. More words on the screen. *I'm too weak, my star. I'm sorry. Please, do not trouble yourself.*

"No! We...we have to figure out a way to get you out of here. I'm not going to let you die!" My back straightens suddenly. I can take the research we've gathered, travel back in time and give it to Gayarnu or some other alien scientist, return to collect the cure when it's done, and return to this moment and administer it to Ethan. Administer it to all the aliens here, really. I saw Agailya dying, but I never saw her die.

As I spiral out of control, Ethan taps a finger on the glass and directs my attention to the screen. The faint sound of a tune in C minor reaches my ears.

We all die, my star, he says. *If you would grant me one dying wish, it would be for you to sing with me.*

I choke back a sob and find myself laughing. "I'm not much of a singer. I...I don't have any instruments..."

Try, he says, in a low E minor.

The person I love is dying and I must heed his request. He begins in E minor, the water rippling in a glorious G and C chord, and I surrender to my senses. The sound from my lips matches the colours, and we harmonize our protest song that we created so long ago. The song that called Campbell through. He's not here now and the buzz in my ear has disappeared too. It's just me and Ethan and the love we have for each other that endures across species and time.

We will endure. The ahmei words of suffering spring forward, and I suddenly understand them in a new way. Yes, I will endure this moment and the next, for him.

The song fizzles out unexpectantly as his tail flicks against the glass. I jump back, but he's pointing beyond me. I swivel, catching a flash of green scaly flesh with pointed, black hairs through the crack in the door I left ajar.

Jadore.

"I'll be back!" I shout, knowing he'll understand. I rush out into the corridor and Jadore dashes out of sight, her hospital gown trailing behind her.

I've seen her look this way.

She glances back at me with a horrified, fear-stricken look on her face.

"Hey!" I run after her.

She's easy to catch. Her legs stagger beneath her, as if she's been drugged. She's still recovering from the rescue. I throw her against the wall, forcing her to face me. Unlike the emaciated woman thrown out of the airlock, this Jadore is pure adrenaline. Her dark alien eyes are sharp and full of malice. Whatever causes her to become sick, it hasn't happened yet.

"How long were you there?" I demand. "What did you hear?"

The frightened, smug look on her face says it all.

Everything.

This whole time, she knew about the Final Battle. Because I'm the one who told her.

"You won't succeed," she says, through fanged teeth.

"Neither will you," I reply, with equal venom.

And that's why I let her go.

She darts down the hallway as my right ear clogs. The Untrakeepers are close.

I'm not here anymore. My mind is in the past. *This* present. The puzzle pieces, previously floating, click together with an echoing thud in my brain.

Jadore can never be redeemed. Her attack on the Collective had not just been opportunistic, but pre-meditated, based on her ill-gotten knowledge of the future. She alters and releases the vitaphage upon the Collective and humanity to weaken everyone, so that she is free to construct a new portal. And order her followers to fly there, en masse, during the chaos of the battle. So that she can escape the Collective's influence, forever. This whole time, she knew what was coming.

My friends hadn't been fooled, even after spending a year with her trapped on an island. Had my friends not killed Jadore, she could have commandeered the *Blind Elephant* and could have populated her home world with phage-resistant offspring that would have quickly multiplied and taken over.

They had been right about her, and I, wrong.

I sink to the floor. I don't like being wrong.

If I'd been wrong about Jadore's ability to be redeemed, what else had I misjudged?

I reach a hand back towards Ethan's tank room as I sink to the floor. I can't think that way. I wasn't been wrong about Ethan. I saved him. He's alive. For now. I can travel the multiverse; I can travel back and forth through time. But I can't rescue him from this place. We can't even breathe the same air. Even if I figure out a way to return him to human form, he will not remember his true self. The ahmei in the water is who he is. I can't deny him his heritage, his mind, for my own selfishness.

Here in this moment, he isn't dead. When I figure out a way for us to be together, I will return and help him.

Right now, there is one sentient being who has asked for my help repeatedly during our tenure together; someone I can prove my usefulness and power to.

Grasping the knowledge that Ethan will always exist here, safe, in this moment, I whisper to the walls, "I'm ready to see Campbell at the end."

Green fog spills out of the portal. It's a near-perfect, half-sized copy of the portal in the underground library, complete with the consoles and the apparatus Jadore had strapped me into to power the thing. The portal takes up most of the room in this enclosed space. Domed exits lead downward, possibly into an engineering room where the technology responsible for gravity, air filtration, and other such things are housed.

The main difference between this portal and the one at Sparkstone is that this one is in *space*.

The sight of Earth through a floor-to-ceiling, spotless glass bulkhead catches my breath, as if I'm admiring a beautiful person with whom love is not meant to be. Around Earth, our fleet of *Blind Elephant* copies zip around, carrying out the Final Battle dance in all its glory. If I have to guess, I've arrived somewhere close to the beginning of the fight. The show has just begun. If I squint, I can see the first version of us arrive, dead in the water.

I'm here, at the end, like he asked me to be. Campbell has been waiting in this structure for me to help him. That's why I keep returning here. Because *he's* here.

And within less than half an hour, Jadore's convoy will arrive at this portal, expecting a speedy trip to the promised land. It's possible that Gayarnu and the ahmei might divert the ships and rescue the humans. If not, I might have to take matters into my own hands.

I feel the heat of his observational gaze as I cross the room towards the humming portal. I don't understand the depth of his power and tether to me. "Six months. To the second. You are looking rather distinguished for eighteen."

Is he calling me old? I haven't looked at myself in a mirror in a while. I try not to be offended. I am a time traveller with all of space and time at her fingertips. He needs me to complete his mission. I am Chosen. I go along with it. "Must be all that recycled air."

"Even at this hour, you're in good spirits. I'm pleased."

His words paint a picture in my mind. I hear a pleasant man with a pep in his step as he approaches and settles into a slow pace behind me. Yet within his hard-toed boots, I hear the anxious dance of responsibility. I have arrived at the exact moment, as promised, but now the moment has come for both of us to take a leap into the unknown. Neither of us have been here before or have seen what comes after. I must help him, though I don't know how. I clasp my hands before my navel and revel at the technology that once taunted me, that birthed Sunni into this universe, and I steel myself for my terrifying, fated task.

"She built it, feverishly," he says.

He's talking about Jadore and her ill-fated plan, inspired by Campbell's treatise. The portal seems too small for the ships in the convoy. Upon closer inspection, I see mechanisms for enlarging the frame. Perhaps the glass bulkhead opens as well? Not that it matters. Jadore will never live to see her plan completed, and sometime soon, we will stop the ships.

I feel an unexpected twinge of guilt. She went to all this trouble to build a portal, and he helped her...for his own gain.

But he's helping me. I'm helping him. It's me whom he favours and this is how I can use my power *for good.*

A warning tugs at the back of my brain. Didn't the Untrakeepers tell me not to trust him? Well, they also burn doors in the Untraver. They certainly can't be trusted.

"I can't imagine how long it's been for you, waiting here for me," I say quietly, puncturing the hum. I remember when he told me to meet him—he had sounded old and tired.

"Even you can't envision Time's passage like me. You aren't built to." The tone comes off as harsh, although he doesn't mean to be. Again, he speaks of the concept of time as if it is a person. He softens. "Your concern for me is touching. Jadore kept me busy, and I, her. You're meant for something greater than dashing around the universe, I assure you."

I fight every fibre that wills me to turn and shake my purpose out of him like a vending machine that has eaten my money. The portal emits a loud crack and a twisted bolt of lightning snakes out of the circular frame. It disappears, although its visage has been seared onto my eyeballs.

"What am I meant to do for you now?" I ask. Gingerly, I approach the portal, ready to leap through at his command.

"You'll help me ensure all of reality remains intact." He moves away from me, towards the control panels. *Clack, clack, beep.* Hesitation. A sharp sigh from the omnipotent alien who has lived since before the beginning of time. Then, a final long *beep.*

The fog within the portal swirls and evaporates towards the frame, revealing a familiar sight. Although I don't know the exact location, I know by the gut-punch of awe and sadness that this place exists somewhere in the Maritimes. The dense trees, the winding rural road, and the shimmering water reflecting the clouded sun screams rural Nova Scotia. Other than the road, no human has touched this area of nature in a long time.

"This isn't in my universe." The smell of the evergreens beckons me closer, and yet the scent of green is sharper, by one quarter note. Where Alt-Ethan's universe has a dense sweetness like cheesecake, this one is earthier, as if I've sank my teeth into chocolate mousse and discovered the chocolate is seventy-percent cocoa, sweetened with a touch of raw honey.

This place *could* be my home. I can bring everyone I love there, and with time, we will know each other again. Perhaps that is how I will save my people.

"If you can bring up this image in the portal, then why do you need me? You know that I can take you through the Untraver without a portal, right?" I wonder dimly if he needs something large brought through from another universe, just as Jadore envisioned for her devilish plan.

"What you see is only an image. A future memory, converted to bits and bytes, that you can use as reference for where we need to go." I hear the amusement in his voice. I wonder if he thinks that having access to *future memories* impresses me. It does, but part of me doesn't want to let on that it does. Campbell approaches me again, his footfalls light and deliberate. "As for the portal itself, it will help you focus your energy. Transporting me is no easy feat. In there, I want to help a girl like you who knows what it's like to go home and be greeted by the blank faces of her loved ones."

I frown. *Help a girl like you.* He has talked about this before. I wonder if he's talking about my past self, or if there truly is another version of me in this other universe that needs saving. I play along. "Help her, how?"

I hear the flapping of pages. I sneak a glance. Campbell's treatise. Jadore had said she'd given it to him. "She needs this as a gift, to guide her."

Now I'm really convinced this *girl* is me. As he turns a page, I hear a faint, familiar voice cry out in a delicate B-minor from somewhere within the spine. I cock my ear, but Campbell slaps the book shut.

"Take you to a girl to deliver a book. I can do that." I have to be useful. Anything to numb my grief and pain.

"No." The word echoes, thunderous, aloud and in my brain. The wind whips the trees like a sudden gale has afflicted the home that isn't my home.

"What do you mean, no?" I turn and stare at his hands again. They're no longer normal and the book has disappeared. His hands have a strange geometry that my brain can't fully comprehend. Four fingers, one thumb, and yet they're in motion, falling and rising. Is this what four dimensions looks like? I squint against it, because I feel a headache coming on, and I definitely can't travel anywhere if I'm not well.

He sweeps his hand away from my sight. The gesture is a kindness; he doesn't want to distract me. "The honour rests in your power to help me. Only you, in all of the verses, can do this. Just as I am the only one who can help this poor girl, in there." He points to the lake and the trees, which have thankfully settled into a relative serenity.

I feel silly. The woman he's talking about helping clearly isn't me. "Who is this girl? What does she look like?"

"You wouldn't know her. Only I can recognize she who has been Chosen."

Chosen. The word thuds like a dull knife on carpet, but the sound rings through my ears. *She who has been Chosen.*

Does he not recognize *me* as *she?* Am I not the one who called him with my song to this universe? Am I not the one tethered to him, a bond that has endured through space and time?

Campbell is still talking, taking my silence as compliance. "That's why I must go, and why the portal is needed. You must stay and keep the door open, to bring me back when needed. It will not be long, for you."

"So, I send you through the portal. You help some random young woman. Then what?"

"Then the worlds—every world—is saved."

"That's it?"

"That's all you need to do."

That's all I need to do.

"That's...*all*...I need to do?"

"At this point, opening and closing the space between places may seem like nothing for you. You've done it hundreds of times. It is quite extraordinary. A gift. Not everyone can traverse the land between Time's domain."

Something in how he says the word *Time* again makes me feel like it is capitalized, as if he is speaking about a person, and not the passage of seconds and minutes. "What happens after the worlds are saved?"

"What do you want to happen?"

"I want things to return to how they were. Before Sparkstone. Or, at least, I want the ability to pick up the pieces. Gain control over what little I have left."

"Of course. You can have that, once I'm through."

I think about it some more. "I want Ethan to have peace. He doesn't deserve the lot he suffers. He deserves to see his home too." Saying 'home' out loud ushers forth another wish. "And I don't want the Earth to explode. Can we prevent that? Like, the results of the battle, happening out there?" I thrust a finger toward the glass wall.

He seems surprised when I mention that Earth will explode. But the reaction is brief. "Possibly. Now, when you're ready—"

"I've seen so many things. There is so much I can teach our world. I could have my own school. Or why tie myself down, when I could continue to explore? There are so many planets to discover, other parallel worlds—"

"No," he says so firmly that my skeleton nearly crawls out of my skin. "Do what you wish here. But this is the end. You will open this door for me, now that you're able. And then when I'm back through, you will shut it. Forever. Once that door closes, you will never be able to travel again."

"But you said I'm—"

"Chosen? The young woman I desperately need to help is Chosen. You? An anomaly in the multiverse. There are very few of you, Ingrid. And of all of them, I was able to reach you. That makes you unique. Your ability to peel away this reality and reach the Untraver, well, even more remarkable, once I made the adjustments to your placement in the Verse."

I'm too stunned to speak. *Adjustments to your placement in the Verse.*

"You have prepared, haven't you? You've seen enough for many lifetimes? Your world *has* been saved. And it will be saved again, by letting me through. That's all you have to do and then you have earned your rest. That is what you want, isn't it, above all? To rest?"

My body resonates with his voice. To sleep and not wake up with the heavy weight of time and travel laying on my chest. To breathe real air. To look out a window and see nature, not the endless vacuum. To be with my family again.

"So, if I help you through there...the Earth won't explode?"

He approaches the portal. "Your universe will be saved."

"That wasn't my question. If I help you help this girl—"

"The *prolege*—" He cuts himself off, as if he has said too much. "She is not *some girl.* Show some respect."

"My home will still be destroyed. How does this supposed Chosen One save us if everyone I love will still die?"

"Do you not have a spaceship? You walk through time and space because of me. You could have helped them at any time. Shipped them to a new Earth, a new planet, built a space station, formed a new Earth or regime in your image. And yet, you waited."

"You're saying it's my fault that I haven't saved everyone?"

"You could have come to me at any time in your life."

"I was busy saving my friends and my people."

"That wasn't the task I gave you. I need this so I can play my role, as you have now played yours."

"Wasn't it my task to save the universe? Even if it's through another person? If not me and my friends, then who would have pulled this off? Do you even know what I've sacrificed, just to get here today?"

"So self-centered. Maybe in the next loop, I will tell myself to coddle you less."

"What has happened before will happen again!" I shout at him, hating the words.

"Yes, it will," he says with finality. "Every time you see yourself, you will never tell her what is coming, because of your primal self-preservation. And when you help me, now, you are ensuring the continuation of that existence."

"I changed the future." I pull on my shirt. It feels too silly to explain.

"You think an outfit qualifies as a real change? True, the Untrakeepers have burned universes for less, but it is insignificant in the grand scheme, far more insignificant than a nudge or a spoken word. What has happened before will happen again, regardless of what outfit you wear."

I wipe tears from my eyes. I'm quiet for at least a minute, considering his words. "Why does this cut off my power? Can't you give it back, when you're done?"

"I'm sorry, Ingrid. That's not the arrangement I negotiated."

The *arrangement*. The *alteration* of my fate. I can't accept that. "Fine. I'm leaving, and when I'm about to die, I'll return here and help you."

This frightens him. "No, no, no. Far too risky, now that you are already here."

"What we're doing out there is risky." I point out to the raging battle.

"Precisely," he says. "The Untrakeepers, as you called them, don't like it when your life crosses over like that. Very messy."

I gaze out into the calming nature through the portal, and then back to planet Earth. A rush of blood fills my cheeks as I step up into the apparatus designed to enhance my power. "The last time I did this, Jadore tied me up?"

"A crude method. You don't need it. Try."

His voice has become gentle again, like a kindly grandfather speaking patiently to a child about the ways of the world. I tilt my head, considering the portal. The serene wilderness within is fading into rolling green fog. I'm reminded of the Untraver, and the calm waters we crossed.

A dark hole stabs at my brain. Someone had grabbed me when I was in the Untraver, but it hadn't been an Untrakeeper. Something ancient and desperate.

Understanding blooms in my gut. I keep it hidden there, in case Campbell can see through to my brain. The Maritime rural scene has disappeared into the green mist.

"What are you doing?" Campbell asks, his tone laced with warning.

"Go through," I tell him, gesturing to the mist. It takes immense concentration, to be half in this existence, and conjure the other side of a door through the portal. I'm stretched thin, as if I've been asked to perform music on an hour of sleep. As before, the portal amplifies my power. I feel it feeding on me, and I recall how the portal was supposed to be powered by the Hunger. Us destroying the creature put a wrench in those plans.

He puts one boot through the portal. But something is wrong, and he knows it. He turns his face, and I see it in profile. He looks so blandly human. Come to think of it, there have been times when I could look upon him without feeling like tearing my eyeballs out. Perhaps he controls this effect.

Hurry, I think. *Let this be done.*

"This isn't the right place, Ingrid," he says, in a cold, somewhat taunting voice. His face distorts, rising and falling like his hands had done previously.

I match his tone. "How would you know?" I return a little more to this reality. I have to be ready.

"I have travelled the Untraver long before your race existed in the flesh. Where do you think you called me from, truly?" He lifts his boot out of the mist and plants it back on the floor. I can no longer look at his face without triggering madness. "You're planning to deceive me and it won't work. You will help me, in this moment, *now.*"

The sound of his voice contains multitudes and envelopes me like a dust cloud. I hear layers of thoughts, colours, and stories beneath the rich texture. His plan to save this girl, who must shoulder a terrible burden, just as great as mine. But beneath that, his loneliness. He can never see his brothers and sisters again, because of a great sacrifice they made to create everything we cherish. He is the only one left, the twenty-seventh of his kind, doomed to exist in a fabric of reality not meant for his species. I hear the voices of his past in his song, clips of a story that doesn't make sense to me, and then I see it: a memory, buried deep in the sound. It plays out of order and I fight to arrange it.

He's in Sunni's bedroom at Sparkstone University. "How would you like to be a part of something greater than yourself, Sunni?"

"You are offering me something I already have," Sunni replies.

"Then I will put it to you differently: how would you like to be an important instrument in a war that will determine the fate of all Verses?"

An instrument. "I am not a tool."

"Again, a poor choice of words. The language." *He smiles and lifts a hand.* "Perhaps it would be better to show you."

And show her he does, in her dreams. A future that will come to pass: a promise of continued normalcy.

"You see the good you will do," *Campbell says, finally.*

"I have already done this, then," *Sunni says flatly.* "It is not a question or a request. You are telling me that now is my time..."

"You understand, then."

Silence. Then: "Yes."

"And you submit?"

More silence. "My friends...they will not understand. Ingrid will not understand. Misty..."

"We may delay briefly so that you may sort your affairs."

And then: the sound of her dying on the mother ship. Her soul, moving through space and time. Arriving, finally, within the spine of that book.

The Untrakeepers had warned me that once Campbell was done sharing his soul with me, he'd take it back.

He snaked into and manipulated not only my life, but hers, to fulfill some kind of grand plan that I can't bring myself to feel for. Sunni died, not just at Jadore's hands, but at his. I step off the apparatus, holding the door open in the portal, as the sound-memory fades in my ears. I'm shaking as I give this ancient creature a wide berth. "I will *never* help you."

The words echo through the space with damning finality. *Never... never...*

They seal our entwined fate. Within my gut, I feel their truth. I will never help him. Campbell will *never* save this other woman, who will save all the multiverses.

Who says they need saving? They are probably fine, anyway.

The echo becomes an ugly ringing in my ears, like two discordant notes played together and called the same. It stabs my eardrums and a cacophony of colours and tastes overwhelm my senses.

"You were supposed to agree," he says, confused. "I was told you would agree."

"By who? Your Future Self? Are you sure he wasn't *lying* to you, as you have been to me, this whole time?" I advance on him, ready to seal his fate. "You made me think I was..." It sounds stupid to say out loud, so I hold it back.

"No one except one is cosmically important. And even she is such that her very construction has doomed her to obscurity. You wouldn't have brought me this far, had I told you the truth, instead of..." He trails off, distracted, as he touches his ear. He can hear the ringing too. "They've heard you. You have doomed us all. Unless they can convince you otherwise."

"What do you mean, *I* can convince them? You're their great-great-great-whatever uncle!"

"That's why they will never listen to me. I'm...well, that's a different story. The Untrakeepers, as you call them, they control any divergence. The separation of one multiverse from another. They carefully prune the multiverse garden of needless weeds."

The scorched doors.

"No, don't—!" I hear him crash to the ground, the annoyed grunts of the Untrakeepers as they materialize like physical dark shadows and struggle against him.

Campbell doesn't want them to hurt me. He needs me. But he doesn't care about me.

He must see my intention as I barrel forward, palms outstretched, shoulders tensed, head down like a football player, or maybe a boxer.

His feet are square with mine, turned outward, as if to say, *we can talk this out*. But I'm done talking. My fingers touch his surprisingly warm body and I thrust him into the Untraver. He disappears through the portal with no sound of surprise. Just the thud of boots against metal.

He's in there now. I'm going to be running from him too. He's going to do everything he can to convince me to let him out and complete his task. But that's for Future Me to worry about. Present Me has to get out of here. I draw back from the portal and paw at the air, and this slows the turbulent, green swirl of fog. I feel the door to the Untraver closing.

The Untrakeepers continue to spill out of the walls, the ceiling, and the floor like viscous black fluid desperate for form. Their aggressive thought-language assaults my senses. I turn and dart between them. They rip at my clothes. I don't need to run. I just need to close my eyes and move, because the movement distracts me.

All this time, they've been after me not because I've zipped in and out of my own timeline, stole Wil prematurely from Sparkstone, or saved Ethan, Gayarnu, and the others.

This is about, and always has been about, this moment. My rejection of him here and now has caused a cascade that ripples throughout my life.

They reach claw-like hands for my throat.

What has happened before, will happen again. It has already happened.

The Untrakeepers have and will continue to chase me wherever I go, but there's one last thing I can try. It might mean my own undoing because if I succeed, my friends will never meet. But it will prevent Ethan's death, the vitaphage, and all of the evil the Collective has ever done in our universe.

I conjure images of my friends, and happier times. I hold desperately to these thoughts that may unravel, because of what I'm about to do.

I'm going back in time to prevent the formation of the Collective.

❧345❧

CHAPTER 16

What a silly plan, to map the infinite. So vain and small of me, to think that I *could* do that, when all I need is my big, beautiful brain. The Untraver tells me where to go, or perhaps, I tell it my will, and it obliges. Regardless, I get where I need to be, every time.

I don't know *when* in time I appear in a flurried huff in the mess deck of the *Blind Elephant*. But I know from their tans that it's post-island. Misty and Wil leap from the booth, their surprised movements ruining their card game. Playing cards scatter all over the floor. Jia, her cheeks flushed and hair wet from bathing, flattens against the lockers.

"Hey," I say shortly, and beeline for the cockpit.

The three of them race behind me, calling out their questions and concerns. Wil knows my intention, of course. He voices his concern telepathically. *Don't do this, Ingrid. Don't make me stop you.*

He can't stop me. I have very little left to lose.

Sunni mans the ship. From a distance, I spot Earth, a tiny blue globe. Jupiter shines brightly. I don't know why we're cruising along here, and it doesn't matter. Sunni spins in the chair, nimble as a cat. Her tan makes her freckles dark and handsome, and it kills me that her greeting is just as cheery. "Hey, you're back!" Then, as I barge into her space, "What are you doing? Ingrid, stop!"

I've been watching him and Sunni. They're not the only ones who know how to manipulate the controls. I don't need the ship to go back in time, nor do I need to be in control of it before I make the jump, but I'd like to be in the driver's seat the moment I arrive. Better to commandeer the ship I know instead of risking a violent, unnecessary encounter with the real enemy.

Besides. When I'm done with this, they won't know me. And I won't know them. My friends and anyone involved in the Collective. I will have never gone to Sparkstone, because it will never have existed. Maybe I would never have developed my powers.

My gut roils at the thought, seizing control of my trembling hands. If I don't have my powers, who am I?

My friends take advantage my moment of weakness. Misty takes hold of my arms and Sunni leaps from the chair, ready to help. They're chattering around me. Wil's calm voice seems to be relaying information. All I can think is I'm on a roller coaster that I can't get off, and I have to see the ride through to its conclusion, even if it means not everyone will survive.

I'll figure out my powers when I get there. First, I need to take care of the Collective. It doesn't matter that my friends are holding me. I summon hopeful thoughts—despite Wil's intrusions in the back of my brain, attempting to keep me here—I can feel us entering the Untraver. I'm in the liminal space, between sleep and wakefulness. I hear the tittering of the sh-winil and the lapping of waves against the hull. I just have to let go a little more.

We don't have to go to the beginning, Wil says telepathically. *We can go anywhere you want in time. Even home.*

Home. The thought fills me with a painful longing. I haven't seen my parents in so long. They don't even know me. But I can take us to a time when they do know me.

Except I can't. The thought slams into my gut like a hammer to a nail, bringing me fully back to solid reality. I can't go back to Earth, not without the Untrakeepers following me. Because this is what happens when you defy Campbell. This is what happens when you try to change the course of fate.

But I can't let it go. What are they going to do, come after me *more?*

I feel Wil parsing all of this. I feel as if all of my friends can hear my internal monologue at this rate.

"I don't know...I don't know *how...*" I say in response to the silence between us. I've become a problem and I don't know how to not be one at this point.

"It doesn't have to be this way," Sunni says softly, putting a comforting hand on top of Misty's, which still grips my forearm.

My face feels fiercely red. "I just wanted to prevent it all."

"You could have asked us," Misty says.

"You didn't ask..." I trail off, overwhelmed with guilt. They didn't ask me if I wanted to kill Jadore. But they'd been right to do so, in the end. They also don't need my permission to act. I'm not in charge. I'm not Chosen enough.

"Let's all take a deep breath," Wil says, not unkindly.

"I was about to make some tea," Jia says. "Let's go have some, Ingrid."

I nod. Misty and Sunni guide me back into the mess. Their bodies are comforting against mine. I remember the last time we all hugged, at the island. It had been a lifetime ago for them. For me, a torrid few days of emotional upheaval. Misty guides me into the booth and as my buttocks appreciates the softness, my eyes start to droop. Rest. I could lay down and go to sleep, and maybe this has all been a terrible dream, and I'll wake up, and my parents will know me again...

Soothing music is put on from a small speaker and Sunni crawls in next to me. Wil and Misty clear off the card game and slide in across, while Jia piles up a few of the bean bag chairs and plops on top of it.

"Tell us what's going on," Sunni says, stroking my back affectionately.

The story comes out in drips first, like a leaky faucet. When I get to the part about Ethan being at Sparkstone, and a secret ahmei, it starts to pour. The words and my tears. With more kindness than I deserve, they interrupt little, only to clarify events that become tangled from my scattered retelling.

"What Campbell did to you? That's messed up. Not that it totally excuses what you tried to do," Misty says shortly.

Wil looks pensive. He appears like he wants to ask a question, but doesn't want to change the subject. He raises his eyebrows at Jia instead, urging her to take the floor.

"Misty's right. We'll have to figure out some kind of punishment, but..." Her eyebrows knit together at the word. "You did it. You saved Ethan, like you said you would. It sounds like you were predestined to do that, even if the result isn't what you'd hoped."

I'm in love with an alien. Someone who is supposed to be our enemy. Our love had been so brief, and now, unless I can figure out how to cure the altered vitaphage, he will be dead, permanently. It seems so unlikely we'll be able to create something meaningful at this point.

"Whatever punishment, I accept it," I say dully. Nothing matters anymore, anyway. "And I shouldn't have interrupted...whatever you were doing. If you want me to leave, and that's the punishment, that's fine too."

"Where will you go?" Sunni asks. She climbs out of the booth, allowing me to freely leave.

I shake my head. "I guess I'll need to go back at some point and give you all supplies."

Jia leads me now, towards the loft, where there are freshly laundered blankets. I smell them from down here, and they're inviting. "You can nap first, if you want."

I wipe my face. My limbs are so heavy. Sleeping feels like a luxury. "But..."

"We have lots of time, Ingrid. Lots and lots," she promises me.

I don't remember climbing up the narrow staircase and opening the hatch into the loft. I fall into a squishy air mattress, soft fluffy blankets, and a fresh pillow, and I descend into welcoming darkness.

My dreams are curiously uninteresting, and when I emerge into consciousness again, I'm groggy, but refreshed. The woman sending me dreams is here now, so I have no reason to suspect any answers will come from sleeping. But a thought does occur to me upon waking. The nagging sensation from my glimpse of Campbell's final destination has jogged an instinct. I have to follow it, to see if I'm right.

I descend the spiraling staircase into the mess and find my friends: Jia and Sunni are poring over a tablet loaded with historical texts on Buddhism in the cockpit. Misty leans back in the booth, earbuds in and eyes closed as she listens to music. Wil communes with the sh-winil in the engineering room.

"If you're up for it, I think I know where we should go," I tell them.

Roads wind in and around the greenspace around the Alexander Graham Bell Museum. The land slopes gradually down to the water, immaculately kept. I'm overwhelmed on this perfect day by the tamed ruggedness; my mother's homeland.

Jia and Wil stay with the ship, which Wil parks in one of the small lots near the museum. Tourists mill about the grounds, but with Wil's presence, no one will get within three feet of the ship. I don a black toque to cover my signature hair, but otherwise, there's no reason for us to be invisible.

"What are we lookin' for?" Sunni asks as we cross the parking lot and step onto the pathway leading to the museum.

I search the green space before us to ensure I'm right, and when I do, my heart pounds darkly. Yes. The *photo*. There had been a reason I'd sought it out, after dreaming about him. My heritage, my music, it's all tied up in my bond with him, so of course he inserted himself here, so I would be inclined to sing to him and trust him with my soul.

"What is that?" Sunni asks, gesturing with her chin towards a figure standing beneath a large tree.

And there he is. In human form, without the aura of madness. Just a regular, unassuming man, dressed as a tourist and welcomed as such.

"Him," I say, fearful that saying any moniker will alert the powerful being. "You can see him?"

Misty and Sunni make noises of agreement. Usually he doesn't appear in public and takes pains not to be seen by others. I lead us a little closer. Campbell could only materialize in our reality after I pulled him through with my music. I wonder where in his timeline he is, and if he knows I am here, watching him.

I see the corner of his lips twitch. He knows. He always knows. Well, not for long. Soon he will be trapped in the Untraver and I will never, ever rescue him.

An Untrakeeper slips out from a tree trunk like a walking shadow. This one is not angry and it doesn't seem to notice my presence. I don't even hear it speaking or that familiar ring in my inner ear. Crisp black robes, slightly too large for its skinny features, billow in the sea air as it lumbers towards Campbell's human form.

It stops several feet from him. They share a look I cannot see. I strain to listen. The wind picks up and swirls the Untrakeeper's robes. I see no shoes, no feet. It is floating above the ground.

This is the moment of change. The wind carries a long, E-minor note to my ears, emitted from his beautiful mouth. I straighten, and so does my younger self.

My younger self stands with my parents, who are distracted by the boats in the water. She squints and shields her eyes from the sun, staring at Campbell. Recognizing him. *Knowing* him.

Her red hair flows gracefully in the strong wind. I'm a vision. I'm only a year younger than when I started at Sparkstone, but God, I look *young*. There's so much to come.

The change is cemented quickly. My parents see my younger self staring and touch my shoulder. They call him over to ask him to take the photo. I call up the memory, and it's surreal, remembering it, while watching it unfold. Human memory is notoriously bad, so it's no wonder I don't remember the finer details of Campbell's face. My parents exchange pleasantries with him. He tells them he's a tourist from Scotland. I don't recall if he has a strong accent—he never has, to my ears.

I could still stop this, I think pointlessly. I could launch myself at him, and the Untrakeeper, who promptly disappears into the tree again. I could step in and politely insist that I take the photo instead.

I could do any of these things, but I don't.

I remain at my friends' sides, watching the scene unfold. It's so banal, it's hilarious. My body trembles with laughter. And sobs. It's stupid that this day, of all the days in all the worlds, my entire life changed, and I didn't even know it. No one knows it. Two aliens got together in a little-known part of a well-to-do country on this Earth and agreed that it was okay for one of them to become tethered to me, so that someday, he could ask me to send him to another universe. Because for some reason, one alien can't directly help the other, nor can he help himself.

All of this, because of that. My throat tightens and my eyes stare dryly at the freshly mowed grass. My body becomes one with the grass, much to the displeasure of my knees. The shock of pain through my legs and torso feels like it's happening to someone else, far away. Every strand becomes an intense object of focus as I attempt to banish the terrible, haunting truth.

Nothing I do can change the past or the future. It's all been for nothing.

I cannot save Ethan; he will die of the vitaphage in a tiny tank on a foreign planet. I cannot save Earth; I can't even go there without being overwhelmed by an alien force. Apparently, I can't even save Campbell or Campbell's special girl because I'm too resentful that I'm not this time-travelling alien's favourite and that he will revoke my power—the very thing making me *special*—the moment I've served my purpose. Every moment I've disregarded because I thought I could fix it later has been wasted.

"I was wrong." The words are fumbling sobs from my swollen

lips. I gaze up at my friends through blurry tears. "I don't know how to be wrong."

"No one does," Sunni assures me, pulling me gently to my feet.

The words are hard to say and I hate them. Saying them means I have been defeated and I truly can't win against the forces of space and time. "I'm sorry."

I don't want them to see me crying. I can't escape this moment when I'm so deep in despair, so maybe if I bury my face in my hands, my friends will politely turn away and pretend I don't exist for a while until we can all forget my transgressions.

When I look up, Campbell, my parents, and my young self have disappeared. We're in the museum, and we will be for the next hour or so, until we go for supper. Visitors mill around the park, and a few do double-takes at me, checking to see if I'm all right. One family looks determined to approach me but Misty and Sunni step in front, hauling me to my feet and signalling to the family that I'm okay.

"It's so stupid," I keep muttering. I don't know if they fully comprehend what we just witnessed, but it doesn't matter. They're here with me, now. We stroll back to the parking lot, linked arm in arm, because I don't know if I can walk without their support.

"It's not," Sunni replies gently. "We got so much goin' for us, because of all of us, includin' you. You already trapped that demon, so he can't bother you. Jadore's defeated. We have almost everything we need to make a cure for a powerful disease."

I wipe my nose on my sleeve. "We do?"

Misty nods. "We're real close. Helps that we aren't stuck on an island in the past."

"We have a ship and we have *you,* and all of us are well," Sunni continues. "We can go to any point in time and space, in any reality.

Maybe we can't save everyone on Earth or stop it from exploding. But we have the means to try, if that's what we decide. We can save who we can and help our race, *every* race impacted by the tyranny of the Collective, rebuild."

Rebuild. The word sparkles with an intense magenta.

"We don't have to be Chosen Ones to rebuild," I say softly.

"Don't have to be Chosen to do anythin'," Sunni agrees. "We can just...be."

CHAPTER 17

We return to the Final Battle, but instead of watching invisibly from the fray or participating, we speed past the asteroid belt, towards the outer planets. Wil has restored most of the data from the crash, but wants a broader picture of the battle before we jump back in.

From Jupiter's orbit, with long-range sensors, we once again watch the battle for our planet unfold. With everything that has happened, I still expect our actions to have impacted the future. But the Collective still quarantines Earth. Earth explodes. Jadore's army speeds for the portal, for all the good it will do them.

"Nothing has changed," Jia says flatly.

"We are creating the future, we're not changing it," Wil says, exhausted from beating the dead horse. "But taking Jadore out of play, that's not nothing. Now we know our fate with certainty."

Easy for him to say, the man who has had the most time of all of us to come to terms with his personal fate.

After Earth explodes and the participants in the battle go their separate ways, Misty, Sunni, and Jia retire to the mess. Invisibility isn't necessary this far out. Wil asks me to stay in the cockpit.

"The Collective was never going to uphold their end of the bargain," he says. "They were never going to help us save Earth. They banked on our hatred of Jadore and hoped we'd deliver."

I raise my eyebrows at him. "Is now the best time to tell us that?"

He smiles a little. "Well, funny you should put it like that." Tapping on some of the controls, he brings up a digital overlay over the canopy. "Your question to the Collective, way back when we met them at their nebula, had me puzzled. So, right before we snuck on the mother ship, I had the *Blind Elephant* access the mother ship's mainframe. Managed to download some files. I plan to download more, each time we reappear here, if I can."

"Which question?" I ask him.

"The one you asked that neocortex about first contact. If first contact was less than a hundred years ago, but the first research facilities on Earth opened about ten years ago, what was the delay? At first, I thought it was bureaucracy, but that didn't sit right. Then your adventure with Ohz and the hafelglob got me thinking. I did a little digging in the more classified edges of the computer, and found something interesting."

Wil taps another key and a grainy video appears on a digital overlay. I squint and rest my hands on the cool pleather backing of the empty co-pilot seat. Wil plays the video. Grains from the turbulent wind pixelate and block a lot of the action and the colours are limited to blue, black, and white, yet my own image is unmistakable. Long hair, waving angrily up at the camera, surrounded by dead hafelglob.

I feel butterflies in my stomach. "No audio?"

He shakes his head. With another button-tap, the timecode appears in the video as it loops repeatedly. The clip is about ten seconds long. Text also accompanies the video in three different alien languages.

"How many years ago is this from?" I ask.

"This clip was recorded on the exterior sensors of the mother ship approximately eighty Earth years ago," Wil says.

Eighty years ago, I saved the hafelglob. I took Ohz from the Untraver and put him on his dying planet, and helped him save his people.

"Can we translate that text entry?" I ask him.

"Misty and I have been working on a program to speed up some of the decryption on the alternate universe hard drive. Let's see…"

A few moments later, the alien text disappears and is replaced with English.

From the desk of Councillor Ari-Faur. Subject recognized from Earth trials. Sparkstone division. Councillor was on mother ship during hafelglob planet cleanse attempt. Time interference confirmed. Power threat, confirmed. Recommendation: human race cannot be allowed to propagate unchecked. Wrap ongoing trials. Select specimens for containment and study. Terminate planet.

The black thud of dread hits me in the stomach. The timestamp on the text is March thirteenth. Probably just after our meeting with the Collective. That councillor had recognized me. I sink into the co-pilot chair as my vision narrows. I can see why he didn't want the others in here with us.

It was me, not Jadore. I'm the cause of Earth's destruction. If I hadn't trapped Ohz in the Untraver, if I hadn't been so determined to save Ethan…

…then who knows what would have happened to the hafelglob race? If I had not saved Ohz as a child, who would have saved me and my friends in the future?

Every time I try to change something, I end up causing trouble.

"Don't blame yourself," comes Wil's soft baritone.

"How can I not? If I hadn't gone off on my own, I wouldn't have gotten us all into this mess—"

"And you wouldn't be the person you are now," Wil finishes. "You wouldn't do what I know you're going to do, despite my opinions, despite the futility and absurdity."

"You're not going to stop me?"

He shrugs. "I could, I guess. Do I want to?" He presses a hand on the bulkhead as he swivels in his chair. "Surviving on rations, babysitting a genocide perpetrator, fixing the ship over the course of the last year—gives a man time to think things through. If we're going to choose a cause that doesn't directly change a fixed event, it might as well be saving our species. We only got one life, Ingrid. I want to believe that before it's my time to return to help you, and Kimberly, and the rest of them, that I can contribute to something with meaning."

"That's all I want too, Wil." I have to do this, to make up for everything I've done wrong to my friends and family. It's my responsibility to make the most of my power and to use it not to serve myself, as I've been doing. If other humans naturally develop this power, I have to be a good example.

Standing firmly in the cockpit of the *Blind Elephant*, the entire universe at my fingertips and the weight of time upon me, feels stifling. The intimidation of having it all before me, waiting to be done by me, and the hesitation of staring, wide-eyed, at its weight.

My plan? Save humanity, one person at a time. For as long as it takes to remove everyone before the Earth explodes. But for that to happen, we need two things: a vaccine for the altered vitaphage and a new home for humanity.

We scratch the days into the bulkheads. The first year crawls by and we fall into a comfortable rhythm.

Misty teaches us a smattering of French, German, and Chinese to pass the time. Jia leads us in a morning meditation each day. We're reluctant at first, but after a month, I see the benefits of increased concentration and focus. In the evening, we do yoga, or Sunni will teach us advanced hand-to-hand she learned from her guerilla warfare days.

But it's not all work. We take advantage of my time travel powers and create our own traditions. On our birthdays, we allow ourselves one excursion—dealer's choice and never the same date twice, preferably one where smartphones and street cameras aren't capturing our movements. Jia chooses China on her birthday, so we visit the Great Wall and eat street food. Misty shows us around Paris. We eat ice cream from a local place in Houston, Sunni's favourite. Wil nerds out at an aviation museum.

But everywhere we go, the Untrakeepers follow. The further back in time we travel, the more time we have before signs of their arrival appear. We have to run on the Great Wall and through the back alleys of Paris to drink in what we can of Earth.

I want to take them to a dance in Cape Breton, but I'm afraid of gossip and friendly inquiries that might be hard to answer, so we travel back several decades to get my fix. I want to accompany the fiddlers and teach my friends to dance, so we can stay up all night and become drunk on the music. But because I've angered the keepers of reality, we're stuck running from place to place, doomed to experience our home in tiny increments.

In late December, we each choose a specific day from our childhood and travel there to observe our families, always from a distance, and never longer than ten minutes. If the future is fixed, then we have already been to these places, and there is nothing we can do to affect a major change.

Although Earth's destruction has been proven inevitable by our experiences, it doesn't stop us from trying to prevent the explosion at the Final Battle. Because if we're going to move forward with my plan, we have to be sure we've done everything we can to try and stop our home from being destroyed.

But our every attempt is countered, as if some higher power has foreseen our moves.

"It's not a higher power, unless you think Campbell or the Untrakeepers have something to do with it," Wil explains pointedly. "Everything we're about to do, we've already done. Which means, it's been thought of and countered. It feels like a malicious force outwitting us at every turn because we naturally perceive time as linear, but our current experience is non-linear.

"It's normal to feel that living this way is futile. What's futile is fighting against these natural laws in the name of fairness and individual freedoms. It's not meaningless to live even though we know that someday, we'll die."

This speech doesn't sit well with Misty and Sunni, who continue to create and carry out plots to save the planet Earth. During one run, we confirm that the planet has truly exploded, and *not* teleported. Because if I can jump a ship, why not jump a planet?

"It's almost as if not knowing the future gives us the advantage," I say to Wil after a particularly harrowing run, as I study our holographic map of the Final Battle.

"Knowledge is always power," he replies.

"Sure, but if during our first run of the Final Battle we had thought to do a complete scan of all life forms on Earth, we would know that all of those people will die when the Earth explodes.

Because we don't have concrete data of the population on Earth during the explosion, we'll be able to evacuate as many people as we can."

"I don't know if the *Blind Elephant* had that kind of detailed scanning technology, even if we wanted to do that," Wil says. "We could attempt to run a kind of general scan during our next run, to see how many people are on Earth during the Final Battle, if you want."

"No!" Misty, Sunni, and Jia join my voice in protest.

Wil scoffs, but he's smiling. "I'm sure the result will be what it will be, because—"

"Because we've already decided we're doing it, it will be zero," I declare. "Or, close to zero."

"What about the animals and non-human life?" Sunni asks.

"Ugh," Misty says. "We're gonna Noah's Ark this Elephant?"

"Animals deserve to live just as much as humans. Some would argue more," Jia adds. "We might be returning to an agrarian age. If the planet or environment doesn't have livestock, we may need to bring some. Unless you want cats and other animal protein-eaters to die of malnutrition."

"What planet wouldn't have meat that could be hunted?" Misty asks.

"That's part of the biggest issue we have to consider," I say. "I feel like we're in agreement that we can't settle in this universe. Wherever we go, the Collective or any malicious alien invaders will find us. And who knows? Maybe the Untrakeepers too. I am game to search the Untraver for an alternate universe where the Collective has never materialized. But does that mean I'm searching for an alternate Earth where humans, and no other sentient species, have ever evolved? And if so, when we re-settle there, what do we tell humanity?"

"Nothing," Wil says.

"So that means I'm also searching for a place where Earth exists, and all of the same infrastructures of our modern age, but all of the humans have raptured into the heavens? Or are we migrating all buildings and structures and objects from Earth too?"

He waves his hands. "Point taken. This is why I'm against the idea of saving all of humanity. And yes, point taken again, saving a select few puts us in a moral quandary."

"We should experience the Final Battle on Earth," Sunni says suddenly. "It doesn't have to be in a populated area. If we learn what it's like in the days leading up to the battle, we'll learn how to handle their mindset."

"Good idea. We can also gather the world's science on the altered vitaphage, see how close they came to a vaccine," I say. "Did we ever get any concrete information from the alternate universe drive detailing how to make the cure, or alter ahmei or human DNA to resist the vitaphage?"

Sunni and Misty shake their heads. "A lot of scientific papers on theory, but nothing on practice. Even if we gave it to the Collective or the ahmei, they'd have to sift through it and create methodology, which would take time."

Time is something we have. "And Sunni, you said that the vitaphage cure in your universe meant there were more ahmei around, which meant they ended up with a majority stake in the Collective. Right?"

"I don't think I said it in those words," she began hesitantly. "But, yeah, that's basically true. Why?"

Wil sees the idea bloom into a full-fledged plan in my mind and raises a disapproving eyebrow. "No."

"Yes," I say. "It'll work."

"It might," he concedes. "We're going to need help, and—" He reads the response in my mind and sighs. "Okay, then. I guess it's time."

About twenty minutes after the *Blind Elephant* disappears from the alternate universe, Sunni and I materialize in the cockpit of Alt-Ethan's personal ship. It cruises above the Pacific, flanked by other Collective ships, searching for the *Blind Elephant*.

Alt-Gayarnu and Alt-Ethan—to my surprise—sit closely at the helm. Two armed fishmen man posts on either side, and immediately draw weapons as Sunni and I flicker into existence from seemingly nowhere.

"We're back," I say to them, smirking.

Alt-Gayarnu leaps to their feet, steadying the ailing Alt-Ethan. They sing something to the fishmen, who promptly surround us. It's then I realize that Alt-Ethan isn't piloting anything. He's resting limply in the co-pilot chair, wearing an aquatic breathing mask, his wounds hastily patched.

My insides feel sick, looking at Alt-Ethan, who I'd thought had been killed by Misty. That's history. This Ethan knows he's ahmei, and has always known, and became a poster boy to mislead humanity.

"I'm sorry that you ended up like this," I say to Ethan, because I truly am. But to Alt-Gayarnu, I say, "Please help me, so that my Ethan doesn't share his fate."

"No reason," says Alt-Gayarnu after Sunni translates, patting Alt-Ethan's gurgling form affectionately.

"I'll take you to a new world," I say.

"No," they reply steadily.

"The Gayarnu I know doesn't want anything to do with a war against humans. They want to be in their lab and conduct their experiments in peace, without having to report to a superior, who reports to a greater authority who doesn't care about them." I'm extrapolating and generalizing. Hopefully I'm going in the right direction. "That I can give you."

Sunni gives me a look that says, *You can't be serious.*

Carefully resting Alt-Ethan on the floor, Gayarnu rises like a lithe spirit and floats towards me. I feel the familiar wooziness of her pheromones wash over me. We're all friends here. The ahmei don't mean me harm. They just want to use my body parts and DNA sometimes. That seems reasonable.

"Say truth," Alt-Gayarnu says.

"I want to save Ethan and my people," I reply dreamily.

"No kill?"

A presence in my mind cradles the truth and my lips move accordingly. "We might, if we don't get what we want."

"Hmm. Weapons?"

"Yes."

"New portal coordinates for enemy universe?"

Again, I feel my brain lifting from my skull and another voice speaks through me.

Alt-Gayarnu whistles and the ship changes course. They smirk. "Many thanks." They peer closer, and then side-eye Sunni, and the guards. "Now kill."

Our deception unfolds at lightspeed. It's too late for them to counter us now.

Jia manifests with Wil, Misty, Lynn, and Elisha. Wil doesn't have to look at the fishmen. One blink is all it takes to halt the fishmen's minds. Their webbed fingers freeze on their triggers dangerously. Sunni scrambles out of their grip, pushes Alt-Gayarnu out of the way, and commandeers the craft. Jia removes all weapons from the guards and throws them in a reusable bag. Lynn grasps a grassy talisman around her neck and weaves vine ropes around the fishmen's wrists and ankles. They tumble harmlessly to the ground.

Alt-Gayarnu staggers back as Wil advances on her. The scent of her pheromones returns, yet Wil is immune. Jia and Lynn stand far back to avoid the effect. Elisha, who steps beside me, stutters and blinks, gripping her forehead with one hand and a portable flash drive in another. I feel a sudden strong urge to stop Wil, but Wil has my mind in his grasp too. I'm as frozen as the guards.

He places his hand on Alt-Gayarnu's forehead. The other hand rests on Elisha's flash drive. Heat radiates from her and I smell dust motes burning. Her large tufts of hair contort like staticky angel wings. She squeezes Wil's hand and I feel the squeeze in my brain too.

I feel better than I have in months. Rejuvenated. Wil looks equally revived. Elisha's power refreshes, amplifies, and redirects energy.

Which is handy when we need to download an alien brain that helped to cure and modify the ahmei vitaphage.

His booming voice makes my teeth vibrate. *Tell us everything.*

Alt-Gayarnu's lips part. Their fish eyes lose their gleam and their cheeks shrink, as if we're squeezing the juice from a grape. After a minute, the alien collapses to the floor, bumping into Alt-Ethan's form, who also tumbles on top of her.

Wil relaxes his grip on me and Elisha. "Got it?" he asks her.

Elisha convenes with the flash drive. "Yes. I also have a back up in my mind, of some of their most useful memories."

"Hey, if we're stealing knowledge, we might as well take this ship too," Sunni says, surveying the controls of the fighter with interest. "It even has shields. We can replicate this technology, I think. And I don't want this"—she hums a derogatory word in the ahmei language in unconscious Alt-Ethan's direction—"to have it. Deal?"

"Yeah, we can add it to our fleet!" Misty adds excitedly. "We can rename it. *Stacked Elephant? Sleek Elephant*? Or you can name it." She smiles at Sunni with deference.

"No, I'm not fixing up another ship," Wil says.

Elisha surveys the cramped cockpit and peers into the cabins in the back. "I think we're going to need it. No offense, but the *Blind Elephant* is starting to stink like one."

"I thought we weren't going to tell them that," Lynn hisses at her. "It's so rude."

Elisha shrugs. "Just being honest."

"Sometimes the ship doesn't handle sewage very well, it's true. What do we do with them?" Jia asks, toeing Alt-Gayarnu's zombified form, reaching out in brain-death for Alt-Ethan, who might as well be dead.

I close my eyes to their bodies. I run through the justifications in my head one more time. That isn't my Ethan. We've done this to save the human race, and the ahmei, so we can escape the Collective together. This person did unspeakable things to Sunni. I am not responsible for saving him. I can't save him, not now. "Throw them out."

Sunni stands from the cockpit seat. I've said her deepest wish aloud. "Are you sure, Ingrid?"

I nod. "Let's go save the human race now."

✦

We return with our new ship to the newly rescued Greg and Kimberly, who had been left in charge of the *Blind Elephant*. While not the most technologically capable, Kimberly and Greg keep an eye on Jia's family, who huddle in the mess in shock and disbelief. I would too, if I was suddenly transported to an emergency room, watched a team of nurses and doctors administer care, and then witness said doctors not remember what they had done as we escape onto a stolen spaceship. It's going to take time and research to undo what they have forgotten and witnessed.

Elisha has a point. It's getting crowded on the *Blind Elephant*. I stay long enough for a quick christening of the new ship, which we call the *Pacific Rescuer*, and I write down a list of needed supplies for my friends in the past, and in this present.

"Will this have a cure for...?" Jia points to the portable drive containing Alt-Gayarnu's brain, and then juts her chin at her family. Paige snuggles closer to Mrs. Fields, whose gaze sweeps over us like a wounded animal, ready to strike at the first sign of provocation.

"There's only one way to know. Is it done copying?"

Elisha pulls out an identical black portable drive and hands it to me, and puts the original drive in a safety box we've since acquired. "I've made multiple copies. We'll upload it to our new mainframe I'm working on, once I'm done amalgamating the data from the *Blind Elephant*, the original drive you stole from the other universe, the new ship, and now this drive. You got any other data that needs digitizing? Don't worry. I'll get us organized soon."

I don't doubt it.

Finding the right door while avoiding the Untrakeepers and

an insane Campbell becomes trickier with each trip through the Untraver.

I confirm the date on my phone. I'm about a day off, but that's all right. It's a few days after I rescued Ethan, Gayarnu, and the others from the underground library. Ethan's alive here. I brace myself on the wall, already hearing the buzz of the Untrakeepers. Perhaps I am here early enough to make a difference.

Gayarnu emerges from the emergency room and nearly drops their clipboard at the sight of me.

"You're back?" they say, startled. "Where did you—?"

"No time." The buzzing in my ears increases. I thrust the drive into their sternum, along with the vial they'd given me previously, and a handwritten letter that contains a summary of what's on the drive, details of Jadore's betrayal already in progress, the date of my upcoming return to Sparkstone, the Final Battle, what they should and can't say to me on those dates, and everything I know about Jadore's plan and how they can stop it.

"Read it and then burn it. Good luck with the rebellion. And the cure for both of our peoples. And..." I falter. "Please, try to make Ethan comfortable. But if you can't save him...save as many people as you can."

Their stunned face sparks joy, which I use to promptly disappear back into the future.

I thread my own timeline, doing everything I can to help myself succeed. I distract the Untrakeepers while my Past Self grabs Wil and takes him out of time. I arrange the meeting with the Collective. I return to Jadore's escaping fighter during the Final Battle to hand

Past Me a spacesuit. I recognize her fear and horror, remembering how it gnawed my stomach. I smile at her, knowing it will be all right, that she will suffer then to become me now. I remember the confusion and indignance of staring at that amusement. She can't believe that things will get better, why I have something to smile about. I want to tell her that she'll see Ethan again. That there is a moment beyond the explosion where he is dying, but okay. That I visit that moment again and again when I have a spare second, so I can fill him in on our adventures.

Like a revolving door I track the minutes I'm with him, carefully entering and exiting Ethan's chamber so that I don't catch sight of my past or future self, and ensuring I don't overstay past the point where the Untrakeepers will manifest. The most I can manage is ten minutes before the buzzing becomes unbearable. I won't risk them destroying the lab and Ethan's tank, so I'm fastidious about leaving at the seven-minute mark.

"Gayarnu may create a cure, but I am still doomed, my star," he tells me. *"I cannot return to human form without losing memories of you and creating a past that doesn't exist. That has been programmed into the DNA my aunt has created."*

"That's why I will keep coming back here. Even if you're asleep." So that if he is fated to die, he doesn't have to die alone.

I think about pestering Gayarnu again for progress—and think better of it. I won't waste my precious minutes with Ethan. Even if he dies in the future, the most important thing is he's with me, here, in *this* moment, and we will always have this time.

The Untraver is near-infinite. Key word being *near*. It takes far longer than expected for patterns to emerge, and even when I start seeing them, I have trouble believing they're real. When one seeks patterns in near-chaos, it's easy to trick yourself into seeing connections. One trip after another—especially as I venture back to help my friends stuck on the island in the past—we see similarities in my arm scrawls. I'm returning to the same hallway but going through different doors, as evidenced by the variety of symbols.

The number of doors steadily decreases. The burn marks from the Untrakeepers scar the walls at every turn. Time doesn't pass in the Untraver, and yet, I have a sinking feeling that the landscape of this place is shifting, and if I don't find a new home soon, we will be doomed to a nomad spacefaring existence, forever.

One day when I return to my love, he tells me, *"They will inject a new formula soon."*

Fear grips my heart. His time is coming, and I don't want it to be *this* moment. "How soon?"

"This afternoon, maybe?"

I press my forehead against the tank and smile. "I can stretch that out."

And stretch it I do. Whenever I get a free moment, I leave my friends on the *Blind Elephant* and travel to this room, and make each seven-minute interval count. Sometimes I spend ages in the Untraver, evading Untrakeepers and a crazed Campbell, darting in and out of doors, just to extend the time between my present and the time when I'll arrive and find an empty tank.

Finding an alternate Earth without a Collective, where humanity also doesn't exist but neither does an alternative dominant species on Earth, takes time. It means taking the cartography of the Untraver to a whole other level. My arm's running out of space anyway. It means leaving my friends on Earth in the weeks before the Final Battle, while I spend months dipping in and out of the Untraver. Round and round we go, me coming in to scoop them up in the days before war breaks out in space.

At last, I think I've found it. It's our Perfect New Earth. I visit it a few times to be sure. Manmade structures have been erected but strangely abandoned. I wonder if a plague disrupted this Earth, and everyone was evacuated? I try to access digital and physical records, but whoever was here had seen fit to take or destroy them.

Overjoyed, I exit the Untraver, straight for Ethan's tank. I want him to be the first to know about our new home.

When I arrive, attached to the tank, at precisely my eye level, is a tablet programmed with a single text note:

My star. Today is the day I live or die. We will see each other again, if not tomorrow, then tomorrow under different skies.

I throw the tablet on the floor. No. Not today.

He's gone for good, now. Even though I've delivered the research for both vitaphages to Gayarnu, there's no guarantee that they developed a cure in time to save him. I can't bear the thought of losing him again.

I wait in place on my knees, ignoring all pain, knowing it will be worth it when he walks through the door.

The seven-minute mark arrives.

No one has entered this room.

I feel in my heart that no one will again.

The buzzing and familiar itch in my ear intensifies. I must leave. If I don't seek out Ethan's fate, my ignorance may keep him alive. Schrödinger's Ethan, both alive and dead.

Just as I'm about to jump away, Gayarnu opens the door, cradling a rattling box of vials and disposable syringes. I raise my eyebrows with hope. But they shake their head. And I realize why they'd been so confused when I demanded to know Ethan's fate.

He's gone. My Future Self will never see him again.

"Early tests on humans are promising for this," they say, handing me the box and the syringes. "Um, that's the initial batch, so if you could come back and tell me the results...?" Silent tears roll down their face, even though their voice remains steady.

I did my best to save him, but my best wasn't enough. I clutch the box tightly, nodding.

I cradle my memory of him and abscond from that dreadful building, vowing to never return. While I wander the Untraver in heavy sadness, ducking in and out of doors when I am chased, a numbness settles over my heart. I saved him from the portal explosion, and I did everything I could to save him a terrible plague. I saw his true face. We've shared our deepest thoughts and stories in those precious, stolen moments together.

Now, I hold the key to our peoples' futures in my arms, which he died for. I can't let his sacrifice and suffering be for nothing.

Even though spending twenty-four hours under artificial light deceives the brain, the body still continues aging. Misty's dark hair sprouts handsome white strands. My feet and lower back ache more, especially after a particularly difficult jump. I note similar issues with Jia, though she weathers them with a stoic comment. She spends a great deal of her time in meditation and studying the dharma. Wil slowly becomes the man I remember. *Older.* I hadn't seen it clearly before. I hadn't been ready to accept the truth. Everything from my time at Sparkstone is a daze of innocence. Now is clarity because I can create now, forever.

Those first few years are a frenzy of activity. After what we went through with Jia's parents, we decide not to remove any more of our families until we have a better process for reinstating their memories.

Sunni begins using her power to soothe the human race, to assure them that they will be rescued, and to not fear us when we come. Still, the first few inoculation runs are rough. People see us. They freak out. Wil calms them down, using methods we at first despise and question, and later learn to accept. It's better for Wil to control their flailing minds, and then for Jia and Lynn to administer the vaccine. It's not a perfect system, and we do our best to catch as many people as we can. It takes a couple of more visits to Gayarnu to settle on the right dosage and formula.

Getting our species *off* planet is a whole other problem. Sure, I can jump a couple of people at a time, but it's far easier to jump a group if we can contain them in—

"The mother ship!" The words come out like a prophecy, unbidden, in the middle of a group yoga session in the mess, about a month after Ethan's true death.

Wil sees my line of thought. It's easy. Teleport an entire population onto the mother ship. Get the engines working. Jump the ship to a new, habitable planet in another universe.

"It won't fit the entire population of humanity. And the ship would be filled with aliens."

"We can deal with them," Misty says confidently.

"Our data shows the mother ship drifting for at least fifteen minutes after the battle, away from the solar system. We're not there long enough after that to know what happens next," Sunni adds.

Wil doesn't argue further. Kimberly gives him a quizzical look from her downward dog position, and then smiles at me and Sunni. "We should try it!"

We can't teleport everyone on Earth onto the mother ship all at once, and it's the most complicated threading I will likely ever do. Elisha coordinates the logistics. Once we have finished the inoculation of a population, Sunni and I jump the *Pacific Rescuer* to a central location. Wil beckons them to the ship, sometimes with Elisha's help, and we jump back to the mother ship, unload, and repeat the process. Sometimes Paige joins us, when she is well enough, as she has recovered her memory enough to remember her sister and is excited to join our mission.

It's not perfect, and it's time consuming. It is a process we will continue doing for the rest of our lives, if we're going to rescue every survivor on Earth before it explodes.

"I think it's nearly time," Wil says one evening.

Misty, Jia, and I look up from our card game. Sunni's asleep in the loft.

"You sure?" I ask.

Wil nods. "Yeah. Definitely."

A heavy silence falls between us—until Misty abruptly leaves the booth. "We should have a party. All in favour?"

Jia, Misty, and I raise our hands, and Kimberly dashes into the mess. "Did I just hear you're having a party?"

Wil's resolute smile falters as she enters. He stands, shoving his hands into his pockets. She had been there for his death, and that is his future. Her face falls as they share a silent, private moment, very much in public.

Over the coming days, Sunni and Misty try exchange jokes about attending your own funeral. Wil buys into it, probably to keep the mood light. Kimberly disappears with Wil for stretches of time in the private cabin. The party planning starts as a team effort, but eventually Elisha takes over and efficiently organizes us and delegates tasks. I act mostly as a shuttle service to take people where they need to be, and once we've gotten the supplies, I take us back to a time in Earth's history where there were no satellites or alien monitoring systems that can pick up our signals as we orbit our beautiful home.

Wil, Sunni, and Elisha have created an airlock extender so we can connect the two ships during our downtime. Both ships are decorated with streamers, balloons, and photos of happy memories stuck to bulkheads. Fold-out tables host a feast of cakes, shepherd's pie, sandwiches, fruits, chips, and dips. Lynn has crafted an elaborate berry punch. Music pipes through speakers in both ships, though the party's mostly in the mess of the *Blind Elephant*.

Misty and Greg trade barbs and Sunni patiently mediates. "You know, the machete was *my* idea," Greg brags, gesturing to the weapon sheathed next to Wil's sack, which rests in the cockpit.

"It wasn't!" Misty counters. "We knew he had one!"

"Well, I didn't know that you *knew*!"

"You were literally *there* in the past—!"

Sunni waves a hand like a referee. "Indoor voice, Greg! Also, I think I remember Kimberly sayin' that machetes were a neat weapon, so that probably had the most influence over him pickin' one up, no?"

Near the engineering room, Elisha speaks intensely with Wil. Kimberly hangs on his arm, smiling sadly. Elisha slips Wil a USB drive and covers his hand with hers. Something about that drive is important, apparently. I wonder if she's attempting to send information to the past. I smile at that. Do your best, Elisha.

Even Jia's parents and Paige look relaxed as they engage Jia in pleasant conversation. The therapy they've been undergoing with

Greg and Jia has tugged loose some memories, but it will take time for their neural pathways to mend.

"I need a favour," Wil says, when Kimberly has excused herself for a moment to use the water closet. He throws a glance over at the others. "There are some things I need to wrap up, before you put me back."

I try to shove the future from my mind, even though it's pointless, and we're literally in the middle of the party celebrating his own life. We both know what is to come. I still want to pretend Wil doesn't. "Yeah. Of course. Where do you need to go?"

Our first stop is the music trailer. It's strange being back at Sparkstone, after everything. Somewhere out there, my parents know me. Ethan is a human being and not an alien—and alive.

I duck out of our hiding spot and walk down the quad. Is it a good idea to be wandering around campus, when I might affect the past? Wil's probably going to be a while. He said he had to do something with the cameras that will make the coming days easier. Am I taking a constitutional around campus, hoping to catch a glimpse of human Ethan again? All right, sure. I don't see him. After about ten minutes, I return to our meeting spot, just between the trailers.

He emerges from the trailer, a little perturbed. I hear Past Misty and my Past Self calling after him. He shakes his head. "Need another date."

"Oh?" I realize where we are in the timeline. I'd found him in there, fiddling with the camera, and he'd used the banana line, and I'd had no idea what he was talking about. I smirk and take hold of his arm. "When did you want?"

I jump us a couple of days in the future to the same spot, and he enters the music trailer again.

Standing in the cold, once again without the best protection, I'm struck again by Ethan's closeness. What would he say if I came to him in the early evening, or jumped into his art studio as he painted, and we just...hung out? Maybe I have a couple more wrinkles than before, but it's only been what? A year? Two years? That time wouldn't make much difference.

I laugh quietly to myself. No. I have to leave that be. Gayarnu did everything they could for him, but the vaccine didn't take in time. At least here, on this day, he's alive and relatively safe.

Campbell's predictions about my friends haven't all come true yet. We have some life to live yet. Besides, he'd even said that Ethan seemed to have no fate.

That's because Ethan the human hadn't been real. He was a construct, created for suffering. He was never meant to be saved.

My ears are ringing by the time Wil returns, scratching the back of his neck. He gives me a funny look.

"What?" I ask.

"Nothing," he says, a little too quickly. When he sees I'm not going to let that go, he repeats it. "Nothing. For real. Now...now I guess, we say goodbye."

I'm a little taken aback. I thought he'd need more jumps.

"I can manage here. Got a few tricks up my sleeve."

I take in my dear friend, with whom I've shared my entire brain. The one person who has been unafraid to keep me in check. Without him, I probably would've been a villain.

"Same," he says, to my errant thought.

His glasses are a little cracked. I wish we could have fixed that before leaving. "Bye, Wil," I say, for at least the third time.

He nods, and touches my shoulder. I wrap my arms around him. He's surprised by the hug and I try to apologize my way out of it, but he laughs a little, and returns it with equal force. "I'll see you soon."

Wil's absence is sorely felt. Without him, our rescue mission becomes infinitely harder. Communication begins to break down, as Wil did so much mediation between us. Easy when one can hear everyone's thoughts and desires. Elisha, Lynn, and Jia step up to fill his role, both on our ships and in the field.

A couple weeks after Wil's departure, I find Kimberly in the *Blind Elephant* mess. Her usual chipper mood has taken a hit.

"Are you ready to get your family back tomorrow?" I ask her, trying to distract us both.

She slumps in the booth. "Yeah. I guess. They're not going to remember me though, and they'll freak out...I dunno." She throws her head back and lets out a frustrated groan. "It's not fair. I should've found a way to keep him here, you know?"

"I know," I say.

"Like, he was able to fix *some* of our family's memories! Why leave in the middle of all that? I know it's for time-travel reasons, blah, blah, blah, but...still. Are you *sure* we can't change the future?" Her round, brown eyes plead with me, as if I am the god of death.

I touch my skirt pocket. "We change the future by living in the now."

"Ingrid. I *don't* know what that means. But at least tell me you heeded Wil's final words to you."

My face runs hot. I frown and reach deep into my memories.

She sees I don't remember. "The music trailer! Remember! He told you to meet him there?"

"I keep forgetting," I mutter under my breath. "Did he tell you to remind me?"

She grins. "Go get 'em."

I return to that late December, in the dark time when dystopic whispers had gripped Sparkstone University, black-jacketed humans unknowingly paraded their allegiance to invaders, and my powers had just begun to bloom.

The smell of the music trailer greets me. A hint of dust, hot plastic, and wood. I hear the echoes of songs recently played on the keyboards, which have been pushed against the wall. A simple tap on the wristband, and the cameras blink, deactivated. Not a perfect solution. Present Jadore will suspect something. It doesn't bother me anymore. This has already happened. She reigns here, but in the future, she is dead.

I settle on one of the only benches and wait. He will sense my presence and hopefully this time, he'll get the right Ingrid.

I only have to wait five minutes. The distinctive, deliberate steps climbing into the trailer make me smile. He pushes open the inner door and keeps a hand on it, ready to flee, just in case he's wrong.

It's been some months since we've seen each other. But this Wil is in the thick of his ending at Sparkstone—our beginning into our cosmic journey.

"Banana," I say to him.

He smiles as he shuts the inner door of the trailer. "Banana. I guess I'll tell you at some point to meet me here since I didn't before

I left the ship. Although technically, you should know I'm here, since *you* were my ride."

"Yeah. I almost forgot all about it myself. So..." My throat feels tight. "Wil, I'm really—"

"Don't. We've been through all of this a couple times already. And it's not really over for either of us. We're still out there." He gestures to the sky, and then out the window. "We've transitioned into the final stage of it. Helping ourselves get to where we need to be." He reaches into a pocket and hands me a flash drive. "That's what I'm here to give you."

I take it, and turn it over. "What's on it?"

He shoves his hands in his pocket. "Remember I was downloading the mother ship's database?"

"Yeah. I thought that was just you getting specific pieces of information."

"Yes, but the more we went, the more questions I had. I became curious."

"What happened to not investigating the future?"

He shrugs. "We're already there now, Ingrid. I figured you'd want to know. After the portal exploded in the underground library, the Collective got curious and started sniffing around. That was when Jadore altered and leaked the vitaphage. Anyway. Gayarnu got suspicious. During their efforts to integrate ahmei and human DNA, they modified and falsified some of the recordkeeping."

I don't follow. "Meaning...medical records?"

Wil heads for the door and opens it. "Ethan's record, Ingrid. He doesn't die. We saw him that day on the ship, when we captured Jadore. He was one of the hybrids in their entourage, helping to take over the mother ship. Gayarnu saved him. He's out there, somewhere, in some time. Waiting for you. I don't know specifics, like if you'll be able to live on land together, but..."

Tears spring to my eyes. I run to him and wrap my arms around him and squeeze him tight. Dammit, the man found my heart.

Before he can escape me, I press the hidden gadget into his neck. It injects the precious nanotechnology into his skin.

He recoils, stunned.

"Wil," I say softly. "You didn't think I'd spend years of my life trying to find an empty Earth, without also finding a reality with technology able to save you? I couldn't meet you in the music trailer empty handed."

He leans against the door. "But...my body..."

"Yeah. You still technically die. That's the best kind of death, a technical one. You'll hibernate for a year or so. At first in the ground, and then later, on a ship. Well, spoilers. That will give us enough buffer time for things to settle down, and get you transported to the other reality. Which is what I'm going to do now. Before I go and..." I grin at the flash drive. "Just make sure you tell me to meet you here at some point."

"Sounds like I'll see you soon, then," he says.

"Sleep well," I reply.

We grin as our minds resonate. Finally, I'm unafraid to share everything with him. Soon, he will share what I need to know with me in the past, so that I can become the me of now.

My next stop is a no-brainer. I step through into the war-torn halls of the mother ship, on the day of the Final Battle, just as Gayarnu and her crew of hybrids leave the engine room. They stop abruptly before me, confused. Gayarnu's hand hovers over their weapon. I don't take offense. I've darted in and out of their timeline enough times for them to be suspicious of me, just as I was of Campbell.

My voice shakes as I search each person standing behind Gayarnu with intense longing. "I'm sorry, but I can't tell. Which one of you is—?"

"My star." The rightmost hybrid steps forward, and *of course* it's him. Tall, with a dark mohawk revealing blue-green scales on the side of his head. Pointed green-tipped ears. Brilliant blue-green eyes. I see the outline of the man I love, mixed with his ahmei heritage.

"I thought..." My eyes brim with tears and I can't say it, because saying it will make it real.

I collapse forward. In doing so, I narrowly miss the swing of a heavy sword at my neck.

Ethan grips my shoulders and draws me closer as I spin around. Councillor Ari-Faur clicks his mandibles, dripping in sweat and blue blood as he brandishes a sword, backed by Emily Foller and Shane Richmond. Flames engulf Emily's arms as she looks at me like I'm a tasty snack. Shane trains a gun on my chest.

"You tricked us. Ja'Dor'Esss has escaped with her followers and you have no cure. You have squandered our deal. As I knew you would," Ari-Faur says through a translator emanating from a wristband. He fights to keep his balance. He gestures to Emily and clicks an order. "Kill her."

As the modified ahmei draw weapons behind us and Gayarnu sings orders, Misty and Jia pop out of thin air beside me and Ethan.

"Attacking Ingrid wasn't part of the deal." Jia fires two precise shots at Ari-Faur. One hits him in his sword arm, causing his weapon to drop. The other grazes his neck. Blue blood drips from his wounds onto the floor and he staggers back, clicking wildly.

Emily's fire retreats as she narrows her eyes at Misty. Shane whispers something to Emily, and Emily hits him again. In a loud stage-whisper, she says, "Temporary! Until we get the Mistress back!"

"You don't have Ja'Dor'Esss!" Ari-Faur shouts.

"We did have her," I mutter. "You just didn't speak to the right version of us."

Jia turns her head in alarm at me. Ah. This is Past Jia and Past Misty, escaping the mother ship while Jadore had me in her clutches.

The alien clicks again at Emily. "Kill them!"

"So um, I don't actually take orders from you. I'm only doing this because—!"

Misty leaps towards the demonic woman, presses her fingers into Emily's eyes and blasts her brain with ice. She grapples the young demon and freezes her head to the floor.

Shane's gun clatters to his feet as he sees the writing on the wall. He turns tail—and halts, mid-run.

Wil's voice in our minds sounds like it's coming from far away. *You will free the superpowered humans on this ship and guide them to the appropriate location. Then, your current identity will be replaced with one of my choosing.*

"I...will free the humans," Shane says, as if convincing himself that this is the best use of his time.

"Yeah, that's your superpower," Misty mutters.

He gives her a quizzical look and then shuffles off down an adjacent hallway with renewed determination.

As Gayarnu assesses the wounded among her people, Jia considers me with a mixture of fear and admiration. "Banana?" Jia asks.

"Not banana," I say. "Jadore has me. Do what you gotta do and get back to the ship. But everything's going to be okay. Where's Wil?"

"Somewhere ahead, clearing the way," Misty replies, frowning at me. "You're not...?"

"I'm Future Ingrid," I say, pressing my hand against Ethan's chest. I'm grinning wildly. I know I shouldn't be right now. But seeing my friends as they were, in what feels like so long ago now, fills me with hope. They have a lot ahead of them, and so do I, but I know that together, we'll be all right.

Jia takes this in with a nod. "Right. Let's leave her to it."

"So, this isn't...?" Misty trails off as Jia takes her back into invisibility. I hear her mutter as they dart down the hallway, "Is Future Ingrid gonna make out with that fish guy?"

Gayarnu nods appreciatively to me, and gathers her team of ahmei. They seem a little rattled, but all right. "We'll follow Shane and make sure the humans—and our people—are safe."

"We'll catch up," Ethan promises.

And then it's him and me, alone with two dead bodies, staring out at a planet that's about five minutes away from being completely decimated.

"I'm sorry," he says. The British accent lilts with a hint of the tonal sing-sing quality of the ahmei language.

"It'll be all right," I say, and to my surprise, I mean it this time. "We'll continue to save everyone we can."

"I'll help you," he says.

"Really?" I stare up at him, hand pressed against his hardened chest. "I don't know how much of a life it is. I can't even stand on the surface of my own home for more than fifteen minutes without aliens invading from beyond. There are millions we haven't gotten yet, and the new planet exists in another universe, and..."

He leans towards me and kisses me like he's afraid he's going to lose me again. But he never will.

EPILOGUE

Six Months, Eighty Years Later

When I arrive in the Untraver, I fear I've once again forgotten an important life skill.

No longer is it a maze of dark corridors where monsters roam, waiting for easy prey. It's an open field of artificial grass, watched by a hazy blue sky, and tall, floating totems. I touch one instinctively and it glows warmly. Each totem is etched uniquely with markings representative of times and dates and worlds. I note their fragility and the modular design. All it would take is a flick of my wrist, and it would activate, taking me inside its world.

Far fewer totems than doors, of which there are none. I feel no fear here. Perhaps the Keepers completed their work of culling the doors, and have moved on from this place.

Or, they fear the bigger predator lurking here.

"I like what you did with the place," I say, walking along a muddy path that leads further along the plain. Up ahead, I think I can see an ocean. That's a nice touch.

"Had you not been so busy, you could have done something grander."

His voice melts in my brain, warm like butter and just as comforting. That's how he gets you. A lifetime of running, and I have learned to control my base instincts. Smiling, I continue along the path as he matches my stride alongside me. I feel his gaze, evaluating my careful steps, the natural stoop of my back, the spots on my hands and cheeks, and the engraved lines on my forehead.

"What's the matter?" I chide him. "Never seen an old woman before?" I speak as my grandmother did, and her mother before that, carrying the casual cadence of all the women before me.

"Not this one." He seems genuinely surprised to see me. "Although the Untrakeepers did stop materializing, so I surmised you would eventually change your mind and return, despite what I have done."

I still feel the sting of the memory, imparted to me through voice and song. "You may have manipulated Sunniva Harris. But she consented. Does she...live in the book?"

"In a way. She will guide the girl," he replies. "So, I stayed and waited for you to guide us."

"This whole time?"

"Time kept me company. As she did you, occasionally."

"Well, I don't know how much longer she'll stay with me." I feel an impending change within, an instinctive knowing that keeps me on task. I'm so easily distracted these days. "What's that over there?"

I point at about forty-five degrees into the sky. Because of the reflective, shimmering nature of the ceiling, this object is difficult to see. A silvery thread glints like spiderwebbing from the floor all the way up to the object floating there. As we move further along the path, the thread moves with us, always one step ahead, as such that I can never step on it. Following its path into the sky diagonally, I see the strange floating platform also appears to be moving relative to my position. As I examine the sky further, there are more of them, and more threads, too, all moving closer or further away. It strains these old eyes to look them for too long.

He considers the sky, stopping momentarily in the path. "Hmm. Easier to see everything when one removes the walls and the floors. Well. I suppose I'll explain it like this. If you can go up and down the stairs and ladders of the various realms, and to and fro on this lovely path, why not zip across the line, to someplace else entirely?"

"What's over there? More parallel universes? More time?"

"Oh, it's complicated, Ingrid. Let's call it a different dimension, even though it's not technically correct. There are other points within this geometric shape, but the way we are perceiving the Untraver now, in the forms we are in, makes them hard to see."

I nod. If I had been younger, I'd have fought him and demanded an explanation. While I'm not too old for a geometry lesson, I don't intend to spend my final moments learning math and physics. I smile, thinking of an old friend who would have enjoyed such a lesson. I spent a good deal of time in this place, searching for the right technology to keep him in a near-death status. I remember enlisting the aid of a certain alien to help me retrieve him, too, with somewhat disastrous results. We very nearly left him in the past, because Campbell and the Untrakeepers had been chasing me. That was a long, long time ago, and my dear Wil woke in time to see the birth of his first child.

"You saved them all, did you?" he says, changing the subject.

"With time and hard work, we saved a good many. Your Chosen One will still be there, will she?"

"If we still exist, so does she," he says resolutely.

"Then I don't feel bad for making you wait." I look at him now. And whether this is part of dying, or the madness that comes with gazing upon a higher dimensional being from beyond my understanding, or he has simply willed my sanity—I see a human face. A regular man. Nothing remarkable about him. Incredibly forgettable, in fact, are his features, that I start to question why I'm strolling in the infinite realm of possibility, and not walking in the park at home, with my husband.

"I assume you know where you're going."

"I usually do. Though I've been told I'm becoming more forgetful."

"The beautiful thing about time," Campbell says, as he puts on a vest and zips it up, "is that each moment exists equally and continuously. You are here now, but you are also at home, like you desire."

"Yes," I agree. It seems so obvious when he says it, like asking me to turn on the light in a dark room. How silly. I've always been here, but I've always been back there too, with Wil, Jia, Misty, and Sunni—both when we were free on our spacecraft, and when we were trapped at Sparkstone. And I am also with Ethan when I first saw his true face. And again, when I reunited with him. And again, when we married, and when we reunited with our parents.

"Would you change anything?" I ask him suddenly.

"Would you?" He doesn't look back, and adds, "Have you?"

I hum a tune to myself and say no more. With a casual wave, the kind we'd give to someone you'd see again soon, he stops at the final door, shimmering and bright like the sun. It flies open at my command.

It takes no effort to hold open the door for him. I drift into a light sleep on a nearby bench and wake again, looking up at the sky.

Well, this is certainly a strange place. A door open to whiteness in the middle of a field! I'm not sure I remember how I got here.

Someone told me I can be where I want to be, because I exist everywhere, in every moment, always. Well, I certainly don't want to be here, wherever this is. Good thing someone—perhaps me?—gave me a blanket. I wrap it around my sore shoulders and huddle against its course material.

Let's think of another place for me to be. Hopefully somewhere I don't feel this pain in my shoulder, back, and knees. Somewhere with lots of people—no, just a few. My parents. Their faces—I see them now, and yes, there they are, in that car. Such a silly device when we used to drive spaceships and underwater vessels, so long ago. My, technology has changed.

I'm descending, down, down, and the blanket swaddles me, as comfortable and snug as if it were my own skin.

This time I will know the tune in my head, on that first day of that awful school.

I will try to be kinder to my friends—the people who could be my friends.

I will stop and ask my future self what to do and she will answer, because I provide for her, and she protects me.

And so on and so on. Until I am the end, and begin again.

I will—

—*be* forever.

Acknowledgements

Please enjoy the thrilling conclusion of the story of the Acknowledgements Faery and Sir Copy Right!

Late one night, the Acknowledgements Faery and Sir Copy Right joined hands. Their powers combined in a spectacular shower of literary sparks that illuminated every bookshelf in the world. The spell was the most powerful bit of magic they'd ever created. Any reader who skipped the acknowledgements would find themselves unable to turn to the next page until they'd read every expression of gratitude. And, any publisher who tried to remove these pages would find their ink mysteriously disappearing from every other page in the book.

At first, there was chaos. Readers worldwide found themselves stuck on acknowledgement pages, forced to absorb the heartfelt thanks to agents, editors, spouses, pets, and that one barista who provided the perfect oat lattes during the writing process. Publishers watched in horror as books with removed acknowledgements became nothing but blank pages between covers.

The publishing world was in an uproar. Emergency meetings were called. Legal teams scrambled.

Then, something unexpected happened. People began to *appreciate* the acknowledgements with sincerity. Not just because of the magic, but because the magic had helped to open their eyes.

Publishers, seeing this shift in perspective, began not only restoring acknowledgement and copyright pages but highlighting them. Special editions featured expanded acknowledgements. Book clubs discussed the most touching thank-yous alongside plot points and character development.

Sir Copy Right even mustered up the courage to write his own acknowledgements page, dedicated to the Acknowledgements Faery, detailing his feelings for her. Blushing and beaming, the Acknowledgements Faery announced her reciprocation of romantic feelings, and declared they should be married at once!

From that day forward, acknowledgement pages were never again overlooked, and copyright pages were respected by all. And whenever you find yourself pausing to read those pages at the beginning or end of a book, remember that somewhere, the Acknowledgements Faery and Sir Copy Right are smiling, holding hands, guardians of gratitude and recognition in the literary world.

The End.

Acknowledgements

Thank you to everyone who has endured this series and waited patiently for the conclusion. It's one of the most challenging projects I've undertaken. Thanks to my family, friends, and the staff of the Arthur J.E. Child (and those formally of the Tom Baker), for looking after me. What has happened before hopefully does not happen again, in my case, because of all of you. Thank you to my patrons, Melissa Meunier and Bryan Ronald, for your generous support, I appreciate it greatly! And thanks everyone for the kind messages while I was undergoing treatment. What we do in the here and now, even small actions, can have large ripples into the future.

Website: FaeryInkPress.com

Instagram: @faeryinkpress

If you enjoyed this book, please consider writing a review on Amazon or on Goodreads. Thank you!

About the Author

Photo Credit:
Terence Yung

Clare C. Marshall grew up in rural Nova Scotia with very little television and dial-up internet, and yet she turned out okay. She is the founder and author-publisher of Faery Ink Press, where she has published young adult science fiction and fantasy novels since 2011. Her fantasy novel, *The Violet Fox*, was given an honorable mention in the 2016 Whistler Independent Book Awards and its sequel, *The Emerald Cloth,* was nominated for Best YA Novel in the 2019 Prix Aurora Awards. When she's not writing, fiddling up a storm, or sharing stories on YouTube, she enjoys making silly noises at her two cats, Pinecone and Pavlova. She lives in Calgary with her husband.

www.ingramcontent.com/pod-product-compliance
Lightning Source LLC
Chambersburg PA
CBHW030732310726
48969CB00005B/1192